The fiery brilliance of th[e] you see on the cover is crea[...] *is the revolutionary process in which a powerful laser beam records light waves in diamond-like facets so tiny that 9,000,000 fit in a square inch. No print or photograph can match the vibrant colors and radiant glow of a hologram.*

So look for the Zebra Hologram Heart whenever you buy a historical romance. It is a shimmering reflection of our guarantee that you'll find consistent quality between the covers!

DEFIANT SURRENDER

"You are my wife, and I intend to take full advantage of my rights." Giddeon's voice, though firm, was strangely gentle.

Serita glared at him. Again, he had a vision of a wild mustang—a magnificent animal, proud yet vulnerable, beautiful, spirited, and boldly independent. Beauty, fire, and grace, Serita Cortinas de Duval.

"Now, love," he whispered, lowering his face to hers, "I am going to teach you a few things the wedding vows don't discuss."

Serita held out as long as she could, standing stiffly, her lips listless and unmoving against his increasingly ardent attack on her senses. But his hands heated her neck and shot flames the length and breadth of her body. And his lips, moist and urgent, caressed her senses until she felt as though she radiated heat in all directions, like a star in the sky . . .

THE BEST IN HISTORICAL ROMANCES

TIME-KEPT PROMISES (2422, $3.95)
by Constance O'Day Flannery

Sean O'Mara froze when he saw his wife Christina standing before him. She had vanished and the news had been written about in all of the papers—he had even been charged with her murder! But now he had living proof of his innocence, and Sean was not about to let her get away. No matter that the woman was claiming to be someone named Kristine; she still caused his blood to boil.

PASSION'S PRISONER (2573, $3.95)
by Casey Stewart

When Cassandra Lansing put on men's clothing and entered the Rawlings saloon she didn't expect to lose anything—in fact she was sure that she would win back her prized horse Rapscallion that her grandfather lost in a card game. She almost got a smug satisfaction at the thought of fooling the gamblers into believing that she was a man. But once she caught a glimpse of the virile Josh Rawlings, Cassandra wanted to be the woman in his embrace!

ANGEL HEART (2426, $3.95)
by Victoria Thompson

Ever since Angelica's father died, Harlan Snyder had been angling to get his hands on her ranch, the Diamond R. And now, just when she had an important government contract to fulfill, she couldn't find a single cowhand to hire—all because of Snyder's threats. It was only a matter of time before the legendary gunfighter Kid Collins turned up on her doorstep, badly wounded. Angelica assessed his firmly muscled physique and stared into his startling blue eyes. Beneath all that blood and dirt he was the handsomest man she had ever seen, and the one person who could help beat Snyder at his own game.

Available wherever paperbacks are sold, or order direct from the Publisher. Send cover price plus 50¢ per copy for mailing and handling to Zebra Books, Dept. 2866, 475 Park Avenue South, New York, N.Y. 10016. Residents of New York, New Jersey and Pennsylvania must include sales tax. DO NOT SEND CASH.

TEXAS GAMBLE

Vivian Vaughan

ZEBRA BOOKS
KENSINGTON PUBLISHING CORP.

ZEBRA BOOKS

are published by

Kensington Publishing Corp.
475 Park Avenue South
New York, NY 10016

First printing: January 1990

Printed in the United States of America

For Carin
Editor, Teacher, Friend

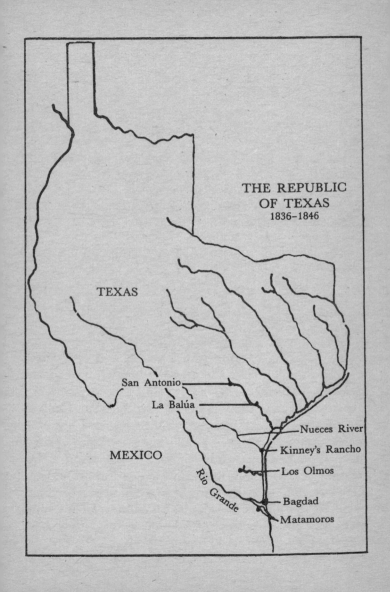

THE REPUBLIC
OF TEXAS
1836–1846

TEXAS

San Antonio
La Balúa

MEXICO

Rio Grande

Nueces River
Kinney's Rancho
Los Olmos
Bagdad
Matamoros

Chapter One

A sudden gust of wind rustled her bedroom curtains and blew its sultry sea-breath over Serita Cortinas's body. In an effort to pull her nightdress from her sticky skin, she kicked her legs, catching a foot in the garment's hem.

When a loose shutter banged against the side of the house again—the same sound which had awakened her—she untangled her legs and struggled to her feet, still half asleep.

A storm was brewing in the Gulf of Mexico. Of that she was certain. All day the wind had gusted hot and humid between spaces of stillness so stifling neither man nor beast could draw an easy breath. And if the weather and the colorless gray sky—a hurricane sky, Tía Ana called it—had not been enough to convince her of stormy days ahead, the playfulness of the animals was proof positive. Old and young, they had curvetted with the friskiness of youth.

By the time she reached the window the shutter lay

7

silent. But other sounds came now—the same, yet different—quickly erasing the last remnants of sleep from her brain. Her blood turned to ice inside the heated shell of her skin; her movements felt stiff, paralyzed. Angrily, she grasped the rifle which stood ready beside the French doors and bolted onto the balcony, shouting into the black night. "Oliver Burton! You bastard! Leave us alone!"

Swallowed by the swirling wind, her words fell like stones tossed into a pond. The sky was so black she could see little, not even a cloud-covered moon, to tell her the time of night. For a moment, she entertained the strange idea that perhaps Los Olmos had been blotted from the continent, as with a dollop of black ink, and existed now only in its own space somewhere.

Would that were true, she cried inside. What difference did it make to her whether Los Olmos was part of the new nation called Texas, or of the older one called Mexico? Some of her neighbors would think that traitorous, she knew. But look at them now, those loyal Mexican *rancheros!* All except one other had already left their land grants and scurried to the safety of Mexico, their *mother* country!

Barb, her Arabian colt, nickered from the stable behind the house. The air, heavy and wet, filled her senses. Having faded briefly into the night, the sounds now rose above the wind.

Young Jorge, her nephew, tugged at her clothing from behind. "What's wrong with Barb, Serita? Are they going to hurt Barb?"

"No, *chico,*" she answered the boy absently. Rubbing the damp sleeve of her nightdress over her face, she blinked her eyes and peered deeper into the pitch-black night. Inky shapes swayed against the backdrop of an even darker sky—elm trees rimming the banks of Los Olmos Creek, from whence came the name of both the creek and the *hacienda*. But it was the shapes she *didn't* see that sent a chill prickling along her feverish skin.

She wasn't afraid of the storm. She and her family had ridden out many a hurricane in this fortress of a home her great-grandfather built back in 1750, when these lands still belonged to the King of Spain. As a child the storms had actually been exciting. But now . . .

Now she was no longer a child. And now she had little family left with whom to share either the good times or the bad. The war with Mexico had robbed her of much more than her brother's life. It had taken, also, her mother's health and her father's will to fight, leaving her alone, at twenty-four, to save the family lands, the family heritage.

And of that she *was* afraid—of failing to preserve her heritage. Deep down inside her heart, in the core of her bones, in every fiber of her being, Serita Cortinas feared losing Los Olmos to Oliver Burton or to any of the other land-hungry gringos who poured daily into the Nueces Strip from the newly independent nation—Texas.

The sounds intensified. Oliver Burton's ridiculous nocturnal visits, his foolish attempts to intimidate her, were becoming so regular she was almost accustomed to them. She was no more afraid of him than she was of a hurricane.

Yet her heart trembled at the baneful tones— shriller than wind whistling through elm branches, softer than a coyote's call, eerie, quivering notes that seemed to hover above the ground, calling from the direction of the family plots. Calling.

Although they were ten miles from the Gulf of Mexico, her nostrils stung with the pungent, salt-filled air. She wasn't afraid, she repeated half aloud. But as the unearthly chant continued, she clasped her arms about herself and felt the prickles still keen along her skin. Her heart thudded against her forearm, despondent, disheartened, finally determined.

The wind tossed her loose black hair as limbs on the elm trees and plastered the delicate cotton of her nightdress to her bare skin. Elevating her patrician profile, she glowered toward the ghoulish sounds. She wasn't afraid. Not of Oliver Burton. He would never drive her from Los Olmos by fiendish pranks. If she could learn to ignore him, in time he would forego this nonsense.

Suddenly Barb's neighs turned to screams, and the racket intensified, shifting from the creek to the rear of the sprawling compound that for generations had been called simply *la casa grande*, the big house.

Serita's heart froze. Instantly, she knew Oliver Burton had changed his tactics from passive intimidation to direct assault. Metal clattered and clanged against metal, against wood. By the second time Barb's hooves thudded against the solid adobe wall of the stable, Serita had raced from the room. She could endure Burton's ghosts and goblins, if she must, but she would not let him harm Barb.

Barb was her dream — and her reality — her only chance to save Los Olmos from the gringo land raiders. Since the war, and with the unrest which prevailed yet in this disputed region, business opportunities were scarce as hen's teeth, as the old saying went. Or as scarce as well-bred horsestock.

10

When Barb was old enough to breed, though, that would change. Serita's plans were made, now all she had to do was keep the filly safe and hold on to her land.

Her bare feet pounded against the sweating tile floor as she raced toward the courtyard staircase with Jorge close on her heels.

Tía Ana met them at the foot of the stairs holding a flickering lantern. "*¿Qué pasó, sobrina?*" Her voice was drugged with a mixture of sleep and age. "What's happening?" she asked her niece again.

"It's Burton, Tita!" Serita glanced anxiously toward the stable from where Barb's thudding hooves could be heard clamoring in panic; her neighs screamed a shrill alarm through the humid night air. The hammering of wood against wood gave warning of the gate being battered down. Serita's brain whirled in a torrent of schemes and counterattacks, equal in force to the rising wind itself.

"*¡Andale*, Jorge!" she instructed her nephew. "Hurry! Ring the chapel bell. Hard. Perhaps if we set up enough racket, we can distract them and gain time to save Barb."

The small-boned nine-year-old slipped past Serita and sprinted for the bell rope hanging inside the front gates. His loose white pants ballooned in the swirling wind; his ribs etched fine lines through the smooth bronze skin on his chest.

"It is beginning to rain, *sobrina*," Tía Ana cautioned her unhearing niece, as Serita ran across the courtyard, her white nightdress flying in the wind.

Just then a door at the far end of the compound opened, and Pablo Ruíz, Los Olmos's ancient and only remaining vaquero, rushed into the dim circle of

Tía Ana's lantern. Grasping a rifle in one hand, he awkwardly pulled his shirt over his head with the other. Nieves, his wife, followed, struggling to cover her nightdress with a *rebozo*.

When Serita stopped in front of the couple, *Tía* Ana caught up with them. Her lantern encased them in an eerie, flickering glow. "Let Pablo handle these wicked men, *sobrina*."

Suddenly the chapel bell pealed through the night, followed by surprised oaths from across the ten-foot-high adobe wall of the stable.

"Bring Barb into the courtyard through the tunnel, Pablo," Serita instructed, while she herself hurried to the ladder leading to the rear roof of the compound, where the housemaids, Abril and Lupe, often hung wash to dry.

Back in the days when the Los Olmos family compound had been constructed, Indian attacks were frequent, so her great-grandfather had devised an ingenious plan to keep his family, his laborers, and some of his prized livestock safe. Built in the shape of a double square, the living quarters surrounded an open inner courtyard, while the stable formed the second square, sharing a common wall with the living quarters. The outer walls were four-foot-thick adobe, and all gates were heavy, iron-clad wood. The living quarters along the common wall were built to house servants and laborers during times of attack. One section was left open with only a gate at each end, forming a covered passageway between the stable and the central courtyard, which the family referred to as a tunnel. During times of peace, the rooms along the stable side were used for guests who attended the many fiestas for which Los Olmos was known as far

12

away as the capital of Mexico, five hundred miles to the southwest.

Serita climbed swiftly up the ladder.

"¡*Chica!*" Pablo called to her. "Do not expose yourself to their rifles!"

She climbed without stopping, clutching her rifle in one hand. "It is *my* gun to be feared," she vowed. "They will not attack Los Olmos without answering to me!"

"It is beginning to rain, *sobrina*," *Tía* Ana called after her niece. "Your nightdress! You cannot run about unclothed!"

"*Chica, por favor,*" Pablo pleaded. "Please. These are dangerous men."

"If they intended to harm us, they would not have attacked the stable," she called down fiercely. "They have come for Barb. ¡*Andale,* Pablo! We have no time to waste!"

"You must not fire upon them, *chica*." He voiced his caution in a tone so severe she cringed. By the time she gained footing on the flat, tiled roof, anger overwhelmed her, and her fingers tightened about the rifle in her hand.

We must not kill an Anglo! We must not kill an Anglo! How sick she was of hearing such sentiments. How could these pale-skinned, weak-kneed usurpers have so quickly humbled her proud and noble people? Her ancestors had come to this country with Cortés; they were the Conquistadors, the conquerors, hailed by the primitives who met them as gods! *Now look at us!* she swore bitterly. *We bow fearfully before an unworthy opponent!*

But Pablo was right. Deep in her heart, she knew that. In order to retain their lands, they must keep

13

their wits about them and defeat the gringos by their ability to outlast them—outlast and finally overcome, but never outfight. They must not kill an Anglo, for there would only be another one to take his place! And another. And another.

Serita picked her way across the rough surface of the roof. But neither would she stand silently by and let them destroy her home.

With the rain had come clouds, which, moved by the winds, drifted across the midnight-black sky like cobwebs, exposing here and there a bit of light and even a few stars. Perhaps they wouldn't have a storm after all. Absently, she glanced to her left, into the solid black wall of night. Somebody to the south wasn't so lucky.

Then she was there—at the edge of the building. Leaning against the outer wall of the roof, she stared down at the dim figures attacking the gate. Her gate. Quickly, she raised her rifle to the sky and fired into the night.

As instantly, all noise ceased. Clutching the rifle more tightly in her hand, she thrust it defiantly above her head. Her entire body trembled so hard she thought for a moment she might tumble over the side of the building. Her breath seemed suspended somewhere outside her body, and she struggled to draw air into her lungs. Using all the strength she possessed, she held herself rigid, feeling already the bullets she expected to be fired.

Gradually fuzzy shapes began to form below her. Hooves thundered from the opposite side of the big house, and for a moment, she thought it was Barb.

Then three very large horses drew rein directly beneath the roof where she stood, and she quickly

14

lowered her rifle sights to them. While the men who had attacked the gate looked on, the two outside riders brought their rifles to bear upon her. The man in the center held an empty hand aloft.

Although only indistinct shapes were discernible in the dim light, she knew no man except Oliver Burton would face her rifle with such arrogance.

"Get off my land, Señor Burton." Her voice was low and steady, and she wondered where it had come from. Certainly not from within her quaking body.

"You might as well give up peaceably, Miss Cortinas. You can't hold out forever. The odds are against—"

"Get off my land!" This time she knew from whence her steady voice came—from the anger embedded deep within her soul.

"Times have changed in these parts, ma'am." Burton spoke no louder than necessary to carry his words to her ears; his air of command infuriated her.

As though he already owns Los Olmos, she thought, steadying her rifle sights on the center of his shadowy form.

"No need to be so pigheaded," he continued. "You Spanish had your day. Now it's our turn to run this land the way it was meant to be run."

With great effort Serita stilled her fingers on the trigger. Pablo's words echoed through her brain. *We must not kill an Anglo. Once the killing starts, we will be the ones who lose.*

As hard as she tried not to, Serita found herself more and more these days believing the words of her father—words she had disputed angrily to his face when he left for Mexico three months back. Don Miguel, however, had been adamant.

15

"There are too many of them to fight, Serita. They will win, because they will keep coming and keep coming and never let up. They will take our lands, because they *want* our lands. If we do not leave like the other *rancheros,* the gringos will destroy us. We have family in Mexico. We can start over there."

"Start over!" she had screamed. "How can you start something over that was begun so long ago? How can you consider giving up our home, the home of our ancestors? The home they fought to build, and us to preserve?" She had looked out at the family graveyard in the grove of elm trees beside the creek. "They died here, Papá. They are buried here, all of them, even our beloved Juan. I will never leave. Never."

The weathered and bronzed old man, the once ramrod-proud Don Miguel Cortinas, stooped to pat the black wool *rebozo* that draped the frail shoulders of his wife of many years. "For your own safety, *hija,* you will leave," he then told his daughter. "Even if I have to sell this land grant to force you away."

"*¡Papa!* You wouldn't . . . !" she began. Then, elevating her chin in a solemn gesture of resolve, she spoke again. "We cannot *sell* this place. You know, as well as I, that those gringos who would have our land would take it by force, not with pesos! They do not intend to *pay* for our heritage, they would steal it."

"Enough, *hija.* Enough. As soon as I have your *mamá* settled with kinfolk, I will return for you. We will speak no more of this nonsense. You cannot beat the gringos."

Serita gripped the rifle tighter in her hands. She *could* beat the gringos; she *would* beat them. At least this one particular gringo called Oliver Burton.

"You are wasting your time trying to take Los

16

Olmos, *señor*," she shouted down. "I will never give up my land. Now, be gone with you. You are not welcome here."

Behind her Serita heard footsteps; then she felt Jorge clutch at her skirts.

Burton spoke again. "Any reasonable young lady would rather see her land go to a reputable rancher than to some scum of a gambler who won it in a card game."

Serita glared without answering. She had heard the tales. That her father was a crazy gambler who, having failed to force her to leave, now spent his time across the Rio Grande River in Bagdad trying to lose his land to someone who could coerce her into fleeing to the safety of Mexico. She also knew the facts, since three of the proud winners had ridden the one hundred miles to Los Olmos, thinking to claim the *hacienda*.

Shifting her weight, she steadied the rifle in her hands. Those were gringos she had not been afraid to shoot. And the surprised fellows knew it to the man of them. Within the hour each had retraced his steps to town, only an empty pocket to show for his foolhardy wager with *Don* Miguel Cortinas.

Grimly, she knew it would take much more than angry threats to intimidate the seasoned frontiersmen sitting their mounts at her feet.

"My land will go to no one except my heirs, *señor*. If you do not believe me, you are wasting your time. Now, be off with you."

"Not so fast." Burton reached into his shirt and pulled out a piece of writing paper. "This invitation here is to a fiesta for Saint Michael something or other—ten days from now . . ."

Jorge darted from behind Serita's legs. "You are not invited to our fiesta! We would never invite wicked men like you!"

Burton shrugged. "Invited or not, boy, we will be here." Then, turning his attention to Serita, his posture straightened to one of even greater authority. "You have until the day of the fiesta to vacate this land peaceably. If you are not gone by sundown, September twenty-fifth, you will pay dearly, ma'am. More dearly than you are prepared to. I promise you that." As he finished speaking, he nodded to his left and right, and the men on foot headed for a thicket nearby.

"You will be the one to pay, Señor Burton," Serita began, watching the man untether their mounts.

Jorge interrupted her. "No *Tejano* gringo is going to take our land. Never. Never."

Oliver Burton pulled the reins against his horse's neck. "September twenty-fifth," he repeated. "Your fiesta of Saint Michael."

Serita gripped the rifle with white knuckles, watching them ride away into the drizzling night, Burton's flat Anglo pronunciation of her beloved mother tongue ringing as a death knell in her ears. How was she ever going to defeat the likes of such cold, evil men? Such persistent men?

Finally, when the riders were out of sight, Jorge tugged at her arm, and they retraced their steps to the courtyard where Pablo had hitched Barb securely to the ancient windswept oak tree around which the entire compound had been built so long ago. The tree, hunched like an old man before the constant force of the gulf winds, had become a symbol of strength for her family. "Because it bent," Papá had

18

told her, "it never broke. Like we ourselves must bow before the winds of change so as to never lose our identity, our heritage."

Tía Ana and Nieves stood to either side of the tree, apart, yet clutched in the same grip of anxiety. Abril and Lupe, the housemaids, had come outside and now hovered beneath the eaves of the porch.

Tía Ana stepped forward and draped her black *rebozo* over Serita's nightdress.

Serita searched the night sky, still midnight black, which made the sprinking of stars even more brilliant. With an almost unbearable ache in her heart, she glared at one particular star, one that shone especially bright and near to earth. "What I wish for is a gingo name!" she hissed. "They wouldn't dare run me off, not with a gringo name."

"*¡Madre de Dios!*" Tía Ana intoned, raising her arms toward heaven. "Mother of God! Pray for this child before she brings the house down upon our heads with such sacrilege!"

Bagdad, Mexico
September 16, 1839

When Captain Giddeon Duval strode into La Paloma Cantina in the tiny seaport town of Bagdad, Mexico, no one in the room would have suspected that his ship with its entire cargo had capsized during a hurricane in the Gulf of Mexico a mere twenty-four hours previous.

Giddeon Duval was well known in every seaport town along the gulf from Campeche clear around the Mexican coast to Vera Cruz and north all the way to

New Orleans.

Known, but not necessarily always liked. Some called him arrogant; some, merely overconfident. All recognized him as a man intent on his own purposes, indifferent to all but his own interests.

A lady's man, only the classiest, most brazen courtesans in the cantinas he frequented dared approach him. Most hung back, yearning for the aplomb to proposition such a handsome devil yet unwilling to suffer Duval's public rejection, should she not please his fancy. At thirty, his volatile temperament had become legendary.

That he was discussed in every hole-in-the-wall where ladies of the evening gathered was public knowledge. Some of the ladies insisted his head was so big it was a wonder he could fit a cocked hat upon it; others, claiming personal experience, swore his head was neither the largest nor the most interesting part of his anatomy.

Dissected thus, Giddeon's friends, consisting of three crew members who followed him everywhere, marveled at his nonchalance. The fact of the matter was, Giddeon Duval paid no notice to the commotion his presence inevitably caused. His mind and energies were always directed on the future—always on the future.

So it was that when Giddeon Duval strode into La Paloma a mere twenty-four hours after witnessing the fortune he had precipitously counted sink to the bottom of the Gulf of Mexico, his attention was already directed to other matters.

Specifically, how in hell he was going to raise enough money to salvage his three-masted schooner, the *Espíritu Estelle*, or at least its cargo.

That he was uncertain of the nature of this mysterious cargo deterred him not. All that mattered was the letter of credit in his pocket — a letter of credit for two hundred thousand dollars, signed by General Anastasio Bustamente, President of Mexico — a letter of credit worth nothing, absolutely nothing, until he, Giddeon Duval, personally delivered the smuggled cargo to Bustamente's representative in New Orleans.

"A whiskey for the captain."

Giddeon turned toward the aggressive Anglo voice at his right elbow. The man immediately seized the opportunity to introduce himself.

"Enos McCaulay, Captain. Have a drink with me."

Eyebrows raised, Giddeon looked to his three crew members.

"All of them," McCaulay told the bartender, indicating the three seamen who flanked their captain.

Giddeon raised the glass of freshly poured whiskey in a salute while he gave McCaulay a once-over inspection. A dandy, his mind registered as he took a swallow of the amber liquid that passed for whiskey, not the sort of fellow who regularly bellied up to the bar in out-of-the-way Mexican seaport cantinas.

Then again, he reflected, hearing the rustle of taffeta, feeling an arm slip through his to his left, he was constantly amazed at the variety of clientele these establishments drew. He glanced at the warm brown fingers that played absently but with purpose against his chest.

"We're in the same business, you and I," McCaulay began.

Giddeon cocked an eyebrow toward the man while he searched the tables at the rear of the room. He had come here hoping to engage some prosperous Mexican in a game. If he expected to salvage the *Espíritu Estelle* while Bustamente still had cash to pay up, he'd best get on with it, and funds for that project were the first order of business.

"Speculation," McCaulay continued. "Only difference, I speculate on land. You, on the other hand, take chances on . . . ah, shall we say, *obscure* cargoes."

To a man, the sailors stared at Enos McCaulay.

"What do you know about my cargo?" Giddeon demanded.

McCaulay smiled, but contrary to Giddeon's expectations, he stood his ground. "Actually, nothing," he admitted. "A deceptive ploy, I'm afraid, Captain. I only hoped to gain your attention. You see, we came in here tonight with the same purpose."

Again Giddeon challenged McCaulay with a stare. Was the man the lunatic he sounded? Or was he a spy, cleverly disguised? And if the latter, for whom?

The whole country was crawling with spies. The Federalists had theirs, as did the Centralists. Santa Anna, a Centralist, had spies on his old rival, Centralist Bustamente. Giddeon had heard that Texas sent spies into the disputed Nueces River region, and he wouldn't put it past the United States to be up to the same shenanigans.

Both the Texas Navy and the French Navy were involved in everything that transpired on the seas between the bickering countries of Mexico, Texas, and, of course, the United States. Rumors had it the Texas Navy was actively aiding the Federalists; facts placed the French on the Federalists' side, also. From the time Giddeon left Vera Cruz with Bustamente's cargo, he had figured himself a damned fool to take on so risky a venture.

He gave McCaulay a decided sneer. To hell with them all. Gulping down the refilled glass, he squeezed the feminine arm, then abruptly dismissed the pretty young thing with a swat on her rear, intending to push her toward another customer.

"I've business to tend to tonight, *bonita*. Find someone who is interested."

McCaulay tapped Giddeon's shoulder. "Here comes our man. Don Miguel Cortinas."

Giddeon squinted at McCaulay, then studied the refined, though obviously inebriated figure of the elderly Spanish grandee who crossed the room toward a rear gaming table. "Speak your mind, McCaulay. You have my attention, but only for the moment. I am here on business."

McCaulay turned his shoulders to the bar, his back toward *Don* Miguel Cortinas, in whom he had professed such interest. "I'm from Texas, Duval. And I'm aiming to get my hands on some of these land grants the old dons are running off and leaving behind."

Giddeon shrugged. "What's that got to do with me?"

"Hell, Captain," McCaulay continued as though he hadn't heard Giddeon's question. "We both know as soon as the United States gets curious about it, she's gonna take Texas into the Union. When that time comes, all the disputed land between the Nueces and the Rio Grande is going to be worth a fortune."

"I'm a sailing man, McCaulay. Not interested in land. If you are, why don't you squat on some of it?"

McCaulay shook his head. "The United States government will require legal titles. I don't intend to fool around and lose the land, once I get hold of it." He turned directly toward Giddeon. "I'm willing to pay, and pay handsomely, for all the land with airtight

23

titles, I can get my hands on."

Giddeon studied McCaulay a moment, then looked across the room at the old man whose entrance here tonight had prompted this conversation. "What's he got to do with it?"

McCaulay's lips curved in a greedy smile. *"Don* Miguel Cortinas, the last of the affluent Spanish land-grant holders. And he's just itching to get rid of his ranch."

Giddeon frowned. "Sounds like a simple proposition to me. If he wants to sell, and you have the money, as you profess, go buy his land. Solve both your problems."

"It's not that easy," McCaulay told him. "A while back the old don signed the ranch over to his daughter, to humor her. Of course, he doesn't consider it binding, her being female and all. Now that things have heated up, and all his compadres have fled the country, he has moved his wife and most of his household to family lands in Mexico, but he can't get the daughter to leave."

Tossing down the last of his whiskey, Giddeon wiped his mouth with the back of his hand and pushed away from the bar. "Thanks for the drink, *amigo*. My business here is of a far different nature."

McCaulay held Giddeon back with a hand to his shoulder. "Not so fast."

Giddeon shook free and prepared to stride away.

"I overheard your men in the bathhouse, Duval. I'm prepared to pay enough to salvage the *Espíritu Estelle*, if you can hand me a clear title to La Hacienda de los Olmos."

Giddeon squinted through the smoke-filled air. "You're crazy, McCaulay." Then curiosity got the better of him. "Why me?"

"Because your reputation preceded you, Captain. You may be Anglo by birth, but you were reared in the Spanish tradition. You are a gambler of some accomplishment . . . and you have a way with the ladies."

Giddeon shook his head. The man was becoming a nuisance. "I'll raise my own funds, McCaulay. Thanks anyhow."

McCaulay held him back once more. "Hear me out, Duval. One more drink and five minutes. That's all I ask. Then, if you don't think it's a gamble a gaming man can't turn down, I won't bother you further."

"One more drink," Giddeon yielded. "But be quick about it."

McCaulay tapped the bar for service and began his tale. When he finished, Giddeon Duval had a smile on his face and the taste of a challenge in his gut.

He patted his pocket, rustling Bustamente's worthless letter of credit. "Fifty thousand dollars, you say? For a clear title to La Hacienda de los Olmos?"

McCaulay nodded.

"How do I know you can pay?"

McCaulay withdrew a sack full of jingling coins from an inner pocket of his jacket. He counted out five hundred dollars. "This should be enough to win the pot. Don Miguel is a fair hand at cards, but if you live up to your reputation, you will have no trouble."

"I mean the fifty thousand. How do I know you can come up with that?"

McCaulay grinned. "I can," he assured Giddeon. "And I will. By the time you win the ranch and convince Serita Cortinas you have a legal claim, I will have the money ready to deliver."

Giddeon toyed with his glass. He had been offered some mighty farfetched propositions in his life, but this one took the cake. On the other hand, the five hundred dollars would go a long way toward winning a pot big enough to salvage the *Espíritu Estelle*.

McCaulay stuffed the coins into Giddeon's pocket. "What do you have to lose, Duval?"

"The most willful, guileful, and beautiful woman in all of Texas, Mexico, and the United States, you say?"

McCaulay nodded. "Don Miguel gambles away the ranch regularly, and Serita runs off every poor sonofabitch who wins it in nothing flat. Her skill with that pearl-handled whip of hers is as legendary as her horsemanship and her marksmanship. She's the talk of the border."

Giddeon turned his back to McCaulay, resting his elbows behind him on the bar. He studied the weathered Don Miguel Cortinas. Slight of stature, Don Miguel's piercing, obsidian eyes warned of a man who gave no quarter. His regal bearing proclaimed his superiority, even to those who would mock his besotted state. Don Miguel Cortinas might be down on his luck at present, but his was a species Giddeon Duval knew intimately, the kind of man whose presence would follow him to the grave, regardless of what the world chose to call him. The fact that the world chose to look down on such a man was, in Giddeon's mind, the world's loss.

As Giddeon watched, Don Miguel hooked his handsome black sombrero on a nail behind the chair which he chose at a far table. A waitress brought him a glass, and the old don withdrew a silver flask from the top of his stovepipe black boot and decanted two fingers worth of amber liquid from it into the glass, as though

26

he poured into the finest of crystal. With hands as graceful as a flamenco dancer Giddeon knew in Campeche, he shuffled the deck of cards, then tapped them on the table.

Three other men sat in on the game, their shabbiness the more apparent for Don Miguel's splendid white shirt and black tie. Apparently they had played with Don Miguel before, because now they grinned in a mocking fashion at the don, then at one another.

One chair stood empty at the table.

Withdrawing the coins from his pocket, Giddeon turned briefly to Enos McCaulay. "You're on." He offered his hand, then strode across the room.

"Con permiso, señor." Giddeon stopped beside the chair of Don Miguel Cortinas and bowed from the waist in an abbreviated yet formal fashion. "Excuse me . . . I would join the game."

When the old man looked up, all the ruckus in the room faded into the woodwork. His eyes were like looking into the sea at midnight with a full moon shining down on it. Bleary on the surface from too much drink, their depths held a strength Giddeon immediately recognized.

"Giddeon Duval, Don Miguel," he said, still staring into the depths of the old man's eyes. "Captain of the schooner, *Espíritu Estelle.*"

If the old man's eyes were obsidian, his features were of stone, for he neither smiled nor in any way revealed emotion. Not on the surface. A brief nod toward the unoccupied chair was all the movement he made.

Yet it was there. A challenge so personal Giddeon felt he had been singled out for the kill. The other players might as well have been engaged in a game of chance with the man on the moon.

"You game, *capitán?*"

"Your pleasure, *señor.*"

Don Miguel shuffled and dealt and the first game went to him. The cards made their way around the table with *Don* Miguel winning one game, Giddeon the next, then *Don* Miguel winning again, and so on until Giddeon felt he might be embroiled in mortal battle with the devil himself.

Never could he recall feeling such rapport with another man. Never had he met a man who at once broadened his horizons and at the same time challenged his image of himself. A fact quite unsettling to Giddeon, though it in no way interfered with his game.

His competitive spirit soared; his gaming instinct was sharper than it had ever been. Each time Don Miguel won, it was by a smaller margin; and each time Giddeon won by more. It was as though he were drawing in the mainsail, hand over slow hand, until finally, he had amassed a heap of coins in front of him, and Don Miguel had enough left for one more game.

The other three participants, if they could have been called such, had departed early on, leaving the game a duel, *mano a mano,* hand-to-hand and personal, between the two competitors.

Don Miguel had spoken only a few words during the entire three hours they had been at the table. Now he tossed his last coins into the pot, Giddeon covered the, and Don Miguel studied his cards.

When he spoke, Giddeon was prepared.

"As you see, capitán, I have no more funds. However, I am in possession of a valuable property, La

Hacienda de los Lomos, which, with your permission, I will now wager."

Giddeon held the old don's poker-straight stare for an eon, or so it seemed. Neither man moved a muscle; Giddeon had the image of two fighting bulls, each sizing the other up before moving in for the kill.

Slowly, almost imperceptibly, Giddeon shook his head. "No, señor." His voice was so low only a few people in the room could hear. "Your daughter's hand. We play for your daughter, Serita."

Again, neither man moved muscle or eye. The noise, as men around them sucked in their breath, sounded like the evening tide being pulled back to sea. Vaguely, Giddeon heard chattering, as those who had heard repeated his words to others who had not been within earshot.

By the time Don Miguel moved, Giddeon knew he had not only been sized up as a competitor. Something much more personal had transpired between the two men. And the old man wagered something of much greater value than an ancient Spanish land grant.

"*Sí, capitán. Mi hija,* Serita, *para su esposa.*"

For your wife.

He lost, of course, Don Miguel Cortinas. Although, to look at him, no one would have ever suspected.

After a handshake, Giddeon signaled his crew, and together the four men, sailors all, left the cantina.

Stopping in front of McCaulay, Giddeon counted five one-hundred-dollar gold pieces from the pot he had won.

"I'll hand it to you, Duval," McCaulay mused. "You have one hell of a style. I never meant you to marry the señorita."

29

"You said a clear title." Giddeon grinned, enjoying the reckless surge of energy victory always brought him. "Don't worry about me, I won't get caught. I've managed to wriggle out of the wedding noose before. When I show Señorita Cortinas her choices, she will not hesitate to give up her ranch and move to the safety of her father's lands in Mexico rather than spend her life married to a gringo seadog who has no intention of remaining on dry land any longer than it takes to sell the ranch and get back to sea." He handed the coins to the speculator.

McCaulay pushed the money aside. "Use it to outfit your men for the ride to Los Olmos. I'll be in touch."

Outside, Kosta, Giddeon's newest crew member, was the first to speak. "What the hell do you mean? Gambling for a wife? I have a stake in that cargo, too. I don't care if she's the most beautiful woman in the entire world, I want my share of that two hundred thousand dollars."

The four men matched stride.

"You should have taken the ranch," Felix told him. "We could sell that."

Giddeon kept his silence. And only Delos, his first mate and oldest friend, held his tongue beside him. He had seen the light in his captain's eyes — the light of a challenge accepted. It rarely shone, but when it did, all hell could not extinguish it until the game was over and won.

Don Miguel Cortinas watched the brash young man leave the cantina with only a handshake to claim his bride. And at last, Don Miguel smiled. Giddeon Duval was quite a man. His good looks matched only

Serita's herself. As her father, however, Don Miguel was not fooled for a moment into thinking Serita would give one tinker's damn for the captain's good looks.

But those eyes. Steady, yes, even cocky, green as the sea itself. You could read a lot in a man's eyes. Leastwise, in the eyes of a man as honest as Giddeon Duval.

Not that Capitán Duval was likely to consider himself honest. If Don Miguel judged correctly — and he had a long history of being able to judge not only horseflesh but a man's character as well — Giddeon Duval had just reached a crossroad in his much publicized life. Oh, he was well aware of Duval's hasty alliance with the speculator McCaulay. His eyes might be old, but they were still sharp, as was his mind. He had seen them in counsel before the game.

But that was before *el capitán* met Serita Cortinas. He puffed contentedly on the last of his imported cigars. From now on, if he were not terribly mistaken, Giddeon Duval's life would be judged in two eras: before he met Serita Cortinas, and afterward.

Don Miguel poured himself another two fingers of whiskey. He would drink this, then he would go back to the *casa* and tell his wife to sleep well — their beloved daughter Serita would now be safe from the *Tejano* gringos forevermore.

Chapter Two

La Hacienda de los Olmos
September 24, 1839

"*¡Sobrina, sobrina!* You must stand still one minute so we can discuss what to do about Señor Burton. Tomorrow is the day he will come."

"I know, Tita," Serita called over her shoulder as she raced from the courtyard. "First, I must exercise Barb; then Jorge, Pablo, and I are going to the pasture to bring in the *manada*. After the fiesta . . ."

"Serita!" *Tía* Ana demanded. "If Señor Burton has his way we will not be here after the fiesta tomorrow. Now, be still and let us figure out how to handle that . . . that gringo!"

Serita's oxblood boots skidded to a stop. Tossing her head, she grinned wickedly at her aunt. "Tita! Such language. You never resort to slang expressions!"

"Serita, *por favor*," the old lady began, "please, let us talk about Señor Burton. You are your father's child— always dashing headlong into trouble instead of taking time to figure things out in a sensible manner."

With a sigh Serita crossed the courtyard and put

loving arms around her aunt. "Tita. Forgive me for not speaking of this matter with you. Let us not worry ourselves today. Don't you see? Tomorrow our house will be filled to the *vigas*—the rafters—with guests. Most will stay overnight. Padre Alphonse is coming all the way from La Bahia to say Mass. All will go well. You will see. Even Oliver Burton would not accost us while the house is full of guests, and a priest of the church among them."

"Perhaps you are right, but I wonder. *Señor* Burton does not appear to be a man who is frightened of anything, not even the church."

"Oh, but he is, Tita. Otherwise he would have taken Los Olmos before now. He could have—anytime he wanted—had he been willing to murder us all."

Tía Ana clasped at her head in her hands. "What about the day after tomorrow, when all the guests have gone?"

Serita kissed her aunt's wrinkled forehead. "We will figure out something, I promise."

Pablo had Barb saddled when Serita arrived at the stable. Jorge danced from one bare foot to the other, holding the reins of the yellow dun filly.

"Let me ride her, Serita. She is broken enough now. I know she is."

Serita tousled her nephew's black hair. "Why not?" she agreed. "First, let me top her off. Open the gates. I will ride down to the creek and back."

The scent of fall was in the air, brisk and cool. The ever-present sea breeze rustled in the elm leaves, many of which were now falling to the banks of the creek.

Leaning low over the saddle, she patted Barb's yellow neck and whispered secrets in her ear—how she was the fairest of all Arabian fillies, how she would bear progeny of great spirit and beauty and intelligence. How together, Barb and Serita, they would save Los Olmos from the gringos forevermore. The wind swept over Serita's back, blousing her white shirt above her, chilling her skin softly as with kisses.

Barb's hooves thudded over the crackling leaves, across the sandy bed of the stream, and up the opposite bank. Serita sat erect in the saddle and let the wind mold her silk shirt to her skin. Her hair flew in a wild flurry. Later, she would drape it about her head, as Tía Ana insisted; later, she would put on petticoats and chemise. But for now her body reveled in the sensuousness of the wind tugging the single layer of silk across her otherwise nude skin.

Lifting her face to the cloudless sky, she drank in the sun's warmth. How she loved this place! How proud she was of her ancestors! How determined she was to preserve Los Olmos not only for her own children, but for Juan's—for Jorge and his heirs to come. Her brother Juan had died fighting against the Mexican Army at the massacre at La Bahia in Goliad, not over fifty miles from this very spot.

Sobered, as always, when thinking of her beloved brother, she lowered her face and prepared to turn Barb toward the stable so Jorge could have his ride.

It was then she saw the men—three of them, walking toward her.

Her first thought was of Burton's vaqueros, the hired men he referred to as his "Cow Boys." Her heart skipped a beat; immediately she recalled her words to Tía Ana, her assurance that Burton would not harass them until after the Fiesta de San Miguel.

Squinting toward the men, she finally decided she

had been wrong. No man who tended cattle did so afoot, and the three who approached her now neither led mounts by the reins nor did they carry saddles, indicating their mounts had gone lame. Besides, the chance of three horses going lame at the same time, for whatever reason, was preposterous.

Her throat constricted, and she drew a deep breath, knowing she should flee to the safety of the compound immediately, yet hesitating.

She sat still while the men drew nearer. Foot-weary, she thought, watching them gingerly pick their way on scuffed high-topped black boots. Their flowing white blouses were dirty, as though they had come a long way . . .

Pirates! Suddenly she recalled the tales Papá told of pirates slipping into Los Olmos Bay. They had come inland with their loot . . . up Los Olmos Creek. How far inland?

Her heart pounded now, and she pulled Barb around and raced for the house. By the time she reached the compound, her mind was in a wild panic, her thoughts in a tizzy. The instant before she turned around, she had caught the eyes of the man in the lead.

Cocky green eyes. Taunting, licentious. Prickles broke out along her skin; the tips of her breasts chafed against the soft fabric of her silky white shirt.

"We've trouble," she shouted to an astonished Pablo and Jorge. "Bolt the gates behind me. ¡Andale! Hurry!"

In one fluid movement, she slid to the ground and raced for the house. The heavy gate creaked, then slammed; the bolts sounded like cannons when they dropped into place. Boots thudded behind hers — Pablo and Jorge.

Grasping the shotgun from above the fireplace in the kitchen, she clutched up a *rebozo* from a nearby chair and tossed it over her blouse, tying it in a firm knot just above her heaving bosom.

"Burton?" Pablo rushed into the kitchen behind her, only to have her dash up the staircase which led to a lookout on top of the main living quarters. He followed, Jorge close on his heels.

"I don't think so," she called in answer. "They're afoot."

"Afoot?" Pablo labored for breath as he climbed the steep, narrow staircase to the rooftop. "Perhaps their horses . . ."

"I thought of that," she interrupted. "Three horses do not go lame at the same time. Besides, they aren't carrying saddles. No horseman goes off and leaves a saddle on a dead horse."

"Where'd they come from?" Jorge asked.

"The bay." Serita's breath was coming short now, too.

"The bay?" Jorge asked. "Are they pirates?"

Serita gained the lookout first. Standing stiff-legged, she pointed in the direction of the approaching men. "See for yourself. They certainly are not *rancheros* coming to our fiesta."

Jorge's eyes grew round watching the three men cross the creek. They approached the house, talking among themselves, apparently oblivious to the enormous compound before them.

All except one of them.

The one with green eyes.

Pursing her lips, Serita fought to bring her racing heart under control. It seemed every day brought a new disaster, lately—a threat from a different quarter.

If they weren't being attacked by land, they were besieged by sea.

The leader stopped dead still in front of the house, yet at a distance which allowed him to look up at her without appearing to humble himself.

The audacity of some men, she thought, studying the figure below her. Up close, his skin was so brown he could pass for one of Spanish blood, but his hair was fair and his eyes—yes, his eyes were definitely green. Green and insolent.

"If you have come for food, I will have some set outside the back gate," she called down.

At her words, he broke into laughter and was joined by his companions.

"Very well," Serita dismissed him. "Be gone with you, then. We have no room for vagrants."

When he raised his eyebrows, she got a better glimpse of the green in his eyes. Green and challenging.

And for some reason, most unsettling. She sighed heavily. Too many problems vied for her attention of late. She was becoming weak and unable to hold her wits together.

Steadying her shotgun on the group, she glared at the silent stranger and pulled back the hammer.

The green-eyed man below her spoke. "Señorita Cortinas?"

She stared, thinking strangely that for a gringo he pronounced her name with perfection.

Sweeping a hand across his waist, he bowed in a courtly fashion, increasing her aggravation tenfold. "May I be so bold as to say, señorita, you are the spitting image of your father—" His eyes swept her form, searing it with a heat which flared from within

37

herself. "—in temperament."

She pulled back the hammer on the shotgun. "State your business and be gone."

Again the stranger smiled. "Before you shoot us, allow me to introduce myself and my men. I am Giddeon Duval, captain of the schooner, *Espíritu Estelle*. These are my men." Indicating each in turn, Giddeon introduced Delos and Kosta. "We bring greetings from your father, Don Miguel."

"My father!" she hissed. The heat in her body coagulated into a mass of pure anger. "If he has lost Los Olmos to you at a gaming table, capitán, you will have hell to pay claiming your winnings."

Again the stranger laughed heartily. His companions joined in. "The hacienda is not exactly what he lost this time, señorita. Perhaps, if we could dismiss the matter in a more civilized manner . . ."

"Civilized!" she cried. "You win my home in a card game, and you expect *me* to act civilized? It is you, capitán, who should learn the meaning of that word."

"Perhaps you would be so kind as to instruct me, señorita."

Serita sucked in a sharp breath. Pablo placed a steadying hand on her shoulder.

"Easy, *chica*. Do not shoot this Anglo."

"This is one gringo no one would mind if I shoot, Pablo. He is nothing more than a pirate come to take my land. The world would be a better place without such scum!"

"One moment." Giddeon held up a pacifying hand. His strong voice turned serious, redoubling her rage. "I had the pleasure of meeting Don Miguel Cortinas, ma'am, and I would be honored to share that meeting with you."

"*Sobrina*," Tía Ana began, "why not invite them in for coffee. They do not appear to be dangerous men, only misguided and a bit weary. If they have word of Miguel . . . I mean, it has been so long since we heard a word. Perhaps we could listen before we send them on their way."

Tía Ana's words came straight from Serita's own heart. How she loved her father! Even if he were involved in this absurd crusade to lose Los Olmos. She didn't have to give over the ranch to these men, but she could learn what they knew about Papá.

"*Sí*, Tita, we should hear what they have to say."

"Toss your weapons toward the gate," she called to the men below her. "Pablo will come down and collect them. Do not mistake me for a weakling. I will shoot and kill any or all of you, if you provide the slightest provocation."

"Have no fear, Señorita Cortinas, your reputation with firearms is as legendary as your . . . ah, your horsemanship."

Heat rose swiftly up her neck and burned the back of her ears at his ungentlemanlylike reminder that she had ridden in such an exposed state before him. The other gamblers had never been so bold—nor made her this angry!

"Then hold your tongue, capitán. Already, you are trespassing. No one would fault a lady who responded with gunfire to such impertinent behavior as yours."

Giddeon folded his arms over his chest, cocked his head to one side, and did not take his eyes from her, while he and his men awaited the appearance of Pablo at the front gates.

She was like Don Miguel, he thought. From the moment he saw her, he knew she was the spitting image of her father. The same obsidian eyes, the same crusty though regal bearing. What was it about her that instantly intrigued him?

Her beauty, of course. She was much more beautiful than McCaulay had described, or than he himself had dreamed these last several days.

And dream he had, to the point of becoming obsessed with the challenge inherent in this mad game of chance. Now, it was the woman herself who bewitched him, standing as she did, so obviously unaware of her own sensuality—clothed in tightly fitting leather breeches, a shawl tied low over her blouse, a blouse he knew to be the only garment she wore over decidedly ample endowments.

Fire, grace, and beauty—the qualities he had only days before attributed to the enormous herds of wild mustangs that roamed the prairies between the Rio Grande River and Los Olmos in such numbers the entire plain was cut and recut by their trails.

He stared at the spirited woman poised expectantly above him. Fire, grace, and beauty. He scoffed. That was before the devious creatures stole their mounts and left them afoot in this devil's playground. Since then, his regard for the mustang had gone steadily downhill.

But they were beautiful animals, he thought again—just as this woman, this Serita Cortinas, was possessed of great beauty.

For years he had head stories of the bands of wild mustangs that ranged in these parts, but the telling compared to seeing them, much as Enos McCaulay's description of Serita Cortinas compared to seeing her in the flesh. McCaulay had communicated none of her true beauty—nothing of her fire and spirit.

For an instant his eyes blurred with a vision of the first wild horse he had seen—a magnificent creature standing on a slight rise, the morning sun bright on the fine details of his physique, glistening on his sleek hairs, his head tossed to the sky, his slender legs poised for flight. As though he were suddenly visited by the devil, the image in Giddeon's mind changed: He saw a rope around the arched neck, a saddle on the proud back, a harsh Spanish bit cutting into the delicate mouth. The master of the wind became a trembling captive. Broken in spirit, his beauty fled.

In that moment, Giddeon Duval glimpsed what he was about, and this mad gamble became a sickening conquest. For without her freedom, Serita Cortinas would no longer be spirited, and, without spirit, her beauty also would flee.

Once inside the compound, Giddeon regained a hold on his senses—and on his intentions. Pablo led them, actually, the old vaquero followed, carrying their weapons, while holding his own shotgun on their wary backs. They passed through a tiled corridor off which doors opened left and right, then entered a sun-drenched courtyard, where they cooled their heels alone with no sign of either Serita Cortinas nor of the elderly woman or boy who had appeared with her on the rooftop.

Although fastidiously clean, the entire fortress of a place showed signs of decay: cracks in the adobe walls, rotting wood on the lintels and *vigas*. Flowers, however, bloomed in vibrant yellows and reds along the porches and around the center fountain. Giddeon stopped beside an oak tree, gnarled with age, bent by the wind. He had seen many such trees on the journey to Los Olmos; the fact that they survived eons of time

41

on this windswept terrain was a testament to their strength. Yet, he wondered at this tree, enclosed as it was by a courtyard which rivaled even the tree itself in age.

Finally, the matron of the house arrived, followed by the young boy and a serving girl who carried a tray laden with coffee and sweet breads—*dulces*.

"Set the tray here, Abril," Tía Ana instructed before she turned to the men with such welcome one would have thought she had invited them for a visit. "I am Señorita Ana Cortinas. This is my nephew's son, Jorge. Please sit, drink your coffee, and tell me about my brother."

Giddeon glanced about the courtyard, around the galleries of the second floor, then took the offered seat. He had finished a brief description of his meeting with Don Miguel, omitting the wager and the man's inebriated state, when the sound of footsteps alerted him. He stared unabashed as Serita bounded down the stairs like a young colt.

"Tell me, Capitán Duval," Tía Ana continued, "whatever induced you and your men to come all this way afoot?"

"We didn't set out on foot, ma'am." Rising to his feet, he watched Serita cross the length of the courtyard in what could only be called angry strides. Still dressed in her riding pants and boots, she had obviously tended to the more delicate concerns of her toilette, for her hair was now draped about her head in a chaste sweep and . . .

"Then whatever happened to your horses, capitán? Surely, three horses. . ." *Tía* Ana paused.

Serita's boots ground to a halt at the table opposite Giddeon. His eyes strayed to her bosom where the

42

white silk blouse was now supported by what appeared to be several layers of undergarments. A pearl-handled riding crop in one hand whacked distractedly against her other palm.

"*Sí, Capitán* Duval, what did happen to your horses?"

Her voice melted over his senses like warm honey, thick and mellow yet dripping with derision.

Giddeon felt color rise along his neck. His eyes held hers, and in that moment he thought perhaps he had wagered in haste.

Serita Cortinas might be possessed with a supple, womanly body, but her eyes were as harsh and black as a winter storm at sea, as unyielding as the iron-bound gates which guarded this fortress of a home, and they taunted him now, as though he were a common peasant. His anger heightened. No spitfire of a woman was going to make a jackass out of him — no matter how beautiful she was.

Drawing on this inner fury, Giddeon casually took his seat and turned his attention back to the elder Señorita Cortinas. "You might say they returned to the wild, ma'am. Being men of the sea, we are not accustomed to the vagaries of your animal life."

"You mean the mustangs stole your horses away from camp?" Jorge asked.

Giddeon looked the boy level in the eye. "That's exactly what happened, son. The second night out from the Rio Grande River."

Jorge looked each of the men over in turn, then quizzed Giddeon. "But . . . I thought you came by sea. You said you are a captain — and Serita said you are pirates!"

Giddeon's eyes narrowed on Serita's where she still

43

stood across the table. At her sheepish look, his mouth quirked in a lopsided grin. "Pirates?"

"Pirates can come by land as well as by sea," she retorted.

"*Sobrina*," *Tía* Ana interrupted. "This man has news of Don Miguel. He says your papá is well."

Serita's eyes glinted fire. "That must be true, Tita, since he is still able to find fools to whom to wager Los Olmos. But you are out of luck, capitán. You have not only lost your horses to the wild, but your folly at wagering with an old man will reap no rewards. You were foolish to allow him to wager Los Olmos."

Giddeon held his tongue. But for the others present, he would leap across the table and shake her regal figure until the mantle of haughtiness fell away; he would kiss those tempting lips until her taunting black eyes melted with desire. But the others were present, so he could not—not at this time, anyhow.

"Begging your pardon, señorita, I am not entirely the simpleton you take me for. I did not allow Don Miguel to wager Los Olmos."

"Then what . . .?" Her lips remained parted in such a manner that Giddeon pressed his own together to keep from reaching to kiss some sense into her stubborn head.

"At least," he continued as though she had not questioned him, "not exactly."

Her confusion gave way to anger. "No matter how you won Los Olmos, capitán, you will never take possession."

As with an iron grip, his gaze held hers—steady, unwavering, demanding. "Make no mistake, Serita Cortinas, what I have won . . ."—moving, his eyes roamed her frame, resting again on her obsidian

44

stare— ". . . I *will* possess."

Her perfect figure radiated such energy, he half expected her to light into him with her crop. Fire, grace, and beauty, he thought again, personified in the flesh and spirit of one Serita Cortinas.

That she was insulted by his improper insinuations was evident in the leashed rage beneath her iron-hard eyes, in the fiery heat which crept up her neck and flamed in her cheeks. His stomach felt suddenly queasy, and he had just entertained the thought that Serita Cortinas's defeat was not something he wanted on his conscience when he saw a change in her.

A subtle change, to be sure. Unnoticeable, had he not been gazing into her eyes with such intensity. But suddenly he perceived a spark where moments before there had been nothing but an iron wall . . . a spark that flared in the center of her eyes and spread to a burning challenge. Her body responded with other telltale signs, which again he would have missed had he not been so attuned to her every nuance. He watched her breasts swell beneath the confines of her garments; the vein at the base of her neck throbbed.

"You are too sure of yourself, capitán." She surveyed the three men as one, then snapped the crop against her leg. "You have had your coffee, now be on your way. We have much work left before our fiesta . . ."

"Fiesta?" Giddeon inquired, and was rewarded with another intense stare, albeit one of pure anger now, no challenge there.

"Tomorrow is the Feast of San Miguel," Jorge informed the men. "It is Tío Miguel's feast day, and we always have a great fiesta. People come from—"

"Jorge," Serita interrupted. "Do not carry on so. The men must be on their way."

45

A bell rang from somewhere toward the rear of the compound.

Giddeon's mind raced. He had no intention of leaving Los Olmos so precipitously. Yet, neither was he ready to spring the truth of the situation on Serita. Finally, he rose, nodded to his companions, then bowed to Tía Ana. "Thank you for your hospitality, ma'am. Perhaps you have horses we could purchase for our return trip to the border. And, if it is not too much trouble, some food for our journey."

"Of course," Tía Ana agreed. "But first you will join us at *almuerzo*. That was the first luncheon bell. You have a quarter of an hour to freshen up." At the flick of her wrist, a housemaid appeared. "Lupe will guide you to your rooms."

Tía Ana turned to her furious niece. "Instruct Abril to serve us here on the patio, *sobrina*. After siesta, Pablo can show these gentlemen some horses."

"Gentlemen?" Serita seethed between her teeth, as Lupe hurriedly led the strangers to a cottage at the rear of the compound. "Tita! How could you invite them to dine with us? We have work . . ."

"*Sobrina*, it is only a meal. Then they will be on their way. We owe them that much for the way Miguel—"

"We owe them nothing! Papá did not twist their arms. They entered the stupid game of their own accord."

But Serita's upbringing stilled her tongue from further outburst, and she acquiesced to Tía Ana's demands, telling herself that *almuerzo* could not last forever.

And for a fact, time went quickly enough at the beginning. When Jorge asked about the *Espíritu Estelle,* Giddeon supplied a daring tale of the hurricane

46

that sank the schooner to the bottom of the Gulf of Mexico, of their rescue by a nearby French vessel, and how he and his crew had arrived in Bagdad with hardly a peso between them. He mentioned his determination to salvage the schooner, but let the rest go unspoken: His agreement with Enos McCaulay and the subsequent game of chance with Don Miguel remained his and his crew's secret.

Until Serita joined the conversation. She had listened quietly, holding herself alert to anything underhanded Giddeon Duval might attempt. She did not know what she expected, but she felt a desperate need to be prepared for whatever he had up his sleeve. Finally, his easy-going manner lulled her into a complacency she soon regretted.

"And what of the game, capitán? You say you did not win Los Olmos. What exactly did you win from my father?"

The question was so unexpected Giddeon almost choked on the piece of tortilla in his mouth. Blanching, he looked from one of his crew members to another, and Serita followed his gaze.

Every man of them concentrated on Giddeon, challenging him, or so it seemed to her, with cocky grins.

"Well?" Serita demanded, returning her eyes to his.

"Ah . . . well," Giddeon began. Damnit, he wasn't ready to tell her the truth, not with the entire household looking on. He had planned to take her aside — alone — explain the situation, her choices. In that manner, she would choose freedom over marriage to a gringo stranger, he had no doubt. But from their brief acquaintance, he knew her willful nature had been, if anything, understated. It would not do to push her into a corner. He must choose his time and place and present the situation with care. "I don't know . . ."

Her mouth fell open. "You came all this way to claim your winnings, and you do not know what you won?"

Her taunting incensed him; caution fled, leaving in its wake an irrepressible desire to silence her ridicule. Perhaps, he thought, a dose of her own medicine would prepare her for the choices she must make later. He tossed his napkin into his plate. "Believe me, señorita, you will find out when I collect." Rising, he belatedly excused himself to *Tía* Ana. "If you will call this Pablo, we will choose our horses."

"After siesta," she answered politely. "Pablo will come to your quarters after siesta."

Siesta did not go well for Serita. As soon as Giddeon and his men had left the table, Tía Ana scolded her for her discourtesy to the guests; then, after she changed to a lounging gown and tried to sleep, all she could do was toss and turn. With everything else which demanded her attention, why had Papá chosen this time to send another annoyance? Did she not have enough to do, keeping their life together, without his continual interference? He should know by now that she would never leave Los Olmos, no matter what he did to wrest her away. No matter who he sent to . . .

To what? she wondered angrily. What exactly had Papá wagered. And why had that outrageous captain been so secretive? Probably to give him time to figure out how to get the best of her!

Storming about the room, she flung garments here and there, unconsciously cluttering her room to a state of disaster.

He would not succeed! she vowed. Disrobing, she redressed in her riding clothes. She had work to do, and siesta or not, she intended to get on with the day's chores. Early guests for the fiesta would arrive in time for a formal evening meal, *cena*.

Tiptoeing along the gallery, down the staircase, past Tía Ana's doorway, she crossed the courtyard, hoping in her heart she wasn't seen. Tía Ana and her mother before her demanded strict adherence to siesta. But today rest was impossible. She needed to be busy . . . to think about Barb, to plan for tomorrow. Tomorrow, which could bring her next and most difficult confrontation with Oliver Burton.

What a time Papá chose to send strangers. She had no time for strangers who wagered for a person's home. This one would leave emptyhanded, like the others, and that was too good for him. The insolent bastard!

She wouldn't see him again.

With a sigh of relief, she reached the stable undetected and headed straight for Barb's stall. Gathering her tack, she began the grooming she had neglected with the arrival of . . . of that dastardly gambling man. First, she inspected each hoof in turn, dislodging a stone from the right front, a hard shell from the left rear. Next, she combed through Barb's silvery tail, then her mane, removing tangles and bits of grass and leaves.

Her mind settled down. As always when working with Barb, Serita began to plan for the future. No matter how uncertain that future might appear at this moment, she knew exactly how she would proceed.

Next year she intended to breed Barb to El Rey de las Estrellas, the most perfect in both form and color of any wild stallion she had ever seen. She named him King of the Stars, because he bore the enduring sign of greatness on his forehead — a perfect white star. With their combined ancestry, Barb and El Rey's offspring would be unequaled, and Los Olmos would take its place as a top breeder of horseflesh.

Picking up the curry brush she swept Barb's golden body with long strokes, bringing a lustrous glow to the filly's coat. Oliver Burton had his own plans for Los Olmos, that she knew. He had taken other ranches, to be sure. But in every case, Serita was convinced the landowners could have held on to their grants had they remained firm and unshaken. He had run the others off by intimidation; she would not give in to his threats.

Suddenly, in the midst of a stroke down Barb's back, her flesh turned queasy, a thing that had happened regularly since Burton's last nocturnal visit. Her backbone went limp. The other ranchers had capitulated under intimidation; she had not. The others had left before Burton was required to resort to violence.

She had not. And his last visit, when he battered down the stable gates, had been vivid proof of the man's intent to take Los Olmos. Tomorrow. At sundown.

At sundown tomorrow. Chills gripped her body. She bent over, holding the brush between her knees, while her stomach contracted in sharp pains.

In two strides Giddeon was by her side. He grasped her shoulders, thinking she had been injured. "What's the matter?"

Abruptly, she jerked around in his arms. The pain in her stomach fled before a surge of blind panic.

"Let me go!" Flailing her shoulders, she attempted to dislodge his hands. To no avail.

"Are you all right?" His eyes searched her face; his mind sought a reason for her pain; his senses throbbed with her nearness. He tightened his fingers about her arms.

Her breath caught in her chest, and she had great difficulty breathing. "Why are you . . .?" She stared down at his fingers, which easily wrapped around her slender arms.

"When you doubled over, I thought you were hurt. I . . ."

"It's siesta," she told him, renewing her efforts to free herself. "You are supposed to be in your quarters."

He chuckled. "What exempts you from this national ritual?"

Fury flamed in her cheeks. "Take your hands off me. This instant. Or I will scream for Pablo."

"And let your aunt discover how you spend siesta?" His face was close to hers now, and her sweet aroma of gardenias weakened him. Her lips trembled; he moved toward them.

She renewed her efforts, jerking her face away from him. "Tita's hospitality does not include accosting me in the stable."

Moving back a bit, he still retained his hold on her arms. His eyes bore into hers, caressing, softly taunting. Then, he turned her loose abruptly.

"My intention was to save you from injury, *señorita*. I gave no thought to accosting you." He smiled in a cocky, lopsided manner. "That must have been your imagination."

"Of all the crude, vulgar, barbaric . . ." She stepped back quickly, raising the brush in her hand. Her face flamed with his insinuations. How dare he accuse her of . . .

51

Gradually, from somewhere deep inside, reason took hold. She dropped her arm and stomped out of Barb's stall. Giddeon followed.

Silently she secured the gate, then began putting away her grooming equipment. "You are wasting your time, *capitán*. My father has wagered Los Olmos before, but as you see, no one has taken possession."

Giddeon propped a foot casually on the lower rung of the gate. Resting an elbow on his leg, he studied her. When she looked at him to lend credence to her statement, he moistened his lips with the tip of his tongue, thinking. "Your father's honor means nothing to you?"

Infuriated by his brashness, she closed the cupboard with a slam that jarred her senses even more. "The honor of my father is not at stake, *capitán*. This land belongs to me." *Of all the boorish oafs!* she thought.

Her thoughts and her emotions, however, were worlds apart. Fingers of fire climbed her neck, singeing her skin; her head throbbed with a strange, unsettling melody. Suddenly, she knew this man was unlike any other; she must get rid of him quickly, before she lost the one thing most dear to her in all the world. Los Olmos.

"Winning Los Olmos in a game of chance means nothing," she explained in as steady a voice as she could call forth. "You see, after my brother Juan's death, my father signed the land grant over to me. He does not think it binding—me being a woman. But I know differently. Los Olmos is legally mine. I have the papers locked away safe and sound, and until such time as I choose to give them to my heirs, they will remain in my possession."

Her impassioned speech notwithstanding, her body

remained under siege by the very nearness of this man. Strive as she did, she could not bring her racing heart under control. Her arms still burned from his touch—a burning that resembled more than anything else a strange and frightening sensation akin to begging.

When she stepped toward the stable gate, he blocked the way. She swallowed the lump in her throat and made an effort at nonchalance.

"So you see, *capitán*, you will save yourself wasted time if you leave immediately. No matter what my father wagered in that game, you will not collect. You did not win Los Olmos, because Los Olmos was not his to lose."

Suddenly, her reticence overwhelmed him. Or was it her nearness? He didn't give himself time to ponder the question. Instead, as she tried to slip past him, he grabbed her shoulders, turned her swiftly, and lowered his lips.

She pulled away; he held her fast. She jerked her head back; he cupped it in his hands and pulled her soft, unyielding lips to his. Fueled by her resistance, he countered with techniques he had not been called upon to use in many a year. Most of his lovemaking had been one-sided, lately; the ladies anxious to please, to pursue, to pleasure.

Serita Cortinas definitely had other opinions of his charms—opinions that challenged his pride. And he rose to the challenge by giving her his full attention.

"Do not fight it, *querida*," he urged, covering her supple yet resisting mouth once again with his own. His hand on her hair recalled the flurry with which it flew in the wind when he first saw her this morning, and his fingers began to take the pins loose.

But she fought so hard, he stopped. Later, he promised himself. One day very soon—before he turned her over to the care of her father in Mexico—he would take her hair loose, pin by pin, and tumble his fingers through its length.

Pressing her closer, his lips plied hers gently, then with greater intensity. Finally, she relaxed her struggle somewhat, and he ran his tongue around the outline of her mouth and was rewarded with a shudder from her entrapped body. For a moment she pressed against him, pliant and warm and willing—

For a moment.

The next thing he knew she had managed to jerk loose, and before he could regain control, she raised her right arm and struck him mightily across the face.

"Get away from me!" Her voice shook from the violent fears he instilled within her. "Get away from Los Olmos! Now. You did not win Los Olmos! And you most certainly did not win me!"

Giddeon moved fast. Grabbing her flailing arms, he imprisoned them to her side. "Oh, but I did, *querida*. I won you for my blushing bride."

It took a moment for his words to penetrate her whirling brain, and when they did, all semblance of thought fled, leaving a void into which instantly rushed terror, cold and black. "You lie, *capitán!* Papá would never do such a thing. He would never betroth me to . . . to an infidel gringo such as you!"

"In the accepted custom," Giddeon continued, his voice strong and calm, "your father pledged your hand in marriage—to me, infidel, gringo . . ."—he shrugged—". . . or whatever I might be."

Serita stood still and deathly quiet, while his words sounded as from a great distance. Why is it, she

54

wondered, that when the inevitable comes to pass, it is never as one imagined? All her life she had known Papá could betroth her at will and without her knowledge or consent. Had known, yes. But she had never believed he would. Certainly not to a destitute sea captain in a cantina!

"Surely now, señorita, you will agree your father's word, hence his honor, is very much at stake. We must negotiate in earnest, you and I."

"Honor!" she spat. "You speak to me of honor? You dishonor my father's name by speaking it! Gather your cohorts and get off my land. Now! And do not ever show your face on Los Olmos again!"

Serita stayed in her room until the bell rang for *cena*. Vaguely, she was aware of horses coming into the stables. She heard guests arrive. Jorge called to her. But she remained locked behind the protection of her bedroom door.

Locked away while the horrible nightmare of Giddeon's angry confession quivered like a den full of rattlesnakes in the pit of her belly. For a long time all she could do was lie on the bed and shake. For a long time, all she wanted to do was die.

How could Papá have done something so ghastly? Wager her hand in marriage! Betroth her to a stranger! He must have gone mad!

When her mind began to clear, she wondered that she had not taken a shotgun—or at least her crop—to the despicable captain. Of course, he gave her little chance. But unlike her usual self, she had not entertained the idea to strike back until she was safely locked in her room. And that was too late.

At the time all she had felt was a weakness, the likes of which she had never experienced. Even the anger that boiled inside her veins was overwhelmed by the sickening prospect of such a wager.

The other oafs she had easily driven away with never a backward thought. But this time things were different. The very nature of this wager was different . . . personal.

The hours passed and with them her emotions shifted from anger and denial to despair. She had labored so long, so hard to preserve Los Olmos — and for what? To be betrayed by her own father? Would he finally succeed in driving her from this land she loved with all her heart and soul?

As dusk set in, guitar music drifted up from the courtyard . . . gay and festive music, mingled with voices raised in laughter. The laughter of guests arriving for tomorrow's fiesta. Perhaps the last fiesta ever to be held at Los Olmos. If Oliver Burton had his way, tomorrow would be the last day she ever spent at Los Olmos. If Oliver Burton . . .

Dear God! she thought suddenly. *A gringo name! You answered my prayer, and I was too blind to see!*

Racing to the door, she flung it wide and rang for Abril. When the young maid hastened to her door, Serita instructed her to bring hot water, *pronto*. And to see that the *capitán* and his men were invited to the fiesta. Pray God they had not already gone!

"Abril, if they are no longer here, send Pablo to fetch them. *¡Andale!*"

Searching her wardrobe, she withdrew her favorite gown — a black watered silk with a ruffled neckline that dipped low at the center of her bosom, then curved around each arm, well below her shoulders.

The full, flirty skirt rustled over layers of multicolored petticoats—red, green, blue, and yellow. Brushing her hair to an ebony gloss, she braided small strands above each ear, then drew them back and caught them in multicolored ribbons, leaving the rest of her near-waist-length hair loose and flying.

That rogue, she thought, flushing still at the feel of Giddeon Duval's lips on hers. He would rue the day he sat in a game of chance with Don Miguel Cortinas!

Her heart fluttered with fear—fear that her impetuous decision could well backfire. But she stilled her fear with the knowledge that, whatever his intention, Papá had handed her the perfect—and at present, the only—means with which to save Los Olmos from Oliver Burton. By tomorrow at sundown.

As the final bell called the household to *cena*, Serita descended the staircase into the courtyard, her heart beating a wild flamenco in her breast. Bless the crazy heart of Don Miguel Cortinas! He had provided her a way to save Los Olmos!

Giddeon rebuked himself soundly for blurting out the truth to Serita. He had intended to wait for the right time when he could lay all his cards on the table at once.

But, damnit! The woman was infuriating. She got under his skin in a way no woman ever had, and he knew he had best watch out for himself when she was around. He sighed, wondering what his next move would be—and how the fiery Señorita Cortinas would react when she discovered him at the fiesta. Tía Ana's invitation to stay made his determination to do so more acceptable, but he was nevertheless wary about facing Serita again.

By the time siesta was over, the housemaids had returned the clothing he and his men had handed over at their insistence, freshly brushed and pressed. The household was aflutter with preparations for the coming fiesta, which, to his surprise, was scheduled to begin with dinner for the early arrivers this very evening.

A germ of dissatisfaction stirred within him. Every time he decided the better part of valor would definitely lie in leaving Los Olmos and the whole sordid wager behind, he recalled the cargo lying at the bottom of the Gulf of Mexico, and the fifty thousand dollars Enos McCaulay agreed to exchange for a legal deed to Los Olmos.

After siesta he and his crew walked around the compound and out to the vaqueros' quarters which now stood empty and virtually in ruin. The entire place was in such need of repair that Giddeon wondered whether McCaulay knew what he had bargained for. The land was what McCaulay wanted, though. The land was the valuable part.

But only to a speculator like McCaulay, Giddeon reasoned, as for the hundredth time Serita's obviously deep love for this land threatened to diffuse his determination to go through with the bargain. A woman like Serita had no business trying to run a huge *hacienda*. The dilapidated state of the place was testament to that fact.

Don Miguel was right. She had no business staying on here. None of them did. As soon as she signed the papers, he would escort the lot of them to *Don* Miguel's lands in Mexico. That was where they belonged; ultimately that was where they would be happy. There Serita would find someone like her father—a wealthy man of Spanish heritage. She would marry and . . .

At that last thought he had returned to the house and accepted Tía Ana's offer of tequila.

That's where Serita found him. When she paused at the top of the staircase, her eyes were immediately drawn to Giddeon Duval, where he sat on the edge of the fountain, tipping the bottle of tequila to his lips. Her blood flowed hot through her veins, flushing her skin, as though she herself had swallowed a swig of the flaming liquid.

Trepidation flooded her senses. What in heaven's name was she about? Would she regret this to her dying day? Was Los Olmos worth such a sacrifice?

The answer to the last question stilled to some extent the flutter in her heart, and she proceeded down the staircase, holding the banister to steady her shaking legs.

When she reached the bottom step, Giddeon offered his arm—*as though she had never ordered him to leave*, she thought. She had watched him cross the courtyard, his crisp white blouse gleaming in the dusky twilight, his tightly fitting black trousers tucked into the tops of highly polished black boots. The combination brought a lump to her throat, and when he offered his arm, she was seized by the sudden impulse to run for her life.

What in heaven's name was she about?!

His eyes pierced deep—to her very soul—searching, questioning. When she placed her hand in the crook of his elbow, he quickly covered it with his other hand. *As though she had never demanded he take his hands off her!*

Neither of them spoke. Later, she thought as how

59

neither of them likely could. Silently, he ushered her toward the *comedor*, as though he escorted her to dinner every evening of the year. When she hesitated outside the doorway of the room full of chattering guests and family, he bent impulsively and ever so gently placed a soft kiss on the top of her hair.

"Ummm . . . gardenias." His whispered touch sent fingers of fire radiating from his lips down her neck, through her body.

They entered the rectangular room in which generations of her family had dined. Suddenly she wondered what secrets her ancestors had carried into this room with them. Had any ever attempted something as unconventional as she was about to? What would they think, should they stand in judgment of her? Would they consider hers yet the latest in a long list of sacrifices required to hold on to the family heritage?

Tía Ana sat at the head of the table with their closest neighbor, Don Fernando Dominquez, to her left and his wife, Doña Maria, to her right. Various guests filled the ensuing chairs, including Giddeon's crew, Delos and Kosta, leaving the chair at the opposite end of the long table, and one to its right, empty.

Serita stopped beside Tía Ana's chair, stooped, and kissed her cheek. "I am sorry to be late, Tita."

She proceeded around the table, smiling, talking, greeting each person, until she came to her place at the foot of the table. Giddeon held her chair, and she sat, feeling like a player on the stage enacting a queen, while inside, she knew herself to be the court jester.

The meal progressed somehow. She tasted nothing, and later she even had trouble recalling who was at table with them. After the main course of roast quail, wild rice, and tamales, Tía Ana rang the bell beside her plate and asked Abril to serve flan and coffee in the parlor.

As soon as Abril departed on her mission, Serita stood at her place. Her heart fairly beat out of her bosom, and she was sure all could see it above the low neckline of her gown. Her knees wobbled so that she held the table edge to gain balance. Then with a flick of the little bell beside her plate, she drew the attention of everyone at the table.

Briefly, she chanced a glance at Giddeon, who looked up at her with a mixture of emotions she was unfamiliar with, but which flushed her skin nonetheless. She stared at him without moving a muscle for a moment, wishing desperately there were some other way out of her dilemma.

Then she turned her attention to Tía Ana. *"Con permiso.* Excuse me, Tita, I have an announcement."

Tía Ana nodded. Serita took a swallow a wine to wet her dry mouth. "Tomorrow, on the feast day of my father, I will be married . . . here in our chapel at Los Olmos. Padre Alphonse will officiate."

An audible gasp filled the silence, and she dared not look down. Neither did she dare stop at this point. Raising her voice, she finished "to . . . Capitán Giddeon Duval."

Chapter Three

"Marry you?! Are you out of your mind?"

Giddeon's words had tolled like the chapel bell through her long, sleepless night, and, now, as she prepared to face this day — one of the most important in her entire life — she pushed aside all thought of what it *should* mean, steeling herself with the sure knowledge of what it *would* mean.

Her wedding day — a romantic day full of happiness and joy. No, her wedding day would be neither joyful nor happy, leastwise not for the traditional reasons.

But her wedding day would save Los Olmos from Oliver Burton, and for that she would be grateful. If not joy-filled, at least she would consider herself fortunate.

In spite of the situation, she smiled recalling Giddeon's outburst the previous evening after she announced their marriage.

Fortunately, he had waited until they were alone.

By the time her announcement registered on the consciousness of the assembled diners, he had risen to stand beside her.

Still, she dared not look him in the face. Tía Ana's

mouth gaped momentarily in a most unaccustomed fashion. Giddeon echoed Serita's previous words.

"Con su permiso, Doña Ana"—he had gripped Serita's forearm in his fist—"with your permission, your niece and I will adjourn to the parlor—alone. We have much to discuss on this the evening before our . . . wedding."

Tía Ana quickly regained her composure, while Serita struggled to retain her own, fighting as she did the guilt of springing such a dastardly announcement on her aunt, in front of guests, no less. Tita rang for Abril and mumbled something about the guests taking dessert here in the comfort of the dining room.

Without further ado, Giddeon had ushered Serita from the room, his grip tightening by degrees with every step they took until they entered the parlor and the massive wooden doors were securely fastened behind them.

Then he thrust her in front of him and shook her by the shoulders.

"Marry you?! Marriage is quite unnecessary, besides being the most foolish idea I have ever heard!"

Her face flamed at the derision in his voice. She jerked free and strode to the center of the room. Turning on him, her black skirts swirled about her ankles, exposing glimpses of multicolored petticoats beneath.

A dancing dress, he thought, dazzled momentarily, as his eyes swept upward from her skirts to her heaving bosom. *A provocative, flirty dancing dress—fit for a witch!*

Serita's eyes flashed in fiery warning. "I agree, *capitán.* Surely to gamble for a woman's hand in marriage is not only foolish, but barbaric." Her heart raced in panic. What kind of sick game was he playing? Winning her hand . . . now backing out . . . ? And Oliver Burton coming tomorrow! "But you are so eager to possess me . . ."

"Possess you!" He returned her stare, spark for spark. "If I wanted a woman, I could have any wench from here to Campeche! It is not a woman I want! If you were not so hard-pressed to marry . . ."

"Hard-pressed!" Tossing her head, she thrust fists to hips and leaned forward in her wrath, exposing much more of her ample endowments than she either knew or intended. "For your information, I have been hard-pressed *not* to marry. It is not a husband I desire. But since you are here . . ."

Giddeon swallowed the passion rising within him and tried to tear his eyes away from her many charms, but he was unable to do so. Somewhere in the back of his brain, he wished he had never heard of Los Olmos . . . had never spent the better part of ten days traveling, mostly on foot, to arrive at this godforsaken piece of land—*land*, forchristssake, when all he wanted was the sea. "There is another way to solve this dilemma, señorita."

For a moment she froze in place, then she slowly straightened her body, to his great relief. "My land?" It was a question in tone only, for the instant he spoke, she recalled the conversation at lunch when he mentioned salvaging his schooner, and she knew. He was no different from all the others. He wanted one thing: her land. The land Oliver Burton intended to take by force before sundown tomorrow.

She glared at him. Somehow her voice remained steady. "To possess my land, *capitán*, you will have to marry me."

He took a step toward her. She stepped backward

the same distance. Her heart fluttered, and inside she felt all trembly and weak. Would this calamity never end? In opposition to the rage boiling in her stomach, she spoke quietly. "Since you clearly desire a wife no more than I a husband, the arrangement should be simple."

The flickering light from the numerous sconces which adorned the adobe walls of this ancient room sparkled in his eyes like the sun on a wintry sea. "A business arrangement," he mused, while running those infuriating eyes over her body in a most personal manner.

She whirled away from his demeaning stare. "A business arrangement." Gaining control at length, she faced him again, her regal bearing intact once more. "If you will be seated, we can work out the details. It is your schooner, is it not? You would use the profits from my land to salvage your schooner?"

He nodded, short and curt, then motioned toward an array of decanters on the sideboard. "*¿Con permiso?*" Without waiting for an answer, he splashed a measure of brandy into each of two crystal tumblers.

Her hand trembled when she took the glass he offered, and she caught her breath for fear he had seen. But he gave no notice.

"Why?" He clinked his glass to hers with a jolt that set the crystal ringing through the room.

Although she kept her eyes on the amber liquid sloshing in the glass, a spot between her breasts burned as with a fever, and she knew his gaze was fastened there.

Steadying the glass with both hands, she took a sip of the liquid heat. "Why what?"

At last he moved away, took a seat beside the cold

fireplace, and she sat opposite him.

The brandy burned her throat, but she was relieved to have some sensation in her body not directly provoked by this . . . this dastardly gambling man.

When again she dared look at him, his eyes bore into hers, hard and accusing. "I am offering you freedom. Your father's honor would not be tarnished if I decided to return to sea instead of claiming my bride."

"My land for my freedom?" she asked incredulously.

"A fair enough proposition," he rejoindered, "given the unstable conditions in this part of the world."

She stared a moment, then quickly looked to the drink in her hand. Her heart beat now with a new fear. Did he already know about Oliver Burton? Summoning courage to continue, she tried to sound contrite. "I wasn't entirely truthful earlier," she conceded. "About . . . Well, you must be aware that a suitable husband is not easy to find these days. One of my own heritage, I mean. And I . . . I . . . ah,"—she felt color rush to her cheeks, but she continued—"Los Olmos has been in my family for almost one hundred years. Since my brother Juan was killed near the presidio at La Bahía, it is up to me to leave an heir."

Giddeon studied her. He was no more of her heritage than the other gamblers to whom Don Miguel had lost Los Olmos. But she could see that without any help from him; she had admitted the same earlier today.

Ignoring this obvious lie, he voiced the other discrepancy in her confession. "What about Jorge," he asked. "Is he not your brother's son?"

She nodded, knowing this man would be hard to fool. "An heir of my own, I mean—of my own flesh and blood. I . . . ah . . ." Suddenly she had enough bowing and scraping. Rising to her feet, she tossed her drink into the cold fireplace. "I refuse to humble myself further. My proposition is simple. We marry tomorrow. Since you admitted your intention to use the profits from my land to salvage your schooner, you will have that as soon as the land provides such a profit. At that time, you will be free to go. I have no wish for a husband. Especially not one who . . ." A catch in her throat stopped her words, and she quickly regained her senses. Wherever had such romantic nonsense come from? A husband who wanted *her* instead of her *land* was indeed a child's fantasy. Certainly such a man would not materialize in time to save Los Olmos.

In one stride he caught her and turned her to face him. His intense stare told her he knew — somehow he had guessed what was in her mind — and she flushed with humiliation.

"Who what? You have no desire for a husband . . . who what?" When he spoke, his face was so close to her own he showered her with his sweet, brandy-flavored breath.

Her skin flamed as though on fire. His fingers burned even hotter around her arms, where he held her beneath the ruffle of her dress. Try as she did, she could not resist the urge to relax in his arms; as badly as she wanted to, she could not keep her body from aching for his touch; and when his lips lowered with infuriating slowness to hers, she was powerless to turn her face away.

"Yes, I want your land, *querida,* but make no mistake, I will have your willing body, too."

Dressing now for her wedding day, the very thought

of the kiss that followed those damning words singed her pores all over again and made her insides go queasy and weak.

What in heaven's name was she about?

Tía Ana had wondered the same thing when she came to Serita's room at the break of dawn to confront her niece.

"You cannot be serious, *sobrina*."

"I am, Tita. Very serious. This is the answer to our prayers."

Tía Ana shook her head slowly. "No, *sobrina*, it is sacrilege. The devil himself is talking to you. You have inherited the worst of both families, I see. Miguel's impetuousness and your mother's stubbornness."

"Call it what you like," Serita tossed over her shoulder. "I will save Los Olmos from Oliver Burton." Turning swiftly, she grasped her aunt's frail hands and drew her to the window. "Look out there, Tita. That is our land. All of it. And sooner or later we will lose it to the gringos. Papá was right; there are too many of them to fight. But with Giddeon Duval's name — don't you see? — with a gringo name they will not touch us."

Tía Ana shook her head sadly. "Is this what we have come to? Perhaps we would be better off in Mexico."

"Tita! Do not worry so. He will not stay around. We made a wonderful agreement last night. As soon as I produce an heir for Los Olmos, he is free to go. I will have an heir with a gringo name."

Tía Ana gasped. "You cannot carry out such a mad scheme."

"Listen to me, Tita. It is very simple. All he wants is money to raise that ship of his. All I want is to save Los Olmos. Working together, we can both have what we most desire."

"You have sold your soul," Tía Ana sighed; then the situation got the best of her. "And your body! This is a thing of the devil. Padre Alphonse will have nothing to do with such an arrangement."

Serita turned to her dressing table. "Oh, yes he will. Padre Alphonse may be a man of the cloth, but he is a practical man, too. He knows what it takes to survive in this land. He does not want us to lose Los Olmos."

"But the banns . . ."

"The banns be damned, Tita! We have no time for publishing banns. Oliver Burton comes today." She turned softened eyes on her aunt. "Tita, please do not be angry. It is the only way. As soon as I have a child, Capitán Duval will be free to go, and we will be alone here at Los Olmos once more . . . alone and safe."

Tía Ana stared at the solemn girl, then her black eyes softened, and she raised a hand to smooth Serita's wayward hair. When she spoke her voice was heavy with gloom. "How innocent you are. Have you given no thought to how you will feel when this man leaves you alone with your child?"

Serita raised her eyebrows.

"What happens then, *sobrina?* By that time you may have grown to love him. What will you do then, when he leaves you alone and safe . . . and empty?"

Serita's mouth went suddenly dry. Tita's gloominess stirred within her own troubled heart and it took great effort to square her shoulders. "That will never happen, Tita. Love is not part of this bargain."

The old woman shrugged her shoulders. "You have much to learn about love, *sobrina*." With that she departed, but the gloominess she had induced remained behind and for a time lingered to confuse the situation.

Love? Serita could not recall ever hearing a woman mention the word *love*. Love was never discussed when a girl was to wed; love was not necessary for marriage. The arrangements included land and a dowry and the lineage each would bring to the union.

She brushed her hair furiously, then looked inside her wardrobe, trying to decide which garment would make a suitable wedding gown. Of course, weddings were important occasions. The gowns, the traveling costumes, the furnishings the bride would take to her new home.

But since they would not be traveling, and since she would remain in her own home, these things were unnecessary.

Love? Whatever possessed Tita to think of such a thing?

While she rifled through the wardrobe, choosing and discarding one garment after another as inappropriate, snatches of a story her mother had told her returned to memory—the story of a beau Tita once had. Just as she tossed aside the last gown in her wardrobe, a knock came at the door and Abril entered carrying an exquisite bundle of white lace. Serita caught her breath.

"The wedding dress of my mother!" She had never seen the gown itself. But Mamá had described it to her with great care, saying one day she would wear it, too.

"Doña Ana had me take it from the trunk and press it for you," Abril said. "You are truly to be married today, señorita? And to such a handsome devil as el capitán?"

"*Sí*," Serita mumbled, her thoughts on Tita and how her dear aunt had risen once more to the occasion, as she no doubt had done for much of her life here on the wild frontier. Lifting an edge of the skirt, Serita fingered the fine handwork in the homemade lace. Someone had been possessed with more patience than she herself would ever have.

She sighed. Her wedding day. The gown her young mother had worn when she wed the handsome Don Miguel Cortinas, the most eligible bachelor in all the country, in the chapel below. As she watched, Abril reverently laid out the undergarments that went with the dress, the stockings, the pointed-toed white kid slippers. The train of the gown was reported to stretch the entire length of the aisle in the Chapel de San Miguel, and she doubted it not, looking on it now. Next Abril brought the heavy lace mantilla and the enormous ivory comb over which to drape it.

Sacrilege? Was Tita right? Dare she wear this costume in such a sham of a wedding? Dare she recite the vows of Holy Matrimony before the altar of God? Vows she had no intention of honoring? Racing to the window, she again flung back the draperies and stared out at the land she loved beyond reason — the land her ancestors had fought and died for, the land where they were buried. Was what she was about to do sinful? A sacrilege?

No! A thousand times no, she screamed inside. Would not any one of her ancestors have done the same? Turning a loving eye on the wedding gown of her mother, a light-headed giddiness overwhelmed her. Her mind swirled with the image of Mamá and Papá on their wedding day. But as she stared back through the years, the faces on the images changed from those of her parents to her own and that of Giddeon Duval. Handsome, green-eyed, Giddeon Duval.

The gringo Giddeon Duval! Suddenly, her spirits lifted by several degrees. That was Tita's concern! Giddeon Duval was a gringo. Her gloominess had nothing to do with a ridiculous thing called love; she simply did not want a half-gringo heir running about Los Olmos!

Dressing quickly but carefully—even given the circumstances, she felt an obligation to savor the activities of this her only wedding day—Serita slipped the five-tiered lace gown over six layers of elegant petticoats. Then, surveying herself in the looking glass, she began removing the petticoats one by one, until she wore only one. Twirling now before the glass, she preferred the image, and definitely the comfort. Five tiers of ruffles provided enough bulk and shape. When she moved, the skirt swished rhythmically around her legs and hips. A perfect dancing skirt for the fiesta.

The fitted bodice of the gown dipped low off her shoulders, as had her black taffeta the evening before, and she tried to imagine Mamá, wearing such a dress. The only costumes she could recall her mother wearing were high-necked with proper lace collars, and since Juan's death, everything she put on her body had been black.

The silk stockings skimmed deliciously over her legs; the shoes were a mite too tight. Likely because she herself spent most of her time in boots, Serita surmised.

She parted her hair in the middle and swept it around her ears, forming her customary low knot at the nape of her neck. The comb fit easily into the mass of hair at her crown, but it was heavy and awkward, and finally she relented and called Abril to help secure the mantilla. Her mother's single strand of pearls completed her wedding costume. With Abril's compliments ringing in her ears, Serita draped the length of the train twice over one arm and started for the staircase.

When she reached the door, however, she turned back to her dressing table, where, on impulse, she stuffed a tiny lace sachet filled with dried gardenia leaves into the cleft between her breasts.

Poor Tita! Giddeon Duval, the gringo, was her fear! Serita chastised herself for being so short-sighted? Why had she not recognized her aunt's concern? Tita would discover the truth soon enough—that it would be a thousand times better to have a half-gringo heir to Los Olmos than one of pure Anglo blood, the heir of Oliver Burton!

Approaching the stairs, Serita's thoughts turned to the green-eyed sea captain waiting below to become her lawful husband. Eager to have the ceremony completed before he learned of Burton's threat—or, worse yet, before Burton himself arrived to carry out that threat—she had planned for the service to take place this morning, before the luncheon, which always was held in the courtyard preceding an afternoon of cock-fights, matched horse races, and music and dancing.

The patio was aswarm with guests when she descended the staircase, but she saw neither her aunt nor Padre Alphonse—nor Giddeon Duval. A gnawing came in her stomach, and she worried that he might have had second thoughts and fled the scene.

Her foot had but touched the bottom step when three separate gentlemen reached for her elbow, their compliments meshing in her ears.

Lupe came to her aid. "Doña Ana asks you to join her in the parlor, señorita."

"Not so fast, cousin dear."

Serita's eyes found those of her cousin, Trinidad Cortinas, who shouldered through the throng and took her arm from the gentlemen in attendance.

"Trinity! I'm glad you're—"

"What in hell is the meaning of this?" Trinidad jerked her behind the staircase, away from the crowd.

"Be careful, Trinity," she pleaded. "You will tear my mother's gown."

"Have you lost all concern for our heritage?" he raged into her face. "Marrying a gringo! A man you have known less than twenty-four hours! Whatever has come over you?"

Serita stared at her handsome, volatile cousin. "No, Trinity, I have not lost concern for my heritage. By marrying Capitán Duval—"

"By marrying him, you will put all that is left of our land into the hands of a gringo you do not even know! I will not let you do it!"

She jerked her arm free and adjusted the gown across her bare shoulders. She favored her cousin with a grin. "You cannot stop me, Trinity. And I won't let you hold up the ceremony, either. Time is very important. How important, you will discover before the day is out."

Trinidad changed his tactics. "Serita, Duval is after Los Olmos, like all the other gringos. By marrying him, you are putting the last of our land grant into his hands without so much as a fight. Don't you know the law says a husband holds control over his wife's property?"

"I know, Trinity. But Giddeon does not want Los Olmos. In fact, he is probably the only gringo in the entire country who doesn't. We worked out a suitable agreement last night: All he wants is enough of the profits to salvage his sailing ship. Then he will leave us alone to run Los Olmos like always . . . except for one very important thing. I will have a gringo name. The Texans will not bother me when I have a gringo name."

Trinidad shook his head. "This is not the way to stop los Tejanos, Serita. I bring wonderful news today. We have formed the Republic of the Rio Grande I spoke of last year. The first recruits for my army are with me. We will set up headquarters here on Los Olmos. No one will . . ."

"You will not! You will not turn my ranch into an armed camp. I have told you that before . . ."

"Neither Mexico or Texas will interfere with our new republic. We will be our own masters—"

Serita scoffed. "I want nothing to do with this! I do not belong to Texas or to Mexico, and I do not need the Republic of the Rio Grande, either. All I need is my land and the peace to run it without interference from anyone."

As she turned to walk away, her anger subsided. Poor Trinity. When his own father, her uncle, died two years ago, Trinity lost his part of the land grant. Now he had become a true revolutionary. She sighed. Perhaps she would have reacted the same without Los Olmos.

Turning back to him, she held out her hand. "Come, Trinity. Let us not darken my wedding day with discord. Come with me to the parlor. Once you meet Capitán Duval, you will understand that he has no long-term designs on Los Olmos." She winked at him. "Besides, as my only adult male relative in attendance, you must give me away."

Trinidad jerked her around to face him. "In giving you away, cousin dear, I would be giving away Los Olmos and the last of my heritage. Do you think I am a *lunático,* also? I will not let you go through—"

"Trinity, please trust me," Serita implored.

"If I have to kill this gringo, I will not let you wed him."

Serita bit her lip a moment. "How big is this army you brought with you today?"

Trinidad glared at her. "I have only three men, but that is more than enough to take care of one sea captain and his gringo sailors."

Serita shook her head sadly. "You don't understand, Trinity. Three men will not be enough for all the fighting necessary today if I do not wed Capitán Duval. Oliver Burton and fifty or more of his gringo Cow Boys are coming to take possession of Los Olmos before sundown. If I have not married Giddeon Duval by the time they arrive, neither of us will have a heritage left to defend."

Trinidad stared at her. "Oliver Burton?"

She nodded. "Please do not say a word. Capitán Duval does not know of this . . . yet."

As she watched, Trinidad's jaw clenched and a deep frown etched his broad forehead. "There must be another way."

Straightening her shoulders beneath the weight of the heavy mantilla, she slipped her hand through his arm and drew him toward the parlor. "There isn't. Perhaps if my father had stayed and fought for his land—for my land—things would have been different. But he didn't, so I must."

Giddeon Duval paced the length of the parlor while he awaited the arrival of Serita's maiden aunt, who had summoned him abruptly an hour earlier. His heels clicked against the polished tile floor. Even though the room was enormous, he felt trapped. Accustomed to the deck of a schooner in the midst of the mighty ocean, one room, one house, one ranch resembled—to his mind—a prison.

And from the looks of this room, he was on the verge of being incarcerated in a medieval institution. In the corners stood several massive and complete suits of armor, on the walls hung a Toledo steel sword, steel-tipped halberds, daggers, and a single-shot matchlock, along with a more modern nail-studded cowhide shield. The tiled floor was covered with a threadbare Spanish carpet, and the heavy, uncomfortable pine furniture included a richly carved and painted chest, a *traster* with four shelves, and a sanctuary bench on which to sit comfortably one would be required to wear layers of women's petticoats.

Perhaps Delos had the right idea last night when Giddeon returned to their quarters on the opposite side of the compound.

"I vote to get the hell out of here," he told Giddeon, while Kosta nodded in agreement. "Walking across country is better than what you're fixing to get yourself into."

Giddeon shrugged. "No one ever said it would be easy."

"You didn't count on going through with the marriage, though," Delos reminded him. "What will you do with a wife, for God's sake?"

"Take her to Mexico to live with her father," Giddeon replied glibly.

"She wouldn't go for him, what makes you think you will have any better luck getting her away from this place?"

"Don't worry, old friend, I'm not in the habit of abandoning people, and I certainly do not intend to start with Serita. If she won't go to Mexico, I'll work out something."

Kosta shook his head. "For a seasoned seadog, capt'n, you're about as bright as the evening star . . . covered over by a thick fog."

"Speaking of seasoned seadogs," Giddeon laughed, "you two are carrying on like a bunch of old maids. We had a long talk, my bride and I. Let me assure you, everything is going our way."

"I don't like it . . ." Delos began.

"Hold on, mates. I'm not getting us into any trouble. As soon as Felix returns with word about the taxes . . ."

Kosta laughed. "Not us, Capt'n. It's you who's headed for the stable."

"Temporarily," Giddeon assured them.

Frowns creased the foreheads of his crew, one by one.

"Divorce?" Kosta asked.

Giddeon shook his head. "Much simpler and more acceptable," he told them. "The señorita is no more eager for a husband—in the permanent sense—than I am for a wife. All she wants . . ."—a smile of conquest broadened his face—"is a child . . . an heir." He shrugged again. "And that doesn't look to be a challenge I can't handle."

The men laughed. Then, a somber mood replaced their jocundity at Delos's next words.

"Take care, old friend. Many's the man who was not

infected by the thing called love until it was too late to prevent a disease fatal to his freedom."

Pausing to catch her breath outside the great double doors to the parlor, Serita was conscious only of a need to hurry, to be done with the deed before Oliver Burton arrived to take Los Olmos.

Trinidad squeezed her arm. When she looked up at him, his eyes had softened, his anger replaced by obvious concern for her. "We will find another way," he said.

She shook her head, a wistful smile playing on her lips. Without further ado, he swung wide the doors, and she preceded him into a bedlam she had not anticipated.

"Begging your pardon, Doña Ana, I do not ordinarily carry around my baptismal certificate. If my word will not satisfy your demands, then be damned with you all."

Furious, Giddeon whirled on his well-polished boot heel, bringing himself face-to-face with the vision of an angel.

His eyes lightened by degrees as he drank in her loveliness — softness and light, heady with passion and promise. His body responded with a suffusion of heat; his mind swayed beneath the aroma of gardenias; his voice, when he opened his mouth to speak, was husky.

"Querida."

Serita hadn't recognized him at first, attired as he was in black pants and cropped jacket. Then he turned, and she drew in her breath. Yes, such a handsome gringo, she thought, feeling her body throb at his nearness, swelling and cresting like waves on the beach at Los Olmos Bay at high tide.

"You cannot be married in the church unless you have been baptized," Padre Alphonse insisted.

Gradually, the padre's words sank through the muddle Giddeon's nearness made of her brain, jolting Serita back to the problems of this day. With difficulty, she turned her attention from the unsettling green eyes of Giddeon Duval to the quiet, brown-robed padre standing at the other end of the parlor.

"Padre Alphonse, will you not take the word of Capitán Duval?"

"My child, this is highly irregular. Give me a few weeks . . ." he began.

"We do not have a few weeks," she told him. "My father sent this man to me. Is that not enough?"

"How could your papá know a man's religious history? Why, the *capitán* isn't even—"

"He may not be of our blood, padre"—she looked quickly at Giddeon and flinched at the resolve she saw forming in his eyes—"but can you not see how well he speaks our language? Why—"

"Con permiso, señorita," Giddeon's voice grew strained. "This is where I return to the sea."

Stepping past her, he started to leave the room, but she clutched his arm, and he stopped in his tracks. His muscles bunched beneath her palm. When she met his gaze, his eyes communicated his disgust with the entire situation.

"Giddeon, wait," she pleaded, feeling his muscles throb into her hand. His stare was hard, definite, determined.

"Wait," she repeated, louder this time. "Padre Alphonse is a reasonable man. Perhaps . . ."—her eyes darted to the padre and back—". . . perhaps he can baptize you again." Her words were tentative, and as Giddeon's expression hardened, they died on her lips. He jerked his arm to shake her loose, but she held on.

"Padre, please. Giddeon Duval is a respected sea captain. Surely, you can take his word that he has been baptized. After all . . ."

Suddenly, Serita's heart froze. As surely as the sun was traveling its path through the sky, Oliver Burton was on his way to Los Olmos. Every moment was precious indeed. Resolutely, her gaze moved about the room from Padre Alphonse, to Tía Ana, to Trinidad, to Giddeon, where her eyes stopped, held by his own intense stare. Without taking her eyes from him again, she spoke to the group.

"Capitán Duval and I wish to be married today, and we shall. If we cannot do so in the church, so be it. We hereby proclaim ourselves married under the laws of the land, as is the custom in this unsettled . . ."

Tía Ana's gasp closely resembled a swoon; Trinidad's was a sigh of disgust; and Padre Alphonse . . .

"My child, that would be a sin. I cannot allow such a thing." He sighed heavily. "Very well, seeing you are determined, I cannot stand by and allow you to live in sin. I will perform the ceremony in the chapel."

Serita heard his pronouncement as an accompaniment to the expression in Giddeon's eyes. She had been admired by men before, by handsome men, sons of neighboring *rancheros* who admired both her beauty and her land holdings.

This man was different. That he admired — desired — her beauty was obvious from the enraptured look on his face. That he wanted her land — or the proceeds from it — was also a fact. But he was like none of the others. To none of the other suitors had

81

she herself ever felt such a reaction. None of the others had quickened her heart, slowed her breath, nor brought a burning ache to her flesh. None of the others.

Only this man. This sea captain, Giddeon Duval, with his misty green eyes that penetrated to her very soul. With his husky voice that set her nerves on end. With his most masculine presence that offered her both sanctuary and jeopardy in the same instant.

Later, Giddeon was glad his crew hadn't been around to see him make a complete ass of himself. But at the moment, all he could do was stare into her black eyes, inhale the heady scent of gardenias, and watch Serita's shallow breath pump against her low-cut bodice, tantalizing him by the suggestion of what lay beneath the snow-white lace. Her skin took on the sheen of warmed honey, and he had to clear his throat before words could escape.

"I didn't realize you were so eager to get on with this business of . . . making an heir."

At his suggestive remarks, she blushed; Tía Ana's earlier warning flashed briefly through her brain. Suddenly she saw beneath the veneer of passion in his eyes, and she blanched. She was not eager for that aspect of his agreement. Not at all. But if that's what it took to save Los Olmos, she could do it.

Thoughts of Oliver Burton overrode even the fear of sharing a man's bed, and she knew that come nightfall, she could well be either a widow or an abandoned wife, depending on how Oliver Burton took to her new gringo name.

And how Giddeon Duval took to being duped by a woman.

The wedding began immediately, giving neither of

them more time to dwell on the consequences of their actions. Jorge was set to ringing the bell, Delos and Kosta were advised of their duties—Delos as best man, Kosta to stand with him.

Trinidad gripped Serita's clammy hand in his as she clutched it through the crook in his elbow. They stopped in the doorway to the chapel. A measure of Tita's earlier gloom descended over her, and she took several deep breaths to dispel it.

This was certainly not the way she had envisioned her wedding day. However, with the nearly one hundred guests assembled for the fiesta, the chapel was full, and when, at Padre Alphonse's indication, they stood and turned to see her in the doorway, she felt their admiration. For a moment the magnitude of what she was about overwhelmed her.

"I still don't like this," Trinidad whispered, but the heavy mantilla masked the harshness of his words.

After the confrontation in the parlor, Giddeon and Trinidad had faced off like two rival mustang stallions fighting for the same mare. Except, they were not fighting over her, of course, but for control of her land. Well, they would both have a surprise. No one, not even a duly married husband would control Los Olmos. This was her land, and if she thought for one minute Giddeon wanted anything more from this union than enough money to finance his salvage operation, she would have sent him packing last night.

Jorge, robed in white, finished lighting the altar candles, and Serita stepped forward, her heart pounding with . . .

With all the wrong things, she thought sadly, as she neared the man who would in a matter of moments become her husband.

What in the world was she getting herself into? What in heaven's name was she about?

"Who gives this woman . . . ?" Padre Alphonse intoned.

Serita, head held high, looked to neither right nor left. She felt Trinidad step backward, felt her arm being transferred to another . . .

"Giddeon Duval, do you take . . ."

She felt, rather than heard, Giddeon clear his throat. Her heart lurched. He couldn't back out now! She gripped his arm tighter.

". . . in sickness and in health . . ."

He fidgeted beside her.

". . . for as long as you both shall live?"

Silence.

Her heart raced.

Silence.

She turned her veiled face toward him, and through a haze of white lace she saw him staring at her.

For a long moment his troubled eyes held hers in silence. Outlined as he was against the adobe wall, he appeared encased in candlelight. The only color she could see was the sea-green of his eyes.

The sea, she thought. Freedom. He ran his tongue around his lips. Then his eyes took on a strange, foreign glaze, and he turned his attention back to the padre.

"*Sí, yo la tomo.*"

"*Yes, I take her . . . yes, I take her . . . yes, I take her*
. . . The words ricocheted from side to side in her mind so that for a time she was unable to concentrate on the continuing ceremony. Then the question was put to her, and she responded quickly, conscious now of time . . . precious time . . . racing time . . . escap-

ing time.

They came to the part concerning the ring, but no one had thought of one. Giddeon looked sheepish, and Serita shrugged. The ceremony continued.

A homily. Padre Alphonse rambled, or so it seemed, about the responsibilities of marriage, about the solemness of the day, about the finality of the vows they took before the altar . . . in the sight of God.

Serita's heart ached. She tried not to listen, so afraid was she of tarnishing her eternal soul. Giddeon stood beside her more steadily now, sensing her own discomfiture, she supposed. The infidel! He likely hadn't been baptized after all! That would only further deteriorate her cause for her own soul!

Her pulse raced. Would Padre Alphonse never end the merciless sermon? Then he did finish, but her mind was so abuzz she wasn't aware for a time that his words had ceased.

The pounding in her heart traveled throughout her body. Padre Alphonse motioned them to kneel. She felt him take her right hand and twine it with Giddeon's; she watched him remove his stole and wrap their hands together; glancing up, she caught and held Giddeon's eyes.

Taunting now, his eyes danced in the candlelight . . . accusing, laughing, enjoying her discomfiture.

The pounding increased. Padre Alphonse unwound his stole and touched their shoulders, indicating they should rise.

"I now pronounce you . . ."

Behind them the chapel doors banged against the adobe walls.

". . . man and wife."

Serita's spine turned cold. Boots thudded against

the tiled floor, stomping down the aisle toward the altar.

Giddeon turned her by the shoulders. His green eyes pierced hers. His hands fumbled with her mantilla; finally he tossed it back from her face.

The stomping boots grew louder.

Giddeon's eyes bore into hers, as though they, he and she, were the only two people in the entire room. Lowering his face, his lips covered hers, and all she could do was clutch at his arms.

His lips, warm and moist, stroked hers, commanding her full attention. She tried to pull away, to turn toward the person who now stood within inches of them here in the aisle of the church. But Giddeon would have his due. His arms encircled her and pulled her to him; his lips plied hers with such sensuous sensations that she could but respond in kind. Her arms crept up his, then encircled his neck, and she gave herself up to kiss and be kissed by this man . . . her husband.

Her husband. The reality settled in her brain along with the fact that she had, in the very nick of time, accomplished what she set out to do.

To save Los Olmos from Oliver Burton.

When, at length, Giddeon raised his lips from hers, she smiled sweetly into his face. Slipping her arms from around his neck, she turned him to face their visitor.

"Mr. Burton, may I introduce my husband, Captain Giddeon Duval."

Chapter Four

With one sweep of his eyes Giddeon recognized Oliver Burton for what he was: trouble. Trouble for Los Olmos. Trouble for Serita.

Trouble for him. Taking in the rancher, he felt Serita tense beside him. When he turned his eyes to her, she winced, then quickly looked away.

"An *heir, querida?*" he hissed.

She held her breath, half expecting him to run down the aisle and away from her, away from Los Olmos. The other half anticipated his slap across her face, so intense was the fury she saw in his eyes.

He did neither. But the grip he placed on her elbow communicated his wrath, as did the set of his mouth and the length of his stride, when, without another word, he proceeded to escort her toward the brilliant morning sunlight that streamed through the open doors of the Chapel de San Miguel.

Her face flamed; her feet stumbled over the tile in her too-tight shoes, as Giddeon towed her back down the aisle. With great difficulty, she achieved the un-daunted expression for which she strove. She had made it in the nick of time. She had beaten Oliver

Burton by a hairbreadth. And the shocked look on his face would have been worth marrying the very devil himself.

Outside, Giddeon's heels ground against the tiled steps. After the dimly lit interior, the intense sunlight blinded them both for a moment. The congregation stirred behind them.

"An heir?!"

Face-to-face, his eyes challenged her to deny the truth; hers, him to accept it. Suddenly they both became aware of the commotion in front of them.

Horses, a good fifty or so, stamped and swished just this side of the grove of elm trees. Their riders held shotguns trained on the doorway of the chapel. No one moved.

"What the hell is going on?" Giddeon spoke through his teeth.

She inhaled a deep breath, striving to appear in control.

"What kind of trouble are you in?" he demanded.

"It's nothing," she said, hoping her voice carried a measure of assurance. "Nothing you can't . . ."

His eyes found hers again. "Nothing I can't handle?" Fury seethed in every word. "You overestimate me, *querida*. When I decide to lay down my life for a woman, *I* will choose the time and place—and the woman!"

Her eyes widened. "Fool! No one is going to die. You are a gringo. They will not kill you."

The congregation crowded behind them. Delos and Kosta pushed through to stand at Giddeon's side. Oliver Burton shouldered his way to the front of the group.

His breath came short and fast. When he spoke, it

was in clipped tones. "The documents, Miss Cortinas."

Serita felt Giddeon's eyes on her. Without looking at him, she answered Burton in a steady voice. "My husband is in charge of Los Olmos."

"Our arrangement has nothing to do with a husband."

Giddeon raised an eyebrow. "Most everything involves a husband, Burton. What's this all about?"

The rancher stammered, and Giddeon spoke again, this time a harsher threat. "It had better be important, since you chose to disrupt our . . ."—he glared at Serita—"wedding day."

Burton snorted. "That was no wedding! Not in the legal sense. It changes nothing."

Padre Alphonse spoke up. "I am duly licensed by the State of Texas, señor. This wedding is as valid as . . ."

"Married or not," Burton fumed, "nothing is changed. I am here to take possession of this ranch."

Giddeon moved one step away from Serita, his legs spread. His men followed suit. The fact that they wore no weapons detracted little from the message intended by such a stance. "By whose authority?"

Burton cleared his throat, but held his ground. Serita glanced at the riflemen and wondered whether Giddeon and his crew were lunatics or merely blinded by the morning sun that glinted from the gun barrels held by Burton's Cow Boys.

"This ranch has been reclaimed by the State of Texas. I am . . . an agent of the state."

For one sickening moment, Giddeon's heart stopped. He looked to Serita for confirmation.

"You lie, Mr. Burton." Her voice was firm, and Giddeon marveled at her self-assurance; then he recalled her ace in the hole — him. He winced.

"Show me your proof," he demanded of Burton.

Oliver Burton nodded to the men behind him. "They are all the proof I need. The Cortinases are traitors to the state."

Audible comments broke out behind them, and Serita glanced quickly to Giddeon to deny the charge.

He never looked her way. "As my wife says, Burton, that's a damned lie. Her brother, the only son of this household, gave his life for Texas at the battle of Goliad."

Burton fumed. "That has nothing to do with . . ."

"It has everything to do with the situation," Giddeon replied. "The state specifically instructs that land grants belonging to martyrs of the independence be left alone."

"How do you know that?"

Giddeon stared hard at the man, thinking instead of the fifty armed men behind him. Before he could answer, Serita spoke up.

"Surely you have heard of the Texas Navy! My husband is *Captain* Giddeon Duval."

A smile tugged at Giddeon's jaws. Was there no end to the guile of this female? Staring relentlessly at Burton, he continued the charade in a calm voice. "It is my business to know the laws of the State of Texas."

Burton's eyes shifted. Giddeon paused, giving the man time to think. "Now, get off our land," he ordered. "And instruct your men to stay off. If I catch any or all of you on Los Olmos property again — or if any of you so much as raises a finger against my . . ." — in a gesture born of vengeance, he drew Serita to his side — ". . . my *wife* . . . let us say my crew and I have firsthand experience dealing with

90

pirates. Whether they come by land or by sea, as my *wife* stated recently, makes little difference."

Burton huffed and puffed. Serita could see he had no liking for the situation; he hadn't intended to ride away empty-handed. But the Texas Navy consisted of nothing more than a bunch of pirates, and she knew he would take time to rethink his position. She straightened her shoulders and held her neck at a regal angle, despite the strain of the heavy mantilla.

After what seemed like an eternity, Burton shifted his feet, and she sighed.

"I'm not finished, Miss Cortinas. You can bet on that."

"My name is Duval, Mr. Burton. *Mrs.* Giddeon Duval."

Giddeon stared at her. His name, dropped comfortably from her lips, sounded like sweet music. Burton turned to leave, and at that moment Trinidad eased up beside Serita.

Burton stared hard at him. Then he riveted his attention on Serita, and she cringed. "Traitors," he repeated. "You haven't heard the last from me."

The instant Burton was out of earshot, Giddeon addressed his crew. "Find your weapons. Keep them at hand at all times."

He grabbed Serita by the shoulders with such force she fully expected him to shake her here on the steps of the chapel before all her family and friends. "The next time you set a man up, at least give him a chance to arm himself."

She stared into his furious face. "Giddeon, please. Oliver Burton has nothing to do with our agreement. This changes nothing."

His eyes bore into hers, causing her to wince. When

he spoke, his words carried a foreboding almost as fiendish as Oliver Burton's nocturnal visits.

"How right you are, *Mrs. Duval.* Nothing is changed. Except that now you are my lawful wife, a fact you may very soon regret."

With that he dropped his hold on her, stormed around the side of the compound, and she did not see him again for several hours.

For an occasion with such an inauspicious beginning, the fiesta soon got into full swing. While musicians strolled the grounds, Lupe and Abril set long tables under the *vigas* for *comida,* the heavy meal of the day. Serita was besieged with questions about Giddeon: where she had found such a dashing husband, when he had come into her life, and, more specifically, where he was at the moment.

The last, she wondered herself. His men were about. They joined the festivities as though they were longtime acquaintances of the family instead of newly arrived interlopers.

The first course of corn soup — *sopa de elote* — gave her a chance to escape the crowd, since Giddeon's place remained empty to her right, and Padre Alphonse was seated to her left. She answered his question in monosyllables, searching still for any sign of Giddeon.

Instead, she saw Trinidad. The second course, a golden rice Nieves called *arroz gualdo,* had just been served when she spied Trinity dining beside Delos.

He had played the crowd all day, drumming up support, Serita was sure, for the Republic of the Rio Grande. Her heart skipped now at sight of him in deep conversation with Giddeon's first mate. Instantly, she recalled his demands to headquarter his army here at Los Olmos. That, she doubted not, was the topic of their conversation. By the time the table had been cleared and the next course served—Nieves's special red fish caught fresh in Los Olmos Bay—Serita's nerves were a jangle. Delos had left the table, but she still saw no sign of Giddeon. What if he had left, too—for good? She could not let him go—not until . . .

Just when she started to excuse herself to Padre Alphonse, Trinidad slipped into Giddeon's chair.

"I stand corrected, cousin dear. You may have found the perfect way to save Los Olmos after all."

She glared at him. "What were you and Delos discussing?"

Trinidad studied her. "For gringos, these men are going to come in handy—pirates, Texas Navy, or whatever they turn out to be."

"Trinity, I have told you, you cannot bring your army to Los Olmos."

"Serita, you are married now. Your husband has legal rights to your land, and he thinks . . ."

"To hell with what Giddeon Duval thinks," she retorted. "Los Olmos is mine—only mine—and I alone will run it."

Trinidad took a healthy bite of the meat course April set before him. "Ah, *carne de res con napolitos*," he enthused. "Beef with pieces of cactus—my favorite."

"Trinity!" Serita insisted. "You are not to bring your army here. No matter what Delos or . . . or even Giddeon himself told you. I will not stand for it."

Chilies rellenos stuffed with *frijoles* followed, and, after that, frothy cups of a cinnamon and chocolate drink accompanied by platters of *tamales de dulce* and sugar cookies.

93

Trinidad, however, had raised a dreadful new fear in Serita's already overburdened brain. Had she taken the easy way out, marrying Giddeon Duval so quickly? It would have been hard getting rid of him . . . but should she have tried? Without him standing beside her this morning, as her lawful husband, Los Olmos would even now be in the hands of Oliver Burton. And Burton would surely return as he promised. Still she worried. What new conflicts awaited her now that she was legally married? Trinidad's words rang through her anguish: *You are married now; your husband has legal rights to your land.*

Tía Ana rang her tea bell for quiet, and Serita watched several of the menfolk slip out the side gates. Although siesta was a required part of any day, even fiesta days, everyone knew that a certain number of men would slip away to the row of old vaqueros' quarters where they would hold cockfights. If the noise was kept down, and if the younger children were not enticed away from siesta, no mention was ever made of the fact.

Serita looked around the gathering. Delos hadn't returned, but Kosta was here, acting like he owned the place, she thought furiously. Then she admonished herself. She should be glad to see him: it meant Giddeon hadn't left Los Olmos. Gathering her train in her arms, she excused herself from *Don* Fernando. The first thing she intended was to remove this ridiculous wedding costume. It might have been perfect for her mother's wedding, but her mother's wedding was not a sham. She should never have worn this special dress for such a travesty, she admonished, taking the tiled steps carefully, so as not to trip.

Suddenly Pablo caught up with her, and at his

whispered plea, all though... ...her mind. With both arms... ...train, she ran as fast as her cramp... ...her to the corral.

True to Pablo's words, Barb was gone, along w... one of the other horses. Her heart raced with fear, with anguish.

"You are certain . . . ?"

Sí, chica, it was *Señor Capitán* himself, and his man called Delos."

"What did they say? Where did they go?"

Pablo shrugged. "When I saw them, they were already riding out the gates."

Fury seethed inside her with such an all-encompassing impact that she forgot her clothing and dropped her skirts to the dust.

Trailing her garments, she rushed across the corral, flung open the heavy gates, and stared into the empty countryside. No one was in sight—neither horse nor man. For an instant she thought he might have gone for good, and her head swam with one thought: Barb, Barb, Barb. Kosta was still here, however, and she regained a measure of her senses. Surely he would not have left Kosta behind. "Go on back, Pablo," she told her vaquero. "I will await the return of Señor Capitán."

Her heart pounded against the boning in her corset, pulsated in the veins in her neck, throbbed painfully in her head. Pacing back and forth in front of the open gates, she let her train sweep behind her, kicking up swirls of dust.

Silence settled over the compound as the household retired for siesta. She glanced at the sun. Where had he gone? The bastard! He didn't know the country

not even know how to ride a horse—
valuable as Barb, leastwise.

With ominous gloom, the last words he spoke to her echoed in her brain—the threat outside the chapel that she would soon regret marrying him. Anger quelled the gloom, however, and quickened her pace. If he got lost, if he injured Barb, he would be the one sorry over the whole affair.

The sun moved steadily across the sky and still she paced, unaware of her attire—of the heaviness of her mantilla, of her tight-fitting shoes, of the damage she was doing this heirloom dress—of anything except her growing fear for Barb. Barb, on whom rode the very salvation of Los Olmos.

Finally, after what seemed like an eternity, she heard horses in the distance. As she watched, Barb, with Giddeon riding easy on her back, almost carelessly, she thought, approached the corral. Serita searched the mare from muzzle to heel for any sign of injury or abuse.

Hands on hips, she stood in the center of the gateway, her head tossed up to stare at him as he passed through. "Where have you been?"

He reined, looked hard at her, then maneuvered Barb past her into the corral. He rode without stopping to the stalls, where he dismounted and began to unsaddle the horse.

She stomped after him, her garments trailing in her wake.

"Where have you been?" she demanded again.

When he turned, his eyes were still hard and cold, and she flinched inside, suddenly conscious that she knew nothing about this man? Was he violent of nature? Most likely, she assured herself. Was he cruel?

Was he . . .?

"Making sure *our* enemy departed," he replied in clipped tones. "No sense letting him take us unawares. Delos is guarding—"

"You are not to ride this horse again!" she interrupted, jerking Barb's reins from his hands. "Not ever. No one rides Barb without my permission. No one. Not even . . ."

Giddeon grabbed her arms. His eyes bore into hers. "*Mrs. Duval,* everything you have belongs to me. Everything. Don't you ever forget it."

He held her so long and stared into her eyes with such intensity that she was sure he intended to kiss her. Pressing her lips together, she practically dared him to try. Finally, he pushed her away, and she stumbled backward but caught her footing before she fell to the corral floor.

She wanted to turn and run to the house, but she could not, would not, leave Barb unattended. Silently, she approached her horse and helped him tend to her. She hoped he would leave when they finished and she could remain behind with Barb.

But such was not to be. Surveying his work for a moment, he looked Serita up and down in the same manner, but with less attention. Then with a fist to her arm, he ushered her toward the compound, from where she now heard activity.

Siesta was over, and she hadn't even changed from this ridiculous getup. Just as she thought she would slip away to her room, however, Giddeon changed that plan, also.

He stuck by her side for the rest of the lengthy afternoon. Holding her arm, slipping an arm about her waist, resting a hand lightly over her shoulder.

Only when she tried to escape did he tighten his hold on her by the slightest, almost imperceptible pressure from his hand, his arm.

His mockery soon became evident. When she introduced him to first one then another of her relatives and neighbors, he conversed in a most pleasant manner. She heard him laugh easily in a deep, rumbling voice. From time to time he drew her to his side with a tenderness that belied the reality of the farce they had entered into this day, and for a moment she would relax in the security she felt beside him.

But each time she looked into his eyes, she realized his every action was a facade for the benefit of her guests. At those times she was hard-pressed not to tremble with fear at what she had gotten herself into — marrying this man . . . a stranger — in such haste.

Jorge, she noticed, saw Giddeon only through the wanderlust of youth. Not as a gringo whom he should despise but rather as the dashing and gallant man who had stood up to Oliver Burton.

She smiled at Jorge now as he tugged her toward the center of the courtyard, where the children had gathered to break the *piñata*.

Padre Alphonse stood beneath the decorated clay pot which was suspended by a strong leather *reata* from a high limb of the old oak tree. In one hand he held a blindfold, in the other a stick which the lucky child would use to break the *piñata*. When the group had assembled, he called for silence. "Whoever will go first must tell me the symbolism of this game."

Eager hands waved in the air. Louisa, granddaughter of Don Fernando, answered the padre's question loud and clear. "The *dulces* that fall to the ground symbolize God's blessings raining down upon our heads."

Padre Alphonse nodded approval, but before blind-folding her, he smiled benevolently at Serita and Giddeon. "On this most solemn occasion, we must remember the special blessings of Holy Matrimony and the responsibilities of the wedded state, especially that of showering the world with their descendants."

Serita's face flushed. She tried to move away from Giddeon's side, but he pulled her closer, and she felt him chuckle against her shoulder. Glancing up, she caught a glimpse of amusement in his green eyes . . . and something more. For a moment, only a moment, she saw a measure of tenderness when he grinned that lopsided grin.

Then in the next instant, he looked away, his eyes hard as emeralds once more.

Blindfolded with the strip of black cloth, Louisa swung a wide swath at the *piñata*, sending the crowd staggering backward out of her path. Her three tries swiped large circles in the air, but accomplished nothing toward breaking the *piñata*. The next three contestants had no more luck than she.

The musicians who had strummed guitars and a fiddle in the background all day came to stand on the opposite side of the fountain from the *piñata* and played a feisty accompaniment to the contestants. The crowd joined in, helping and hindering each child with calls to strike to the right, to the left, higher, lower.

Jorge's turn came last, and on his third and final try, he smashed the clay pot to bits. Pieces of candy and trinkets flew into the crowd. Everyone scrambled for a souvenir to take home or a *dulce* to eat.

During the confusion, Serita sought a chance to

dash up the stairs. She would lock herself in her room and gather her wits. A flash of red caught her searching eye. Immediately she recognized Abril's red skirt. The housemaid disappeared beneath the staircase with Delos behind her. "I thought you left Delos outside to guard against Oliver Burton's return!"

Giddeon had followed her gaze. A grin played on his mouth. "My dear Mrs. Duval, just because you have caught your man . . ." Seeing her chin tilt up in that regal, holier-than-thou attitude, he winked. "The men are taking turns guarding the *hacienda*. Surely you would not deny them each a spot of pleasure."

"You are insufferable, *capitán*. Your attempts at humor are unwelcome." Gathering her skirts in her hands, she tried to pull away from his hold, and in her efforts she bumped into Tía Ana, who surveyed Serita's dress with a critical eye.

"*Sobrina*, you have just enough time to change into fresh clothing before *cena*. I will take charge of *Señor Capitán*, while you retire to your rooms and freshen up for dinner."

Rescued at last, Serita ignored the impulse to smirk at Giddeon in a most immature fashion. "Thank you, Tita. I will return to help you with the rest of the preparations for *cena*."

Not until she stood in the opened doorway of her bedchamber, however, and stared into a room empty of anything she recognized, did Tita's word ring true: *rooms. Tita said rooms.*

Nieves appeared as if on cue. Motioning Serita to follow her, the old cook led the way to the other end of the compound, where she flung open the double doors to the salon of the suite shared by Serita's parents. Serita stared in awe. Gone were the multitude of mementos belonging to her parents; gone were the ivory jewel box, the silver mirror and brushes. Every tabletop instead held her own collection. The heavy draperies had been drawn back, the windows opened wide, the rooms cleaned and polished.

"Doña Ana had these rooms prepared for you and your bridegroom."

"Tita?" she whispered, burying her face in a bouquet of freshly cut hibiscus.

Nieves drew Serita to one of the sofas flanking the large fireplace. "Sit, *chica*. Doña Ana asked me to speak with you."

Serita sank to the heavily padded brocade sofa, frowning. Her mind swirled with curiosity, with uncertainty.

"This is the day of your marriage," Nieves began. Serita stared at her, her brows knit, trying to discern the meaning for this strange turn of events. Nieves continued, and Serita didn't have long to wait for answers.

"In a few hours, you will come to these rooms with your new husband."

Serita quickly averted her eyes from the older woman's. She felt color rise along her neck.

"There are certain things you should know beforehand," Nieves was saying, "and your aunt, being a maiden lady and all, asked me to . . . ah, to tell you about what will go on between . . ."

"Oh, no," Serita jumped to her feet. Crossing the room, she opened the doors and walked onto the private balcony where her mother and father had shared morning coffee and evening brandies.

"With a man like *Señor Capitán* . . . ah, it is our opinion that he is much experienced, and you will

101

have little to worry about. He will be able to teach you . . ."

"Stop!" Serita swirled to face Nieves, who had come to stand behind her. "I know what goes on. You cannot very well run a ranch without knowing about . . . about those things. After all, I have been involved in breeding horses for some time. Why, there's nothing . . . nothing to it. It's just . . . just . . ." Shrugging, she clamped her teeth together to still her trembling jaws. When she looked at Nieves, the woman was studying her curiously.

"There is a difference in what goes on between a man and a woman and what you are acquainted with."

"Difference?" Serita questioned, agitated. "What could possibly be different, Nieves. Thank you for doing my aunt's bidding, but there is no need . . . no need at all to educate me along these lines. I know exactly what . . ."

"*Chica*"—Nieves used a firmer tone—"your aunt also asked me to instruct you . . . ah, to remind you . . . of your duty . . . under God . . . to fulfill the vows you and *Señor Capitán* took this morning."

Instantly, Serita recoiled at the guilt she felt rising in angry swirls within her. Holy vows recited with the sure knowledge they would be broken. Had she placed her soul in eternal jeopardy? "Yes, yes, Nieves. I am well aware of my duty to beget children."

"It is more than that."

Serita stared at the old lady, her brows knit. What else? she wondered impatiently. "Nieves, please inform my aunt that I intend to be a dutiful wife for . . . for as long as necessary. I will conceive a child to—"

"There is more you must do than beget children. You must . . . you must submit yourself to your husband . . . whenever . . . whenever he wishes."

"Submit myself?! Submit . . . myself?" Giddeon's words of the evening before when he had sworn to possess her willing body rang through her gloom. And what had he said at the corral this very day? *Everything you have belongs to me. Everything.*

Everything! Fury rose by giant degrees within her. First Los Olmos, then Barb, now herself. *We will see,* she raged inside. "Thank you, Nieves." Crossing the room, she held open the door leading onto the gallery. "Tell Tita you have done your duty."

"But, *chica,* we have not discussed . . . I mean, *Señor Capitán* will expect you to know . . ."

"You have instructed me on my responsibilities as a dutiful wife well enough, Nieves. I am sure I will be able to manage *Señor Capitán* on my own from here on out."

From the look on Nieves's face when she left Scrita's suite, Serita knew the old woman wasn't sure she had succeeded in her mission.

Neither was Serita, but she did know she had heard all she intended to listen to. From below came the first bell for *cena.* She sighed; she should change and hurry to dinner, but her spirits certainly were not of the festive sort.

Walking to her mother's bedchamber which opened off the salon to the west, she saw it for the first time as something other than the secluded place she and Juan had on rare occasions been permitted inside. The once-elegant blue brocade bed and window draperies were now shabby from wear, as were the sofas and the two large-sized chairs in the salon. All the furniture had been in the Cortinas family for many generations, having come from Spain with the first settlers.

Suddenly her eyes fairly popped in her head as she stared at the bed. The blue coverlet had been carefully turned back, exposing lace-edged white sheets, and at its foot . . .

Across the foot of the enormous walnut bed, in which her mother had borne her children, lay the most elegant heap of white lace she had ever seen, aside from the wedding costume she had worn all day. Fingering it, Serita's heart fluttered with anxiety. A sheer nightgown of Spanish lace and flowing dressing coat to match.

As quickly as she touched it, she jerked her fingers away. Returning to the salon on shaky legs, she wondered for the hundredth time what she had gotten herself into.

The salon was large, enormous, and she had the unwanted vision of Giddeon Duval sitting on the sofa, his long legs stretched out in front of the fireplace. Giddeon would fit well—comfortably, she corrected—into these large rooms. The tall ceiling was vaulted and beamed and hung with two enormous chandeliers of flickering candles.

A sudden thought grasped hold of Serita then, and she hurried to the other room in this suite: her father's own bedchamber, located off the opposite side of the salon from that of her mother. But the room obviously did not belong to *Papá* any longer. Giddeon's belongings had been transferred here, as her own things had been placed in the room which belonged to her mother.

Fighting back the resentment rising within her at Tita's presumptuous actions, Serita turned her mind instead to more pressing matters. She despaired that she would have to sleep so near this stranger, yet each sleeping chamber had its separate door onto the passageway. She and Giddeon could come and go separately. Actually, she reassured herself, they need never see each other, if she so desired.

Suddenly the weight of her newfound despair deepened, and she returned to the balcony her parents had shared through a lifetime of happy married life. Why had she made so hasty a decision? If she had given the situation more consideration, perhaps she could have come up with a different plan . . . a better solution.

Staring out at her beloved countryside, the brilliant glow of the setting sun held her transfixed.

Sundown.

Sundown, September twenty-fifth. As the sun sank in the western sky, Serita's spirits rose in equal proportions. Sundown, September twenty-fifth. She had saved Los Olmos from Oliver Burton. No matter that this wedding day was not one of a young girl's fantasy. A young girl's fantasy did not belong in this troubled world. Only a woman's strength and determination would save Los Olmos.

The bell pealed again, the final call to the festive *cena*, prepared as the final meal for this year's Fiesta de San Miguel. Thoughts of the future lay suddenly heavy upon her heart, and her guilt returned. She stared down at the now-begrimed lace gown. This day, this feast day of her father, her own wedding day, certainly had not been what she would have ever dreamed. What if she had made the wrong decision? What if . . .? Pray God, she had not brought sacrilege upon this house and eternal damnation upon herself by wearing this dress for such a travesty.

"Dear Mamá," she sighed aloud, "look what I have done with your wedding dress."

"It is *your* wedding dress, *querida.*"

At his voice, Serita whirled about, steadying her headdress with one hand as she did. He lounged against the door-facing and studied her with the most benevolent expression she had yet seen upon his face. Her heart beat in her throat.

"What are you doing here?" Her voice came out as a whisper.

Crossing, he stood beside her at the edge of the balcony. "Sundown," he mused, staring not at the sky but into her eyes. "I'll hand it to you, Serita Cortinas de Duval, you have lived up to your reputation."

She tried to get angry with his words, but they were couched in such an innocuous tone, she couldn't stir her fury. Disconcerted by this and by his close scrutiny, she looked toward the fiery sky. "In what way, *capitán?*"

Turning her gently by the shoulders, he gazed at her face as it was illuminated by the golden glow of the setting sun and thought about Enos McCaulay's claim that she was the most beautiful, willful, and guileful woman in three countries. He grinned.

"Sundown," he repeated. "What would you have done if I had not ridden into your life before sundown today?"

Her heart lurched at the knowledge that he knew; but, of course, someone was bound to have told him. Thinking on it, her amusement was roused by his choice of words.

"You did not *ride* into my life, *capitán*. As I recall the situation, you more nearly *trudged.*"

He laughed, spirited by her teasing manner. "How right you are, and my feet will attest to every step they trudged through your despicable cactus-riddled land."

106

Her brows knit in a defensive challenge. "If this land is so despicable, I suggest . . ."

"*Querida, querida,*" he soothed. "Let us not quarrel. I came to your rescue, and you to mine. Is that not what we agreed to last evening?"

With a sigh, Serita shrugged. "You are right. Since we are partners, after a fashion, we should strive to be amicable toward each other." Slipping her hand over his arm, she indicated the open French doors behind them. "Shall we go down to *cena?* I fear we are terribly late . . ." And recalling their late entrance to dinner the evening before, she added, ". . . once again."

Giddeon placed a hand over hers as it rested in the crook of his elbow, but he made no move to leave the balcony. Slowly, then, as though he approached an unbroken filly, he let go her hand and reached for her mantilla, all the time studying her skittish eyes. Lifting the ivory comb and veil above her head, he frowned. "Your neck must feel like the mast of a sailing ship, after carrying this thing around all day."

Without thinking, she raised a hand and rubbed the back of her neck.

He stood so near, towering over her with his arms extended above her head, his eyes riveted on hers, that she scarcely dared breathe. "*Cena* . . ." she whispered, wondering why she didn't move around him and away from the balcony . . . why she stood so still.

"We won't be missed," he whispered back. Pulling the yards of her veiling from behind her, he laid the mantilla aside, and suddenly she felt silly. Two grown people whispering on this secluded balcony, off empty rooms, at the far side of the compound where no one would . . .

He turned slowly back to her, and her eyes flashed.

"What . . . ?" Her mouth felt like it had been swabbed with cotton wool. Touching her dry lips with the tip of her tongue, she watched him do the same thing, and her heart lurched.

But as she stepped to the side, prepared to dart away from him, he caught her shoulders. Gently. Later, she knew she could have twisted out of his grip. Later.

At the moment, all she could do was strive to tear her transfixed gaze away from his eyes — green and oh so captivating with the setting sun glinting from their depths.

His hands again traveled slowly to her head, where she felt him remove the pins from her hair . . . one, two . . .

"Don't. We must go downstairs . . . what will they think?"

He grinned. His green eyes expressed a depth of passion that sizzled to the very core of her being. "They will think . . ." As he spoke, his fingers discarded the last of the steel hairpins and played through the lustrous strands of glistening black hair. ". . . that it is high time the bridegroom spirited his bride away from the crowd." His last words were muffled, though, because his lips had gradually descended upon hers.

This kiss, unlike the early ones, began in such a tender way, her defenses were quickly shattered and she responded quite without intending to.

When he pulled her closer, his body felt lean and hard against her own. His hand swept from her head down her back, molding her to him, and she relaxed beneath his sensual demands.

Heat rose within her, while he caressed her lips with

his own, then traced the outline of hers with the tip of his tongue. Before she realized what was happening, she had opened her lips to his questing kisses, and when he pulled her closer she felt her heart throb against his chest . . . or was it his heart? she wondered crazily.

His hand moved boldly down her back, teasing her senses. Cupping her bottom through the layers of clothing, his broad palm pressed her body to his, suffusing her senses with a rush of heat. She felt his own lean frame press through her clothing, and instead of pulling away, she relaxed against him, encircled his broad shoulders with her arms, and pressed her now-tantalized breasts to his chest.

A knock at the door brought her back to reality, and she pulled away from his embrace.

"It is only Abril," he whispered, his lips brushing hers in a breathtaking manner. "I asked her to bring a private *merienda* for us here."

Serita's eyes flew open, but before she had time to struggle, he released her and crossed into the salon, where he held the door for the housemaid to enter with a heavily laden supper tray.

Serita stepped to the doorway. Scarcely breathing, she stood as still as stone, bound in an entanglement of fear and shame. The intense pleasure she had experienced in his arms, the thrill of his disgracefully wicked kisses and caresses, doubled the guilt she felt inside. If she had been afraid of consigning her soul to eternal damnation by her superficial marriage, surely she had sealed the pact with her actions now. Why, she would be fortunate if a year's penance erased her burden of guilt.

Giddeon closed the door behind Abril, then examined the tray. "Ah, tamales, sweet breads, and a bottle of port. All we need for *merienda*."

Serita hadn't budged an inch. Now she stared from him to the tray of supper, then back to him. Apprehension rose by giant leaps inside her breast. "I don't understand . . ." she began weakly. "Why . . .?"

Dropping the tea cloth back over the food, Giddeon turned to stare at her, uncertain what caused her confusion. The sky behind her was pink with the afterglow of sunset. The dress fit her exquisitely, and now, without her cumbersome veil, her cheeks flushed from his kisses, she looked inviting, even though her words sounded a trifle confused.

Coming to stand before her, he took her hand and lifted it to his lips. "What's troubling you, *querida?*"

She swallowed. "The fiesta." She watched his lips brush her fingers. "We should go down to *cena*." The touch of his moist lips against the back of her hand sent tremors straight to her brain. "I have never missed dinner, not during a fiesta . . ."

Aggravation worked against his rising passion. "You have never been married before, either."

"What does being married have to do with missing *cena?*"

Giddeon raised his eyebrows, then stepped forward to kiss her, but she dodged.

"Don't . . . Not like that."

"Not like what?"

She shook her head, thinking, wondering how to tell him what was on her mind. "Polite people do not behave like that," she retorted.

"Like what?"

She swallowed. "In such a wicked . . ."

"Wicked? Kissing? We're married—by your own

urging, I remind you. Do you intend to deny me my connubial rights?"

Serita's eyes flew open. She stared, astonished, into his serious face. "I certainly do not." She sucked in a deep breath, recalling Nieves's words. What had the old woman said? *Submit yourself.* Serita clamped her lips together, then continued. "I will submit myself, but only to fulfill our vows. I do not intend to become a brazen floozy in the process!"

Now it was Giddeon's turn to stare wide-eyed. "A brazen floozy?" he asked. "You mean, you don't think married people kiss?"

"What *you* . . ." Inhaling deeply, she rephrased her thoughts. ". . . what *we* did just now has nothing to do with proper kissing."

Giddeon threw his head back, his lips pursed. "Proper kissing," he repeated as though in thought. Turning, he stared into the cold fireplace. "Proper kissing." Swiveling on his heels, he faced her with a challenge in his eyes. "Would you care to instruct me in what you consider *proper kissing?*"

Serita glared at him. She grasped her train in one hand and swept past him. "You know as well as I do what I mean. Now, with or without you, I am going downstairs to *cena.*"

With lightning speed, he stopped her by a fierce grip to her forearm. "Not so fast, *querida.* We must settle this thing you call *proper kissing.*"

Jerking her arm fiercely to free herself, she glared into his threatening eyes. "Mock me if you wish, but you will not turn me into one of your . . . one of your . . ."

"Brazen floozies?" he furnished.

"My parents have been married for many years," she

reminded him. "Do you think I have never seen married people kiss?"

He grinned. His aggravation diminished beneath the inviting challenge to teach Serita Cortinas the meaning of her connubial duties. "Now I understand," he mused. "Let me demonstrate." He planted a quick, dry, passionless peck on her forehead, then drew back and studied her with mock seriousness.

"Did I do it right?" he asked. "Is that the way your parents kiss?" Before she could reply, he swept down upon her, kissing her fiercely, not with tenderness as before, but with force, separating her lips with his tongue, probing her struggling mouth, renting her resisting senses.

She struggled against him with all her might; she worked feverishly to wrench herself from the madman he had become. What in heaven's name had she gotten herself into this time? His hands burned circles around her arms, and her body . . . her own body trembled with blasphemous sensations. His grip loosened a fraction, his hands moved up her shoulders; her heart pounded, throbbed, and finally, against all her own struggles, she felt herself relax.

At that moment he thrust her an arms' length from him, retaining still his death grip on her arms.

"And that, I suppose," he mused, "is the kind of kiss I would expect from a brazen floozy?"

For a moment she held his gaze, while his insolent green eyes probed her soul. Then desperately she tore her eyes from his, bowing her head in abject shame. What in heaven's name . . . ?

"Serita." His voice had softened dangerously. "Serita, look at me. You liked it; so did I. There's nothing wrong with that. It's the way we begin . . ."

Her head jerked up. "That's what . . . what *putas* are for."

Giddeon glared at her. "Have it your way. But did you ever consider that your kind of attitude is what keeps *putas* — courtesans — in business?"

Fiercely she tore away from his clutches and turned her back on him, burying her face in her hands. "Leave me alone. Just leave me alone."

Stepping closer, he encircled her in his arms from behind. "No chance." His voice, though firm, was strangely gentle. "You are my wife, and I intend to take full advantage of my rights."

Still holding her hands over her face, she felt tears well behind her closed lids. "I told you I won't deny you . . ." Pausing, she stifled a sob. "but, please don't . . ."

Turning her with gentle hands, he encased her face between his palms. "Look at me, *querida*. Look at me."

He held her thus until she complied.

"The doors to this suite are closed and barred. Inside here, we are man and wife, just as your parents were." He had witnessed the fierce passion she possessed, passion her upbringing taught her to unleash only through anger and retaliation, passion that beckoned him as nothing ever had before. "You come from passionate stock, *querida*. Never doubt that your parents expressed their love for one another with all the feelings you are experiencing now."

Serita glared at him, while inside her heart raced wildly. Resistance shone strong. He knew she intended to submit to him — but only, as she said, to what she considered her duty.

"Now, love, I am going to teach you a few things the wedding vows don't discuss."

113

The pulse in his wrists throbbed against her face, causing her heart to respond. Heat flushed her skin. She tried to resist, but she felt weak and queasy.

"When you start enjoying yourself, don't fight it," he whispered, lowering his face to hers. "It is perfectly proper to enjoy honoring your vows. This is the way it all begins."

Serita held out as long as she could. She stood stiff, her neck and shoulders at attention, her lips listless and unmoving against his increasingly ardent attack on her senses.

But his hands heated her neck and shot flames the length and breadth of her body. His lips—moist and urgent—caressed her senses until she felt as though she radiated heat in all directions, as a star in the sky.

As the star she had wished upon that fateful night when she wished for a gringo name.

Look what she got, she thought, tentatively moving her fingers against the fabric of his black jacket. A gringo name—and much, much more.

At the first indication of her surrender, Giddeon intensified his kisses, his caresses, while at the same time he tried not to startle her out of the web of passion he attempted to weave about the both of them.

Again, he had a vision of a wild mustang—a magnificent animal, proud yet vulnerable, beautiful, spirited, and boldly independent. Beauty, fire, and grace. Serita Cortinas de Duval.

Against the backdrop of pensive Spanish guitars, he had watched her this long day, and at all times she had glowed with passion—the warmest welcome for her guests, the most fervent arguments with her reprobate cousin, Trinidad, the most blistering anger against Giddeon himself. Only when he forced her to stay by his side did her spirits dampen. Then, she became quietly defiant; then, he knew he would have to handle her with great wisdom for his mission to succeed.

Serita's hands slipped up his chest, encircled his neck, and Giddeon clasped her head in his hands, pulling her back to stare into her eyes.

"What did I tell you?" he murmured, nipping kisses across her face in the gentlest, most seductive manner. "Kissing can be a pleasurable experience." She stood still beneath his loving touch, her skin heating his palms, her flesh trembling against his lips. Scooping her into his arms, he held her steady a moment, while his lips again caressed hers passionately so as to quiet any fears his movement might have engendered within her. "But kissing is only the beginning, *querida*," he soothed, carrying her now through the salon into the large bedchamber.

"No . . ." she began, when he stopped beside the bed.

"Serita, love . . ." After kissing her soundly, he continued. "Tell me what you're afraid of."

Her eyes darted to the bed, then tentatively back to him. "Not here," she pleaded. "This is . . . was . . . my mother's bed."

Again, he kissed her face softly. "It was your mother and father's bed," he corrected.

"No," she insisted. "No, *Papá* slept in the other room."

He studied her quietly, amazed that so passionate a woman could have grown up so ignorant of lovemaking; amazed that he hadn't expected as much, owing to the fact that the females of his acquaintance fell into the category she so aptly labeled brazen floozies; amazed, most of all, that he felt nothing but gentle-

115

ness and patience and a great determination to teach her the extent of her own passion. Far more characteristic behavior for him would have been to toss her on the bed and stalk out of the room. He brushed aside this sudden change of attitude with the thought that were he to win Serita's confidence, her undying loyalty and dependence, he had no time for impatience.

"Perhaps your father *slept* in the other room, *querida,* but we are not going to sleep—not just yet." Standing on her feet, he felt her body stiffen beneath his hands. Fumbling behind her, his fingers found the first of the multitude of tiny buttons running down the back of her wedding dress. "When we do sleep"—his voice now caressed as his lips had earlier—"we will sleep here together, as man and wife." The last button slipped loose; his hands retraced their path. Grasping now the neckline of her wedding gown, he slipped it over her shoulders.

Her eyes stared at him, round as black pools of ink, but she moved not an inch. As he edged the lace off her shoulders, his fingers further tormented her prickly skin; when the garment fell to the floor at her feet, she gasped.

"As man and wife . . ." he repeated, deftly untying the ribbons on her corset cover and pulling that garment over her unprotesting head. Then he unbuttoned her petticoat and let it follow her dress to the floor. ". . . as our vows instructed we should."

Serita's body trembled so hard by now, she feared she might topple onto him at any moment. She opened her mouth to speak, but her heart was in her throat. Finally, she managed a whisper. "Are you certain . . . ?"

His eyes found hers; all his attention immediately

transferred from her clothing to her worried mind. He kissed her softly. "I have never been more certain of anything in my live, love." Without removing his lips from hers, he swept his arms beneath her legs, lifted her out of her heap of clothing, and deposited her in the middle of the bed.

"I'm not sure I . . ."

"Don't think about anything but this moment, Serita. Let me prove to you that our bodies were made to give each other pleasure."

Nieves's words came suddenly back to her, and she blanched at her innocence. Nieves had suggested there was more to this than begetting children; why had she not listened?

Giddeon swiftly removed his clothing and the rest of Serita's while she lay as if in a trance — of embarrassment, of curiosity, of intense anticipation. Nieves had also said Giddeon would teach her. She blushed.

Why did everyone know these things but she herself? Why, even Tita, who had never experienced married life, knew there was more to . . . to . . . A heavy sigh escaped her trembling lips. She didn't even know how to think on this anymore. Giddeon stretched beside her. The touch of his flesh against hers sent heat quivering with expectation along the length of her body.

He kissed her deeply, but now she was more aware of her naked breasts nestled into the soft fuzz on his chest. Her fingers stroked his face, sending needles of fire along her arms, while his hands roamed her back. Suddenly she thought of the wind blowing kisses along her skin through her silk blouse, and she knew he was right.

This was even better. Returning his ardent kisses in

kind, she felt his hand move to one of her breasts, where he plied her with undreamed-of torment, bringing a moan to her lips. At the sound, he trembled against her, and her own body blazed with strange and unfamiliar yet wonderfully felicitous sensations.

Her response emboldened him. He shifted to one side and trailed his lips across her cheek, down her neck, finally replacing his hand with his lips over her now-erect nipple, where he called forth even more uninhibited responses from her gardenia-scented body. *Yes, my wife,* he thought while his mind swam in a blazing lake of passion, *your body was made to love.*

He wasn't sure when he became aware of the change in his role. Perhaps it was while his lips set her very soul on fire with caressing kisses deep and moist; or while his fingers manipulated her heated flesh as a smitty would wield a piece of iron into a priceless work of art. But somewhere along the way, Giddeon Duval ceased to be the teacher and became instead the willing pupil.

Later, he was reminded of the times he had consumed too much tequila and hadn't been aware of his inebriated state until too late to stop the process.

Not that he would have stopped Serita's eager lovemaking if the very roof itself were falling in on top of them; and at times it felt that might be the case, as she went from timid and submissive to master of the craft in one fell swoop.

Her lips that so recently cursed him now set his soul on fire, and her hands—hands trained in the expert care of the horses she loved—now kneaded and massaged his quivering flesh, drawing passion from his very depths in such quantities that by the time he finally moved to enter her, it was only in the nick of time that he remembered her virginal state.

Poised above her heaving body, he focused on the now-unrestrained passion in her obsidian eyes. Catching his breath, his words still faltered. "This first time . . . it will hurt . . ?"

Her face glistened with perspiration; her eyes shone with passion. "Nothing this wonderful can hurt too much. Please hurry." Without hesitating, she lifted her hips, he entered her body, and they stared deeply, each into the other's eyes, as he tore her past away, branding her as his, forevermore.

Her breath whispered against his cheek, when, afterward, they lay entwined in each other's arms. "Did you ever wish upon a falling star?"

He drew his thoughts back to the present. Since the first time he saw her, riding with the wind across the meadow, he had known she was possessed of great passion. But he hadn't been prepared for her to unleash it in such a triumphant manner their first night together.

Not that he minded, he thought sardonically. Once her doubts concerning her immortal soul had been put to rest, Serita threw herself heart, soul, and body into lovemaking, producing, in turn, the most magnificent performance he had ever been a party to.

"A falling star?" he asked, half attentive, moving his head back to stare at her through the flickering candlelight.

"That's what it was like . . ." She paused, then corrected herself. "More like a thousand falling stars."

He kissed her nose along its straight, patrician bridge; he kissed her love-swollen lips soundly. "A thousand falling stars? Yes, at least a thousand."

Then his sultry seductress of a moment before

turned into a precocious child, her voice soft and dreamy. "Do you know why you came to me?"

He studied her, an inquisitive look on his face. "Why?"

"Because I wished upon a star for you."

He tensed in her arms. Enjoying her passionate lovemaking was one thing, but becoming a part of her romantic fantasies was quite a different proposition.

When he spoke, his voice was gruffer than he intended. "I don't believe in such nonsense."

For a moment she was silent. Her heart beat painfully in her breast. Why had she spoken so boldly? The rules they set for this game were quite clear: They might include sharing a marriage bed, but they definitely did not extend to revealing personal fantasies.

As soon as she was sure her voice would not betray her innermost feelings, she responded in terse tones. "Do not flatter yourself, *capitán,* I wished for a gringo name, nothing more."

Chapter Five

By the time All Hollow's Eve arrived a month later, Serita had settled into her new life with much greater ease than she had thought possible on the night of her wedding. For a while during the long hours following their tumultuous lovemaking, she had despaired of her—what had Tita called it?—her impetuousness. Surely this time her hasty decision was one she would rue to her dying day.

Thinking on it now while she helped Tita and Nieves prepare flowers for the graves of her ancestors, she recalled vividly her surprise at learning that Nieves had been correct, after all. Yes, there was a lot more to lovemaking between two people than she would ever have dreamed possible! The mere thought gave her a warm glow, even yet.

Never mind the fact that Giddeon Duval had not so much as cast a passionate glance her way since their wedding night. Of course, she hadn't encouraged him, knowing, as they both did, that their missions in life would prevent their being together any longer time than it took to get Los Olmos back on a paying scale.

Fortunately, they had not been required to discuss

the matter. No sooner had their lovemaking ended than a group from the fiesta assembled beneath the balcony to serenade them. At first she was reticent to show her face because of what had just transpired inside this suite. Could they read it on her face? Passion so great must surely leave telltale signs.

But Giddeon assured her their musicians would remain below all night unless they made an appearance on the balcony. And she knew it to be a fact.

"Besides," he told her, struggling into his pants and shirt, "they may *think* they know what will eventually take place in this room, but they have no way of knowing it has already occurred." Leaving her to dress, he went into the salon, and she reached for the dressing coat at the foot of the bed.

One glance at the filmy garment told her it alone would provide no shield, so she hastily pulled on the matching gown. The two garments were fashioned of so many yards of lace that together they managed to conceal her nudity quite well.

When she stepped into the salon, however, she felt completely unclothed by the magnitude of passion she saw in Giddeon's eyes. Clutching the lace about her, she averted her glance, then realized foolishly that he had already turned his back.

She took the glass of port he offered and sipped the fiery liquid, hoping it would soothe her quivering flesh. It didn't, but neither did he touch her, so she began to relax.

After listening to the musicians and thanking them by tossing down hibiscus blossoms Giddeon handed her for the purpose, she turned at his word and reentered the salon, where they ate the meal Abril had brought up for them earlier, drank another glass of port, and sat stiff and awkward on opposite sides of the fireplace.

"I am sorry if I . . ." she began, intending to let him know she hadn't meant to overstep the fine line of their agreement.

He shook his head. "No, Serita. No regrets. No apologies." She looked across at him briefly, and his hand seemed to tremble on the wineglass. No, she thought, it was only her imagination — or her own vibrating senses.

When he spoke again, she chanced another look and he was staring into the cold stone fireplace. His features appeared made of the same stuff. "We enjoyed ourselves tonight, as well we should have. That's what a wedding night is all about."

With that he retired to the small room which once belonged to her father, and she did not see him again for two days.

Now, as she arranged the flowers for All Souls' Day tomorrow, she suddenly had the strange idea that she had learned more about Giddeon Duval this past month — through their distant relationship — than she knew of anyone else on earth.

The time they spent together at meals, in the corral, and in the pasture, helped her adjust to her status as his wife; the magnificent occasion when she had been his lover receded into the world of her dreams and fantasies. This distance gave her a chance to carry on around him and their household as though it had never occurred.

The only physical contact they shared was when he seated her at meals. After moving her chair toward the table, he always planted an ever-so-chaste kiss upon her forehead. At first she had been offended, thinking he mocked her words spoken on their wedding night. In time, however, she came to realize that he, like she herself, remained dedicated to carrying off this charade that passed for a marriage.

Even now, however, she did not regret the fact of their marriage. How could she, when her plan appeared to be working? They had seen neither hide nor hair of Oliver Burton since his appearance at their wedding. Heartened by this evidence that her decision had, after all, been the right one, she had proceeded with her plans for Los Olmos.

And here, too, Giddeon's presence proved to be of value. He and his men, though born to the sea, as each of them told her more than once, took to ranching with a purpose. Her heart swelled to see activity around the place once more.

Within the month, everyone at Los Olmos had in his own way taken the seafaring men to hearth and home. The zeal with which the housemaids accepted the handsome men concerned Serita. She determined to keep a watchful eye on Abril, who spent more and more time of late, serving Delos or merely watching him when he was around.

Jorge, of course, fell immediately under the spell of *Señor Capitán,* dogging his footsteps until Serita worried that he might be rebuffed. And even Pablo grudgingly admitted he was glad to have the extra hands.

"They do not ride like our people," he had told Serita only this morning when she went to the corral to tend to Barb, "but they ride well enough to be of help on the *rodeo* tomorrow." Serita knew she appreciated their promptness: Giddeon and his crew did not tarry long at the house but arrived at the stable every morning ready for whatever task Pablo had for them

124

after a light *desayuno* of nothing but coffee. By time for the late breakfast, *almuerzo,* much had been accomplished around the compound: rotted *vigas* were replaced with new wood, cracks in the adobe chinked. Kosta, a master shipbuilder, turned his talents to house repair. Los Olmos began to shine under the attentive hands, which probably accounted for Tita's surprising response to Giddeon and his crew.

Tita quickly appeared to forget the disturbing fact that Giddeon Duval was a gringo. Of course, he did pay more attention to her than to anyone else, more even than to Serita herself. He fawned over her hibiscus, asked her advice before he undertook any changes around the place, and even held her chair at meals. So thoroughly charmed was she that Tita gave no notice to Abril's attraction to Giddeon's first mate, Delos.

As if on cue, Tita broke into Serita's thoughts. "*Sobrina,* find Jorge to ring the bell for *almuerzo.* We will leave the rest of these flowers until after the meal."

In the past month everyone at Los Olmos had settled into such a state of predictability that she knew instantly where to find Jorge—with Giddeon, of course.

And Giddeon, too, had become predictable. Climbing the stairs to the rooftop lookout, she knew he would be there, spyglass in hand, searching the distant horizon.

In fact, he spent so much time doing just that, that even his crew had taken to teasing him about it. No one bothered to tell her what he searched for, however, and she had come to believe he felt more at home high in the air, where he could survey the surrounding countryside, as he would view the limitless spaces at sea from the vantage point of a ship's bridge.

True to her expectations, upon reaching the roof, she found Giddeon with spyglass to his eye and Jorge at his side.

"Jorge, Tita says to ring the bell. We are ready to serve *almuerzo*."

At her voice, the boy turned his head to look at her, but Giddeon kept his vigil without acknowledging her presence. "*¡Andale!*" she repeated, and Jorge rose obediently.

"I will return, *Tío Capitán*," he told Giddeon.

"*Un momento, hijo*," Giddeon replied absently. "I will follow in a moment."

Serita stared at the two in astonishment. Jorge dashed down the staircase. "Uncle Captain?" she asked.

Giddeon turned, at last acknowledging her with a sheepish shrug, followed by his lopsided grin. "Jorge chose the name," he offered. "I suppose he is entitled . . ."

"Yes . . ." she admitted quickly to cover her unexpected nervousness at his presence. They were seldom alone these days, and she had not given thought to how it would be . . . how she would react to his nearness.

"Yes," she repeated, "he is entitled to call you whatever he wishes, but . . ."

Giddeon telescoped his spyglass. He studied her a moment before returning his gaze to the horizon. "The boy needs . . . Well, I *am* his uncle . . . after a fashion. Surely you don't begrudge him . . ."

"You misunderstand. I do not . . . I mean, I think it is wonderful that he . . . You're right. He needs a man in his life." A strong man, she thought, like you. But a man who will stay around to see him grow up, a man who . . .

Following his line of vision, she strove to calm her racing thoughts, to quiet her raging emotions, to steady her trembling legs. A burning sensation seared up the back of her neck, and her lips quivered. At this moment, all she could think of was that she wanted him to kiss her . . . to hold her . . .

Furious with herself, she tore her thoughts away. "What is it you have been searching for these last weeks?"

He turned to look at her; she felt his movement, his eyes. His reply surprised her, for she had thought she knew the answer.

"One of my crew members who is long overdue."

His unexpected announcement conquered her sensual yearnings for the moment, and she turned to him with curiosity. "From the north?"

Her question took him aback; looking at her did even worse things. "He's . . ." His eyes sought hers. "He's been to . . ." Their eyes held.

At only the last moment, he stopped before blurting out the truth. "Felix . . . that's his name . . . is on a mission," he sighed, reaching for her. "He should have returned by now."

She came into his arms naturally, eagerly, and their lips met with a fierceness engendered by memories of their wedding night, provoked by emotions once experienced, so long denied.

After that night, Giddeon had sworn himself to abstinence in matters involving his wife. Where before he had thought it necessary to win her compliance by submission, he had since decided upon a different course.

Now, he believed that the fewer contacts he and

127

Serita had, the better off she would be once he departed. For to return to the sea was all he intended. Although her sensuous lovemaking left him craving her sweetness and passion, he now feared permitting her to become too attached to him.

After he sold Los Olmos to Enos McCaulay, she would hate him, and well she should: In order to survive without Los Olmos, she would have to be infected with a sound and solid hatred for the man who robbed her of this land, which was, after all, the greatest of her passions.

Besides, he had reasoned, he did not need her compliance to sell the *hacienda*. Now that he was her legal husband, he had total rights under the laws of either Texas or Mexico to dispose of her property as he saw fit.

Yes, after that night, he had promised himself to keep his distance. But she came to him now, so warm, so soft, so ready to love him. And he was powerless to resist the demands of his body.

While his mouth devoured her inner sweetness, he cupped her body to his, acutely attuned to her fiery response, all the more conscious of her many charms since every crook and hollow were revealed vividly by the clinging layers of her clothing: her customary attire of deerskin breeches tucked into the tops of oxblood boots, and her silk blouse, worn conservatively now over corset and chemise.

But he always saw her as on that first day — patrician profile tossed to the sky, hair flying freely in the wind, one supple layer of silk cupping her breasts . . .

As the wind before him, Giddeon moved a hand across one of her breasts, feeling the heat from her body radiate through the layers of silky fabrics. With his other hand, he supported her regal neck, pressed her head closer while his lips moved across hers, urgently caressing, seeking, devouring. Her response was as free as on their first night together, and soon their bodies moved as one, pulsating as in the very act of lovemaking.

The bell pealed through the passion-charged air. When his hand slid inside her blouse, fumbled beneath her chemise and corset and closed around her throbbing breast, Serita moaned aloud and whispered his name into the humid folds of his lips.

The sounds meshed together in his brain, resounding a warning, clear and harsh. He drew back and stared into the radiant expression on her lovely face. She was his for the taking—everything she had, everything she was, everything she would ever be, and that realization suddenly turned the fire in his soul into a mass of cold ashes in the pit of his stomach.

Quickly, he dropped his hands, then his eyes.

But not before she saw his face draw up in an expression of pure loathing. She made it through the day, but alone in her mother's bed that night, she cried.

Not for the loss of anything, rather for the brashness of her actions, for the boldness with which she had expressed her feelings. For in unleashing her passion in so aggressive a manner, she had become what she feared—a brazen floozy—and now he hated her for it, and for that, she cried.

The chapel bell tolled before dawn the next morning, calling all hands to an early, hearty *desayuno* of beefsteak, eggs, *frijoles,* and tortillas with which to begin the *rodeo*. On roundup days, one meal must last until well into the afternoon. Nieves drove the chuck wagon into the pasture in order to provide the vaqueros with a hot meal in the middle of the day, but the roundup usually kept all hands busy until at least midafternoon.

Serita waited until everyone had already begun to eat before arriving in the dining room for *desayuno,* and she busied herself with her plate until Giddeon and his crew had left the table.

In the stables, Pablo issued riding orders.

"The herding ground is a natural glade beyond the *resaca* over the farthest rise. Never fear, the cattle know it better than most of you. Our task is to ride the outskirts of the range. When the cattle get sight of you, they will move toward the herding ground on their own." He scratched his scraggly white beard. "For the most part, they will. Keep a careful lookout for stragglers and move in a tightening circle toward the central ground. Do not expect the cattle to take the easy way around chaparral. They will head straight for the herding ground, and you will be hard-pressed to keep your mounts from doing the same. *La chica* trains them that way."

At the mention of her, Serita studied the ground at her feet, where she traced circles in the dirt with the toe of her boot. This morning her shame was so real she felt it must surely show on her face, and she had no intention of sharing such a secret with Giddeon Duval, much less with his crew of hardened sailors.

"Delos and Kosta, you take the east side," Pablo was saying, *"Señor Capitán,* you and —"

"I will ride alone," Giddeon broke in.

His obvious determination to stay away from her intensified the shame she felt inside, and Serita knew her face now flamed.

"Let me ride with *Tío Capitán,*" Jorge chimed in.

"No, Jorge," Giddeon retorted. "You ride with your
. . . with Serita."

Quickly Serita glanced at Jorge, whose dejection
showed on his face as plainly as she knew her own
shame had a moment ago. Her shame was a thing of
the past, however, replaced now by anger at this . . .
this dastardly gringo!

"Come, Jorge," she offered. "I want you to ride Barb
today, if . . . if you will."

"Do you mean it?"

She nodded. "Run saddle her. It will soon be time
to leave."

She had not intended to take Barb into the pasture,
but Giddeon's callous rejection of the boy made it
necessary. She seethed at his abrupt tone, calling
Jorge *boy,* when only yesterday he had addressed the
child as *son* . . . when Jorge was so obviously enraptured with this . . . this . . . despicable gambling
man!

Her anger lasted most of the morning, assuaged
now and again by Jorge's pleasure at riding Barb in
the *rodeo,* then finally replaced entirely by a rising
sense of apprehension.

Jorge noticed the problem first. Later, she berated
herself for letting personal troubles blind her to her
work. To the work of Los Olmos.

"Where are all the cattle, Serita?"

At first she looked around absently. "We must be
riding out too far."

Jorge shook his head. "We always find a lot of cattle
this side of Pablo's Resaca."

Serita pursed her lips. Jorge was right. They always
found several dozen head of cattle among the retama

131

and huisache on this side of the old mudhole into which an outlaw mustang once pitched Pablo, hence bestowing upon it his name.

"Perhaps they have found a better bedding ground," she answered, not too concerned.

They tightened the circle and still no cattle. Then they tightened it again.

"Serita, where are they?"

Before she could answer the boy, a rifle shot echoed from the direction of the herding ground. Together, they sunk spurs to the flanks of their mounts and raced through the chaparral. Now filled with the business at hand, Serita suddenly thought of Barb.

"Jorge," she called. "Bring Barb in slowly. We cannot allow her to step in a varmint hole and break a leg." With that, she herself raced pell-mell for the herding ground.

Giddeon, Delos, and Kosta had already arrived. They sat their horses staring at the carnage; a sickly pallor colored their ruddy faces. At the sound of horses, Giddeon glanced across the clearing and watched Serita bring her mount to a skidding halt.

Wide-eyed, she searched the group, her gaze resting briefly on Giddeon's, before she found Pablo.

"What is the meaning of this?" She spurred her horse to the old vaquero's side. Together they surveyed the several hundred head of cattle, freshly slaughtered.

"No sé, chica," he moaned. "I do not know. I do not know."

Fury amassed like the black cloud of a brewing storm inside Serita, as she took in the sight which was unmistakably designed to keep Los Olmos from selling this herd of cattle. "That bastard Oliver Burton!" Her voice raised by several degrees, and she screamed again. "That bastard! And I thought he had given up. I thought by . . ." In her rage, she had not been aware of Giddeon, who steered his horse around the bodies of slaughtered cattle and now sat at her side.

"No, *querida*," he answered. "It takes more than a name to stop a man like Oliver Burton."

At the sound of his voice, her head swiveled on her neck and she stared at him. Though his words were spoken in anger, his anger wasn't for her. She knew that, as surely as she knew he tried to comfort her . . . calling her querida . . . love. . . . And she wished he wouldn't. She wished he would leave her alone. She wished she had never married him. Before her lay evidence that her impulsive decision had not solved her problem with Oliver Burton.

"Are you sure it was Burton?" Giddeon asked.

"Sí, Señor Capitán," Pablo answered him.

"Then we will go after the man," Giddeon swore. "He will pay for . . ."

"No," Pablo insisted. "There is no proof the perpetrator was Oliver Burton." Then in a voice that revealed his own dejection, he related his theory that Burton's Cow Boys had followed the Los Olmos practice of luring the cattle onto the herding ground, and once there, instead of branding them as the Los Olmos vaqueros would have done, they methodically slaughtered them to the last head.

"All is not lost," he added, turning toward Serita. "The deed has been accomplished but a few hours. If we hurry, we can save the tallow and hides."

She drew a deep breath. "Yes, Pablo. We must hurry. Oliver Burton will not defeat me."

"You must instruct us in this, Pablo," Giddeon told the old vaquero. "My men and I are willing, but hopelessly ignorant."

In spite of herself, Serita smiled. Then she blushed at her own thoughts. *Would this dastardly gambling man were ignorant of other matters!*

When Jorge arrived, Serita soothed him, and Giddeon did his best to ignore the boy. Pablo sent him back to the compound to instruct Nieves to send along their supply of skinning knives and sharpening tools. The next few hours passed in back-breaking physical work, during which the seamen-turned-vaqueros learned to remove a cowhide without shredding it to bits with the thin, sharp blades of their knives.

"Ain't much different than skinning out a shark," Kosta joked.

"Or tuna," Delos replied. "Remember that time we spent three months tuna fishing off Sitka?"

"The only tuna we have around these parts," Pablo joined in, "is what you see yonder with all the thorns. Prickly pear, we call it. The Indians, though, walked halfway across the country to harvest prickly-pear tuna."

The talk of food was fine at first, but by the time Nieves rang a cow bell attached to her chuck wagon, every stomach in the group was far too queasy to consider a meal. They took coffee and worked until, finally, Pablo stopped them.

"We have done enough for today," he told the exhausted group. "We will go home and return again at sunrise. With dusk approaching, we are more likely to skin ourselves or one another than these cattle."

They washed the blood and gore from their hands in a nearby stream, the headwaters of Los Olmos Creek, Pablo told the seamen. Serita sent Jorge back on her mount, saying she wanted to ride the kinks out of Barb before she brought the filly in for the night. The fact was, she wanted to ride alone, away from the carnage, the destruction. Alone, away from Giddeon Duval.

Once she left the group behind, she gave Barb the reins and let her race to a far rise. At the bottom, she hitched Barb securely to a heavy, low-growing limb of another windswept oak tree.

Then she crept up the rise on all fours and lay on her stomach in the short grass, watching El Rey—an enormous chestnut-colored mustang stallion—and his *manada*. As heartsick and weary as she was, the sight of El Rey restored her hope for Los Olmos.

Alerted by a noise behind her, she tensed at the sight of Giddeon. He dismounted beside Barb, hitched his own mount, and started toward her, stooped at the waist.

Pablo was right about one thing, she thought sardonically, these sailors were fast learners. He dropped to his knees, then to his stomach beside her.

"Are those the sonofabitches who stole my horses?" he whispered.

In spite of the anger she had felt for him all day, she grinned. Without answering, she turned her attention back to the stallion who stood sentinel at the far side of the group of twenty-five or so mares.

"Do you know the story of the first horse God created?"

Silently, he shook his head.

"It was a chestnut," she whispered, "with a star on his forehead. The star is a sign of glory and good fortune."

Giddeon studied the magnificent stallion as he sniffed the air, peered over and beyond the backs of

135

the twenty-five or so mares that formed his *manada*, searching for danger . . . always searching for danger.

"The stallions can never relax their vigil," she told Giddeon. "Not for a moment, or their *manada* will be stolen by a rival."

"Before my experience on the trip out here, I would have thought Indians or mustangers were the only threat."

She grinned. "Don't be embarrassed at falling prey to the mustangs. It happens to everyone who sets foot in this country, not once but any number of times. Lucky we're upwind, or our own horses would be straining at their bits."

Giddeon watched the stallion toss his head up. "Can he see us?"

"Not this close to sunset," she responded easily. "In full daylight we would be easy for him to see."

As she spoke, the rays of the setting sun glinted from the chestnut hair of the stallion, and the wind suddenly shifted. The horse snorted, turned in their direction, then, in a matter of seconds, he had signaled his band with some unseen yet effective method, and the entire *manada* appeared to have taken wing. Trailing his mares, encouraging them with nips and snorts, the stallion's long mane and tail floated in the air behind him like a stream of liquid gold.

"You've convinced me," Giddeon laughed.

"About what?" Serita rose to her feet and brushed dirt from her hands. "The mustang's sense of smell or . . .?"

"His beauty." Giddeon rose along with her.

"In another year, I am going to breed Barb to him." Turning, he studied her, a curious light in his eye.

"That's how I will save Los Olmos," she continued,

136

sharing with him her plan which she had not so much as spoken aloud before. "Can't you see their progeny? Endurance, hardiness, speed, intelligence . . ." She stopped, embarrassed that she had opened her thoughts to his ridicule. "I will do it," she finished.

"How do you plan to go about it?" he asked. "Without turning Barb loose in the *manada?* And if you do that, you will never . . ."

Cocking her head, she studied him a moment, then looked away, irritated with herself for sharing this secret passion without first thinking it through. "You don't think I can do it?"

"I think you have stars in your eyes."

She glared at him, then turned toward their horses. Shame replaced her irritation at his mention of that . . . that distasteful night. "Doubt me if you will," she retorted. "I have set out to breed Barb to El Rey, and I will do it. Believe me, I will."

He stared at her while the setting sun glistened on the strands of hair that played about her face, and he thought of that night on the balcony . . . of sundown . . . and something stirred in the pit of his stomach, sounding an alarm in his brain.

"*Sí, querida,*" he answered in her own tongue. "*Yo te creo.*" And he did believe her, somewhere in the depths of his intellect, he believed she could accomplish whatever she damned well set out to do. Turning, he started toward his own horse. He would ride back to the compound, away from her. Quickly. Now, while he still could.

"Do not call me that again."

Pausing, he studied her curiously with knitted brow. "What?"

She returned his stare with fire in her eyes. "You

137

know very well what," she retorted. "I am sure it is what you call all your women—*querida*. Well, I am not your woman—I am your wife, so do not call me that."

As she often did, she took him by surprise, and he knew the truth shone in his eyes. Followed closely by fury. "So what if I do?" he challenged. "You happen to be the first to complain."

Whatever she had expected, his admission shocked her. She reached for Barb's reins, then another thought struck her, and she pivoted to find him still staring at her.

"And another thing . . ."

He bowed in an exaggerated fashion. "I suppose I should be grateful you chose this out-of-the-way place to dress me down," he fumed, intending to ride away and leave her standing in her pool of wrath.

His ridicule sharpened her anger—and her hurt. "Even though you loathe me for my . . . for my wanton conduct on the . . ." She swallowed, then continued. ". . . on the night of our wedding and . . . and yesterday on the rooftop, you do not have to take out your feelings on Jorge. The boy . . ."

With angry strides he advanced on her, stopping only when the toes of their boots touched. "What are you talking about? I have never . . ."

"Jorge adores you," she continued as though she had not been interrupted "and you encouraged him by . . . by letting him call you that outrageous name . . . and yourself calling him *hijo!*" She shook her head, carried away by her anguish. "First you call him son, then you brush him aside with abandon . . ."

"Not with abandon," he broke in. "You don't understand . . ."

"Just because you think me a . . . a brazen

floozy . . . you've no right to . . ."

He stopped her with his hands, by shaking her shoulders and staring desperately into her raging black eyes. "What in the hell are you talking about? I never called you . . ."

"You don't have to say it in words," she cried. "I saw it . . . in your eyes. I felt it in your—"

His lips crushed the words from her mouth. He kissed her wildly, with a fervor. When she didn't respond in kind, he drew back and stared into her distraught face.

"Serita, I never meant you to think . . ." Pursing his lips, he studied her lovely features. "You are wonderful . . . magnificent . . . perfect. If every wife treated her husband to the kind of lovemaking you gave me, why, no husband would ever stray from his marriage bed. It's just that . . ." His words broke off at the admission, and he sighed.

Her brow knit in confusion. "But yesterday on the rooftop you . . . you looked at me with such . . . such revulsion," she whispered, not understanding. His words and his actions were worlds apart.

"The revulsion . . . was for myself, *quer—*" Favoring her with a sheepish grin, he continued. "Serita, I'm going to leave Los Olmos. We both know that. When I go, I don't want you to be hurt. Your lovemaking is by far the most wonderful experience a man . . . any man . . . could ask for, but . . . well, it can lead to feelings . . . to commitments far more difficult to break than the wedding vows we took so lightly."

She listened, assimilating his words and actions in her brain. "What you are saying is that you intend to be cruel and mean to everyone until you leave?"

"Forchristssake, Serita!" he implored. "Yes! If that's

139

what it takes to keep you from falling in love with me."

Her eyes widened. "You would rather have me angry with you all the time than . . . than in love with you?"

"Dear God in heaven! Will you not listen? I don't want to *hurt* you."

She stared at him, while his hands held her as with heated bands around her arms. Tita's words on the day of their wedding came to mind unbidden: *How will you feel when this man leaves you alone . . . by then, you may have grown to love him.* Right now, that eventuality seemed eons in the future. Right now, she was too busy rejoicing in his affirmation of her . . . he said she was wonderful and magnificent and perfect; well, maybe she wasn't all those things, but what a relief to know the wondrous feelings she had when she was with him did not mean she was a common floozy.

Smiling now, she whispered into his downturned face. "Giddeon Duval, in case you haven't noticed, I am quite capable of taking care of myself. Why don't you let me worry about being hurt after you leave?" And with that, she stretched to meet his lips and kissed him ardently, uninhibited by unfounded fears.

Chapter Six

By the time they arrived back at the compound, dusk had settled among the elm trees; its pink glow enveloped the old adobe walls of *la casa grande*. Serita rode weary but peaceful with Giddeon by her side, the magic of their relationship restored. Today they had rebuffed one more attempt by Oliver Burton to take Los Olmos—to destroy her dream.

He would try again. She knew that now. Giddeon was right; a name would not stop him. But strength would. And Giddeon Duval possessed the strength.

Strength and so much more. Lanterns flickered from the outer walls of the compound, beckoning them home. She had just entertained the delicious thoughts of a bath and the big, soft, walnut bed when a ruckus in front of the compound startled her out of her reveries.

Unidentifiable noises reached them first. Then they saw shapes—bulky, stationary . . . moving. Serita and Giddeon exchanged puzzled glances, instantly alert. Both drew rifles from saddle scabbards. Giddeon motioned her back with his hand.

"Let me see what we're riding into."

141

She squinted through the hazy night air. Several wagons, their contents covered with canvas, stood here and there under the trees. "It isn't Oliver Burton. He wouldn't bring wagons, unless . . . Dear God, he's moving us out!"

Spurring Barb, she raced ahead, with Giddeon on her heels, calling after her to be careful.

The first person she recognized upon reaching the compound, however, was not Oliver Burton, but her reprobate cousin, Trinidad Cortinas. Immediately, her fright turned to anger, made all the more fierce for the scare her had given her.

"Trinity! What is the meaning of this?"

"Thank God you're here, Serita. My men were bested in a fight with General Arista south of Las Palmas today."

Serita stared at the melee of wounded, groaning men. The horses stamped and neighed nervously, and she herself felt sickened by the same nauseating odor of blood she had inhaled all day. Uninjured men rushed about carrying litters of wounded into the compound.

"Stop! All of you! Stop this minute!" She slid to the ground and confronted Trinidad with hands on hips.

Giddeon drew to a halt beside her, jumped from his horse, and scanned the area, silently taking in the feverish activity.

"What's the rush, Cortinas?"

"My men are dying, fool!"

Giddeon grasped the startled Trinidad by the collar, fairly lifting him off the ground. "Who are you running from? Who have you led to this house?"

Serita's mouth flew open at the suggestion.

"Trin—"

"No one." Trinidad twisted away from Giddeon's hold. Angrily, he straightened his shirt. "My men are dying," he repeated.

Half listening, Giddeon strode toward one of the wagons. "What do you have here?" Without waiting for an answer, he lifted the canvas covering its cargo. Then he raced from wagon to wagon, tearing back the canvas at each stop, scrutinizing the contents. "Where did you get this stuff?"

"Supplies for my men," Trinidad spat. "An army cannot live without supplies."

Serita stumbled to one of the wagons and peered into the bed. It was crammed to the brim with foodstuffs—canned foods, sacks of flour, and coffee. The next wagon was loaded with ammunition, and the next with supplies for horses, equipment used to repair wagons—metal rims, braces, axes and crowbars, and a full keg of nails. "Trinity, answer him. Where did you get these supplies?"

"What difference does it make? This is war, Serita. A man has to do a lot of things in wartime."

"You will not bring stolen goods to my home. You will not turn Los Olmos into your camp! I told you that before."

Giddeon seethed into the man's face. "If you bring harm to this household, Cortinas, you will pay with your life."

"Giddeon, please," Serita interrupted. "Let me . . ."

He glared at her, then pushed Tinidad aside and scanned the gathering. "Do what you want with him. I'm taking the wagons away from the house so those following him can retrieve their goods without attacking us."

143

"No one is following me," Trinidad reiterated.

Paying no attention to him now, Giddeon spied Delos in the crowd and motioned him to come forward. Then he turned to Serita. "See what you can do for the wounded. Delos, Kosta, and I will unload these wagons down by the old road."

When Delos approached, however, he was accompanied by a man Serita had never seen before. She paid no attention, assuming him to be one of Trinidad's soldiers, until Giddeon embraced the man jovially.

"Felix, mate! I'd almost given up on you!"

Without pausing to introduce her, Giddeon hurried away, Felix in tow, and Serita became engaged in swabbing this man's wounds, binding that one's arm, while Tita, Nieves, Abril, and Lupe tended still others.

As she dressed wounds, however, she gave Trinidad a proper dressing down for coming to Los Olmos with his army.

"I want you gone by dawn," she told him.

"Serita, be reasonable. That row of old quarters is doing no one any good standing empty. My men will not harm you. I promise."

"Their presence is harm enough," she insisted. "By letting you remain here, I have as much as taken sides with your . . . your ridiculous new republic! You know the Texans are watching and waiting for an opportunity to take over this land. And Mexico . . ."

"Mexico!" he spat. "If Mexico had not ignored us so completely and for such a long time, we would have no need for a new republic."

Progressing from one man to another as they were

144

laid out on pallets around the fountain, Serita ceased to argue with her cousin. "We will discuss this no further. Los Olmos is my land, and I say what goes on here. I have enough on my hands keeping this *hacienda* out of the clutches of Oliver Burton."

Again Trinidad scoffed. "Your *marriage* was supposed to do that, cousin dear."

"Little you understand," she stormed. Herds of slaughtered cattle stampeded across her mind. "Without Giddeon Duval, Burton would have run us off already."

Silently, she resumed tending the wounded until finally, upon reaching the last man, Tita sent her off to dress for *merienda*, saying Lupe and Abril would feed the men broth. "From Pablo's account," Tita told her, "all of you had a miserable day. You must have some nourishment before retiring."

Serita found a tub of steaming water sitting in her bedroom, thanks to Lupe. And it did feel good to wash away the blood and gore of this day, even though she could hardly keep her mind from worrying over what tomorrow would bring.

Dressing hastily in clean breeches and shirt, she brushed and tied her hair back, then secured a *rebozo* around her shoulders to ward off the nip in the night air. Though the first of November could hardly be considered winter in this part of the world, the nights were cool, sometimes even cold.

She met the others in the *comedor*, where Giddeon's reception, though not as warm as she had expected, at least was not as cold and aloof as during the past month. He introduced her to Felix, who greeted her in an offhand sort of way. Giddeon and Trinidad kept their peace by remaining silent throughout the

145

meal of tamales and cold fish, served with mugs of steaming broth.

After *merienda,* however, the two men set to it again in the parlor. No sooner had Tita excused the table than Giddeon turned to Serita.

"We have business to discuss. Bring all the documents you have concerning Los Olmos." He nodded toward Trinidad. "You, too."

"In order to save Los Olmos from Oliver Burton . . ." he began when the three of them had assembled in the parlor. Standing before the fireplace, he addressed them as though he owned the place, which Trinidad accused him of thinking he did.

"If you think I don't own this place . . ." Giddeon replied with steel in his voice.

Serita squirmed. At times he took his position as her husband to heart more than . . .

". . . then you do not know very much about a husband's rights under the law," he finished.

Trinidad jumped to his feet. Serita crossed the room to stand beside Giddeon. She smiled at him, but only with her lips. "Do you have a suggestion?"

Her voice carried an air of absolute command, which Giddeon could see at a glance had a strong effect on Trinidad. He continued in a firm tone of voice. "Our mutual interest is to save Los Olmos from Oliver Burton and from those who would come after him. We must obey the law. That means you, Trinidad, cannot quarter your army here. In fact, you are not to bring another soldier on this place. Serita has requested as much of you before; now I am ordering you to leave here as soon as your men can ride, and to take your stolen property with you. You will find your wagons on the north side of

Pablo's Resaca."

Trinidad jumped to his feet once more. "Like hell I will leave. This *hacienda* is a part of my heritage; it does not belong to you."

Ignoring him, Giddeon spoke to Serita. "Where are the papers on Los Olmos?"

"All I have are the land-grant documents and the deed."

"She probably has them hidden beneath her bed in that old trunk like our great-grandfather did," Trinidad sneered.

"I must go over the papers," Giddeon told her, "in order to figure up the taxes."

"Taxes to whom?" Trinidad questioned. "With whom do you intend to align yourself, gringo?"

"Trinity," Serita soothed.

"Don't Trinity me," he retorted. "Are you stupid? Or merely blinded by this . . . this gringo raider. Can't you see what he is trying to do?"

Giddeon held his breath; Serita turned on Trinidad. "I know perfectly well what he is trying to do," she answered. "It is you I doubt, Trinity. You of my own flesh and blood; you who are trying to bring us to ruin by labeling us revolutionaries to those who look for any excuse to become our enemies."

Giddeon laid a possessive arm around Serita's shoulders. "She's right, Cortinas. You are the blind one. The United States is getting ready to annex Texas all the way to the Rio Grande River. That includes the very spot we are standing on; it includes every acre of La Hacienda de Los Olmos. Unless the back taxes are paid in full, nothing will save this land from being taken over by the state. Nothing. No matter how old the land grant; no matter how respected the owners. All that will hold water is a legal deed, upheld by tax receipts."

Trinidad scoffed, and Serita pulled away, staring incredulously at Giddeon. "How do you know all this?"

He shrugged, attempting to appear casual. "It stands to reason," he told her. "The United States—"

"I mean about the taxes? How do you know they are not paid?"

He studied her at length, trying to decide whether to tell her the truth, that Felix had just returned with proof the taxes had not been paid, or . . .

Finally, he answered her with a question. "You mean to say you paid taxes to a country you have never claimed to be a part of?"

"No," she admitted, "and I never will. Los Olmos is not a part of Texas; it will never be part of the United States. It is *my hacienda;* that is all it is—all it will ever be. So you are wasting your time, both of you."

"Serita," he began cautiously, "you are too intelligent to take such a narrow view . . ."

"She did not show much intelligence by marrying you!" Trinidad blurted out. "Both of you are stupid not to realize that what we need is a new government—our own republic, the Republic of the Rio Grande. We will use the Mexican Constitution of 1824. If Mexico had kept that constitution, Texas would never have revolted in the first place. Now—"

"I will hear no more talk about this country or that," Serita cut in, "nor about taxes nor armies nor constitutions. Los Olmos is all I care about."

Giddeon's eyes glinted green and cold. "Then your stubbornness will lose you the one thing you love

148

most." Turning abruptly, he stalked out of the parlor, slamming the heavy wooden doors behind him.

He did not come to her bed that night, and she doubted she would have let him in had he tried. The next morning she arose early, but upon entering the *comedor,* Giddeon and Felix were already leaving the table.

He paused to seat her, but when he began to tell her of his plans for the day, she bristled.

"Since most of Trinidad's men are unable to travel right away, we will use their wagons to haul the hides to Matamoros. Pablo suggested it."

Her aggravation lessened somewhat at his last words. At least he still listened to Pablo. "That's fine," she agreed. "I will be right along."

"Serita, about last night . . ." His voice faltered, her eyes darted to his, and he planted a chaste kiss on her forehead.

As always, that simple gesture brought a rush of memories—their conversation on the night of their wedding . . . and what had followed that conversation.

She felt her face flame. "I'll get my . . ."

Lifting a hand, he stroked her cheek with the back of his knuckles. "Yesterday was a rough one. Why don't you stay at the house today? Trinidad has enough uninjured men to help finish the skinning before nightfall."

She hesitated, but only a moment. Yesterday had been rough—a messy, gory job she had no desire to repeat two days in a row. "All right," she agreed.

Leaning forward, he planted a sound kiss on her

149

lips, then grinned his lopsided grin. "I will return, *querida*."

She watched him leave the courtyard, her hand to her mouth, that wretched name singing through her senses. Yesterday—last night, at least—forgotten.

The day sped by as she helped tend the wounded, who had been moved from the courtyard to the cottages beside the stable. Then she exercised Barb; and finally, after siesta, she inspected the horses and equipment she would use to bring in the *caballado*. With the present price of horses, she must break a herd to drive north before spring.

Throughout all her chores, the confrontation in the parlor the evening before haunted her, and she began to worry that Giddeon might be right.

If the United States did take over Texas, would they confiscate her property? She wasn't totally ignorant of the law; she knew land could be sold for unpaid taxes. And with the almost daily increase in the number of gringo raiders from north of the Nueces River, she doubted not that the United States would find a ready buyer for Los Olmos.

At last, determined to discover the extent of her debt to the state, she withdrew the land-grant documents from their resting place in the flat, nail-studded leather trunk of her great-grandfather, which lay, as Trinidad had said, beneath the heavy walnut bed in her mother's—now her own—bedchamber.

Pulling aside the window draperies, she lighted a lamp and spread the documents on the desk in the salon of her suite. As a child she had been fascinated by the scrawlings and markings; studying them now took her back in time—to when she used to watch Papá study these same documents.

They were all here: the original land-grant petition, dated 1752, with the governor's signature and recording fee; the first survey, with its elaborate signatures, seals, and ribbons; and the more recent survey, not over thirty years old, when the three brothers divided the original three hundred thousand acres into equal portions of one hundred thousand each. Being the elder son, Papá had been given the most desirable piece of land—that bordering on Los Olmos Bay.

Bringing her mind back to the present problem, Serita pursed her lips. How much would the taxes amount to? Dismayed with such things, she had no idea where to begin to discover the facts. Was it really important? She couldn't take a chance otherwise.

Sighing, she retied the ribbons about the documents and restored them to the trunk. Giddeon Duval had come into her life at exactly the right moment. Not only had he provided her with the name and power of a gringo fighting man, but he must surely have an understanding of legal matters which far surpassed her own. She would talk to him.

While she bathed, she made plans. But running just below the surface as accompaniment to her conscious thoughts . . .

Undermining her schemes, while she dressed for *merienda* in a yellow watered silk, while she twined her hair about her head and secured it with a set of ivory combs . . .

Diverting her concentration from schemes to save Los Olmos and plans to pay the taxes . . .

Tantalizing her very soul with sweet promise . . . were his farewell kiss, burning still upon her lips,

151

and his parting words—I will return, *querida* . . .

As the first bell calling the household to *merienda* tolled through the dusk, Serita grabbed a small sachet filled with dried gardenia leaves and stuffed it inside her corset, into the dark hollow between her breasts.

Her heels clicked across the tiled floor from her bedchamber to the salon in rhythm to her singing heart. I will return . . . I will return . . . love . . . love . . . *querida* . . . love.

Reaching to snap a yellow hibiscus blossom from the bouquet on the table in the salon, her toes tapped out the rhythm—*querida* . . . *querida* . . . *querida* . . .

Suddenly, the stem was drawn from her fingers, and she turned to stare directly into his smiling face. Heat, like flares of lightning, raced up her arms.

"Allow me." Snapping the stem, he tucked the flower in her hair, low, behind her ear, then leaned back to scrutinize his work.

She stood transfixed, scarcely breathing, while her heart did a dance on its own. "When did you return?" she asked, drinking in huge drafts of his intoxicating scent.

By way of answering, he lowered his face to hers. His warm, moist lips touched, caressed, then possessed her won.

Tidal waves of heat surged through her veins, crested in her brain, and broke into a score of fragments pommeling her pores as with needles of fire.

His hands spanned her waist, then stroked her girted back, and she pressed closer to his racing heart. The ardor with which she returned his kisses activated yearnings inside him that needed no help in the first place, and he kissed her as if he would never stop.

She, in turn, tightened her arms around his neck and held him as though she would never let go. But their passion was soon interrupted by the last call to *merienda*.

She tightened her hold on him, but he drew back. For a moment he couldn't speak, so lost was he in the open invitation beckoning him from the depths of her obsidian eyes. He cleared his throat. "Tita said to tell you the candles are in place."

Serita sighed. "Dear Tita. She is determined to save my wayward soul."

At Giddeon's raised eyebrows, she continued, while freeing herself gently from his embrace. "With all the commotion last night, we didn't light candles in the chapel for our ancestors."

Gideon frowned, watching her pluck a yellow lace mantilla from the back of a chair. "I thought flowers, not candles, were the requirement for All Souls' Day."

She slipped her hand through the crook of his elbow, gaiety bubbling from her lips. "Tita believes in leaving no stone unturned on the road to salvation."

They walked down the corridor, still wrapped in a soft web of smoldering desire. "I suppose it's natural," she mused. "The church is all she has."

Coming to the staircase, Giddeon steered clear of her billowing skirts. "Why did she never marry?"

Serita held the edge of her skirts with one hand and stepped down the stairs lightly. Her heart fairly burst with his nearness. "She did have a beau once, or so Mamá told me." She shrugged. "I don't know

153

what happened." But when she reached the table and bent to kiss her aunt's withered cheek, an unsettling thought stirred within her. The conversation had called to mind Tita's admonition on the day of hers and Giddeon's wedding. Did Tita know first hand that one could fall in love without intending to do so?

Although Trinidad was morose, Giddeon refused to let himself be badgered into reaction to the man's verbal stabs. The day in the field had given him time to think out his strategy, and sparring with Trinidad Cortinas did not fit into his plans.

His silence continued after the meal when he escorted Serita from the comedor. He guided her toward the chapel, but she stopped.

"You don't have to come."

"I will," he responded quickly. On the walk over, the thought struck him that perhaps he had spoken in haste. Attending family vespers was no more a part of his strategy than was arguing with Trinidad. But he did not turn back.

The chapel was dimly lit by only the altar candles. As they made their way down the aisle, Giddeon felt the old uneasiness return. His religious education had stopped before his mother's death, and his habits along with his education. The extent to which this family's life revolved so completely around the church surprised him. Los Olmos was far removed from civilized society, where he would have expected religious practices to be in keeping with that of one's neighbor. At Los Olmos, vespers and morning prayer were a daily practice, with or without guests or feast days or even priests.

By the time he and Serita knelt before the altar,

154

Tía Ana and Jorge had already lighted several of the line of white candles. Serita took the taper, and, as she lighted each one, she whispered the name of the person for whom she issued the prayer. The last two were supplications: *"Para Mamá. Para Papá."*

When she finished, two candles remained. She looked up at Giddeon. He stared at her with such a curious expression that she suddenly felt faint—not with passion—at least, not passion of the sensual kind. Without speaking, he took the taper from her hand and lighted the two remaining candles himself.

"Para Mamá." His whispered supplication was barely audible even to Serita. Then as she watched, he lighted the last of the candles, while staring solemnly at her. *"Para tú,"* he whispered. "For you."

Afterward, she questioned him. "For me? Why did you light a candle for me?"

He squeezed her to his side and changed the subject. "What now?"

She shrugged. "Come, you will see." And sure enough, some of the candles they had lighted at the altar they now carried, with a great deal of care against the wind, to the plots in the grove of elm trees, where one was placed on each of the family graves.

Back in their suite, it took two glasses of port and Serita's babbling about the land-grant documents to dispel the pensive mood brought on by the candle-lighting service. Never again, he vowed, watching Serita unroll the sheepskin documents. Never would he set foot in that chapel again. Feeling sorry for Serita was no more a part of his strategy than was squabbling with her cousin.

In the end it was the land-grant plat that brought

him back to his immediate goal: selling Los Olmos to Enos McCaulay. She rummaged through the ancient trunk, laid several yellowed documents on the low walnut table, then sat cross-legged on the floor and beckoned him to her.

"Come look at these. You must advise me."

His self-deprecating groan turned to a low whistle as the plat came into focus in the flickering light. "This was some piece of property."

"Three hundred thousand acres, in the beginning."

Giddeon turned the land-grant petition over in his hands, thinking about the remaining one hundred thousand acres — four bits an acre, McCaulay's offer. Not bad at all. "The governor's signature means the petition was accepted?"

She nodded, then pointed to the seal, bearing the words *dos reales,* the recording fee. "The fee was never accepted until after all three steps had been completed," she told him, recalling the story she had heard told since her earliest memories. "First came the petition, then the order, signed by King Ferdinand VI himself. Before the grant could be recorded, the petitioner had to physically take possession of the land from a representative of the king. In our case, my great-grandfather took possession at Resaca de las Palmas, where the first stake was laid to begin the survey."

After pointing out this spot on the plat, with her finger she traced the present boundaries of the Miguel Cortinas land, then showed him her uncles' property: "Tío Pepe, my uncle at La Bahia, traded his land for the townsite; *Tío* José, Trinity's father — at his death two years ago, *Tío* José's land was taken over by his wife's brothers. By rights, of course,

Trinity was his heir." She sighed. "That is why Trinity is so possessive of the remaining Cortinas land. He feels his inheritance was wrongfully taken from him. It was, of course."

Giddeon studied the plat. "And since Tía Ana never married, she has no property."

Serita shrugged. "This is her home. She was born here, and she intends to stay right here until we carry her to her place in the family plots. Those are her words. She argued mightily with Papá before he left; he tried in vain to convince her to move to Mexico with my mother."

In spite of his rising uneasiness at discussing this situation, Giddeon grinned. "You must be cut from the same cloth, you and your aunt." His teasing brought forth laughter, bubbling like music from her lips. "From the tales I've heard, Don Miguel had his hands full with his lovely daughter."

Her laughter died slowly, leaving only a studied smile. She held his gaze; a regal solemnness masked the passion he knew simmered beneath the surface. Her father's daughter, Giddeon thought. The spitting image of old Don Miguel.

When she spoke, he knew he was right. Her passion was there, all right, but it was not for him. Her passion was for this land . . . her land.

"Los Olmos is my birthright, Giddeon. My ancestors fought untold odds to hold on to it, to carve this . . . this empire." Flinging her arms around, she included the shabby room, the run-down compound, the now dwindled acreage. But these were not the things of her vision.

"Do you know what I have dreamed of almost every night since I was a child?"

Studying her silently, he tried to keep his mind unattached—away from this lovely woman who was his wife, for whom he felt such a raging passion even at this very moment; away from her hopes, her fears, her desperate dreams—dreams he would destroy for his own purposes.

Her hand swept the face of the plat. When she looked at him, her eyes flamed. "I dream of reuniting this land—buying it all back and reestablishing the original Hacienda de los Olmos . . . all three hundred thousand acres of it, just as King Ferdinand gave it to my family in 1752."

With a ragged sigh, he slid to the floor beside her and pulled her into his arms. He held her tightly against his chest, striving to still his runaway senses.

Finally, she drew back, and with an innocent look that called forth fidelities long since abandoned, she further rent his wits asunder.

"I am so thankful you have come to help me, Giddeon. We must find some way to pay the taxes."

In the end his only defense was to make love to her. And even in that, it was Serita who led him out of the maze of despair and into a new and glorious state of enchantment.

With his back supported against the sofa, he cradled her in his arms and reveled in her kisses, in the way she twined her fingers in his hair, played them down his neck, around his ears, and in so doing, riddled his body with physical pangs of desire.

Lifting his lips from hers, he ran kisses down the slender length of her patrician nose. Deftly he removed the combs from her hair and dropped them to the rug; then he set her back against his knee and studied her face, while he played his fingers through the silky lengths of her hair.

"Do you look like your mother?" he asked, suddenly wondering how she came to be so beautiful.

She answered with silence, her face a lovely mask. Her words were in the tips of her fingers which tormented his skin, tracing his nose, the outline of his lips, his chin, and downward past his neck to where she massaged his chest through his shirt.

And there he pinned her hands, by drawing the brief shoulders of her bodice over her arms. With feather-light strokes he pushed aside the top of her gown and exposed the rosy nipples of her breasts. A flood of heat radiated from her skin through his fingers to the nether-reaches of his body.

Without warning, then, the sachet of gardenia leaves tumbled into his hands, and he immediately raised it to his face. "Hmm . . ." he inhaled. "Gardenias . . . my favorite thing . . ." For an intense moment, one that seemed to last an eternity, he gazed into her inviting eyes. ". . . *almost* my favorite thing." Scooping her reverently in his arms, he rose and carried her to the bed.

The pleasure she brought to him that night was magnified by his knowledge that she had planned the evening: from the flirty yellow dancing dress she wore to dinner, to the hibiscus she let him tuck behind her ear, the gardenia leaves she planted for him alone to find, the single lacy chemise she wore beneath the dress. For him, Giddeon Duval, alone.

The fleeting thought that she might be trying to entrap him in a manner in which he had no desire to be trapped died quickly beneath the assault she ravished upon his senses. Once she had allowed him to disrobe her, garment by slow garment, she did the

159

same for him. Her long fingers tormented with each movement as she slid his shirt over his head, then unbuttoned and removed his breeches.

When as last he stood unclothed before her, she clasped him fiercely about the neck, pressed her body to his, and kissed him ardently. With a desperate moan, he lifted her once more in his arms and lowered them, together, to the bed, where she became his willing partner, giving as much as she took, and taking everything he in his great passion could give.

When at last they lay limp in each other's arms, he kissed nips at her nose, her eyes, her ears. "A thousand falling stars?" he whispered.

"At least," she sighed.

Chapter Seven

The following morning a pensive mood accompanied Giddeon when he left Serita's bed at dawn to see the shipment of hides off to market. Felix's report on the unpaid taxes had delivered a major blow to his plans to finish this sordid job with dispatch, and last night's session in Serita's bed was one of the results. He had solemnly vowed to stay away from her, but . . .

Tempted, teased, and tormented as he had been by her these past few weeks, the fact that she was his legal wife made denying himself her passion more difficult and at times absurd. His body flamed now, merely thinking on the night spent in her arms. Uninhibited and natural, she lavished him with her fiery passion in a way which could soon become addictive, and the thought of her lying alone at this very moment with only a threadbare sheet covering her satiny skin caused his feet to hesitate on the stairs. From the grumblings of most married men of his acquaintance, a wife so responsive was rare indeed.

Yet a wife was not what he wanted. He continued toward the courtyard, taking the stairs now two at a time. The sea was in his blood and his soul; he must return to the sea. And he must—he *would,* he vowed once more—stay away from Serita's bed. No matter her protestations that she could take care of herself, he knew otherwise. Women like Serita—ladies of genteel upbringing, especially ones who had been reared in such a strict religious environment, ladies such as Serita regarded marriage as sacred. No matter what she might profess to believe, Giddeon knew well enough that when a lady such as she gave her body, it was with her heart attached.

Delos and Kosta awaited him beside the fountain in the courtyard. Kosta was in a jovial mood, while Delos appeared more subdued, not quite meeting Giddeon's eye when they shook hands. Likely the weather, Giddeon observed silently. The muggy gray day, typical of November weather along the Gulf Coast, presaged rain at best, a wet norther, if they weren't so lucky.

Giddeon took a cup of coffee from the tray Abril held for them. "No need to tell you, we want the best possible price for these hides. Burton shouldn't give you any trouble on the way to Matamoros, not with Cortinas and his army along. But stay alert. We cannot afford to lose these hides."

Lost in instructions for their trip, Giddeon watched without observing as Abril offered the tray to Kosta, who took a cup. "You may be required to stay in Matamoros a while in order to make the best deal."

Absently still, he studied Abril, saw her favor

Delos with a coy glance. She took the remaining cup from the tray herself and handed it to Delos. Their hands touched briefly; Abril smiled, curtsied, and vanished. Delos blushed.

"I'll have my hands full with or without trouble from Burton," Kosta mused. "Keeping Delos away from the *hacienda* looks to be a full-time job."

Delos cleared his throat. "Everything loaded?"

Giddeon nodded.

"Sure you won't come along, Capt'n?" Kosta invited.

"And give Burton the opening he's looking for?" Suddenly Giddeon's eyes and half his attention were drawn to the staircase, where Serita appeared, attired in her usual buckskin breeches and silk blouse — chastely worn over layers of undergarments since that day on the prairie.

Their eyes held, hers beckoning, shattering for the moment his vow to stay away from her. He grinned. She smiled. Quickly, then, he regained his determination and turned away, furious at his own inability to control the sensual emotions with which her presence always flooded him. He felt like a man overboard, incapable of rescuing himself from the man-killing waves. "I'm sending Felix to inform McCaulay that this business will likely take until after the first of the year . . ."

He knew the men were watching Serita walk toward them. Finally, just before she came into earshot, Kosta waggled his eyebrows at Giddeon. "Guess you have *other business* to keep you around the *hacienda,* too, Capt'n, being a settled man now." He shook his head in mock sadness. "Never thought I'd see the day when two old seadogs like the both of you would rather be fenced in on dry land than—"

Giddeon scanned the four high walls of the courtyard. "Don't count me in such company," he retorted. "I'd die a slow death, shut away in this prison. I'll be the first one on board the *Estelle*, as soon as we have McCaulay's money tucked in our pockets. And make sure you return with all the money from these hides. Don't squander it in a cantina on some female. There'll be time for that, later."

Those remaining behind—Tita and Jorge, and Nieves and Pablo, Abril and Lupe, Giddeon and Serita, and those of Trinidad's men who were unable to travel yet—gathered in front of the compound to watch the heavily loaded wagons pull away into the fog of this typically muggy fall morning.

"Poor Trinity," Serita sighed, watching until the last of the riders was out of view. "If only he wasn't so bitter." Slipping a hand through Giddeon's arm, she smiled at him. "I do understand him, though. Without Los Olmos, I would likely be a rebel, too."

Giddeon grunted and immediately drew away, leaving her with a blush of embarrassment on her face. Her heart ached painfully beneath the bones of her corset. Twice already this morning he had openly rejected her—and after the night they just spent together! Every time she thought she was beginning to know this restless gambling man, he changed and became someone cold and distant.

As in a flash of lightning, her embarrassment turned to anger. She did not deserve such treatment, and she certainly did not have to put up with it! With a whack of her ivory-handled crop against her

164

breeches, she strode past him in a huff. "The profits you bargained for will not fall from the trees into your lap, *capitán*. You will have to work for them. Saddle up. We ride out immediately."

Two hours later, along with Pablo and Jorge, they sat their horses on a slight rise a good ten miles from the big house, and he still smarted from her words. Leaning his forearms across the leather-covered *poma* — saddlehorn — of his Spanish range saddle, he studied the herd of mustangs grazing in the valley below them and wondered what she intended. His questions on the ride to this spot had received only cryptic replies.

"Capture a herd of wild horses?" Sometimes her schemes were so farfetched as to leave him speechless.

She had bristled at his skepticism. "I suppose you have a better way to come up with the tax money, to say nothing of the profit *you* bargained for."

"Capturing a herd of mustangs isn't as practical as salvaging the *Estelle*," he had retorted. "In fact, it isn't even in the same category of folly."

"For your information" — she had kept her voice low and steady, as though she instructed a child with a thick head — "saddle horses are in great demand, especially in the swamp lands of Louisiana, where horse's hooves cannot develop well. We can sell saddle-broke stock in Galveston for three dollars a head, but in Louisiana, a good saddle horse will fetch upward of five dollars."

"I don't doubt the value of horseflesh," he began, "but . . ."

She had averted her patrician profile in her own

particularly arrogant manner. "You do not believe I can break horses?"

"Break horses?!"

At his outburst, she turned, their eyes locked, and he stared long into the obsidian wall she had erected between them. He was reminded instantly of Don Miguel and the night they played poker—the night he won the hand of Serita Cortinas.

For as hard as she tried to conceal it, behind the wall of stone her eyes still beckoned him and he in turn wanted nothing at the moment quite as desperately as he wanted to respond.

That's what all the bickering was about, he knew. A smokescreen to hide herself from the enemy—from him. For an instant, he gave thought to surrendering to her then and there, to restoring the peace between them, a peace he had deliberately severed this morning with his cool treatment of this oh-so-hot-blooded woman.

Each time he restored the peace between them, however, it would only be that much harder to break when the final moment came. So he straightened himself a little taller in the saddle, squared his shoulders, and returned her stare with an insolence of his own.

"It isn't that I doubt your wrangling abilities, *querida,* but first you must corral the horses."

It was the appellation that finally broke their gaze, an endearment she always responded to with passion: If she was already angry with him, that one word never failed to add fuel to the flames. And if she wasn't . . . He sighed recalling her great, at times engulfing, sensuality. This time, with a gesture of

166

haughty superiority, she flipped her chin up and away from him.

She moved quickly, but not not quickly enough for him to miss the crack in the wall she had erected. Through the crack he saw not the sultry beckoning she had favored him with earlier, but something equally as passionate—anguish.

And in that moment, he knew he had been right not to restore the peace between them. A shaky, short-term truce would not be enough for Serita Cortinas de Duval.

They rode the rest of the way to the valley in a strained silence, and the countryside soon mesmerized him. The endless vistas of waving grass, puncuated here and there by a large mesquite tree or a grove of live oaks, reminded him of the sea stretching around him, of a sail sighted upon the horizon. The horse he rode galloped over the prairie, soon lulling him as did the swells and crests of waves when he stood on deck. No sun shone today; the horizons were not sharp, but softened by blankets of fog. His sea bones told him they were in for some bad weather. They would be lucky if the weather held until they returned to *la casa grande*.

Now, sitting their mounts on the rise beside a grove of wind-whipped oaks, they watched a herd of mustangs graze blow. Giddeon pulled himself back to shore.

On their approach, a sleek black stallion stopped grazing. His head and tail came up like flags on a ship's mast, and Giddeon fully expected the band of horses to take flight. But they didn't. Instead, the stallion gazed majestically at the horsemen, then circled slowly in and about his band, lifting his head to view the intruders on the hillside from time to time. Finally, the ebony stallion actually started to approach them, apparently unafraid of the men on horseback. Tossing his head, he sniffed the wind in their direction. For a moment Giddeon thought they had come upon a *ladino,* one of the outlaw stallions he had heard about who protected their *manadas* in a violent fashion. This one certainly did not appear violent, but neither did he act in a normal manner.

Serita watched as *Ebanol* the stallion they had raised from a colt, approached them in his usual roundabout way. One glance showed Giddeon's confusion, and she grinned in spite of herself. Somewhere inside, she longed to share with him this part of the ranching operation she was most proud of, but deeper within, she still smarted from his unprovoked rejections. So she stared straight ahead and refused to so much as acknowledge that anything irregular was in progress.

At her nod, Jorge lay down in his saddle and whinnied in imitation of a young colt. Immediately Ebanol flicked up his ears. Then, flinging one last protective glance toward his herd, he trotted toward Jorge as though he were a pet dog called for a treat.

Giddeon's mouth dropped open. Had he been on board the *Estelle* when his crew called a whale to deck, he would not have been more surprised than he was at the stallion's actions.

Pablo came to his rescue. "This is Ebanol, *Señor Capitán.* We raised him from a colt, and he is now a superior herd stallion."

"He's tame?"

Pablo nodded. "But do not mistake the meaning of that word. Were you to try to take his *caballado* away from him, he would react as a true *ladino*."

Jorge whinnied again; Ebanol nickered, then approached the boy, tossing his head in greeting. The boy untied a sack from behind his saddle and offered it to the magnificent stallion, who allowed Jorge to lean forward and stroke his mane, while he devoured the offering of corn.

Giddeon listened intently to Pablo's explanation. "We brought him out here a few months back with four or five tame mares. The rest are wild mustangs he has picked up since—mares and a few outcast stallions with no *manada* of their own. This is a true *caballado*, rather than a *manada*, which consists of all mares."

Giddeon frowned. "What has kept him from returning to the wild?"

"We keep him on this side of the *hacienda* where there are not as many bands of wild mustangs," Pablo told him, as though that were all the explanation needed.

What followed was one of the stranger things Giddeon could ever recall being involved in. When Ebanol finished his treat, he tossed his mane and headed back toward his heard. A couple of mares had drifted away, and he immediately brought them back into the fold by kicking and biting their already scared shoulders.

Jorge, in the meantime, had ridden to the head of the small valley. Lying prone in his saddle, he once more imitated the whinny of a colt. This time, however, instead of waiting for Ebanol, he guided his own mount in the direction of the *la casa grande*. Close to three hours later, the entire *caballado* of horses and riders pulled into the compound, led by a boy imitating a colt calling its mother and guided from the rear by the vigilant slave-driver, Ebanol.

Giddeon, Serita, and Pablo rode at a distance to either side of the *caballado,* where they deflected runaways. Although, Giddeon suspected, their roles were totally unnecessary with the attentiveness shown by Ebanol. He raced back and forth providing a complete rear guard defense, moving the three dozen or so mares and ten to twelve outcast stallions forward, bringing any who strayed back into the fold.

Upon coming in sight of *la casa grande,* Pablo rode ahead to open wide the corral gates, and Jorge led the balking mustangs inside.

The ruckus raised by the corraled horses could surely be heard halfway to Matamoros, Giddeon decided. But by the time they were seated at the table in the *comedor,* the noise had quietened to a few thudding hooves, an occasional screaming neigh, followed by silence.

A silence which immediately brought to mind the treatment he had received from Serita all afternoon. He knew he should be grateful; wasn't that exactly what he had in mind by ignoring her this morning? Watching her now, however, he was mesmerized once more by her beauty . . . by her presence. Her bronze skin glistened deliciously in the candlelight, and he had the sudden desire to stroke his fingers across her cheek, down her neck. He felt himself overcome by an unreasonable desire to hear her voice, even if it were raised in anger.

"I'll say this for old Ebanol," he mused, his eyes fairly caressing her face, "he certainly knows how to handle his women."

Her throat constricted when she swallowed the sip of wine in her mouth. Her glass slapped against the tabletop, but she did not look up. Still he studied her, and he knew she felt his gaze.

"He isn't at all nice to them, is he *Tío Capitán?*" Jorge questioned in all seriousness. "I have often wondered why the mares stay with a leader who treats them so viciously."

Serita smiled sweetly at Jorge, then stared with hard, angry eyes at Giddeon.

Her embarrassment of this morning had turned into anguish by noontime. Throughout the afternoon it had boiled and stewed inside her, until now she was consumed by anger, fierce and hot. His intense green eyes added fuel to her fury. Her explanation began as a simple lesson to Jorge, but it ended with a warning, delivered in a voice low and intentionally seductive, directed to Giddeon's begging green eyes.

"It is the way of nature, Jorge," she instructed the boy. "As we have told you before, living here on the *hacienda*, you will discover that wildlife does not always reflect what we humans regard as right. Without the control a herd stallion has over his *caballado*, we would be the poorer, believe me. We should be grateful for the help we get. But always remember, human females do not tolerate abusive treatment."

For Giddeon, the days and weeks that followed were filled with Serita and the mustangs as she began to break the wild horses to the saddle in order to drive them to market and fetch a price that would

171

pay the taxes and enable him to take Los Olmos away from her forever.

Whether for that reason, or because when she was in the corral her safety was always in question, Giddeon found himself unable to sleep at night for the nightmares of Serita being kicked or thrown or otherwise injured by these animals, who were several times larger and heavier and often even more passionate in nature than she herself.

A number of times a day his presence, along with Jorge's and Pablo's, was required in the corral to help her. Other times he went to the rooftop lookout and tried to settle his nerves by gazing to the distant horizon — to his beloved sea — away from the melee of hooves and teeth and tons of horseflesh which moment by moment endangered Serita down in the corral.

As soon as they had finished *merienda* on the evening they brought Ebanol and the *caballado* to the corral, Serita began the long and arduous work of breaking the herd for market.

Dressing for the occasion, she donned carefully chosen buckskin pants, shirt, chaps, and jacket. Although the norther they feared earlier in the day had not materialized, she knew that before she was finished with this task, the weather would turn cold, and she dared not introduce a new piece of clothing once the breaking process had begun.

She advised Giddeon to do the same. "Since you expect to share in the profits, you will be required to help," she told him in formal tones. "Wear exactly what you intend to wear the next few months. After the breaking begins, you will not be allowed to wear

172

any other clothing into the corral."

Her tone infuriated him to the point of madness. He wanted to shake her by the shoulders until he shook the pretense from her lips and the high-minded tilt from her stance. He wanted to . . .

Furiously, he regained control of his emotions. That, he insisted to himself, was *all* he wanted to do to her—nothing more . . . absolutely nothing.

Yet when he descended the staircase into the courtyard and saw her standing alone in the dim lanternlight, his body definitely came up with a few other choices.

Pablo and Jorge, anxious to have the day's work behind them, had gone ahead to the corral, leaving Serita to await Giddeon, a situation her weary mind did not question until he stepped toward her.

He had dressed in work clothes and chaps furnished by Tita from Don Miguel's vast wardrobe, and her throat constricted at the sight of him. In the days when Los Olmos was a leader in Spanish ranching, Don Miguel had had his clothing tailored to fit, and the fact that they fit Giddeon Duval as though they had been tailored for him personally both amazed and aggravated her. He was so much like *Papá*—in height, in build, in . . . No!

Averting her head quickly, she refused to let herself think further. Giddeon Duval was as far removed from Don Miguel Cortinas in character and in deed as was the moon from the sun. Giddeon Duval could not hold a candle to *Don* Miguel—not even in *Papá's* present demented state of mind.

Without so much as a word, she led him out the main entrance to the compound. Giddeon matched her angry stride. The gate closed behind them, and they headed toward the back of *la casa grance*. From somewhere ahead of them came the voices of Pablo and Jorge.

"Are we taking a late-evening stroll?" he asked in as mild a tone as he could muster.

"We will walk around the training corral several times in order to accustom the animals to our smell," she told him.

He inhaled deeply, dispirited by her hostility. Her nearness in the filmy night air brought unwanted yearnings close to the surface, and before he so much as had time to think the word "gardenias" slipped from his tongue.

Serita's sharp intake of breath was followed by the slap of her crop against her leg. When they rounded the corner of the corral, she gathered her wits and began to talk in soft tones. "If you plan to speak in the corral during the next weeks, you should talk now in a low, quiet voice."

"You mean we can't nip and bite at each other like a couple of mustangs?"

Her boots ground to a complete but soundless halt. Her voice when she spoke was low and controlled, but her message contained the full measure of tension they both felt inside. "Whether you take it to be or not, this is serious business. The wild animals in that corral are frightened of us, as well they might be. Try to put yourself in their place, if you can manage something so foreign to your nature. They are free-spirited, liberty-loving animals. Today they were betrayed by their lord and master, and now they are imprisoned. They have no way of understanding what has happened to them. In order not to break their spirits while we condition their behavior, we have found certain methods work best. I am sure you do not understand, but at least try to cooperate."

She had a way of silencing him, he thought angrily. Her scathing tongue would silence even the most salty seadog. Nevertheless, he walked with her around the corral and around and around. An occasional hoof struck the corral wall, only to be followed by the sound of Ebanol subduing a frightened horse. A bullfrog croaked down by the creek, a shrill, unearthly noise he was sure he would never get used to. The first time he ever heard that sound was when he and his crew were camped beside the Arroyo Colorado, the same night their horses were stolen. He laughed to himself, remembering.

The sound of his laughter—actually, it was no more than a soft chuckle—smoothed somewhat the tattered edges of her hostility, and, without thinking, she responded to him in a civil tone for the first time today.

"What's so funny?"

The stillness of the night had closed about them, incarcerating them in the prison of her anger. Now, at her amiable tone, he answered with a warm laugh, then related the story. "You should have seen Kosta on the trip out—and Delos, too, for that matter. They were fit to be tied, until we discovered where that unearthly sound came from, and, even then, we had a time convincing them that anything which emitted such a horrendous noise wasn't automatically trouble." He shrugged, comfortable for the first time today with the nearness of her. "In fact, Felix was the only man of us who had ever heard a bullfrog before."

"So you sent him to find out about the taxes," she concluded innocently, "because he is the only one of you not afraid of the dark."

"Something like that," he answered lightly, but the reminder of the lie he had told her concerning Felix's mission thudded as the blow of a mustang's hoof against his chest.

They walked without talking once more. Giddeon listened to the efforts of Ebanol to subdue his captured herd.

"Why don't you breed Barb to Ebanol?" he asked suddenly. "He's a fine stallion and much more easy to corral than El Rey will be."

"You are right. Ebanol is a fine herd stallion. But he doesn't possess that . . . that certain spirit I want Barb's offspring to have. Only El Rey has that." They walked and she thought about the difference, finally expressing her ideas in words. "Only one so free possesses such spirit. Only the free are . . ."

"Serita, I'm sorry about . . ."

"Don't . . ." Her pace quickened.

"I didn't intend . . ." Ever since the first time he had turned away from her in the courtyard this morning, he had been sorry, now . . .

"You did nothing." Her heart thudded against her ribs; she thrust her fists deeper into her pockets. If he touched her, she would die, she thought. And if he didn't . . .

They rounded the last corner of the corral and headed for the house, marked by a flickering lantern at the entrance a good rifle shot away. His anguish increased. "Tell me about Barb." His words came more as a command than as the opening to a neutral topic of conversation which he intended. "I mean, even her name is unusual."

Candles shone from various windows in the big house, which loomed dangerously far away. "Barb," she repeated. "She is named for her ancestors. Hannibal, so the story goes, brought the first Barbs to Spain two hundred years before the birth of Christ. They were a mixture of hot-blooded North African horses and cold-blooded Norse stock. Later, a little over a thousand years ago, the Moslems added Arabian blood to the original Barbs before they brought them across the Strait of Gibraltar."

As she spoke, her voice lightened a bit, as did Giddeon's spirit. "Where did you get her?"

"Papá bought her mother after she had been bred. Her ancestry traces directly back to the Andalusian Barbs Cortés brought to Mexico."

Giddeon nodded in the darkness. "As I recall," he joined in, "the Arabians were bred for desert warfare."

"Yes," she added, becoming more animated now as her interest in the topic overcame her more fragile emotions. "Desert warfare requires swift dodging and twisting. Don't you see what the combination of Barb and El Rey would produce? Beauty and swiftness, hardiness, endurance, intelligence, that indomitable spirit, and . . ." Stopping in midsentence, she tossed her head back to stare into the black night.

"And a white star on the forehead," he offered quietly.

177

"Yes." She caught her lower lip with her teeth to still her sudden trembling. Then with a sigh, she lowered her head and quickened her pace to the house. "I will certainly have a hard time parting with a colt with a star on its forehead."

During the weeks that followed, as Serita went about the business of gentling the mustangs, Gideon learned much more about wild horses, and about Serita Cortinas de Duval, his beautiful, spirited wife, who rivaled the liberty-loving animals in many ways—ways he was coming to rue, and to admire. Sometimes, during the often futile struggle to keep the animals quieted, he would look at her through the dust in the corral and see a star. But it wasn't a falling star. He was the one falling, and he didn't know what in the world to do about it.

That Serita actually tamed the wild animals herself left Gideon thunderstruck for a time. She learned the art from her grandfather, Pablo told him, who in turn had learned from an old Indian, of what nation, no one recalled. From the time she could toddle into the corral, she had a way with wild horses, Pablo had said. *And with wild men,* Giddeon thought, but he didn't say anything, because the last was something he could change—or at least keep from becoming general knowledge.

Her way with wild horses at once fascinated and frightened him. The method was simple, so simple, in fact, that had someone bellied up to a bar and told him the tale over a whiskey, he would have accused the man of being a fabricator of tall tales.

She used a blanket. The first course of action was to isolate the horses, one at a time, from their peers.

Pablo and Jorge each dropped a rope over the neck of the horse Serita chose, then led the animal from the pen—pulled was more like it—with the help of Ebanol whom Giddeon came to think of as an extra vaquero, so attuned was the stallion to the work going on around his *caballado*.

Once they brought the animal to the portion of the corral Serita had chosen for her work, two more ropes were put on the horse. While Giddeon held the rope around her neck, Pablo expertly placed additional ropes on her legs, by which he and Jorge then held the animal, as well.

The first time Serita approached one of the plunging, nickering horses on foot, Giddeon almost shouted at her to go back. He scarcely dared breathe while she inched her way across the corral, making slow, strange motions with a blanket she held in one hand, all the while emitting soft, guttural sounds with her lips almost closed.

Giddeon's heart raced so fast he did not immediately notice when the horse itself stopped plunging and began to watch Serita in a likewise curious fashion. Closer and closer she came, steadily crooning the low, soothing melody. Finally, she was near enough to pass the blanket gently in front of the animal's face. Then with equally slow movements, she reached to touch the horse's nose.

With difficulty, Giddeon resisted the overwhelming urge to grab her hand away. His own rope, he held so taut he feared it might break. That thought called to mind the other ropes held by Jorge and Pablo, and he began to worry whether one of those ropes might give way, or whether the man or the boy might lapse into inattentiveness and let the animal loose.

At Serita's touch, the horse's nose shuddered, then the animal relaxed a bit. Serita let him smell her thoroughly, and Giddeon immediately understood the meaning of their walks around the corral. Slowly, with movements ever cautious and calm, she removed a rawhide strap from the waist of her breeches and haltered the horse.

That was actually the end of the operation, as far as Pablo, Jorge, and Giddeon were concerned. Giddeon, however, had no intention of leaving her alone in the corral with a wild horse, never mind the fact that she had been raised here, and this was his own first experience.

Controlling the horse now by the halter, she began a process that looked more like witchcraft than breaking horses. Over *merienda* Giddeon learned that the rawhide strap—a *jaquima*, she called it—tightened around the horse's muzzle and behind its ears in a manner that wrought a sharp pain to the nerves in both places when pulled.

The first day's work lasted many hours, during which Serita never stopped her crooning to the animal, and Giddeon never budged from the corral fence where he perched, ready to come to her aid. All this time her fingers and hands rhythmically massaged the animal's entire body, beginning with its face, then its neck, ending with its flanks and inner legs. Each time she finished stroking one section, she flicked it with the blanket, then moved on to the next portion. Every time the horse bucked or started to kick, she tugged the rawhide *jaquima*, and the animal immediately quieted down. As the hours wore on, Giddeon became concerned that she might not see the movement in time, that she might become too tired to react quickly enough.

After she kneaded and stroked every inch of its body, she stood beside the animal and struck its back with the blanket three times. Then she laid the blanket gently over its back. The horse bucked it off; Serita tugged the *jaquima,* then replaced the blanket. Never once did she hush her soothing, crooning song. It took three tries before the animal let the blanket stay on its back, and by this time, Giddeon had begun to worry that her voice might play out.

Next she fixed her elbows on top of the blanket directly in the center of the mustang's back, then lifted herself several times. When the animal made no resistance, she raised herself higher and, on the last attempt, she slipped on to its back. A wave of anxiety swept over Giddeon, and his eyes closed of their own volition.

When next he looked, she sat easily, stroking the horse about the neck, still crooning, as she had for so many hours now. At last, with only the slightest flick of her eyes toward Giddeon, she urged the horse forward with her knees, and together they moved around the corral, conqueror and conquered. From the looks of them, Giddeon couldn't quite tell which was which.

Except for the light in Serita's eyes when she glanced at him, a light that shone brighter than a thousand stars in a midnight sky.

Over *merienda* Jorge excitedly reported every phase of the day's events to Tita. Giddeon watched Serita sip the wine and eat very little.

"It is a gift, *Tío Capitán*," Jorge told him. "Pablo says Serita has a gift few people have. She has promised to teach me, though. Haven't you, Serita? Can I try one tomorrow?"

"Perhaps not tomorrow, *chico*. But soon. Let me narrow the field a bit first."

"Do you think you will be finished in time for Christmas?" Tita asked.

Serita shrugged wanly, then took a sip of wine. Giddeon answered for her.

"Let us take this one day at a time, Tita. I agree Serita has a great gift . . ."—he studied her, his green eyes mellowed with concern— ". . . but it is an exhausting job, nonetheless."

By the end of the second week, Serita had narrowed the herd of forty horses only slightly. However, she let Jorge help her with a mare. The process took twice as long, but the success on her face and on the boy's was reward enough.

After the second day, when Giddeon remained on the fence the entire time, Serita admonished him. "Do you not trust me, even now?"

His mouth flew open. "Not trust you? You are magnificent with those animals." He had sighed deeply. "But what if you become so tired your reactions are slowed? What if you can't pull the *jaquima* in time . . . ?"

She shrugged off his concern. "Even inside the corral, you would never be able to get to me in time to prevent an accident. I do not want you to spend your days sitting on that dratted fence."

So he didn't. Instead, after the initial rope holding

was over, he left the corral with Pablo and Jorge and worked around the place. The vaqueros' barracks where Trinidad had wanted to house his army were in bad repair, and together with Pablo and Jorge's help, he began getting them livable.

"Whatever for?" Tita asked him at *merienda*.

He looked at Serita and wondered what he could say short of either lying or destroying her. Serita came to his rescue.

"Why, Tita, we aren't always going to be poor. One day we will need those quarters for all our vaqueros."

A few weeks later, Tita returned to her question concerning Christmas. "Do you know now whether you will be finished with the horses by Christmas?"

Serita sighed, then she turned to Giddeon to explain. "Every year we travel to the chapel at La Bahía for *posada*. It is a ritual we have not broken for generations. Since it is the place where Juan was killed, it has special meaning, now."

Giddeon thought about it overnight and had planned to suggest they go and leave him behind, but Serita came up with her own plan the next morning.

"I can't stop work on the horses; the ones I have already gentled must be ridden every day. But why can't Tita and Jorge go to La Bahía? Pablo and Nieves could accompany them. Do you think . . . ?" She sighed, then continued. "I was thinking of Oliver Burton. If he should strike with everyone gone, we would have only the two of us and Lupe and Abril. That wouldn't be enough . . ."

"Serita, if Oliver Burton struck with his full force,

183

all of us here right now wouldn't be enough to stop him. Surely you realize that."

She nodded.

"I don't expect him to strike again, though, not directly at the compound. Besides, Delos and Kosta should return from Matamoros before long."

That settled, Jorge and Tita, accompanied by Pablo and Nieves, left the compound the following morning, ten days before Christmas. The three days' journey would cut down on the *posada* activities, but Tita was relieved to be able to receive Mass at Christmastide. Her worry was that Serita and Giddeon would miss the sacrament this year.

As it turned out, she should have worried over other matters.

Serita spent the days before Christmas riding the ten horses she had gentled since they brought in the *caballado*. Giddeon took over Jorge's job of feeding Ebanol his rations of corn and tamales twice daily. When he grumbled at the insignificance of the job, Serita informed him that the tamales were the secret which kept Ebanol on their side.

Several times daily Giddeon climbed to the rooftop lookout and surveyed the countryside with his spyglass. After searching the distant horizon for sign of his men, he inevitably discovered himself studying the corral and the captivating woman who had such power over wild horses — and wild men.

"Where the hell were Delos and Kosta?" he stormed to himself one afternoon. He slammed his spyglass back into its case. "Or Felix? Or anyone? Would *someone* not come soon to support him in his battle against her . . . and against his own weakening senses?

Christmas came and went without either of them so much as acknowledging it, other than a brief exchange over coffee, before Serita headed for the corral and Giddeon to the vaqueros' quarters.

"I hope Tita made it to La Bahía," she said.

"They arrived," he assured her. "Otherwise we would have heard."

She nodded, then paused in her stride on her way to the corral. *"Feliz Navidad,* Giddeon."

He grinned, then headed the other way with an equally brief, "Merry Christmas to you, too, Serita."

They did not meet again until after dark when they both arrived at *merienda* in the work clothes they had worn all day.

Serita stopped short at the sight of him, then proceeded to her place at the long, empty table. He quickly drew back her chair, but when he seated her he omitted the perfunctory peck on the forehead he had foregone since the day they brought in the *caballado.*

Looking down at her own disheveled attire, she felt suddenly ashamed. "I haven't been running the household very well," she admitted, feeling more miserable by the moment. "I've let Christmas come with no preparations."

"Don't worry about it," he reassured her. "I'm not used to anything special for Christmas. We are usually out at sea somewhere."

"Christmas is always festive at Los Olmos." She sighed. "At least it always has been in the past. After our journey to La Bahía, we have twelve days of fiestas and fandangos." She shook her head, her discontent growing steadily. "We should have taken time to change our clothing."

Giddeon tried to shrug in a lighthearted fashion. He dipped his spoon into the *sopa de elote* Abril set in front of him. "It doesn't matter. We worked all day."

Serita suppressed her rising despair. She knew as well as he why they came to dinner without dressing. For weeks she had busied herself with the horses — pushing aside the unbearable feelings this man stirred within her. And he had occupied himself with other things, too, to the extent that he no longer treated her with the abruptness that caused her to respond by throwing verbal arrows at him.

But if she had come to dinner in rustling petticoats, with ribbons in her hair — if he had shaved and dressed in fitted breeches and flowing shirt, then all would be lost, she had no doubt. They would end up in bed together, and tomorrow they would begin their fighting, their ceaseless bickering, all over again.

No, they had come too far during these weeks to risk a return to cold rejection. Fortunately, they were both intelligent enough to realize it.

Still, she could not keep her disappointment from showing. "We could have at least . . ." Dismally she stared at the clothing she had worn so long now while in the corral. "Tita would die if she knew."

"She doesn't. She's in church." Then as an afterthought, he scrunched his brow and added, "Praying for us, I have no doubt."

When Abril set a platter of broiled quail in front of them, Giddeon asked her to bring a bottle of port and two glasses. "We'll have a Christmas toast. Will

186

that do?"

So they toasted the season in solemn tones, but when the meal was done, neither felt much better. "Tell you what," Giddeon suggested as they left the *comedor*, "we'll work on it, and for New Year's, we will come up with a better celebration."

Serita smiled.

On impulse, he planted a quick kiss on her forehead — reminding her, as always, of their first night together. "Run along to bed," he whispered. "I'll check on the *caballado*."

Bleakly, she obeyed, and after she had bathed in the water Abril and Lupe provided and dressed in a white cotton nightdress and lay snuggled alone in her bed, a tiny part of her was proud of her behavior.

But only a tiny part. The rest of her body and soul yearned unbearably for him to come to her. He didn't, however, and before she knew it, her fatigue overcame her despondency, and she drifted off to sleep, only to be awakened hours later by a piercing scream from the corral.

Without taking time to so much as fetch a dressing gown or slippers, she dashed from bed and bounded down the gallery.

Giddeon was fast on her heels. "Stay back and let me see what's going on."

Unheeding, she raced ahead of him to the staircase.

"That was Barb!" she cried, the anguish in her voice quite as great as the young mare's own panicked screams.

Chapter Eight

"Barb! That was Barb!" By the time Serita reached the kitchen and lifted the shotgun off the wall, Barb's cries had ceased, and the finality of her words sank like an anchor to the bottom of her heart. The pandemonium of thudding horses' hooves increased her terror. Her first thought was of Oliver Burton; then she wondered whether Ebonal might somehow have managed to break down the barriers to the compound stable and attack Barb.

With a mighty heave, she flung open the gate to the tunnel. Giddeon grabbed her shoulders, bringing her to a stop.

"Let me go," she breathed. "Something terrible has happened to Barb."

"Wait here, I will see to it." Then, at her continued resistance, he relented. "Stay behind me until we find out what we're facing."

Abril and Lupe had come into the courtyard, where they stood huddled together, their eyes wide with confusion and fear. Giddeon cast them a desperate plea. "Fetch a lantern. *¡Andale!*" Shielding

Serita with one arm, he held his rifle at ready with the other and led them down the dark tunnel.

By the time they threw open the second gate, the one leading into the stable itself, their heads resounded with the thunder of hooves. Inside, they stared directly across the corral to the iron-clad outer gates, which stood open to the rush of fleeing horses. Dust stung their nostrils, and around them the earth fairly rumbled. All her work, Giddeon thought. Her back-breaking, painstaking work.

"That bastard!" Serita wailed, rushing forward. Again Giddeon held her back. "Let me go! It's Burton, the bastard. I will kill him."

"Serita . . ." — Giddeon spoke calmly — "whoever turned our mustangs loose, left ahead of the stampede. You can be sure of that."

Then fears for Barb overcame even her anger at Oliver Burton. Tearing loose from Giddeon's hold, she rushed to the stall, and even before the housemaids came with lanterns, she knew something terrible had occurred — much more terrible than losing a herd of mustangs.

Falling to her knees, she threw her arms about the little filly's head. The stench was always the same, she thought, her mind making the connection quite apart from her emotions. Whether it be slaughtered cattle or wounded men or her precious Barb, the sweet, musky odor of blood was always the same.

Giddeon approached the darkened stall. "Careful, Serita, she could kick you."

Then the maids crept around the corner holding aloft two lanterns, and amid the flickering shadows, he saw the truth. Quickly he knelt beside Serita and closed his arms around her.

Stunned for a moment, she merely clasped Barb's head tighter. When Giddeon tried to pull her free, she flung herself about, almost toppling him in the process.

"Leave me alone," she wailed. "Please leave me alone." Her sobs came, and she rubbed her forehead against the coarse hairs between Barb's eyes and cried.

Giddeon stroked her back and held her hair away from the gaping wound where Barb's throat had been cut. The little filly's life-blood still flowed into the sand on the floor of the stall. Mesmerized by it, he imagined it mingling with Serita's tears, and anger grew and swelled within him.

As the last of the mustangs raced out of earshot, a stillness settled around them, punctuated only by Serita's sobs and the shifting feet of the housemaids. Finally, after the circle of light swayed precariously a second time, Giddeon glanced at the tottering girls. Abril clung to the stall gate, and Lupe stood with one hand clamped over her mouth.

"Go on back to the house," he instructed them softly. "Draw a bath for the señora, then return to your beds."

When neither of them made a move to leave, he continued. "It's over for tonight. We have nothing more to fear."

That, he suspected, was true. Serita herself had claimed more than once that if Oliver Burton intended to kill them, he could have done so on numerous occasions. Tonight, he could have slipped into the big house as easily as he did into this stable; as easily have murdered them in their beds as he did Barb in her stall.

No, the likelihood of Burton returning tonight was slim. The man had accomplished what he set out to do: He had destroyed all Serita worked for . . . all she lived for.

Giddeon swallowed the bitter dregs of truth that swept into his conscience. Oliver Burton had destroyed everything Serita had, leaving her nothing except her land, which he himself intended to take from her.

The thought was momentarily so devastating he had the impulse to jump to his feet and ride away from Los Olmos this very night. But he didn't.

And the fact that he stayed had nothing to do with not having a horse left to ride. He could well have left the way he arrived—afoot. He stayed, because, he told himself, she needed him now more than ever.

Another thought took hold in Giddeon's brain while he held Serita and choked on the heavy smell of blood let by the heathen, Oliver Burton. Serita was no longer safe at Los Olmos. Sooner or later Burton or someone like him would drive her away empty-handed. So he must convince her to leave before that happened.

If she refused to go to her father's lands in Mexico, he would set her and her household up in some safe, temporary quarters with part of McCaulay's money. Then, after he salvaged the cargo from the *Estelle*, he would provide her with a livelihood for the rest of her life.

191

Finally, her breathing became more regular, so he pulled her gently away from Barb and held her against his chest. Although her sobs had stopped, he could tell she was far from quieted. Her heart pounded forcefully against his arm, and soon she struggled to her feet and broke away, running, stumbling in the pale light toward the wide-open gates.

"I'm going after him!" she cried. "Tonight. He will not get away with this."

Giddeon followed. He pulled her resisting into his arms, where he held her tightly against him. "We have no way to follow him tonight, *querida*." Over her head he looked toward the empty corral. "But never doubt that he will pay. If Oliver Burton is responsible for this attack tonight, he will pay. I will see to that, myself."

Huddled against him like this, with his strong arms binding her to him, her heart began to slow, bringing not peace but anguish and hot, silent tears. "If only I had protected Barb better . . ."

"You couldn't have stopped him, Serita. He discovered what was most important to you, and that's where he struck. As soon as Delos and Kosta return . . ."

She inhaled deeply. The futility of the situation seemed overwhelming. "Barb was my only way to restore Los Olmos. Now it will take years before I can afford to buy another colt. Barb was my beginning . . ."

He squeezed her tighter and nuzzled his head on top of hers. "You will find another way," he assured her. "There is always a way to start over."

Scooping her into his arms then, he carried her across the empty corral where she had so diligently gentled the now-lost horses, across the courtyard where Tita's hibiscus looked black beneath the pale moon, up the staircase and straight to her room, where a kettle of hot water boiled on the hearth and a sit tub stood half full of well water.

While Serita stood as in a daze, Giddeon mixed hot water with the cold, then stripped her blood-soaked nightdress from her body and lifted her into the water. All the time he washed the blood from her skin, from her hair, from her face, she sat with eyelids closed and trembling over her devastated obsidian eyes.

When he finished, he buffed her body, then secured the towel around her while he searched her wardrobe for another nightdress, to no avail. So he carried her to the bed one of the maids had straightened and turned back anew, discarded the damp towel, and deposited her on the clean white sheets.

Covering her to the chin with the bedclothes, he returned to the salon where he cleansed himself—his body, at least, he thought grimly. He had every intention of returning to his own bed.

But he didn't. He stood in the doorway to her bedchamber a good while, studying her with a mind that refused to function properly. Then, solemnly, he crossed the room and climbed into the bed beside her, and, at last, holding her in his arms, he drifted off to sleep, comforted.

Sometime toward morning, he awakened to find her arms entwined about him, her body warm and inviting and her lips on his . . . as in his dream.

And as in a dream he proceeded to make love to this very real, warm and lovely, womanly body. Ever so slowly she came to life in his arms, her lips responding to his, her body nudging, nestling, snuggling against his questing hands. Instead of wild and free as the last time they loved, however, her response was subdued now and reminded him of the way she gentled horses—by loving caresses and strokes.

Suddenly, she drew back and stared at him, her features stiff. "No . . ." She tried to move out of his arms, but he held her tight.

"Don't, Giddeon, please."

He gazed into her skittish eyes until she dropped her head against his chest. Moving his hands up her body, he captured her head, felt hot tears against his thumbs, and with his palms forced her face to his.

"We have come a long way since . . . since the last time," she whispered to his unspoken question. "I don't want to . . . I can't go through all that again."

He pursed his lips and studied her. Yes, he thought, they had come a long way—from passion to denial of passion, through a hell of days and nights fighting against their unquenchable desire for each other. "We won't," he whispered. "I couldn't stand it, either. But let me love you until . . . until it's time to go."

He watched her make up her mind, watched the questions fleet in and out of her eyes. "What do you mean?" she asked at length.

194

Bending his head the slight distance between them, he kissed her gently and quick. "I mean, *querida*, every day . . . and every night . . ." — speaking slowly, softly he watched her eyes come to life — "for as long as . . ."

Her lips closed quickly over his, obliterating the end of his sentence, as though by doing so, it would cease to be true.

So while the morning sun rose and cast its light over the world outside their windows, he loved away her anguish and her fears, replacing them with an unspoken promise of things to come — perhaps not his love, she thought, but at least his loving touch.

Subdued by her loss on Christmas Day, the character of her lovemaking changed from lustful to hushed, from aggressive to restrained. Her fingers twined gently in his hair, played languidly on his chest, while her body cuddled against his, offering instead of demanding, and her lips opened to receive his deep, life-restoring gifts.

To the end that he loved her thoroughly, completely with his lips, which laved her face, suckled at her breasts, explored, assaulted, ravished, leaving her breathless with wonder and desire; and with his hands so large yet gentle, so skillful at tormenting and soothing, at tantalizing and caressing.

And when at last she begged, he rose above her, and, joining his body with hers, he brought her to a crest of tempestuous passion that was at once sweeter and more perfect than anything she had ever known.

Kissing his love-dampened forehead with languid lips, she whispered hoarsely. "Thank you."

Her words startled him, and he drew back and studied her thoughtfully, then pulled her to his chest. "Thank *you, querida.*"

She moved against him, and at his question, she admitted, "I'm growing rather fond of that despicable name."

He stared at her, his green eyes intense, for so long she feared what his thoughts might be. At last, he spoke, his voice low and husky. "You are the only woman who ever gave meaning to the word . . . *querida.*"

Somehow she managed to keep tears from forming in her eyes, hope from swelling in her breast. "Then it is mine," she whispered before she kissed him.

When next she stirred, it was to talk about the night before. At first, he discouraged her from discussing Barb, but when she finished, he was glad she had talked it out.

"I know Barb represented your dreams for Los Olmos, Serita," he told her, choosing his words carefully. "But there are always new dreams to take the place of those we have lost — sometimes even better ones."

She didn't answer, and he knew it would take time to convince her of his plan. As things stood at the moment, time was about all he had. It would take time to pay the taxes. "I suppose we'll have to find some other way to raise money for the taxes, though, since Burton drove all the mustangs off."

She smiled, and he returned the smile, glad to see hers. "We will get the mustangs back," she assured him. At his raised eyebrows, she explained.

196

"As soon as Pablo and Jorge return, we will have horses to go after them again. By that time Ebanol will have them under control."

"And you'll have to start over."

"Not necessarily," she said, her spirits definitely on the rise. "Some of those mares I gentled may be as hooked on tamales as Ebanol himself."

But when she moved to get out of bed, he held her back. "Stay here." Rising himself, he pulled on his breeches. Then he bent and kissed her lips soundly. "Don't get up,"—he waggled his eyebrows, bringing a smile to her face—"wait for me . . . right here."

She watched him silently until he reached the door, then she called him back to her side. "Where are you going?"

He sat on the bed and held her head in his hands. "Let me take care of things before you come downstairs," he said quietly.

She stared a moment longer, then nodded. But when he started to rise, she pulled on his arm. "It will be best if you take her as far away from the house as you can," she began, "and burn . . ." With a heavy sigh, she turned her face away and continued. ". . . burn the carcass. That's the only way. It will be hard without horses to pull the wagon . . ."

"Serita, let me—"

"And the stall," she continued. "We won't be able to stable any other animals in there—especially not the mustangs—until the smell of blood . . ."

He held her face gently and wiped the tears from her eyes with his thumbs. Bending, he kissed her softly. "Let me handle this, *querida*." Then with a show of spirit, he kissed her again. "I know more about the ranching business than you give me credit for. Besides, being a pirate, you should know I've encountered my share of blood."

She squeezed his hand, and a smile glistened through her tears. "Come back . . ."

When he tried to speak, his voice caught in his throat. "Wait right here."

As the days progressed, he kept his promise to return to her bed, not occasionally but every night, where they came together as man and wife, loving until both their spirits were restored, both of their lives revitalized.

Two days after Christmas, Delos and Kosta returned, and Abril served a feast of the roast venison the men brought with them. The following day Pablo and Nieves returned with Tita and Jorge.

Tita was fairly bursting with news of La Bahía, of her brother Pepe, who was moving his family to a trading post on the Gulf of Mexico called Kinney's Rancho — nearer Los Olmos — and how Giddeon and Serita would have to travel to the presidio for Christmas next year. "All our holidays are spent in worship there."

Giddeon detected a note of disapproval in her voice, but when she discovered what had transpired with Barb and the mustangs in her absence, she immediately ceased her talk of La Bahía and the family's religious heritage and pitched in to help.

Jorge, of course, was devastated by the news. Serita took him down by the creek and talked to him. When they returned, the boy was anxious to go into the pasture immediately in search of Ebanol and his *caballado*.

On the evening before they were set to round up the lost horses, Felix returned from his visit with McCaulay.

Serita had taken to dressing for *merienda* once more, and Giddeon's response gave her great pleasure. Although Burton's latest threat hung heavy over the entire household, she felt herself on a different plane of life. She knew well enough that her newfound serenity rested as on quicksand, since it was due in large part to Giddeon's temporary place in her life. But she refused to let herself dwell on the future — the distant future when he would go away. Instead she concentrated on the immediate future — paying the taxes and reassembling the *caballado*.

Descending the staircase in a brown silk gown with a matching woolen *rebozo* around her shoulders to ward off the onset of their first really cold spell of the season, she paused at the last step to watch Giddeon. Felix had arrived as she retired to her bedchamber to dress, and the two of them, standing now in earnest conversation beside the fountain, had not seen her as yet.

Crossing the courtyard she felt herself encased in a delicious dream. Even though dreadful things kept happening all around them, Giddeon's presence, his firm yet gentle approach to solving their problems, gave her a more secure feeling than she had had since she was a child. She slipped an arm through his, delighting in the feel of his muscles through the cropped black jacket. When she placed her hand palm down over his arm, he covered it absently with his own hand.

"You are sure?" he was asking. "It was Trinidad Cortinas you saw . . . ?"

"What about Trinity?" Her question brought Giddeon's words to an abrupt halt. She felt his sharp intake of breath against her shoulder.

"What about Trinity?" she repeated, returning his hesitant stare with one of determination.

"Ah . . . wasn't nothing, ma'am," Felix mumbled.

"Giddeon . . ."—her voice held a quiet warning—"whatever Trinity has done, I want to know about it. I am fully aware of the rebel he has become, but . . ."

"Querida . . ." Giddeon began.

She cocked her head in a manner he knew well.

"Serita," he tried again. "You really don't want . . ."

"Con permiso, Felix." Smiling politely, she tugged at Giddeon's arm.

When they were a few steps away she stood on tiptoe and looked him straight in the eye, almost nose-to-nose. "Tell me."

Pursing his lips, he inhaled a deep draft of her sweet gardenia scent.

"Serita, please . . ."

"Tell me."

Studying her intently while he tried to figure some way around her curiosity, he dislodged both her hands and raised them to his lips, kissing them knuckle by knuckle.

"Tell me," she repeated in a soft, seductive voice,

200

all the while wondering what ignoble deed Trinity had performed that Giddeon would take such pain — and tenderness — to keep from her. "You can kiss me later . . . upstairs . . . after you tell me about Trinity."

"You really don't want to know this . . ."

"I must."

So he drew another deep breath and told her. "Felix saw Trinidad in a cantina over on the road to San Antonio de Bexar with . . ." Pausing, he cocked his head in a manner that told her he didn't want to continue.

"Go on," she encouraged. "With whom?"

Giddeon swallowed. "With Oliver Burton."

At first, she merely stared at him. At first, she was more aware of his hands, warm and soothing, than of his words.

Then she frowned. "So . . . ? What does that mean?"

"Oliver Burton," he repeated. "The Oli — "

"I know who you are talking about, but what difference . . . ? I mean, a lot of people go into a cantina for a drink and . . ." She shrugged, trying to communicate her confusion.

"You're right, *querida*. A lot of folks go into a cantina. It is even conceivable that the two of them would go into the same cantina at the same time, but . . . But they were *together*. Sitting together at the rear of the room, in deep conversation."

Her frown returned.

Giddeon shrugged, as if to say he knew no more. "There's no love lost between them," he added. "I'm sure you noticed that the day of our wedding. And

201

later, in the way Trinidad threatened to take care of Burton."

Her mouth fell open. "You don't think he . . . ?"

"I don't know what to think," he admitted. "Except I fail to see how a meeting between those two men could result in anything good for—"

"For Los Olmos," she finished.

Later that night, when they lay satiated and breathless in each other's arms, she again thought of Trinidad, her wayward cousin. "What business could he possibly have with that bastard, Oliver Burton?"

Giddeon squeezed his arms tighter about her, basking in the way her curves and hollows fit against his own. "You know how desperate he is for contributions to his cause."

She shook her head, teasing his face with tendrils of her hair. "Not that desperate," she said.

And he agreed.

The next day they found Ebanol on essentially the same range as before. He aided them in recapturing the *caballado*, to the utter amazement of Delos and Kosta. Felix stayed behind at the big house, saying he had had enough of the backside of a horse to suit his fancy for a long time.

The men were anxious to get back to sea, Serita could see that in everything they did, hear it in every word they spoke.

Delos, however, had turned into a good hand, and Giddeon—she smiled to herself—Giddeon could have been born to the saddle. But, of course, he hadn't been. He was born to the sea, she to the

202

saddle. She wasn't about to let him see how proud she was of the way he had taken to ranch work. In fact, she didn't even want him to suspect his own conversion until . . .

Until it was too late. Quickly, she squelched such idle thoughts—thoughts designed to bring her nothing but a lifetime of despair. Today was what she had been given, and today was what she would take. No questions, no begging . . .

Except, he certainly sat his horse well, she finished in spite of herself. And he was equally proud of her.

That, she discovered the moment he began to explain the gentling process to Delos. "Wait until you see the way those wild horses respond to her, Del," she overheard him say. "It's a gift. They say she learned it from her grandfather, who learned it himself from some old Indian. But when you see her, you'll agree, it's a gift, pure and simple. No one learns that sort of magical mastery . . ."

Serita had expected little from the horses she had already gentled, but in this she was pleasantly surprised. Of the fifteen horses she had worked with, ten of them trotted behind Jorge and his sack of corn straight to the corral. The other five, the last ones she handled, did not respond as readily, but she began with them, and they came around in no time.

When the work began, she had despaired at finishing by mid-February, but as the days wore on, that goal appeared more and more possible.

One night after they retired to their suite, Giddeon poured each of them a glass of port and made

203

her a proposition she had not considered before.

"I want you to come on the drive with us."

"Me?" she asked, tempted by the chance to get away for a while.

"I know you will be even more exhausted when you finish the *caballado* than you are right now, but you won't have to do any work on the trail, and . . ." Pausing, he clinked his glass to hers. "I thought you could stay over at your uncle's new home at Kinney's Rancho while we take the herd on to either Galveston or New Orleans."

"It's a lovely idea," she agreed. "But I can't leave Los Olmos. My absence is the very thing Oliver Burton is waiting for."

Backing up to the crackling fireplace, he sipped his drink before answering. "I thought of that. Delos, Kosta, and Felix will be here. They will stay vigilant, post guards at night. They should be able to keep Burton at a distance until we return. Your absence wouldn't be the same thing as abandonment, under the law."

"Are you sure?"

He nodded, then came and sat beside her and kissed her wine-flavored lips. "The trip would give you a chance to visit, and when I return, I could show you the sea."

"The sea?"

He grinned. "Kinney's Rancho is on the Gulf."

"I know that," she retorted. "So is Los Olmos Bay."

He tipped her glass. "Kinney's Rancho will have ships. I'd like to show you a ship."

She kissed his lips then, and cuddled against his

204

strong, welcoming body. "I would like for you to show me a ship," she whispered.

By the middle of February she had four mustangs left to break. One more week's work. She was sure she could finish on time.

And she was sure of something else, too. She was carrying Giddeon's child.

The thought sent chills chasing heat throughout her system—joy chasing sorrow, and the other way around. She became absent minded, thinking on the coming event, and giddy with anticipation—and dread. She was happy, she was sad, but, thankfully, she was not sick.

Otherwise, he would have known. And that was her problem. How would she ever tell him? When would she tell him?

Certainly not before she finished the *caballado*. He would surely try to stop her working with the mustangs—never mind that Mamá had never given up riding during her two confinements. Giddeon still did not fully trust the animals; he would quarrel with her over it, and discord would disrupt their lovely harmony.

Discord over her working with the *caballado;* discord over money to pay the taxes. Her mind whirled like a rearing stallion when she thought on these things. She would not harm her baby, but she must gentle the horses. For without them, money could not be raised to pay the taxes.

Unless they paid the taxes she would lose not only her husband, but her home.

And *when* they paid the taxes . . . Her dilemma was born of despair, and the solution to it would reap a lifetime of loneliness. When they paid the taxes, Giddeon would leave.

Giddeon, the father of her child. Giddeon Duval, *Señor Capitán*, the handsome, gentle, caring . . . determined Capitán Duval.

The father of her child. The man determined to return to the sea. The man Tita had recognized at once: the man with whom she had fallen hopelessly, helplessly, joyously in love. The man she would find it unbearable to live without.

The man with whom she had an iron-clad agreement.

An agreement she intended to honor to the extent that he would never know her anguish — anguish made all the more insufferable by the joy he brought her every single day now.

Through it all she worked, bringing the *caballado* to a state of readiness for the drive to market. Giddeon and the men held the ropes; then he went about the chore he himself had set, restoring the *hacienda* to its former condition. Often, though, she would see him on the rooftop with his spyglass.

And that act filled her with renewed determination to keep from him her other secret, the one she carried in her heart: her ever-growing love for him. Because now when she saw him on the rooftop, she knew it was not to search for a lost comrade; all his crew was together here at Los Olmos. Now when he searched the horizon, she knew it was for the sea . . . for his ship, his past, his future, his way of life, his one true love.

Late in the afternoon two days before they were to leave for Kinney's Rancho, she was finishing

206

work for the day, when Trinidad arrived with his army. They went about setting up camp, and Giddeon exploded.

Serita came upon them in the courtyard on her way to bathe before *merienda.*

"Serita has worked too hard for you to ruin it, Cortinas," Giddeon shouted. "You are to pack up your army and leave within the hour."

Trinidad spat to the tiled courtyard, very close to Giddeon's boots. "Who are you to order me away? You have no say in what happens on my ancestral lands."

Giddeon grabbed the man's shirt and held him close. "I have everything to do with whether you stay or leave Los Olmos, Cortinas. Don't you doubt that for a minute. This is my land—as well as Serita's—and I am ordering you off. Tonight. My men are prepared to back me up."

Serita stepped from the shadows to stand beside Giddeon. "Trinity," she began, "you must go. As he says, he has every right to make the decision, and I back him completely. I don't know what you are trying to do to us, but I cannot let you stay around and endanger Los Olmos any further."

"Endanger Los Olmos? What kind of lies has he fed you?"

Serita jerked her chin up. "You were seen in conference with Oliver Burton. That is enough for me. Nieves will give you a sack of food, if you are hungry. But you will leave now . . . this very minute."

She worried throughout the night. After all, she told Giddeon, Trinidad was her own flesh and

207

blood. For her father's sake and her grandfather's, she should not reject a member of the family.

The next day Giddeon tried to convince her to rest before their trip. "You've done enough. Those horses are ready for the trail. Take this time to prepare yourself for the trip."

"I won't spend the entire day in the corral," she promised. "Two or three horses still have rough edges. I will exercise them, then quit."

The first horse was a mare, a dun with four white stockings, and Serita worked with her about an hour, feeling satisfied when she turned the animal back with the bunch.

The second horse, a sorrel, also worked out well, after a hesitant beginning during which Serita sat his back for well onto fifteen minutes without moving. Once the horse decided to trot around the corral, however, he moved with a smooth gait, and when she turned him into the pen with the other gentled horses, he trotted dutifully over to the fence where Jorge waited with a sack of corn and a tamale.

The third and final horse proved to be a surprise. A beautiful paint pony, her favorite of the bunch, he had the roughest edges of all the day before, but he started this session as a star pupil. After three turns around the corral, she knew she should put him in the pen and return to the house to finish the packing she had set Abril about this morning. But the day was bright, with a clear blue sky and a golden sun shining overhead, so she bent forward and shoved open one side of the iron-bound gates, intending to take the paint down to the creek and back as she used to ride Barb.

They had barely cleared the gate, however, when the heavy iron lock fell back into place, as it was sometimes wont to do, and the pony panicked. He leaped straight into the air, reaching for the sun. At the top of his arc, he buckled, and his front hooves hit the earth with a jolt that rattled Serita's senses. The next bound took the two of them ten yards farther from the training corral toward the pen of horses. When the pinto saw them, he became even more determined to shake the weight off his back and join his friends.

She had known horses to do almost anything to get to a friend. Once an old bay mare belonging to *Don* Fernando turned up at *la casa grande* with bloody hooves from walking the entire distance between the two *haciendas* to be with a friend—a gray stallion *Don* Fernando had recently sold to *Papá*. At the moment, however, she gave no thought to wayward horses in general, only to keeping her seat on this particular pinto.

The lightweight saddle she used when breaking the horses was girted loosely for corral use, and Serita, intent on a pleasant ride to the creek, had let that necessary fact slip her mind. Now when the saddle started to move, she quickly disengaged her feet from the stirrups and lifted herself by her knees to keep from sliding around the horse's side along with the traveling saddle.

The pinto chose the same moment to execute another pirouette. This one was higher than before, and without the support of the saddle, Serita flew up the pinto's neck, where she clung for dear life.

Then he descended, and she tightened her grip on his mane.

It was the spin which followed that got her, she decided later. A spinning horse is hard to stay aboard, even with knees clamped firmly to his sides and feet pushed tightly in the stirrups.

Without either of those, it was impossible, and she flew through the air, landing with a thud on the hard-packed earth.

Immediately, she rolled away from the pitching horse and curled into a ball, ducking her head to her chest. Her heart constricted, her mind swirled, and her arms instinctly clutched her stomach—all with one thought—her baby.

Jorge was the first to see her. He dropped the sack of corn beside the corral fence and ran for Pablo.

Giddeon heard her first. Turning swiftly toward the corral, he saw her plight from the vantage point of the rooftop lookout; his immediate thought was to jump straight from the roof. It was a trick that might have worked from ship to sea, but not from roof to dry, hard land. Taking the stairs three at a time, he raced through the courtyard, out the corral gates, and reached her side just as she curled herself away from the rearing horse.

His heart pounded against his rib cage with the same force that the pinto's hooves struck the ground. *"Querida?"* he called in a hoarse whisper. "Can you hear me?"

Dazed by the fall, her head reeled. She heard his voice, opened her mouth to respond, then quickly clamped her lips closed. Not over the pain, which was minimal, but over the words that had almost come out. As determined as she had been to keep him from finding out about the baby, she had almost blurted out the fact herself.

He slipped his hand beneath her head for a cushion, but he dared not move her until he knew where she was injured. "How badly are you hurt, *querida?*"

Gingerly she tested her neck, moving it to look into his worried face. "Guess I should have listened to you and stayed away today."

He only shook his head, watching her stretch first her arms, then her back, her legs. Against his will, she sat up and moved her shoulders about; a small, sharp pain in her back, her right shoulder felt . . .

She stopped when he held a handkerchief to her forehead. "What . . . ?"

Scooping her into his arms, he rose to his feet, steadied himself, then kissed her softly on the lips before he carried her toward their bedchamber.

"Send for Nieves," he told Jorge, who met them in the courtyard.

Serita's eyes widened. "Nieves?"

"Didn't you tell me she is a *curandera?*" he asked. "You must let her examine . . ."

"I'm all right," Serita insisted. "I do not need . . ."

"You will let Nieves check you over." For the first time in a long while, the voice he used with her was firm.

She lifted a hand and stroked his lips. "I don't need . . ."

"Shush!" He bent forward and planted a firm kiss on her lips. "If you want to go on that trail drive with me tomorrow, you will let Nieves check you over today."

Serita sighed but acquiesced, unsure how she could refuse without raising more questions than she wanted to answer. Surely, Nieves wouldn't know . . .

But, of course, she did.

After she finished checking Serita, the old woman stirred a good measure of flour into a cup of hot water until she had a substance almost the consistency of paste. She handed the cup to Serita. "You should not have been riding like that with your condition so new."

Serita grimaced. "How did you know?"

"I have ways," Nieves told her sternly. "Drink this all up now. And you must stay abed a week or ten days."

"I can't. The trail drive . . ."

"*Chica,* you mind me or you will lose your baby."

Tears swelled in Serita's eyes and brimmed over. "I must go on the trail drive, Nieves. You don't understand. It is very, very important to . . . to my husband. He wants me . . ."

"I am sure what *Señor Capitán* wants more is a healthy wife and baby," Nieves broke in.

Serita clamped her hands over her mouth. Was this how he would discover the secret? He would never consent for her to go on the trail drive now! And she must. It could well be her only chance to go any place with him . . . ever. He would leave soon and . . . "Nieves, listen," she pleaded, patting the bed beside her. "Come here, I must talk to you."

Misunderstanding, Nieves sat and began to talk

212

herself. "I suppose if you were to ride in the wagon
. . . I will speak to *Señor Capitán*."

"No!" Serita wailed. "Listen to me, Nieves. Just
listen. He does not know about the baby."

Now it was Nieves's turn to stare wide-eyed.
"Why have you not told him? He has a right . . ."

"Nieves," Serita insisted, "listen to me. He would
not have let me work with the horses had he
known. And now . . . After this fall, he will not
allow me to go with him on the drive. Please help
me. It is so very important. I plan to tell him when
we return from Kinney's Rancho, but . . ." She
broke off and covered her face in her hands.
"Please, help me, Nieves. No one knows. Not even
Tita. No one."

Nieves pulled Serita's hands from her face and
stared into her eyes. "If it is that important to you,
chica, you know I will help. You are my little girl.
Why, I brought you into this world and I have
taken care of you ever since. I won't let you down.
I will tell no one your secret. But, *chica,* I am very
happy for you and for *Señor Capitán*."

Serita hugged the old woman around the neck.
Then she dried her eyes and got down to business.
"Now tell me clearly what I must do to save my
baby — and to preserve my secret."

213

Chapter Nine

Together Nieves and Serita agreed on a plan to keep her secret and protect her baby.

"Two days?" Giddeon entered the bedchamber at Nieves's invitation, and quickly knelt beside Serita's bed. "Sure, we can postpone the drive, but . . ." Tearing his eyes from Serita's head wound, he questioned Nieves. "Are you sure two days is long enough. A head injury can be dangerous. I've seen men . . ."

"Dos días, Señor Capitán," Nieves repeated in Spanish. "Two days should be enough, but she must take it slow on the drive. She cannot get wet or chilled or spend long days in the saddle. If you want your wife to bear you healthy children, *Señor Capitán,* you will . . ."

"Nieves!" Serita broke in.

Nieves turned her wagging finger on Serita. "And you, *chica,* you mind what I told you."

"Nieves," Serita warned.

"That is all I have to say," the old woman declared, and with that she left the room, but they heard her in the gallery outside instructing Abril on the preparation of the flour tea Serita would be forced to drink for the next two days.

Serita squirmed under Giddeon's close inspection as he gently soothed the hair back from her face to study the flesh wound on her forehead. "It's nothing," she insisted. "Nieves has always been a mother hen."

"It *is* something," he told her firmly. "You will obey Nieves's instructions to the letter. The first thing is get you well, and the second thing . . ." His voice broke in midsentence, and he gently buried his face in her hair, kissing the top of her head. With a deep sigh, he continued. "When I saw you, I . . . Forchristssake, Serita, you could have been killed. You were lucky, that's all. But it won't happen again. The moment I saw you lying on the ground, I made myself a promise."

He was so serious, she dared not let a smile show on her face. But his words fairly took her breath away. She cocked her head, and with her eyes, dared him to finish. When he didn't, she prompted him. "What sort of promise did you make yourself?"

Still frightened by what could have happened, he failed to understand her meaning. "Take it lightly, if you want, Serita. But believe me, I don't. I have seen men killed or knocked senseless for life by swift blows to the head. You'll not be one of them. I promised myself if you recover this time, there will be no others. You will never ride a wild horse again."

Her eyes flew to his. "*You* promised *yourself* that I will not break horses?"

215

"I certainly did, and . . ."

"Why, *Capitán* Duval, however do you intend to keep such a promise when you are way out in the middle of the ocean? Or with some floozy in a seaport town somewhere?"

He blinked only once, then merely stared at her with a deathlike calm brought on by the fact, he was sure, that his heart had stopped beating in his chest. After what seemed like an eternity, he rose abruptly to his feet and strode to the fireplace, where he rested an arm on the mantel and stared into the burning logs.

Finally, he turned back to her. "I care about you . . . very much. I want you to be safe. I . . . I don't want you to rush recklessly through life . . . endangering yourself at every turn. You're . . . you're too old to be engaging in such things as breaking mustangs."

"Too old? Older men than I break mustangs every day of their lives. Or is that the problem, *capitán?* I am a *woman* . . . ?"

"Yes, damnit! Yes! You're a woman, and you're supposed to be . . ." Having regained his composure with this new, less threatening line of questioning, he crossed the room and knelt beside her bed once more. Taking her hand idly in his, he continued, his lopsided grin firmly in place. "You're beautiful and feminine and gentle and . . ."

She snickered. "I'm not usually considered gentle."

"Well, you are. And you're not bent over and stove up, yet, which is what most of those old mustangers are."

She laughed. "Enjoy my fragile beauty while you

can then," she teased, "because I don't intend to give up breaking mustangs any more than you intend to give up salvaging the *Estelle*."

The conversation had come full circle, but this time he wasn't taken off guard. With a squeeze of her hand, he rose and studied her a moment, a curious grin tipping the corners of his mouth. "Rest now. I will return later."

She watched him walk away, then stop at the door and turn, the same grin still on his face. "By the way, I don't have much use for floozies."

They left two days later, and now Serita kept three secrets locked safely in her heart: her love for Giddeon, his child, and his growing affection for that child's mother. If she could have, she would have left them all at home safely locked away in the trunk with the Los Olmos land-grant documents, for day by day she knew these were the things she treasured above all else in the world.

The trip took ten days instead of the allotted eight, because Giddeon took Nieves's words to heart. Not only did they stop for a noonday meal of tortillas and *carne quisada*, a stewlike dish consisting of cubed meat and gravy which Pablo prepared at Nieves's instructions, but they also made two other stops—one at midmorning and one at midafternoon—before settling onto new campgrounds at dusk. And in between all the stops, Giddeon questioned her continually: Did her head hurt? Was she tired? Was she damp or cold or cramped?

"I have never felt better in my life," she assured him one night after they climbed into their separate bedrolls on the opposite side of the campfire from

Pablo and Jorge. Giddeon at first had despaired that they had no room to carry along a tent, but she assured him she was quite comfortable sleeping around a campfire — after all, Pablo and Jorge were family. They both longed, of course, for more than the stolen good-night kiss, hastily accomplished after the fire had died down.

Fortunately, the weather held to damp, chilly, and gray, instead of wet and cold as they often experienced during February.

Which was good for more reasons than her own health, she told him one evening around the campfire. "Horses will stampede at a mere clap of thunder, especially a mixed herd of stallions and mares like we're driving."

Pablo agreed. "We have been lucky this trip, *Señor Capitán*, but we are not finished yet. Every night and every day, we face the threat of losing our herd."

"Tell him about the time we drove a herd to Indianola, Pablo," Jorge encouraged, and what followed was the retelling of every horse-stampede tale Serita had ever heard. She had just started to suggest retiring when Giddeon told one of his own.

"Have you heard the tale about the Buenos Aires drive back in 1830?"

Pablo shook his head.

"Tell it, *Tío Capitán*," Jorge begged.

"Down in Campeche where I'm from, this story is famous. The herd numbered five hundred when they pulled out of Buenos Aires — that's down in South America," he told Jorge. "One thing or another caused a stampede every night they were on the trail—one night it was thunder, another the scent of panther, then something else, and so on until by the time they arrived at their destination, they had lost all but twenty head of the five hundred they started out with."

Soft swears and mumbles followed the telling of the tale, and all agreed it was by far the most extreme example of the difficulty of driving horses they had heard. Serita stood and glanced toward their bedrolls.

"I guess I'll turn in . . ."—she eyed Giddeon through the smoke of the campfire—". . . if you won't reconsider and let me take my turn at guard duty."

"Not on your life," he responded emphatically. "Nieves would have my hide."

With a sigh, she studied the group. "She wouldn't have to know."

Both men held firm, so Serita went to bed, and Giddeon took first guard. The night was dark with hardly any stars and a pale, white moon. Once she turned over and he had not returned. Having nothing to gauge the time by, she went back to sleep, but when she awoke again to find he still had not returned, she sat up and tried to see across the smoldering campfire.

Finally, her nerves on edge, she slipped into her breeches and boots and crept out of bed. Pablo and Jorge were gone, as she had suspected, and her uneasiness turned to worry. Straining to hear any sound out of the ordinary, she briefly considered saddling up and going to find them.

But only briefly, of course, since she didn't know

the exact location of the men and any noise she might make could be the very sound that set the horses to running. So she stoked up the fire, made fresh coffee, and waited.

And waited. And waited.

At last, when the sky lightened somewhat, she heard a horse's hooves, followed by the jangling of spurs. Giddeon walked into the clearing.

"Where have you been? What happened. Where are . . . ?"

Closing the distance between them quickly, he pulled her into his arms. "Shhh . . ." he whispered. "Nothing is wrong."

"Then where are Pablo and Jorge? Why were all of you . . . ?"

With both hands he held her head back and stared into her upturned face. Her features were barely visible in the still-shadowy dawn. Sighing deeply, he lowered his lips to hers. "You feel so good next to me," he whispered before kissing her more soundly than she had been kissed in several days. "I've missed you."

"Me, too." She snuggled against him, responding eagerly to his kiss, his hands on her back, stroking her spine, spanning her waist, caressing her breasts, setting her skin on fire with desire for more . . . more . . . more . . .

"The next time we go on a trail drive," he whispered in a husky voice, "we're going alone."

She chuckled, cuddling in his embrace. Then suddenly, she had the unsettling feeling that he knew. Her breasts, tingling now from his urgent caresses, already felt fuller than before . . . Did he

220

know?

Her waist was thicker. Could he tell? Her breeches strained across her once-taut belly. Did he see?

"Hey," he whispered, drawing her back to study her face in the dim light. "What's the matter?"

Quickly she covered her disquietude with a question. "Tell me what happened to keep you all on herd duty tonight."

With a peck to her lips, he argued playfully. "I can think of a lot better ways to spend our few moments alone."

"And I can think of no better way to begin paying the taxes than with the sale of this herd. Tell me."

As always when she brought up their arrangement, he sobered. Squatting before the fire, he held his hands, palms out, toward the flames. "We have a visitor intent on joining the herd."

"An outcast stallion?" She handed him a cup of coffee.

He nodded. "We've been trying to keep him a fair distance away from the *caballado*. A fight in the dark would be as good as the whiff of panther to scatter these horses from here to kingdom come."

"You should have called me."

He drank down a swig of the hot coffee. "No sense disturbing your beauty rest."

"Giddeon Duval! I am not an invalid, so don't treat me like one. I demand to be part of this crew. Besides," she finished, "I don't need beauty rest. I have never needed pampering or . . ."

Setting his coffee cup on the ground, he came to

his feet slowly, running a hand up her leg as he rose in a sensual way that brought a catch to her throat. He traveled past her thigh, her hip, her waist, and, gaining his footing, he let his fingers tantalize her breast. "No, *querida*, you surely do not need beauty rest." Seductively, his face lowered once more to hers; his lips descended slowly but with purpose. "If you were any more beautiful, I fear my goose would be cooked."

Again she melted against him, and they kissed and held each other tighter and tighter still and wished for time and privacy to make their dreams come true. But footsteps in the underbrush alerted them.

Drawing her face back, she stared into his green eyes. "So it's my looks you are becoming accustomed to?"

The muscles in his throat tightened involuntarily, and she felt his body tense against hers.

They made Kinney's Rancho in two more days with no mishaps. The outcast stallion hung around, but by staying alert, they were able to keep him away from the herd. Entering the small seaport town, Serita felt a despondency fill the place in her heart where once she had known joy and anticipation. Somehow her melancholy seemed the greater, the threat of loneliness more powerful, because now she grieved for two—for herself and for her unborn child.

They found a flat, grassy plain on the far side of the Nueces River to herd the horses, and Pablo went into the trading post to secure some vaqueros, while Serita and Giddeon visited her relatives.

Numerous businessmen had moved to Kinney's Rancho in the last few years, some bringing their families, as well as their social and religious customs.

Arriving now, as they did on the last day before the beginning of the Lenten season, the town was in the middle of one huge fandango. Serita's blues were quickly overshadowed by the festivities.

Her family engulfed her—by their sheer numbers, Giddeon thought—as first Tío Pepe and Tía Beatriz embraced her, followed by their five married children and spouses, four unmarried children, and so many grandchildren Giddeon didn't even try to count. All were overjoyed to meet Serita's husband, for all heard the story of the now-infamous card game between Don Miguel and Giddeon.

"Wait until tonight. Someone has even written a *corrido* about it all," Rosaria, Serita's favorite cousin, told them.

"A ballad?" Serita paled. "About . . . ?"

Rosaria giggled. "About you and *Señor Capitán,* . . . how he won your hand in a card game . . ."

"Oh, no! They didn't?" She never dreamed anyone would know of that game except *Papá,* Giddeon, and herself. Perhaps his crew. But no one else. Certainly not her family—not the entire community of Kinney's Rancho. How mortifying! Her own father wagered her hand in a game of chance, and the whole world knew! *Her* whole world, anyhow.

"We will sing it . . . but tonight," Rosie enthused. "Now there are other things to take care of." She looked Serita up and down with a wrinkled nose.

"I know how unkempt we are," Serita told her. "Even the clothing I brought along is full of trail dust."

"Never mind," Rosaria responded. "We must get the two of you dressed in time for the parade." She sent Giddeon off with her brother Luis, while she herself dragged Serita into a back room of the sprawling frame house, where she fitted her out in a festive *china poblana* costume, consisting of a full black skirt heavily embroidered in red and green, a white waistband, and a colorful *rebozo*, embroidered to match the skirt.

While Serita dressed, several of the other sisters prepared themselves for the parade. Rosaria donned a confection of a gold lace gown with multi-tiered skirt.

Twirling before the looking glass, she suddenly stopped and hugged Serita around the neck. "Married! I cannot believe you are really and truly married. And to such a handsome man. The *corrido*, it isn't really true, is it?" Drawing Serita back to look into her face, she shrugged. "What does it matter? I wish Papá would wager me in a card game . . . if he could find someone as handsome as your *capitán*."

Serita wriggled uncomfortably out of her cousin's arms. "We'd better go, or they will leave us behind."

"No chance of that," Juana piped up. "Rosaria is the queen."

When Serita emerged from Rosaria's room in the tow of her four female cousins and caught the first sight of Giddeon in a *concho*-studded *charro* suit, she stared as though she had never seen him before.

He grinned. "Don't you recognize me without the trail dust?"

"The gringo Cow Boy is definitely gone," she agreed, taking his arm as she stepped into the second carriage. "But so is *Señor Capitán*." The fitted suede jacket and trousers looked every bit as custom-made for him as *Papá's* clothing had, but then, Tío Pepe and Papá were very close to the same size.

They watched the parade from the front of Tío Pepe's General Mercantile, where she greeted or was introduced to everyone who came by, including people from several foreign countries — Germany, Ireland, and even one couple from Czechoslovakia — all of whom had taken refuge here in this no man's land, hoping to begin life anew.

The parade was led by the *alcalde* — the town's mayor — who rode a magnificent black stallion, his saddle heavily laden with silver trimmings. Following him came a dozen horsemen, garbed also in leather and silver, their *charro* costumes and wide-brimmed hats richly embroidered with gold and silver.

A few yards behind the horsemen, Rosaria, in her golden lace dress, rode in her father's finest carriage, drawn by two spanking palomino horses.

The rest of the parade was a menagerie of dancers and music-makers attired in an array of costumes, both religious and pagan, representing folk dress of many countries. After he passed around the plaza three times, the *alcalde* led the way to the church. Serita and Giddeon, those of her cousins who were not involved in the parade itself, and the other spectators fell in line behind the last of the parade members and hurried along to the church, where the visiting dance troupes began a series of folk dances, while vendors hawked samples of their specialties.

Giddeon guided Serita to the front row of spectators.

"Wise men, those early missionaries," he mused, watching four agile young men perform El Volador, the flying pole dance, to the delight of the crowd. "Instead of forbidding the pagan dances, they convinced them to dedicate the very same dances to God and the Church."

She nodded, surprised he seemed to know so much about such things. "They say this dance once honored the Aztec's sun god."

The visiting dance troupe from Veracruz erected a raised wooden platform, where they performed one folk dance after another, accompanied by a band playing a variety of instruments ranging from violins and a bass guitar to deer antlers, shells filled with pebbles, and even a mandoline made from an armadillo shell, called a *concha*.

When the performers shifted from ritual dances to *malagueñas* and *fandangos,* the spectators crowded onto the wooden platform and joined the dancing.

Through the melee of sounds and languages, Serita suddenly became aware of an Anglo voice beside her.

"The *polca norteña,* Edward. We can do that."

When Serita turned to look at the couple, the woman smiled at her. "A polka is a polka, dear. No

226

matter what the language."

Serita nodded.

"I'm Mary Stavinoha. This is my husband, Edward."

"Yes," Serita acknowledged, introducing Giddeon and herself. "The new schoolmarm. *Tía* Beatriz spoke highly of you."

Mary Stavinoha accepted the compliment graciously. "I hope she feels that way at the end of the term. I am not easy on the youngsters. Learning is too important."

Giddeon offered his hand to Edward Stavinoha. "And you, sir, have an excellent reputation as a cabinetmaker."

"I appreciate that. If you're ever in need . . . Ah, well, with a home like Los Olmos, you likely have furniture to treasure from ages past."

"That we do," Serita agreed. "Things have gotten a bit run down, but *Capitán* Duval is seeing to the restoration. You must come visit us. Both of you. We will return within the month."

"We'd like that," Mary Stavinoha agreed. "We love to travel about . . . see how other folks live."

Through the conversation, Edward had cocked his head in a thoughtful manner. "Perhaps I'll bring along a new crib. You'll probably find yourselves . . ."

"The polka," Serita interrupted to remind Mary. "You are about to miss it."

Giddeon didn't seem interested in the polka, so she didn't insist. The next number, however, was a *jarabe,* and before she knew what had happened, he drew her to the dance floor, where her misery was

227

quickly lost in the coquettish nature of the dance.

Tossing her head, her hair flew about her face, strands of it catching in her mouth. Her hands were busy flicking her skirts about her ankles, while she executed the flashing steps with grace and perfection.

The passion with which she danced did not surprise Giddeon. His heart throbbed with the music as he watched her twirl and whirl in great splashes of color. Her hands clutched her skirts, exposing frilly petticoats and well-turned ankles, glimpses of her exquisite calves. But his eyes did not stay on her shapely legs, nor did they tarry on her heaving bosom, glistening now with perspiration from the exertion with which she danced. His gaze held hers, and again he was struck by the resemblance between Serita and Don Miguel. Her chin was elevated, her patrician nose tilted at a haughty angle, wisps of hair clung to her lips, which were parted— the better to catch her breath, he knew—full and moist and inviting enough to be disconcerting.

Their eyes still united, they executed a near-perfect *paseo*, their taut bodies passing to within an inch of each other, so close he could feel her heart throb, inhale her sweet breath as she lifted her face to his. All he need do was move his arms from behind his back and encircle her, draw her to him . . .

As in a flash, they pivoted apart and finished the dance, then collapsed laughing against each other.

"You dance like you break mustangs," he told her through labored breaths.

Playing the coquette, she tilted her head and

228

studied him with a grin. "Are you suggesting I give up dancing, too?"

With the greatest of control, he lifted his fingers to her face and pulled away the strands of black hair still clinging to her damp skin. "Never." For a second, the din surrounding them did not exist.

Serita's heart pumped almost painfully in her breast. Had she been at home, she would have thrown her arms about him then and there. But here in the middle of Kinney's Rancho with her uncle's family to think of, she kept her composure and waited for the music to begin again.

Instead, a male voice rose above the crowd. "While our band takes a break, we will entertain you with a *corrido,* recently composed, entitled *"Hombres de Juego."*

"Gambling Men!" She had forgotten about the *corrido!* The music, the dance had filled her to overflowing with Giddeon's mesmerizing presence. Now embarrassment flushed her face. Quickly, she slipped her hand through his elbow and moved away from the speaker. "Let's get out of here."

It was all she could do to keep her feet from fleeing, but Giddeon held her to a steady pace. With measured stride he guided them toward the outer edge of the crowd, while the balladeer's words, accompanied by the strum of a *concha,* reached them in whiffs as on the rising and falling wind.

"Don Miguel Cortinas . . . Hacienda de los Olmos . . . Serita Cortinas . . . *la hija de el* . . . his daughter . . . *bella a ver* . . . beautiful to see . . . *pierde el rancho en el juego* . . . he gambled the ranch

229

away . . ."

By the time they escaped the crowd, she was shaking. How could Papá have done such a thing? How could Giddeon? And to think! Someone had the gall to honor the occasion with a song!

He squeezed her to his side. "It has a nice rhythm."

"Joke if you like," she stormed. "The song is about me! And I find it humiliating, not amusing."

With a shrug he cocked his head toward the crowd. "Listen again. They're on my verse now."

El Capitán Duval of the schooner *Estelle* . . . dashing and daring . . . *guapo ojos de verde* . . . handsome green eyes . . . *'No, señor,' dice el capitán, 'jugamos para su hija, Serita.' "*

Giddeon stepped in front of her suddenly and tipped her face to his. "He's right about one thing, *querida. Bella a ver. . . .* You are very beautiful to look at."

She stood still, scarcely breathing, while her thoughts dropped like stones in her heart. *And you, my love, have handsome green eyes.*

Rosaria's animated cries broke into their reveries. "Serita! They're playing your song . . ." Her words came to a halt along with her feet when she reached Serita and Giddeon.

Giddeon still held Serita's shoulders, and they stared into each other's eyes. She felt his grip tighten, and she resisted the urge to flinch. Finally, she saw his Adam's apple bob. Then he spoke in a hushed but harsh voice. "I'm sorry. It was a stupid thing to do. I never meant to hurt you."

"Gidd—" Before she could finish, he had turned

to Rosaria. Serita caught her lip between her teeth.

"Take care of her," he commanded, as though to a member of his crew. "She had a bad fall before we left home." Without a backward glance he strode off toward the bay.

The rest of the afternoon crept by at a snail's pace. She accompanied Rosaria and Juana around the various vendors, but for the first time, her stomach was in such turmoil she could hardly think about food, much less consider eating anything.

The musicians returned and the visiting dance troupe entertained with more of the primitive dances she had always loved. But she could scarcely watch for the *corrido* worrying her mind.

Several of the men, including Tío Pepe, had been off at the plaza holding cockfights; now, as dusk settled in, they returned and the couples again danced.

The ballad was on everyone's lips. Serita tried to keep a friendly smile on her face, while inside she wondered how anyone could think she would enjoy a song about the way her father had wagered her . . .

Suddenly the words of the *corrido* — words she had been too embarrassed to hear at the time they were sung — began to take form. " '*No, señor,' dice el capitán, 'jugamos para su hija, Serita.'* "

We play for your daughter, Serita. We play for your daughter, Serita. She found him at last, sitting on the opposite side of a dune, his back propped against the sand, chewing on a piece of marsh grass and staring out to sea. Overwhelmed by the various emotions that vied within her, she collapsed beside

231

him, her heart pumping wildly. For a time she couldn't speak. And even when her heart quieted enough, she had trouble finding the words.

"Is the *corrido* true?" she asked at last.

He turned to her, a frown on his face. "You know it is."

"I mean . . . is it *really* true? Does it tell the story the way it . . . the way it actually happened?"

He watched anxiety build on her face with a growing sense of despair. "I told you I'm sorry . . ."

"That is not what I want to hear," she stormed. "I asked if . . . Did you indeed gamble for my hand in marriage, *capitán?* Or was it my body you played for?!"

"Your hand, forchristssake!"

"Repeat the exact words you spoke," she demanded.

Her anguish over the ordeal was more than he could stand. He turned to stare at the distant horizon. The sun was sinking fast behind them, and the sea was an inky blue, almost black — *like her eyes,* he thought. "Don Miguel asked to wager Los Olmos, and I told him . . . no . . ." His words died on the wind.

"No, what?" she insisted. "What exactly did you say?"

"Serita, don't . . . please."

Her voice shook with the effort to control her fury. "I have a right to know."

He inhaled deeply. The words came back to him as on the breaking of the waves — words of the *corrido*, words he himself had spoken first.

"Don Miguel asked to wager Los Olmos," he

232

repeated, "and I . . . I said, 'No, your daughter's hand. We play for your daughter, Serita.' "

For a long time the only sound was the lapping of the evening tide as it inched its way toward them. She thought how Mamá had always admonished her to give praise for even the smallest of blessings. But now she found herself unable to do so. The *corrido* had seared her soul with fear, claiming as it did that Giddeon had gambled for *her*, saying nothing about him winning her hand in marriage. Although she knew well enough that *corridos* rarely followed a tale with accuracy, she had sought the truth, thinking it would relieve her mind . . . but it did not. The very fact of the game itself—played in a cantina, no less—left her feeling tarnished, dirty, a floozy. How could a father have done such a thing? "What did he say to your . . . ah, your proposal?"

Giddeon rested his arms across propped-up knees. "He stared at me for what seemed like an eternity. When he spoke, he just said, '*Sí, mi hija*, Serita. *Para su esposa.*' "

"Just like that?" she whispered. "Just like that, he betrothed his daughter to a . . . to a destitute sea captain . . . in a cantina?" Moisture dampened her hair and face and beaded on her arms which, she, too, crossed over her knees, pulling her skirts down over her feet. She had come to terms with the wager at home, but here at Kinney's Rancho, where it was on everyone's lips—where it had been preserved for posterity in a *corrido*—why, even her child would know and judge . . . How would she ever explain such a dastardly thing to her child? That its

233

father married its mother, not because he loved her, but because he *won* her in a game of chance?!

"I know why he agreed," she admitted at last. "To get me away from Los Olmos. He thought you would take my land and force me to leave the Nueces Strip. But you . . . you had never even met me, and it was your idea." Turning, she stared at him, the hurt wild in her eyes. "Why, Giddeon? Why not just the land? Why *me?*"

Her anguish washed over him like a cold wave. "It was a whim! A stupid, foolish whim that I will regret until the day I die. What else do you want me to say?"

Before his words died on the wind, he knew. Their eyes held, and he knew exactly what she wanted him to say. It was written all over her face . . . in the shadows, in the tears. *I love you.* Three simple words that would set everything right—erase her embarrassment . . . eliminate her fears . . . bring joy to her face, happiness to her heart. The words were there . . . in his heart; the truth, however, choked them back. His jaws tightened. His heart pumped with the agony he felt—for her . . . for himself; his voice left his mouth as a breath on the lonely night wind.

"I'm leaving. You know that. I told you . . ."

But before he could finish, she came into his arms, and their lips met. Laying her gently against the sand, he kissed her and held her and felt her heart beat against his and tasted the salt of her tears.

"I never meant to hurt you," he whispered. "If you never believe anything else, please try to believe

234

that."

She touched his cheek gently with her lips, tasting sand mingled with her tears. How quickly his lips and his arms erased reality, like the tide washing the beach clean of debris. "I told you I can take care of myself."

He pressed his lips against her forehead and held them there a moment. "That was before . . ." His words trailed off. *Before you fell in love with me,* he finished furiously in his mind.

Before I carried your baby, she thought.

"I can still take care of myself," she argued, bringing them back to the present. "But you didn't answer my question. Why did you wager for me?"

Her lightened tone eased his gloom, and he grinned when he answered. "I told you once I wasn't stupid. You had driven off every poor sonofabitch who won Los Olmos. I figured if I won *you,* you'd have to keep me around until . . ."

"Until what?" she demanded coyly. "You are certainly a conceited bastard if you thought I would give you Los Olmos for your charm."

"Wouldn't you have?" he teased, kissing her again, because it was far safer and more pleasing than anything he could think of to say.

But when she spoke again, it was to further probe this most unsettling subject. "Tell me how Papá reacted."

Running his tongue idly around his lips, Giddeon remembered every detail of Don Miguel's reaction to his suggestion—the probing eyes that searched his very soul. At the time he recalled thinking the old man saw through his ruse. Now he wondered if perhaps Don Miguel hadn't seen something far different when he peeked so intimately into his soul. Did he think he had found a true son-in-law and heir, instead of a wandering sea captain who would whisk his daughter away from the gringo land raiders, then leave her to return to sea?

"You will have to ask him, *querida*. I wouldn't dare speak for so shrewd a man."

Chapter Ten

The morning following the fandango, Giddeon, accompanied by Pablo and Jorge and the three vaqueros Pablo had hired at Kinney's Rancho, left for Galveston or New Orleans, whichever place they could obtain the best prices for the mustangs Serita had broken to the saddle.

After the festivities, the entire Cortinas household welcomed the somber season of Lent, a quiet time when they could prepare for the coming spring and summer. Serita, too, found the slower pace gave her a chance to unwind from the rigorous task of breaking mustangs, then driving them to market.

"Lucky you're here," Rosaria told her one morning. The rest of the family had departed in various directions for the day, and they took *desayuno* alone. "We can work on your more feminine necessities. Your hands and face are becoming like tanned leather, and your hair needs attention; you spend far too much time in the sun. However do you expect to hold on to a handsome husband like *Capitán* Duval if you—"

237

"I don't," Serita interrupted, her voice flat with despondency.

Rosaria studied her cousin while she took a large swallow of *leche en chocolate*. "It's that *corrido*, isn't it? You shouldn't let things like that bother you. Someone writes a *corrido* about every unusual thing that happens nowadays, and you will have to admit your marriage was a bit unusual."

"You don't know how unusual," Serita moaned, then with a heavy sigh, she poured her grief out to her cousin. "Oh, Rosie, Tita is right. I am impulsive . . . and look where it has gotten me! I will pay for this travesty the rest of my life."

"Serita, don't be silly. The wager merely adds to the romance. After all, he not only won your hand in a card game, he married you."

"He never intended to go through with the marriage. That was my doing."

Rosaria's eyes blinked, then she shrugged. "However it came about, you got an uncommonly handsome and gallant husband out of the affair. I mean, most of us will not be so fortunate in our marriages."

"I certainly hope you are more fortunate than I." Then swearing her to secrecy, Serita told her cousin of the bargain she and Giddeon had struck the night before their wedding.

Rosie sat stunned for a moment. "He won't leave you," she said at length.

"Yes, he will. I won't ask him to stay." Rising, she quickly crossed the room and poured more hot milk into her cup of chocolate. "We made a bargain. Only . . ." Pursing her lips, she tried to keep tears

238

from falling.

Rosie sipped from her own cup. "Only you have fallen in love with him?"

After a painful glance at her cousin, Serita nodded, then burst into tears. She buried her face in her hands and sobbed. "That isn't all. I . . . I am carrying his child."

"A baby!" Rosaria squealed, embracing Serita. "How wonderful! When?"

"By the end of September."

"Of course he will stay with you now. Men love babies!"

"Not all men." Serita pulled away from her cousin's arms and seated herself once more at the table. "Only those who want families. Giddeon plans to leave as soon as the taxes are paid. He tells me that at every opportunity."

"Even since the baby?" Rosaria demanded.

"He doesn't know about the baby."

Rosaria's eyes widened. "Why have you not told him? Your worries will—"

Serita shook her head. "For so many reasons. First one thing, then another stopped me, until now . . . now I'm afraid to tell him."

"Afraid? Of what?"

Serita stared into space and thought of the beautiful yet fragile relationship she shared with this man whom she loved so desperately. Well she recalled the difficult times when they could not speak to each other without nipping and biting, as he had said. Only after she convinced him she could take care of herself did he let her come close. Now, with the baby . . .

239

"Of losing him," she whispered, "even before he leaves Los Olmos. Every time I express even the slightest affection for him, he grows distant and draws away. He says he wants to protect me from being hurt when he leaves, but . . . but I can tell he's growing fond of me. The barrier he erects is as much to protect himself as me; I know that. Oh, Rosie, don't you see? My only hope is time and patience. I must treat him like a skittish mustang . . . gently. I must not threaten him with . . . with love . . . and . . . and babies."

"You cannot keep the baby a secret forever."

"I know. But I need time . . . time for him to come to me of his own accord. Right now all he thinks of is returning to sea." Tears blurred her vision. "I love him so, but I cannot push him. I must remain strong and unthreatening . . . and pray he does not get enough money from this herd of mustangs to pay the taxes."

Rosaria rose and put her arms around her cousin, smoothing her hair in a soothing gesture. "Surely we can find some way to show him what a fool he would be to leave you and his baby."

"No, Rosie. You must promise me to do nothing. I entrusted you with this secret, now you must honor my wishes. If I can keep the secret until we return to Los Olmos, perhaps there I can find a way to explain so he will not feel trapped."

Rosaria promised and no more was said of the situation until one morning three weeks after Giddeon had left. Juan rushed in with a letter for Serita, which had arrived on a freighter with supplies for Tío Pepe's store.

"Papá sent me at once. It is from your *esposo*."

My husband! Serita tore into the letter. When she read it, her despair turned to despondency.

"What does he say?" Rosie asked, subdued now that she knew of Serita's fear.

"He is going on to New Orleans. That means another four or five weeks before he returns." She inhaled deeply, visualizing how much larger she would be by that time. Gripping her emotions then, she read the rest of the brief letter. "Jorge is fine. He is enjoying the trip, seeing sights he has never seen before."

"I'll bet!" Juan interjected. "A seaport town like Galveston is full of things young Jorge has never encountered before."

"Juan!" Rosie admonished.

"Giddeon will take care of Jorge," Serita told them confidently. "He is very fond of the boy, and Jorge thinks the sun rises and sets on his *Tío Capitán*." Thinking on this, Serita's mind drifted away from the baby for a moment. Unconsciously her finger stroked the paper Giddeon had held in his hand, and she felt comforted somewhat by the nearness this symbolized. Strange, she thought, how one could fear and be comforted by the same person. Although, of course, she didn't fear Giddeon.

It was his leaving she feared. That, and letting him know how much she dreaded him leaving her. She had told him she could take care of herself, and she must not let him think otherwise. No matter how much she hurt inside, she must pretend she didn't care that he was leaving. She must. That was their agreement. And that was the only way she

241

stood the slightest chance of winning his love.

"Another month?" Rosaria said after Juan had returned to the mercantile. "We will have to do some fancy disguising to keep him from discovering the truth until you return to Los Olmos."

Serita sighed, thinking as she had, both awake and in her dreams lately, of lying in Giddeon's arms. No amount of disguising would keep her secret, not once she lay in his arms. He wouldn't have to see with his eyes; in time her figure would grow so much his hands would discover the truth.

Jumping to her feet, she forced her mind away from such things. She had heard it said a woman's senses took flight during pregnancy. She must fight to keep hers under control.

Of course, the family discovered her secret in short order. All were overjoyed, with only Rosie knowing the truth of the matter.

At Tío Pepe's insistence, Serita and Rosaria rigged up a carriage a few days later and rode into town to fetch some cloth from the mercantile to make her new dresses.

"You and Rosie might as well put your fingers to work at something worthwhile," he told them. "You will need the clothing before that husband of yours comes back."

"We will make several full *huipils*," Rosie told her, referring to the loose, rectangular dresses worn with or without a wrapped skirt and waistband. "If we have time, we can even embroider some. And some baby clothes. We must make some baby clothes."

Tío Pepe had a pleasing selection of cloth, so much, in fact, that Serita soon became disenchanted with the whole endeavor. She had never cared for sewing, anyway, and had intended to wear some of the many different styles of *huipils* found in trunks at Los Olmos. While Rosaria engaged herself in the selection of cloth, Serita wandered about the crowded store, coming finally to the tack department, where she inspected a group of new halters.

"Mighty fine leather work."

She looked at the man, an Anglo, who examined the halters alongside her. For a moment, she thought she recognized him as someone she knew, but then she realized it was merely that she had seen him several times since arriving at Kinncy's Rancho, first at the fandango, and then on every subsequent visit she and Rosaria had made into town. A dandy, she thought involuntarily.

Nodding politely, she did not speak, but turned her attention to the saddles nearby.

"Señorita Cortinas, may I comment that you have excellent taste in equine equipment."

At her name she tensed, but continued examining the saddles. Immediately she thought of Oliver Burton. Was this man one of his spies?

"Of course, your reputation with horses is well known, señorita."

Turning to him briefly before she rejoined Rosaria, she replied in a cool manner. "My name is Mrs. Duval, sir. Mrs. Giddeon Duval. Please excuse me."

That evening at *merienda,* Tío Pepe commented on the man. "Stay away from him, Serita. His name is Enos McCaulay, and his professed goal is to obtain our land grants — by hook or by crook."

Holy Week came and the women in the Cortinas household busied themselves preparing tamales, molé sauces, and cakes for Easter when they would break the forty days of fasting.

Every evening they journeyed into town to church, and always on these trips she would see Enos McCaulay lurking here or there, staring at her. Once she mentioned it to Tío Pepe, but he received the news with such anger, she let future occurrences pass unnoticed, fearing what action her uncle might take against the gringo.

She wasn't afraid of Enos McCaulay. He couldn't touch Los Olmos. After all, wasn't that the reason she married Giddeon Duval?

But if Enos McCaulay didn't concern her, other things she heard in town did cause her to worry. Trinidad was on everyone's lips. One night at *merienda,* her cousin Estefan brought the latest word.

"Cousin Trinity is headed for trouble," he announced to the group. "He has become a regular bandit. Folks say the Republic of the Rio Grande is merely a front for his renegade army. Everybody in the Nueces Strip is after him, and half the border people in Texas and Mexico, as well."

"What do they accuse him of doing?" Serita asked.

"Stealing," Estefan replied.

"And a lot more," Roberto chimed in. "Why, I heard only today that he has been waylaying stage coaches and not only robbing the passengers, but taking the coach and horses. He leaves the passengers stranded with no food or water. One lady almost died the last time from being left out in the

244

weather so long without nourishment."

The more Serita thought on it, the more anxious she was to return home. She certainly did not want Trinidad making Los Olmos the headquarters for a gang of bandits. In her absence, he could have already done that very thing.

Worrying about Trinidad took a portion of her mind off her own situation. But, since the family was aware of her condition, she was not allowed to forget it long at a time. Tía Beatriz acted as if this baby would be her grandchild, a surprising fact, since she already had ten of her very own. And Rosaria insisted on hearing how she felt morning, noon, and night. The first time the baby moved, Rosie was as excited as Serita herself.

Almost, Serita thought, recalling the incomprehensible joy the action brought her. The baby inside her womb was alive and growing and . . .

And it belonged to Giddeon. The knowledge they had shared in the creation of a human life drew her even closer to him and left her feeling both humble and proud. And overwhelmed with melancholy. The birth of her baby and the loss of her husband became intermingled in her mind to the extent that at any given moment one would overshadow the other, leaving her in a constant state of racing between joy and sorrow.

Then he returned. Three days after Easter, he rode in without any warning and found her in a brilliant, multi-striped *huipil* of Rosaria's design. Seeing the horses approach the house, her heart throbbed in her breast and her baby moved in her womb.

They were in the backyard enjoying an early spring afternoon, she, Rosaria, Juan, and Tía Beatriz. Anxiety rose quickly, filling her senses. Torn between the desire to throw herself in his arms and the fear that he would feel the baby the instant she did so, right here in broad open daylight in front of all her relatives, she turned to her cousins with a stern look.

"Promise me," she demanded. "Promise you will not let on about the baby. I want to tell him myself . . . when we get home." Fluffing her dress about her enlarged body, she cast a worried look toward the hitching rail at the front of the house. "If he doesn't discover it immediately."

"We won't say a word, dear," Tía Beatriz assured her. "But do not worry so, he will not notice right off. With your bone structure and fitness, your condition will not be noticeable for at least another month."

Rosaria patted her shoulder. "You are not as large as you think."

Serita cast her a wistful glance. "Come with me," she whispered. "All of you. Come greet him."

Her legs wobbled on jelly-filled knees, but the sound of her family behind her gave her renewed strength. He wouldn't take her in his arms with her relatives present.

He wouldn't. She licked her lips, trying to bring moisture to her mouth. He wouldn't, but oh how she longed for him to. One look at him reaffirmed her desperate need to feel his arms around her and brought tears to her eyes.

By the time she reached the edge of the house he

246

had stepped down from the saddle and ⌐
reins around the hitching rail without ever
his eyes from her face.

Insolent green eyes, she recalled stupidly. No,
loving green eyes. He had missed her! No doubt
about that. He strode toward her; somehow she
kept her feet from running. She would be calm . . .
strong. She *would!*

He touched her first, grabbed her arms at the
shoulders, but instead of coming into his embrace,
as she so desperately wanted to do, as would have
been so natural to do, she placed her arms along
his, grasping him at the elbows, keeping the distance between them.

When he tried to pull her closer, she resisted.
"Let me look at you," she laughed, striving to greet
him casually, as friend to friend. "You aren't any
worse for the trip."

"And you . . ." he began, then cleared his throat.
"Are you all right? I worried about you . . . about
the fall you took. How is your head?" Even as he
spoke, he knew he was filling space and time with
words, when all he wanted to do was kiss her, but
she seemed hesitant here in the company of her
relatives.

"You remember Tía Beatriz?"

He nodded, then smiled an awkward greeting to
each of her cousins in turn.

Drawing him toward them, however, she reintro-
duced him, saying, "You have probably forgotten
their names." He slipped an arm about her shoulders, then started to drop it to her waist. She
caught it, edged away, and clasped his hand in hers,

247

r arms between them like schoolchil-
she felt his eyes burn into her face.
nt you something," he told her. "Come
.he docks and see it."

She held her breath to still her racing
heart.

At that moment Jorge rushed up, eagerness showing on his face.

"Now," Giddeon repeated.

She dropped his hand and stooped to hug Jorge
around the neck. *"Tío* Pepe will be home any minute; we must have *merienda."*

"It won't take long," he urged.

Her mind swam with heady passion: *I love you. I
love you. I am carrying your child*—with caution: *Do not
rush him; do not push him into a corner with your urgency.*

"Jorge . . ."—she smiled at the boy—"stand still.
Let me see how tall you are. I think you must have
grown a foot." Tousling the boy's hair, she pretended
to measure him. "How was your trip?"

"It was great, Serita. In New Orleans . . ."

Giddeon cleared his throat, then laid an arm
about Serita's shoulders. "Jorge, son, why don't
you . . ."

"Whatever it is, Giddeon, it can wait. He is
anxious to tell about his trip."

"So am I," he whispered.

For a moment his words erased everything except
his husky voice, his arm on her shoulder, and her
desperate need to feel his lips on hers. But the fear
in her heart had grown and multiplied as the baby
in her womb, and it held her back.

"We will have plenty of time to talk," she replied

248

lightly.

The instant she said it, she knew she had injured him. His arm stiffened, then dropped from her shoulders, and he started to move away.

"Of course I'm interested," she assured him hastily. "I'm just . . ." His eyes pierced hers in a moment of anguish; she read his misunderstanding clearly in his face. Then he moved toward his horse.

"Giddeon . . ."

Turning his head, he stared at her, waiting.

"I do want to hear . . ." she started. "Did you get a good price for the horses?"

He nodded.

"Enough to pay what we owe on the taxes?"

"Some of it." He stepped toward his horse.

Some of it! Not all of it! "Where are you going?"

"I have business to take care of down at the docks. I . . . I had thought you might like to come along."

She stared at him, longing to tell him how much she had missed him . . . how much she . . . Ignoring his question, she asked, "When are we going home?"

"In the morning. I booked passage on the *Paisano.* We will take it to Los Olmos Bay. I sent word for Kosta to meet us there with a wagon."

By this time he had reached the hitching rail, where he began to untie the reins. She hurried toward him, grasping the rail from the opposite side.

"Are you coming back tonight?"

He studied her hands on the rail, then covered

249

them with his own. Looking at her frankly a moment, he asked, "Would you like to . . . ah, to spend the night on the schooner?"

Her hands burned with his touch; she stared into his green eyes so long, she got a lump in her throat. "I would like to, but . . ."

"But what?" he demanded, losing patience now.

"I need to stay here. I have to finish packing, and I must tell the family goodbye, and . . . and . . ." Suddenly she could hold back no longer. Caution fled. ". . . kiss me, please, Giddeon . . ."

His lips descended as she raised on tiptoe and leaned across the hitching rail. His hands held her head—thankfully her head, she thought, as her mind swam with his kisses, his nearness, with the desperate longing she had felt for him these many weeks gone by.

When he started to move around the rail, she held him back. He lifted his face a hairsbreadth from hers. "Come with me. I'll wait while you pack. They can come to the docks to tell you goodbye in the morning. Come with me, *querida*."

His whispered plea was almost more than she could resist, yet her resolve remained great. "I cannot . . . not tonight, they wouldn't understand."

"What's to understand," he demanded. "I'm your husband, forchristssake."

She sucked in her breath. "You will return to eat with us?"

He stared long into her stony features. *Don* Miguel Cortinas, he thought, you bequeathed your daughter a stubborn head. "No."

He rode away from the Cortinas house in a huff. The last few weeks, while he went about the business of getting the herd to market, hassling for a reasonable price, and preparing for his meeting with McCaulay, Serita Cortinas de Duval had remained a thorn in his side. Not only did she haunt his every dream, but he awakened most mornings with the feel of her skin soft and warm against his own, only to find the ground rough and reality cold.

Meeting her cousins had created an even greater depth to his problem, he found, as he drove the mustangs through the damp, cold weather. By their numbers, they had overwhelmed him, but that wasn't the worst of it. Most of them were married with children, and seeing their families had stirred feelings inside him he had never experienced.

Having lived on board one ship or another since he was six years old, he had been reared without any knowledge of how families lived. Now, in adulthood, he realized he had spent his entire life outside the normal order of things. Families. The very idea gave him a feeling of being closed in and stifled.

Families. The thought always brought him back to Serita, her laughing face, the way she enjoyed being with her cousins, and the way the children gathered around her, everyone babbling in animated conversation and conviviality. He was beginning to understand her attachment to family . . . to heritage.

Most of all, however, he was haunted by Serita

Cortinas de Duval—his wife. By the glow in her eyes when she looked at him. A glow he now recognized and feared.

Families. No matter how hard she might try to hid it, Serita wanted him to remain with her and become a part of her family.

Finding the prices unsatisfactory in Galveston, he had pushed on to New Orleans. By the time he crossed the Sabine River into the United States, he had begun to sort out his life. He wouldn't send Serita to Mexico. He would buy her a house at Kinney's Rancho. That way she would be close to her cousins, and he could go on his way, assured that she and Tita and Jorge were safely ensconced in familiar surroundings. The port at Kinney's Rancho was accessible enough that he could visit them from time to time.

That was the solution, he decided, as he haggled for better prices in New Orleans. As Serita had said, the going rate for broken horses was much better in the United States than in Galveston. And in accordance with his own expectations, the United States military was everywhere. The air hummed with talk of the imminent annexation of Texas and the resulting war with Mexico.

Yes, he decided, he must get Serita out of the Nueces Strip as soon as possible. Kinney's Rancho would be the perfect place.

Dusk settled around him with the fog as he approached the *Paisano*, still smarting from her rejection. Then suddenly he glimpsed his life as it really was. He could not have things both ways. He could either take Serita and family life, or he could

252

go back to sea. To do half one and half the other would not be fair to her.

Put that way, he had no choice. He would not give up the sea. Especially not for a wife who was so mule-headed she wouldn't even embrace her husband in front of family members — when he had been away two whole months!

If she didn't want to spend the night with him, he reasoned, so much the better. That would make leaving her all the easier.

At the schooner, he checked with the skipper, a longtime friend, who insisted on giving up his own cabin for Serita and Giddeon's comfort during the trip down the coast to Los Olmos Bay.

"That little filly your man brought on board is coming along fine," Captain Swain told him. "She will have her sea legs in no time."

Giddeon followed the captain to the hold, where he studied his latest folly: a one-year-old purebred Arabian filly . . . a replacement for Barb. From the moment he saw the animal in New Orleans, visions of Serita riding Barb across the meadow, wild and free, filled his senses. Finally, he gave in and bought the animal, justifying the expense by the pleasure the horse would give Serita when she moved to town. That it assuaged some of the guilt he felt at deceiving her, he knew also.

"When's the missus coming aboard?"

Giddeon's jaw tightened involuntarily. "In the morning. She has packing to see to tonight."

At midnight, when Giddeon left the *Paisano*, fog

swirled around him like spider webs. Had it not been for the music and noise emanating from within, he would have passed by the tiny dockside cantina, so dim was the lantern glow.

Enos McCaulay stood at the bar, and Giddeon was at once swept by a sense of *dejàvu:* the smoky cantina, the card game in the far corner, McCaulay at the bar. Suddenly, he entertained the strange sensation that he could walk in here tonight and begin all over again; that if he walked backward, step by step, he could remove, as from a child's slate, everything which had transpired these last few months, since the downing of the *Estelle*, since the game of chance with Don Miguel Cortinas, since . . . since Serita . . .

"Captain Duval! Glad to see you made it back." McCaulay ordered another glass, and, with bottle in tow, led the way to a table close to the rear of the jacallike building.

"My man Felix delivered the message?" Giddeon asked.

McCaulay nodded, motioning Giddeon to a seat. "See you didn't escape the wedding noose, after all."

Giddeon shrugged.

"You sure you aren't getting to attached to this . . . ah, family you've started?"

McCaulay's words called to mind Serita's cold reception, and he bristled. Swallowing a swig of the liquid fire, he kept his peace.

McCaulay changed the subject. "What'd you hear about war plans over in New Orleans?"

"The United States is preparing. War is on everyone's lips. War and annexation."

254

"Then time is short. How soon . . . ?"

"By the end of June," Giddeon cut in. "July at the latest."

McCaulay frowned. "That's late."

"It will take that long to gather enough money to pay the taxes."

"How do you plan on convincing the . . . ah, the *señora?*"

Giddeon clenched his jaw, but remained silent once more. No use angering the man. "Leave that to me."

McCaulay shook his head. "It takes one tough sonofabitch to do what you're doing, Duval. Hope that little *señora* doesn't tighten the noose so you won't be able to get away when the time comes."

Without warning, Giddeon rose and spat his mouthful of whiskey to the earthen floor beneath his feet. "You have until June to get the fifty thousand, McCaulay. Let me down, and you'll regret it."

Chapter Eleven

During the night the wind blew a gale and by morning the skies had cleared, leaving the air fresh and clean, the sun a welcome sight.

Serita slept little. By the first cock's crow she was dressed and sitting on her trunk, waiting for the rest of the household to stir.

Jorge had stayed the night with them, and his excitement infected her. As Giddeon had indicated when he arrived, he brought her a gift, and until Jorge went to bed that night, he talked of almost nothing else.

"*Tío Capitán* made me promise to keep his secret," he told Serita a dozen times. "You will be so happy. Can we not go to the schooner now?"

By morning Serita's wits were fairly torn asunder, what with longing to be with Giddeon, anticipation of the surprise he brought her, and despair over the surprise she had for him.

Before dawn Giddeon was on the bridge, pacing, waiting, searching the road leading from town. Don Pepe promised to have Serita and Jorge at the *Paisano* by sunup, and when at last Giddeon saw them coming, his heart slapped against his ribs like waves against the hull of the *Paisano*.

She strode toward the schooner, a determined tilt to her patrician chin. He could tell her resistance to him had not diminished overnight. So much the better, he chided himself. She was better protected, angry. As was he himself. He thought of McCaulay calling him a tough sonofabitch.

Watching her now, he knew Serita Cortinas was the tough one. Thankfully. He must be tough, too, for her sake and for his own. But as she marched toward the schooner, her loose Indian-style gown flowing beneath the *rebozo* she clutched about her, his mind wandered, and he was unable to keep from imagining the pleasure of running his hands beneath her loose garments, of touching her skin with his fingers, his lips, his body.

Her hand was damp when he took it to assist her from the gangplank to the deck. *"Buenas días,"* he whispered, then repeated the greeting louder for her relatives who followed her with several trunks. "Good morning."

"Can we show her the surprise now, *Tío Capitán?"* Jorge urged.

Giddeon tousled the boy's hair. "Tell your kinfolk goodbye, son."

Serita moved as in a trance. She had spoken not a word since leaving the house. All the way to the

257

docks she clutched her stomach, while Rosaria's admonition that Giddeon wouldn't be able to tell yet, not with her hip bones still showing, vied with the truth in her mind.

The truth that Giddeon Duval knew every inch of her body by heart. His hands would immediately detect the mound her belly had become, however slight that mound might be at the moment. Or if he pulled her tightly against him, the feel of her abdomen on his would give her secret away in an instant. Rosaria had never been married. She didn't know the intimate knowledge one person could have of another. Perhaps that was the best part of love, Serita thought.

The beauty . . . the perfection . . . the completeness of being one with another person . . . with a beloved person. The intimacy of knowing before you were told, seeing before you were shown . . . loving before you were loved.

She became obsessed with the thought that if she could cover her belly with her hands, he wouldn't notice it, but she knew the opposite was true. All the way from the carriage to the schooner, she clutched her *rebozo* fiercely with both hands to keep them from shielding her secret, thereby revealing it. So that when he offered her his hand, she had to pry her fingers from the *rebozo* to grasp it.

The deck swayed beneath her feet, he caught her, and she looked into his concerned eyes.

"You'll get used to it," he assured her.

Inhaling, she pursed her lips. Suddenly she knew the future was here upon her. The time had come. She had no choice but to move from this moment to the next. His strong hands held her steady and somehow gave her strength.

"I'm fine," she told him. Quickly but sincerely then she dismissed her family with thanks and hugs and kisses and assurances she would visit again the following spring.

"That's an excellent idea," Giddeon told Tía Beatriz. "Serita spends far too much time away from the people she loves. She needs a place here in town where she can come more often."

"She is always welcome in our household," Tío Pepe responded. "But perhaps a family would be more comfortable with a town house to themselves. I will look around, see what I can find."

Serita glanced, puzzled, from one to the other of the men, but before she could respond, the captain called for the gangplank to be raised.

True to Giddeon's word, she adjusted to the swaying boat quickly enough. With an inner intensity she hadn't known she possessed, she kept her composure intact also, until he ushered her, with Jorge leading both of them, to the hold, where she stared transfixed at the little Arabian colt. In an instant, all tenseness left her body. Approaching the filly, she ran her hands down its back. Her thoughts raced, and she looked at Giddeon. "Where . . . ? Why . . .?"

He stood close beside her. The joy on his face lifted the pall she had carried like a dead weight these last few weeks.

"She's just like . . ." Serita began.

"Barb," he whispered. "I thought you could call her Barb II."

"You bought her for me?"

He grinned his dear, lopsided grin. "Don't worry. I didn't *win* her."

Serita stared at the beautiful filly through blurred vision. "She was too expensive. You should have saved the money for taxes."

"I know," he agreed. Then he turned serious. "But damnit, Serita, you earned her. You worked so hard on those horses . . . and you . . . you lost so much." He shrugged. "Consider her a late Christmas gift."

She studied the glow on his face while he caressed her with his eyes, and they both recalled Christmas Day—the horror of losing Barb, the joy of finding each other.

"I will name her Feliz Navidad."

Lifting a hand, he stroked her cheek with the back of his fingers. "Happy Christmas is a long name for such a little feller."

When his fingers touched her lips, she kissed them. "We will call her Navidad."

Intently, yet gently, he lowered his face to hers. "Or Feliz," he suggested just before he kissed her.

Fortunately, she thought later in the day, they had Jorge to dog their every step. After they fed Navidad, Giddeon showed her around the schooner, and the heat of his hand on her elbow kept her senses in a dither. They lunched with Captain Swain in a makeshift dining area set up on deck, and it was then she learned he had given over his cabin for her use.

"Wouldn't you like to rest this afternoon?" Captain Swain asked.

"Oh, no," she hastily rejected. "I want to see it all . . . to stay on deck and . . ."

"This is my wife's first ride on a sailing vessel, Swain," Giddeon told his friend. "I want her to see everything . . . to get a good idea of what my life is about."

The captain nodded his understanding, and Serita asked, "How long should the trip take us?"

"We could be at Los Olmos Bay by tonight. That is, if we don't get stuck in the mud or hung up on a sandbar."

The casual tone with which he delivered this prospect belied the real threat, Serita discovered late in the afternoon. She and Giddeon had strolled the deck, Giddeon pointing out the tops'ls, the mains'l, a for'tops'l — strange-sounding words that tripped easily from his tongue. She listened and noted, knowing well the words he had spoken at luncheon held more truth than the captain of this vessel knew. After Giddeon left, she would have this day to recall. She would imagine him on his own sailing ship — at the helm, at the stern, standing on the bridge, spyglass in hand. And she would feel closer to him.

Once Giddeon sent Jorge off to spend some time with Navidad, saying, "Stay with her awhile, son. She likely feels threatened being on such shaky ground and all alone, to boot."

As soon as Jorge departed, Giddeon guided her to the railing, where they stood shoulder-to-shoulder looking over the waves to the distant horizon. The sea breeze blew against their faces, their bodies, and occasional mists of salty spray sprinkled them.

261

"It's limitless," she said at last.

He nodded. "Imagine what it's like when we aren't hugging the coastline. The ship is just a speck, a tiny object in the huge universe of the sea."

"It reminds me of the prairies," she said. "Some places you can turn in a complete circle and see nothing to break the eye — nothing but waving grass; here it's water, instead."

"I've noticed that," he admitted.

"But on the land," she continued, "you can move around. You do not have to stay in one —"

"We move around, too. We can go anyplace this ship will take us."

"It isn't the same, somehow," she mused. "Do you not feel trapped here on this tiny ship? Like you are being held prisoner?"

Leaning on the railing now, he stared into the distance and recalled thinking the same thing about the compound at La Hacienda de los Olmos. "The ship is a part of me," he answered. "It's like . . . I don't know if I can explain it so it makes any sense, but the ship is an extension of myself. On land you have nothing so powerful, so . . ."

She smiled at him. "It's the power you like, Giddeon. Here you have complete control over this magnificent sailing vessel. You are free to go anywhere, do anything. To challenge the vast elements of nature. But you are limited, too. You are limited by this powerful contraption, because, in reality, it cannot take you every place. Only the sea is so large, you do not realize that."

He laughed. "You mean I'm so insignificant, I am lessened by this boundless space and I don't

262

even know it."

Facing him, she stared at the side of his face until he turned to look at her. "You are not insignificant, Giddeon. You are simply in love with the sea. And, as always, a person in love is blind to any imperfection in the beloved."

Slipping an arm around her shoulders, he drew her to his side, and while she pressed her cheek against his heart, they both stared back to sea. "Yes, I am in love with the sea," he said quietly. "I never denied it."

She stood beside him, relaxing against the warmth of his body. He couldn't feel the baby now, and if he could, it wouldn't make any difference. Suddenly, she saw him as she knew she would remember him always. Not on board his ship, but at the *hacienda,* standing on the rooftop, searching the horizon.

"All the time you spent on the rooftop at *la casa grande,* you weren't looking for Felix . . . or for anything in particular. You were . . . you were simply lost at sea."

He kissed the top of her head through the *rebozo* she had wrapped around her. "I knew you would understand," he whispered. "That's why I wanted us to come by ship. If you can understand me, it will be easier for you . . . for both of us."

She understood, she thought sadly, but would *he?* How would he feel, when he learned . . . ?

Suddenly the deck lurched forward with such force that her feet skidded out from under her. She grasped for the rail, but Giddeon caught her before she fell.

The captain rushed forward. "We need your help, Duval," he said. "And the help of your men."

"A sandbar?" Giddeon asked.

"Mud," the captain answered, already hurrying to alert his crew.

"What will you do?" Serita asked as Giddeon ushered her toward Captain Swain's cabin.

"Push it out," he swore under his breath. "That's why I like to stay off the coast."

"But you can't jump into the ocean . . ."

"The water isn't over waist deep," he assured her. "You stay in the cabin until we're finished. I'll go get Pablo and Jorge. It won't take long . . . I hope."

She lighted the lamps in the small cabin and tried to read, but the light wasn't strong enough. When she opened a porthole, the sun was already so low it gave little additional light to the cabin, so she closed it against the sea spray.

How could he love the sea? she wondered. Everything was damp and salty and smelled like fish.

At the thought of fish, her stomach swayed and she knew it was time to get off her feet. Turning back the covers on the small bed, she found them to be immaculate, instead of louse-ridden, as she had feared. *Capitán* Duval definitely had influence.

Removing her shoes, she lay her *rebozo* aside and climbed into bed, pulling up the covers to ward off the chill in the late April air.

Two hours later, Giddeon returned. She awoke at the sound of the door slamming, to see him standing in the dimly lit cabin holding a tray of food, clothed only in long johns.

Throwing back the covers, she jumped to her

264

feet. "What are you doing?"

"Delivering supper?" he announced with a grin.

"In your . . . your . . ?"

He placed the tray on the captain's table. "It was a dirty job, digging this old tub out of the mud. Jorge loved it, though, especially bathing off afterward. Even if it was a salt bath." While he talked, he lifted the cloth on the tray of food. "Ugh. You may have hit the mark about being held prisoner. This supper isn't much more than broth and hardtack."

Serita rummaged in the sack of food Tía Beatriz had insisted on sending along. "Tamales," she said, "tortillas, and some of Tío Pepe's special jerky."

Giddeon laughed. "By special, you mean gutburning." One after the other he opened and closed cabinet doors, until he found what he wanted. "A bottle of port to warm our innards . . . in case the jerky doesn't do the trick."

Disarmed by the preposterous look of him, she stared unabashed. "I suppose you intend to dine in your long johns."

As quickly as a blue norther was wont to blow up on the sultry gulf coast, the mood in the cabin changed from casual camaraderie to profound longing. The room separated them, and for a moment neither could move, the space was so charged with emotion.

She pressed her lips together and swallowed the lump in her throat. Then he stepped forward, and suddenly she found herself in his arms. His husky voice sent shivers down her spine.

"How about if we don't dine for a while?"

She answered with her lips . . . on his . . . kissing and being kissed, caressing and being caressed, loving and being loved, forgetting . . .

Forgetting everything except the moment, the moment they had both waited and longed for these many, many weeks.

Clumsy in his haste, he fumbled with the pins in her hair, until he had them strewn about the floor at their feet. The long black strands fell in gentle waves over his hands, and he moved his lips from hers and buried them in her hair, groaning then, when she kissed his neck and nibbled at his ear.

With his fingers, he traced her spine from her neck to its base and back, sending fingers of fire through her body with every touch. 'Hm . . . no corset." He nipped her lips with his own. "I like this kind of dress."

"I made it," she whispered into his lips, moving her body against his even though she had promised herself she wouldn't.

"I didn't know you liked to sew," he mumbled. Gathering clumps of fabric in his hands, he finally reached her petticoats and blindly felt for the ties.

Instinctively, she moved back. "I don't . . ."—she untied and dropped the petticoats to the floor—"but you were gone, and I didn't have anything else to do."

While she spoke, he managed to pull her dress over her head and drop it to the floor with her hairpins. He studied her in the dim light, then ran his hands from her shoulders over her chest, to her breasts, which he clasped in his hands a moment, before he untied and discarded her chemise.

When she stood before him half naked, she was glad for the dimly lit cabin. His hands, rough, firm, and wonderfully familiar, soothed away her tension. But when he reached her waist, she moved aside, untied her own pantaloons, then began to unbutton his long johns, keeping him at a distance in this manner until they were both unclothed.

Then she grasped him about the neck with clasped hands and pulled him urgently toward the bed. "Come to me quickly." For a time, however, she kept her arms between them, twining her fingers in the hair on his chest.

Kissing her desperately all the while, he ran a hand up and down her back, across her buttocks, and down one thigh, tantalizing her with unbearable, quivering yearnings.

"I knew the time you spent at Kinney's Rancho would be good for you." Moving his lips across her face, he rested them at last on her forehead. "You've put on some weight."

She froze at his words.

"It's all right," he soothed. "I don't mind. In fact, you had me worried. You lost too much while you worked with those blasted mustangs."

She exhaled and moved her face back, reaching for his lips with her own. Oh, how she had missed him. His voice, his touch, his kiss, his body.

He kissed her deeply, as he had in his dreams. This, he decided, was definitely more pleasing. And she responded to his deepened kisses—drawn into a web of confidence. Since he hadn't already discovered her secret, perhaps he wouldn't—not this time. And right now, *this* was the only time that mattered.

Gliding his fingers through her hair, he traced the outline of her face, her neck, her chest, at last capturing one of her breasts, where he kneaded its pliant tip to a rigid peak, all the while thinking how his memory had failed him.

She was even better than he recalled, when, in fact, he had thought her perfect to begin with. It must have been the absence, he decided, covering her breast now with his lips, teasing its tip with his teeth, feeling her writhe with pleasure beneath him.

It must have been the absence, he thought again, for everything about her was heightened, somehow, larger, more full of life, more beautiful and radiant.

Yes, she was tense, but so was he. This mess they got themselves into would not be easily resolved. Very likely, the only good thing to come of the madness they created would be their few moments of pleasure, like tonight, when the masks dropped away with their clothing, leaving them free to express their deepest, most fervent desires.

Lifting his lips, he traced a trail of kisses back to her lips. "Do you feel it, too?" he whispered, his lips brushing hers in a sensual manner that caused hers to tremble.

Afraid of his meaning, she tried to wriggle her hips farther away from him. Instead of answering, she pulled his lips to hers, but, after a moment, he lifted his face once more.

"It's even better now than before, isn't it?" he asked. "I mean . . ." As he spoke, he caressed her breasts one in each hand. ". . . even your breasts seem fuller, like you are bursting with . . ."

Serita felt as though a battle were being fought

inside her body—one side pommeling her with fear, the other with unbearable, sweet desire. Did he know? Did he not know? Would he find out to-night? Or did she have time left . . . precious time in which to win his love?

"I've always known you were the most beautiful woman in the world, but now . . . from the time I first saw you yesterday . . . somehow you've grown more beautiful in my absence."

As he spoke, one hand left her breast and began tracing a trail of fire down her body. Deftly, she twisted her hips, and his fingers brushed across her hip bone, instead of over her abdomen. Without appearing to notice, he traveled on to the curly black patch of hair, and she relaxed and pressed sensually against his questing hand, eager to love and be loved by this beloved man—her husband.

She wanted to tell him that if she had changed, it was because of him—because of his love and his loving, because he had left her with the seed of his progeny growing strong inside her, because he had returned to her . . .

For however brief a time. But she didn't.

Caressing his back with her hands, she kissed him fervently, kindling them both with passions raging out of control. No thoughts now of discovery or abandonment, not with his lips on hers. No thoughts of rejection while his hands plied her flesh to a fevered pitch. No thoughts of sorrow, only of joy, as his body curled around hers, wrapping her in a cocoon of sweet, unspeakable yearnings, desperate to break free.

Finally, at her urging, he moved above her and

filled her with the physical presence of his love. Joined once more, their bodies moved as on a tumultuous sea, cresting at length with such might that they lay for a time, entwined in a tangled heap.

Their bodies were damp and their skin clung together, reminding her of her own impulse to cling to *him*, though she knew she could not. Shifting to one side, she looked into his eyes; he stared at her through the dim light.

For a time they gazed quietly at each other, neither anxious to break the magic of the moment by expressing joy in something they knew was limited. Finally, he planted a firm, solid kiss on her forehead.

"You taste like salt water," she whispered, nipping his neck with her tongue. Clasping his head in both hands then, she drew his lips to hers and kissed him deeply, urgently. And he reciprocated, finally tracing kisses down her neck, across her damped chest, tasting, then urgently plying a breast with his lips, his mouth, his teeth.

"And you taste like heaven." Staring again into her loving eyes, he moved his hands over her satiny skin, caressing once more her breasts, the hollow between them, her midriff. At the feel of her fingers in his hair, he sighed deeply, enjoying to the fullest this magnificent, loving woman, who, knowing he would stay with her but a short time, nevertheless gave herself so completely to the task of loving him. Eager to touch all of her, he suddenly splayed his fingers wide and ran his flattened palm across her ribs from side to side, then lower, spanning her abdomen.

"Serita, Serita . . ."

The baby moved—a slight, almost imperceptible flutter which could have been the protestations of an empty stomach, except for the other telltale signs, except for the intimacy they shared. His hand stilled over the spot, then continued to gently, but methodically now, stroke the mounded surface of her abdomen.

Her heart had stopped with his hand. Tears sprang quickly to her eyes, but she squenched her lids against them.

"Serita . . . ?"

She couldn't answer; the words stuck in her throat. Looking at him now, scarcely breathing, she watched the truth grow in his eyes. Quickly, she covered his hand with both of her own, holding it firmly over her belly.

He turned his face away, and for what seemed like an eternity, she watched him stare at her belly and wondered desperately what he was thinking. But he said nothing, and she couldn't recall ever feeling so lonely in her life . . . not when Juan was killed, not when *Papá* left. Finally, she could stand it no longer.

With trembling hands, she turned his face to hers. "Talk to me, Giddeon. Please."

His eyes expressed a helplessness she had never seen there. "How long have you known?"

"A while," she whispered.

His brain swirled like a hurricane with debris from the past, the present, the future. Nieves's warning came back to him, clear and certain.

"When you fell . . . you knew?"

Pursing her lips, she nodded, still holding back tears, holding in her escalating fears.

"Yet you went right ahead breaking horses? And the trail drive . . . ?" She could have been killed . . . or the baby could have . . . The *baby* . . . His hand tightened over her abdomen—

As though he intended to clutch the little thing and pull it out through her skin, she thought frantically. "Giddeon, don't . . ." She stared at his eyes; her words died away. He didn't even hear her. He looked at her, but his thoughts were someplace else.

His baby. The idea flooded him with emotions both familiar and foreign. *His* baby . . . and hers . . . *Their* baby. Husband and wife and child.

Family. Home.

Land.

Prison.

Jumping from the bed, he found his grip and drew out a fresh shirt and breeches, which he proceeded to struggle into. The urgency which gripped him was unfamiliar—only the fear was real. It was like standing on the beach when the tide went out, stranding him on shore . . . away from his beloved sea. And every grain of sand that washed from under his feet was another dream lost to him forever.

She sat up, giving no thought to clothing. "Giddeon, talk to me. Please."

Her soft voice sent tremors through his anguish . . . tremors of desire and guilt—sickening guilt— and anger. Enos McCaulay's words came to him through his runaway senses: Hope the little señora

272

doesn't tighten the noose . . . tighten the noose . . . tighten the noose.

"I am not staying!" he shouted.

Unsteadily, she rose to her feet.

"You have known that from the beginning of this . . . this arrangement. I am not staying!"

She watched him pull his breeches on, thrusting one leg at a time into the garment with such ferocity she fully expected to hear the fabric rip. "I didn't ask you to."

Buttoning the placket, he grabbed for his shirt. The walls of La Hacienda de los Olmos closed in around him, smothering . . . "You can't hold me."

"Hold you?!" Although she strove to remain calm, her anguish turned to anger. She understood his fears even if he did not, even if he lashed out at her when it was also himself he blamed; but her own hurt was great, as well, and would not be denied. "I have no intention of trying to hold you. I can take care of myself, I told you that."

"Yes," he responded, angrily stuffing the tails of his shirt into his waistband. "You can take care of yourself. But what about a . . . a baby?" He spat the word with such vehemence, she cringed.

"It is *my* baby!" she yelled at him, tears spilling now against all her best efforts. "Do not give it another thought. I can take care of myself *and* my baby."

He grabbed her arms with the same ferocity he had used to put on his clothing. "It's *my* baby, too." His eyes swept her body, still unclothed and trembling, then without warning he clasped her to him fiercely. "Forchristssake, Serita. You and you alone

273

are all a man could ever desire. Now a baby . . . ?
Will there be no end to the misery I wrought with
that damnable wager?"

Chapter Twelve

He left the cabin then, before she had time to gather her wits and tell him the only misery wrought by the wager would be his leaving, that, though unplanned, the baby was not a disaster, but a wonderful accident — a fateful gift to keep and to hold, to love and to cherish . . . for her alone.

A permanent sense of numbness settled over her while she redressed, then sat in an armchair beside the table. Memories and dreams washed over her in great swirls, like a cold tide in wintertime. She dosed in the chair, and when morning came, the fear she had awakened to for so many weeks now — Giddeon discovering her pregnancy — was gone, replaced by an emptiness of which she became acutely aware the moment she stepped onto the deck and saw him standing at the helm.

Jorge had come for her, saying the landing at Los Olmos Bay was in sight. And sure enough, when she went on deck, she saw the familiar beach in the distance, and as they drew nearer, the shape of a wagon took form. Kosta had come for them. He would take them home; they would capture another herd of mustangs; she would break them; and in that manner they would pay the taxes, and Giddeon would leave.

How simple it all sounded. Until she stepped onto the deck and saw him standing with his back to her, Jorge already close by his side.

Fortunately, she thought later, his back was turned, giving her time to collect her wits.

Because *he* was definitely composed. The instant his dispassionate green eyes swept her, she knew the events of last night had set the course their lives would follow until he left. The fear inside her heart turned to a leaden sort of dread. He might as well have already left Los Olmos, the distance between them was now so great. How would she bear it? How would she ever bear it?

Without so much as a flicker of recognition, he acknowledged her presence, then turned to Jorge. "Help your aunt into the dinghy, son." After which, he began issuing orders left and right: "Load the supplies. Bring *Navidad* on deck. Lower the dinghy."

To her dismay, everyone obeyed him—Jorge and herself in a small boat with one of the schooner's sailors to row them ashore; Pablo and Giddeon swimming Navidad to shore.

All the way to the beach, Serita's mind revolved around one inconsequential thought: How fortunate she had not named the new filly Feliz. Happy was something she did not expect to be for a very long time. But with Navidad and the new baby, she assured herself, she would learn to enjoy life. In time.

Kosta helped her ashore and handed her onto the wagon seat. She watched Giddeon tie Navidad to the tailgate, while Jorge climbed into the bed and took a place next to the filly's lead rope. After they loaded the supplies into the wagon, Kosta started to climb into the back with Pablo and Jorge, but Giddeon stopped him.

"Drive. I'll ride back here."

Shrugging his disinterest, Kosta climbed onto the wagon seat beside Serita, flicked the reins, and they started home.

The sun was already bright by the time they began the ten-mile journey to the compound. In the six weeks since they left, the grass had greened up and a multitude of various-hued wildflowers blossomed gaily. Huisache bloomed yellow and delicate. With a deep draft of air, she filled her lungs and let the essence of springtime recharge her spirits.

How relieved she was to be home! Here, she was safe. Here, she could deal with heartaches and disappointments. Here, where her ancestors had survived before her, she, too, would survive. As she had told Giddeon, she could take care of herself. Here at Los Olmos she could take care of herself and her baby.

"How are things at the *hacienda?*" she asked Kosta.

He shrugged. "Same as when you left. Delos and me, we've been keeping an eye on ol' *Ebanol*. His new herd is coming along fair."

"Good," she responded, quickly filling her mind with plans for the next *caballado*. "We can bring them in this week. I will begin work —"

"No, Serita. You won't."

277

At the command, her head spun around; her eyes caught the startled look on Kosta's face, then settled on Giddeon's icy stare. It was the first time he had spoken directly to her this entire day, and she had half-hoped he would keep his silence. His presence was difficult enough, but she knew she could handle it, if she didn't have to deal directly with him. Now, like hot coffee poured into a cup on a cold morning, his voice diffused her numbness, until at last the intense hurt within her rose and turned to anger. And in that moment she knew how she would handle his distance—the same way he intended to, the way they had handled it in the beginning: their love and hopeless longing would smother beneath a blanket of anger and bickering.

"What do you mean?" she challenged, staring into his cold eyes.

"I mean you won't . . . you can't . . . break any more horses," he repeated.

With raw determination, she elevated her chin and pierced him with a steady gaze. "I certainly can—and what is more, I will."

Kosta drew up on the reins, and Serita turned to see a mother roadrunner flutter across the road on stubby wings, followed by two very small duplicates of herself.

"If you don't have any better sense than to endanger your own life," Giddeon continued in a truculent tone, "at least think of . . ."

She felt Kosta turn to stare at her, and her face flushed with embarrassment, which only fueled her disappointment . . . and her anger. "That I should have had better sense has already been determined,

278

capitán. But that has nothing to do with breaking horses—a chore which I intend to commence within the week."

"Like hell you will," he spat. "A woman in your condition cannot do that kind of work."

"This woman will."

The road ran along the creekbank for the most part, and now they passed beneath new-leafed branches of a stand of ebony trees; their graying seed pods mingled with green leaves and twigs to form a crunching carpet beneath the wagon wheels. From high overhead bickering calls of a family of Green Jays broke through the charged atmosphere in the wagon, and she looked up to see emerald-green bodies with royal-blue heads bobbing about in the treetops. The thought that all families argue and fight crossed her mind, but the notion quickly fled before an onslaught of despair. Hers wasn't a family . . . not in that sense. Hers was only half a family. And all the bickering in the world would not change that fact.

Suddenly Kosta broke into the battle with one word which brought them all to attention. "Smoke!"

Following his pointing finger, they saw an ugly black stack of smoke billow above the far trees.

"*¡La casa grande!*" Pablo intoned.

Serita caught a ragged breath. Giddeon swore. Kosta whipped up the horses, and they raced toward the growing black plume.

"So much of the house is adobe," Kosta said. "I doubt if much of it will burn."

Giddeon had moved to a position behind the wagon seat, while he and Serita exchanged their

279

previous barbs. Now he stood behind them, holding to the back of the seat. "Except the interior . . ." — he spoke as though thinking aloud — "all the relics . . ."

"Relics?" she questioned, furious with his choice of words. "To you they may be relics; to me they are heirlooms."

"Sorry," he answered in a sheepish tone. "I didn't mean it that way."

"What about Tita?" Jorge asked from directly behind her. "And Nieves?" Serita heard his voice tremble. Turning, she intended to help him onto the seat beside her. But Giddeon had knelt, and now held the boy close.

"Don't worry about them, son," he said. "Delos is there . . . and Felix. They're good men in a crisis."

"Good men!" Serita scoffed. "If they are so good, how did the fire start?"

No one answered her, and too late she realized that in her anguish, she had lashed out not only at Giddeon, but also at Kosta, who had done her no harm at all.

"I'm sorry," she mumbled. "I didn't mean . . ."

Her words died away on the wind, and no one answered. Each person in the wagon was entangled in his own fears. When at last they crossed the creek and topped the rise, the sight they saw multiplied their terrors by tenfold.

True to Kosta's predictions, most of the walls were still standing, but flames leapt from every window and doorway within sight, and smoke billowed from the center of the compound, where the courtyard was. Curiously, Serita wondered what could have been in the courtyard to cause so much smoke.

No one spoke, because, Serita thought later, every one was like herself, having nothing sensible in his brain. Only after he jumped from the wagon, leaving her neck suddenly cold, did she realize Giddeon had had his hand on her shoulder, and that knowledge assuaged her fears with a small bit of comfort.

Stupefied by the horror before them, one by one the occupants of the wagon stumbled to the ground. Serita felt torn by two separate forces: one to find Tita, the other to turn and run for fear of what she would find when she started looking.

Suddenly the need to choose was taken from her. Felix bolted from around the north side of the compound.

"Thank God you've come, Capt'n."

The assemblage raced toward him.

"Where's Tita?" Serita demanded. "And Nieves . . . ?"

"And Abril and Lupe?" Jorge interjected.

"They're safe," Felix told them quickly. "They're at the old vaqueros' barracks west of the house. But Delos . . ."

"What happened?" Giddeon asked, and, without thinking, Serita grasped his arm in support.

"He got himself pretty burned up," Felix said. "But Nieves says he'll make it through."

By this time, the entourage trailed at a brisk pace behind Giddeon, with Serita fast on his heels. Felix kept up, answering Giddeon's questions while the others strained to hear the story themselves.

"A dozen or so armed men," he said. "They

281

swarmed over the place like bees, Capt'n. No way we could stop them."

Giddeon nodded. "We've always known they could invade at will. I just didn't figure—"

"What did they do?" Serita asked. "How did you escape being slaughtered?"

"It was mighty peculiar, ma'am," Felix answered. "Most battles, the assailants go for the people, but these folks were set on burning the house, and that's what they done."

"You mean they let everyone get away?" Giddeon asked.

Felix nodded. "They came at us from all four sides. Hit as soon as Kosta was out of earshot, the way it looked. Took us unawares by creeping up with the shadows at daybreak. Before we knew what was what, they were swarming all over the place. The womenfolk went to screaming. I tell you it was enough to raise the dead. Delos and me, we got off a few shots, but there were so many of them, all over the place. We run out of ammunition, and they wasn't about to let us get another stock. When they started breaking up the furniture and burning the place, we figured we'd best get the womenfolk away from the compound."

"How did Delos get burned," Serita asked.

"It was when he went back to fetch that trunk. *Doña* Ana, she carried on like it was more important than anything in the world. She kept on fretting over it, and finally Delos tried to slip in and bring it out. But by then the fire had pretty much destroyed the second story. A timber landed on his back, and he crawled out."

He shook his head and studied Giddeon a moment. "They just watched him. Didn't shoot or nothing. Of course, they didn't help him, neither. On top of that, they carried off the blasted trunk."

They reached the barracks out of breath. Everyone talked and laughed and cried at the same time. Giddeon knelt before the bunk and examined Delos. Nieves rushed to Pablo's arms, and Serita and Jorge fell to their knees in front of Tita.

The voices were but a jumble of comforting words, until Tita raised hers above the crowd.

"Capitán," she called. When Giddeon came to her, Serita moved aside. He knelt and lifted Tita's frail hands to his lips.

"I'm so glad you are unharmed, Tita," he told her before bestowing a kiss on her forehead.

"I am unharmed, yes, but we are missing a valuable document. You must go now, while the trail is still fresh. You must retrieve the land-grant documents or Los Olmos is lost to us."

He didn't actually tell her goodbye, Serita thought after he rode away. But he did tip his hat and nod in a curt fashion. And his eyes . . . his handsome green eyes showed signs of worry. She chose to think he worried over her.

The trail was still fresh and easy to follow, although it led in an unexpected direction. When Giddeon questioned whether the Burton ranch wasn't north instead of west, Felix scratched his head.

"We're heading straight for the road to San Antonio de Bexar."

Giddeon turned in the saddle. "Where you saw Burton and Trinidad? How far is that cantina?"

"Not far," Felix responded. The men sunk spurs and raced across the new stand of switchgrass.

Taking only Felix with him, Giddeon had left Kosta to help Pablo protect the womenfolk back at the *hacienda*. In doing so, he had briefly thought of Serita's playful rejoinder that he sent Felix on missions because he was the only one of them not afraid of the dark. Images of Serita, smiling and playful, flitted through his brain, bringing a lump to his throat and an ache to the pit of his stomach. Serita and her baby.

His baby. It was already moving, he reflected without design, feeling again the intimate flutter against his palm. Did that mean the child would be strong? Then his memories became visions of the future and his resolve hardened. He would have to be strong, his son, what with the uncertain course his parents had set his life upon.

Turning to the side, Giddeon spat his wrath to the ground below. His son would survive. Hadn't he himself been orphaned at an early age. Perhaps his own life hadn't been all roses, but neither had it been bitter. His life was what he had made it, and he hadn't turned out half—

With a disgusted grunt, he brought his train of thought to a halt. "What do you make of this nonsense?" he asked Felix.

Felix frowned at Giddeon a moment, then shrugged. "Burton likely hired the job done."

They crossed a marsh, climbed a rise, and sat

beneath a spreading liveoak. The country before them had become increasingly barren and flat. "This may turn out to be like our first trip to Los Olmos. Fields of prickly pear, a few mesquite trees, and salty creek water."

"We should find fresh water, traveling this far north," Felix responded in an inattentive tone; then his voice turned serious. "We've lost some of the tracks."

Giddeon studied the ground, nodded in acknowledgment, and the men painstakingly retraced their trail to the opposite side of the marsh. Finally, Felix called, "Over here." And when Giddeon rode around the marsh, he saw where at least six horses had veered to the north.

Giddeon looked north, toward Burton's ranch, then back west. "How far to that cantina?"

"Not over half a mile," Felix told him.

"It doesn't stand to reason they would take the documents to a cantina, but—"

"We haven't lived this long by taking the reasonable bet, Capt'n. Want me to ride to the cantina, and you go ahead to Burton's place?"

Giddeon pursed his lips. "We'll stick together. Burton didn't steal that deed to destroy it. There's time enough to go both places."

It was already midafternoon, and by the time they reached the jacal hut that served as a cantina, both men were not only tired but hungry.

Situated in the middle of a scrawny grove of liveoaks, the nameless cantina looked as if a good wind would blow it over. After skirting the perimeter at a distance, Giddeon studied the lathered horses hitched to the trees.

He nudged his mount alongside Felix's. "I'm going in. Hold my reins, and keep a lookout on that window . . . and on those horses over yonder. When I flush them out, make note which direction they scatter."

The same packed earth that surrounded the building on the outside formed the floor inside. Six men occupied the room, a small room that could accommodate no more than twenty customers at the most.

Giddeon stood in the doorway scrutinizing each man in turn. He finished with the bartender, who was a mirror image of the others, from his nondescript loose cotton clothing to his drooping black mustache matted with the residue of meals past, which gave him a perpetual hangdog expression.

Giddeon's hunger pangs disappeared as if by magic. Combined with the filth, the combative expression on the faces of the men would in other cases have sent him packing. Instead, he sauntered to the bar, his eyes vigilant, his back smarting from an expected attack, either by gun or by blade.

"Drinks for the house . . ."—speaking in fluent Spanish, he tossed a handful of coins onto the plank counter—"to honor Don Miguel Cortinas, the father of my wife." Wary and unwelcoming still, the men nevertheless shuffled toward the bar, where the bleary-eyed bartender poured mescal from an earthen jar into filthy tin cups.

Giddeon stopped at the end of the bar, his back to the window protected from the outside by Felix. As soon as each man had taken his cup, but before any had swallowed the foul-smelling liquor, he drew his guns on them. The bartender moved, and Giddeon fired, splitting the plank bar in half. "I am not alone," he told them, still speaking their own tongue. "One false move from any of you, and my men will open fire on everyone here. Now, very carefully step apart, so I may inspect you further."

"Señor," the bartender implored, "we are poor but honest *peóns*. We have nothing that would be of value to a man of your means."

"I seek only the truth," Giddeon replied, "and the evil men who betrayed those of their own heritage."

"Such men will not be found here," the bartender told him.

"Then have no fear." Motioning to the man at his left, he continued. "Step closer now, one at a time. If you were not involved in the burning of *la casa grande* at La Hacienda de los Olmos, you have nothing to fear."

No one moved a muscle at his words. Not even when Giddeon stared hard at each man in turn did any of their eyes waver. Then he sank in the spurs. "My compadre is waiting outside the door. You will go out now, one at a time. If you had nothing to do with the raid on Los Olmos, you will be free to go. If he recognizes you from the raid, he will shoot you on sight."

It was as though he set loose a can of worms, Giddeon thought later, for no sooner had he spoken those last words than the men in front of him began to tremble and shake.

"*Por Dios, señor,*" the bartender cried. "Your man could make a mistake. An honest man could die."

Giddeon shook his head as though unconcerned. "My man is good," he replied. "He spent many years at sea, executing pirates."

A ruckus set up among the men. *"Por favor, señor."* "I am not a thief, *señor."* "I have a large family, *señor."* "Do not kill me, I am an honest man, *Señor Capitán."*

"Felix . . ." — Giddeon raised his voice and called behind him out the window — "I'm sending them out. Do not let a raider get away."

Then suddenly he appeared to have second thoughts. "There is one way to save all this trouble," he told them. *"Mi esposa* — my wife — daughter of Don Miguel, has lost not only her home, but treasured possessions of her family, valuable only to her. Any man who can guide me to the trunk that was stolen from Los Olmos — its contents still intact — will be free to go, no questions asked."

Again he watched the group of men closely, but no one stepped forward. He shrugged and motioned to the man to his left to leave the jacal.

He had to cock his pistol and threaten to execute him on the spot to get him out the door, however. All the while, the other men pleaded and begged and Giddeon watched them carefully. When Felix called to him, he sent the second man out.

All eyes were white, as those inside waited for a gunshot. When one did not come, Giddeon shrugged. "Two honest men, let us see if we have three in this wretched group." The barrel of his pistol moved to the third man, then suddenly, without any indication as to why he changed his mind, he motioned for the bartender to leave the building,

288

and the overweight, middle-aged man staggered toward the door with the halting steps of advanced years.

Still no shot, and those inside the hut were becoming more brave, all except the third man, whom Giddeon had bypassed in favor of sending forth the bartender. Next, he motioned to the sixth man, then the fifth, then the fourth, giving the impression of having reversed the order of his interrogation, when in fact he had other plans.

The third man in line had given Giddeon cause to think, and thinking, he saw a guilty man. The man had begun sweating profusely at the mention of the trunk. Then as his turn approached, instead of beseeching Giddeon directly, his eyes darted from one man to the next, as though he had something to say, yet was afraid . . . He looked guilty as hell, Giddeon thought.

When the room was empty save for the two of them, Giddeon stared at him hard. Idly he twirled the chamber of his pistol, while the man shifted from foot to foot.

"What is your name?" Giddeon asked.

"Tomás, *Señor Capitán*."

"How do you know me?"

The man's eyes widen into saucers.

"You call me *Señor Capitán*. How do you know that name?"

Tomás licked his lips. Giddeon watched his Adam's apple bob.

"I am a man of my word. If you tell me where to find the trunk, we will not harm you."

Tomás's feet shifted on the hard-packed earth,

and Giddeon noticed for the first time the man's boots.

"Where did you get those boots?"

No answer.

"Such fine black boots on a *peón* like yourself. I have a notion to take you back to the *hacienda* and let my wife examine those boots." The man squeezed his eyes shut. "Better yet, I will send you out the door to Felix."

"No, *Señor Capitán. Por favor.*"

"I am reasonable," Giddeon replied. "The trunk for your life."

"They will kill me."

"No. They are already gone. My man sent them away as they came out the door. But the longer you take to join them, the more suspicious they will become."

Still Tomás hesitated.

Suddenly, Giddeon grabbed the *peón* by his grimy shirtfront. "I am out of patience, Tomás. Talk to me or walk out that door. Now."

"*Sí, Señor Capitán,* I talk. *Sí.*"

Tomás directed Giddeon to another jacal a mile away from the cantina, he said, and Giddeon prepared to leave the jacal, but the frightened young man called him back.

"Take me with you, *Señor Capitán.* They will kill me now, for certain. *Por favor,* take me with you."

Giddeon squinted at the man through the dim light.

"Please . . ." Tomás repeated.

With an indifferent shrug, Giddeon agreed, and the three of them mounted and rode off toward the

290

second jacal.

"We'd best take care, Capt'n," Felix warned. "This is the way three of the men headed, lickety-split."

And sure enough, when they arrived at the thicket of retama surrounding the jacal, they spied three of the horses they had seen previously outside the cantina.

"A precaution," Giddeon said, as he bound Tomás with a piece of rawhide from his saddlebags, then gagged him with an old kerchief. "Friends gained in the manner we acquired you are not always the most trustworthy."

This hut had no windows and, like the cantina, only one door. Giddeon gulped a draft of fear, wished it were courage, and nodded with a grin to Felix. "No better time." With that, the two of them burst into the hut, firing their pistols at the ceiling.

Giddeon immediately holstered his handgun and gripped his rifle at hip position, pointing it directly at the three men who sat cross-legged on the floor, a candle burning in a tin cup in the middle of the circle where they played cards. "Hold still, boys, this will only take a minute."

While Felix trained his rifle on them, Giddeon searched the premises, found the trunk, and, with an audible sigh, pulled the land-grant documents from its interior. Quickly, he stuffed them inside his shirt and slammed the top of the trunk.

"Looks like two of you boys will have to ride double," he mused. "Get up from there now, and carry this trunk outside."

Outside, in the diminishing daylight, he studied the men with consternation. They didn't look like

Oliver Burton's men. For the second time, he wondered why Burton would take to hiring out his dirty work, when he had Cow Boys enough to accomplish any job he dreamed up. After killing Barb, burning *la casa grande* should not have been too harsh a task.

While Felix held a gun on the men, Giddeon helped secure the trunk to one of the saddles.

"Did you find what you were looking for?" Felix asked.

"No," Giddeon answered. "The contents of this trunk have been disturbed."

"Are we going to Burton's from here?" Felix wanted to know.

"No. We're taking these boys back to the *hacienda.* They can help rebuild some of the property they destroyed today."

On the ride back to Los Olmos, Giddeon wondered why he had felt the need to lie to Felix about the documents. The words had come out on impulse, but now he decided he had chosen the right road. If whoever stole the documents thought them still missing, perhaps they could flush the culprits out of hiding. And until they had all their enemies front and center, they would run the risk of being shot in the back.

The buildings on La Hacienda de los Olmos did not matter to Enos McCaulay. McCaulay wanted the land; he also demanded a clear title, and, for that, Giddeon needed the original land-grant documents. He patted his shirt and felt the ancient sheepskin scratch his skin. Today, he had been lucky.

When they rode up to the barracks at Los

Olmos, however, he began to think it was but a brief streak of luck.

Smoke still circled above the crumbling adobe walls; the stench of it filled the air for miles. In lieu of candles or lanterns, which had all burned with the house, torches glowed along the front of the old barracks.

"Looks like we've got company," Felix said.

Giddeon studied the dark figures moving like ants against the backdrop of the building, silhouetted in the glow of a campfire.

"That bastard Trinidad Cortinas," he swore. "And his *army*."

"His army seems to have dwindled," Felix said. "Or else he only brought part of it."

Lupe and Abril worked beside the fire: Lupe cooked the tortillas from the dough Nieves prepared, while Abril took a cooked tortilla, wrapped it around a hunk of cheese and fried it on a flat skillet.

Drawing rein outside the ring of light, Giddeon and Felix pushed their motley prisoners ahead of them toward the campfire. Nieves looked up from where she prepared tortillas. "It is good you brought supplies, *Señor Capitán*. At least we have food."

"Yes," he answered curtly, his attention on Trinidad and two of his men who sat cross-legged on the ground behind Nieves, stuffing their mouths with tortillas and beans, oblivious to—or ignoring, Giddeon decided—the goings-on around them. Their clothing was filthy, their appearance ragtag, at best, and they ate as though they were half starved.

Lupe took an uncooked ball of tortilla dough

293

from Nieves, slapped it back and forth against her palms until she had a thin, flat circle. Then she dropped it onto a sizzling skillet.

When the tortilla was done, Abril gingerly removed the finished product, added a hunk of goat cheese to the center of it, flipped it in half, and fried it front and back. "Have a *quesidilla, Señor Capitán.*"

"Thanks, Abril." Handling the steaming *quesidilla* gingerly, he bit off a hunk and watched her cook one for Felix.

"How's Delos?"

"Much better. We rubbed his burns with ointment made from the cactus, then we swaddled him in fresh cloth. He is not in as much pain as before."

"Good." Giddeon took another *quesidilla,* refused a bowl of beans for the time being, and sauntered over to Trinidad, trying to keep his anger from bursting forth. He had watched the glances exchanged by Trinidad and one of the prisoners when they approached the campfire. Not recognition, as such, yet . . .

He stopped in front of the insolent young man. "What are you doing here?"

Trinidad favored Giddeon with his usual disdainful stare, then stuffed another bite of tortilla into his mouth.

The situation had puzzled Giddeon all the way home. He wouldn't put it past Trinidad, not for one moment, to steal the documents, yet what reason would he have for burning the entire compound?

"You are not any more welcome here today than you were the last time we drove you away," Giddeon hissed. "As soon as you finish that plate of food—"

"Giddeon." Suddenly Serita stood beside Trinidad, her chin tilted, her eyes hard as uncut diamonds. "Can you not see how destitute these men are? Trinity is my family. He is welcome to stay at Los Olmos as long as he needs to."

Giddeon stared at her cold eyes. She had come a long way from the meek woman he had left behind in Captain Swain's cabin on board the *Paisano,* from the angry woman in the wagon this morning. She had returned to the Serita Cortinas of old—proud, defiant, and as arrogant as this despicable cousin of hers.

"No," he told her in precise tones, "he is not welcome here. I thought we had that understood."

"We have nothing understood," she declared. "Nothing, except the fact that you are part of this arrangement in name only. You have no voice in the operations of Los Olmos, nor in whom I choose to welcome to my . . ." Her voice faltered, and she finished abruptly, ". . . to my home."

Without warning, the anger he felt at seeing Trinidad flashed through his senses like a bath of burning liquid, directed now at this infuriating woman. He grabbed her arm, and she attempted to pull away. He held her firm.

"I have every say," he whispered, drawing her away from the crowd toward the barracks. "I am your husband," he reminded her, "and as such, I have—"

With a fierceness he hadn't expected, she pulled loose and slapped him across the face. "You have *no* rights. Not with Los Olmos . . . not with me."

He seized her by both arms and drew her face close to his. "I am your husband, *Mrs. Duval,* by your own choice. Blame me for that baby, if you wish. But we both know the baby is as much your doing as mine."

"We have an agreement . . ." she began.

"Yes," he returned. "But our agreement does not include endangering the ownership of Los Olmos by embracing our enemies."

"Enemies! Who are you calling my enemy?"

He squinted at her through the darkness, unable to see her eyes, wishing somehow that he could, knowing his cause was better served since he could not.

"Doesn't it strike you as peculiar that every time some disaster occurs around here, your scoundrel of a cousin always turns up?"

For an instant she went limp beneath his grip. "Trinity?" Then she resumed struggling against him. "Let me go. I don't care what you say, who you accuse. I know the truth. Oliver Burton is involved in all this. I know my enemies, and Trinity is not one of them. You and your men, on the other hand, are also always in a position to have had a hand in the shenanigans."

Her accusation struck him like a falling mast, then he sighed. "We may be in a position, *querida,* but, believe me, burning a household is not my style."

"Well, it isn't Trinity's, either."

"I know." He exhaled in disillusionment. "I've thought of that, too." He returned, however, to the original argument. "But he still has to go."

"No, Giddeon. Trinity is my cousin, and I will not drive him away again. Can you not see how worn down he is. The Republic of the Rio Grande is falling apart. He has no place else to go . . . no one else in the world but me. Besides, you found the documents, so—"

"No," he lied quickly. "Only the trunk. The documents . . . are no longer inside."

Chapter Thirteen

He hadn't intended to lie to her. Not to Serita. But once the words were out of his mouth, he knew he had done the right thing, at least with Trinidad and his band of . . .

Of what? he wondered later, while he sat alone in the shadows watching for something to confirm his growing suspicions of Trinidad Cortinas.

After leaving Serita, Giddeon had looked in on Tita and assured her he would do everything he could to recover the land-grant documents. Didn't one lie always lead to another and another? he fretted. Then he sat beside Delos until Abril finished at the campfire and came to relieve him.

From the tender way she treated him, Giddeon suspected Delos's days as a roving sailor were numbered. He started to kid his friend about it, then thought of his own situation and decided to let any reference to husband-wife relationships pass.

Now, from his place away from the fire, he had a good view of the bedrolls of Trinidad and his men, as well as of the prisoners he and Felix brought in today.

Felix had secured each man to a separate tree with strips of rawhide he threatened to wet down if they didn't shut up and go to sleep. After a plate of frijoles and tortillas, they did exactly that.

As hard as he studied the situation, Giddeon couldn't put his finger on what he thought Trinidad was up to. More important, he couldn't figure what the man's motives might be. That he would steal the land-grant documents made sense, after a distorted fashion.

But nothing else did. Why would he burn the house? He might set a fire to drive them away, but he would have no cause to destroy the valuable furnishings inside, furnishings that should hold the same sentiment for him as they did for Serita.

Watching from the shadows, he began to doubt his own premonitions. He considered himself a good judge of people, but this looked to be one time he had misread the situation. The fire died down. Trinidad's breathing became deep and regular. Giddeon himself relaxed then and slept, and morning found him in a foul mood.

Tossing the dregs of his coffee into the fire, he missed and hit Felix's boot.

"Looks like you need to go back to bed and get up on the right side, Capt'n."

"Sorry," he apologized sheepishly. "I'll look in on Delos while you check the prisoners."

Giddeon coughed against the stale, dusty air inside the barracks. "What say we move you outdoors today, friend?"

"Fine by me, Gid. I've spent enough time inside

299

adobe walls to last a lifetime."

Giddeon moved closer and watched Abril unwind the bandages on Delos's burned back and hands. Without touching the sticky surface she had treated with cactus pulp, she examined his hands first.

"Move your fingers like Nieves said," she instructed.

"Aw, do I have to?" Delos complained.

"If you want to use your hands, *sí*, if not . . ." Delos's eyes had softened as she talked, and now he waggled his eyebrows suggestively. "You know I want to use my hands."

"Then use them now," she demanded in mock anger, and he obeyed.

Listening to their exchange of intimacies, Giddeon felt the intruder, and he flushed with embarrassment. Then, angry at feelings the scene invoked within him, he headed for the door. Delos called him back.

"Gid, as my best friend and captain, we . . . ah, we want you to be the first to know . . ."

"The *only* one to know," Abril corrected.

Giddeon squinted through the hazy light. "What's happened?"

"Nothing," Delos replied. "Nothing, except . . . well, while you were away, we got ourselves hitched."

Giddeon blinked. "You what?"

"We got married, but you can't tell the folks out there just yet."

"How the hell did you get married?"

"A judge came through, spent the night here, and we got him to tie the knot."

Taken aback by the unexpected announcement,

300

Giddeon shook his head. When again he could find words, he asked, "Why don't you want anyone to know?"

"Doña Ana would be very upset," Abril answered, speaking so fast they could hardly keep up with her. "She thinks marriages performed in the church are the only good ones."

Giddeon grunted. "Shows how little she knows."

"Abril means," Delos added, "that Doña Ana doesn't believe a marriage is valid unless it is performed in church, and since she wouldn't consider it valid, she wouldn't want us to . . . ah . . ."

A smile tipped Giddeon's lips. He cocked his head, enjoying his friend's discomfiture. "Yes?"

"Well, you know . . ." Delos began, then again could find no appropriate words.

Giddeon laughed, patted his friend on an uninjured part of one shoulder, and kissed the blushing Abril on the cheek. "Don't guess we have to worry about that right now," he told them. "Perhaps we should pray for a priest to show up before those hands get well."

The sun shone a little brighter when he left the room. Then he saw Serita bending over the campfire beside Lupe, and for a moment he felt like the stars and moon were shining, too. Gritting his teeth, he cursed the only thing he could think of — springtime.

Fragrant blossoms flourished everywhere, uplifting spirits and causing people to . . . to sneeze, he thought bitterly. Nothing about springtime gave a person reason to be cheerful: spring always brought too much rain, the flowers gave off too much pollen, every female critter around thought she was in love, and . . .

As he approached the campfire, Serita stood up, unaware of his presence. She clasped her hands at her back, arching, stretching . . . He studied her a moment, then turned around and headed the other way. Silently, he finished his previous denouncement of the rites of spring . . .

. . . and babies are born.

If his temperament needed an additional blow, Felix provided it when Giddeon found him at the corral.

"They're gone," Felix told him.

Giddeon instinctively looked back toward the campfire where Trinidad was still rolled in his bed. "Who?"

Felix turned and frowned. "Our prisoners," he responded matter-of-factly.

Immediately, his eyes swept the ground around the three trees where the men had been secured. "But they were . . ."

"Yep," Felix admitted. "They were tied. Right there. But as you can see . . ."

"Could they have gotten loose on their own?"

Felix shook his head. "Don't see how. I checked 'em over good and proper. No knives nor anything that would serve as one. Checked the ground around them, too."

"What about horses?"

"They took 'em. The three we caught them with, nothing more."

Turning on his heel then, Giddeon strode toward the campfire. He jerked Trinidad, half naked, from

302

his covers and shook him until Serita intervened.

"You miserable sonofabitch!" he shouted into Trinidad's startled face. "Where are they?"

"What do you think you are doing, Giddeon?" she demanded. "Stop this at once!"

Shaken awake, Trinidad's insolence returned quickly. A grin played at the corners of his mouth, below his dirty mustache. " 'Mornin', Capt'n. What's got you in such a dither? My cousin not satisfying you in bed at night?"

In one swift movement Giddeon turned Trinidad loose and backhanded him across the face, sending him sprawling to his blankets. He stooped to follow him to the ground, but Serita held on to his arm.

"Stay out of this." He shook her hand from his arm with a fierceness that sent her toppling. She lost her footing, and her hands instinctively grabbed her belly.

Giddeon caught her before she fell to the ground. "Are you all right? Did I . . .?"

Regaining her balance, she tried to shrug away from him. "Turn me loose."

He stared at her, and all thoughts of Trinidad and the prisoners temporarily fled. Her face, soft as warmed honey, radiated a rosy glow from within, her lips were full and moist, and her eyes were hard as ebony. Suddenly, all he wanted in the world was to kiss her until her eyes melted with the desire she was so capable of showering on him.

She pursed her lips, and just before she cursed him, he covered her mouth with one of his hands.

"Forchristssake, Serita! Listen to me. He turned those prisoners loose. Last night. The men who

303

stole your trunk . . . who burned your home . . . who . . ."

Furiously, she wrenched away from him. "How do you know that?"

"Who else would have done it?"

With a blank expression she studied him, then turned to Trinidad. "Is that true?"

By this time Trinidad had struggled into his breeches. He stood by the fire holding a cup of coffee. "What?" he asked, as though he had been oblivious to the entire scene.

"Did you turn the prisoners loose?"

"Me?" He shrugged. Then he shouted angrily. "*¿Por qué?* Why? Why do you accuse me? Why do you listen to . . . to this gringo? I told you not to marry him, but you said it was the only way. Now you see I am right. Only it is too late . . . too late, do you hear? Your house is burned to the ground. The land-grant documents are gone. And what do you have? A bellyful of gringo, and a husband who is after nothing but your land!"

With a sudden leap, Giddeon delivered a blow to Trinidad's jaw, knocking him backward into the fire. The young man caught his balance long enough to step sideways away for the flames, and Giddeon caught him and hit him again.

"Kill each other!" Serita stormed. "Kill each other. That would make me very happy." And with that she strode away from the camp toward the smoldering ruins of her home, leaving the two men who had become so entangled in her life to fight for theirs.

They didn't kill each other, and she didn't return until noontime. She walked around and around the perimeter of the compound, quieting her rush of anger, dealing with her anguish in a way she had become accustomed to lately, talking to her unborn child.

After all, she reasoned, this child was all the future she had. Her child and her land. Even her house now was gone, and soon her husband would be . . . if he could be considered a husband.

Studying the smoking timbers, she began to re-build the house in her mind. A new house and a new baby. She must not dwell on the past — the past was lost with this house — or even on the lost documents. The land grant would surely be recorded in Monclova.

As she walked, she stroked her daily-enlarging belly. All that mattered of the past was growing within her at this very moment. Her child was a testament to the strength of her ancestors, a witness to the future of the Cortinas family.

Her child would inherit this land and make it better. But she, in the meantime, must improve the land for her child. And what better way to begin than with a new house?

So, as soon as the timbers cooled, she put them to work — Trinidad's scraggly crew, Giddeon and Kosta, Jorge and Pablo, and even Lupe and Abril and Nieves, when they weren't cooking for the workers or caring for Delos. Tita wandered about wringing her hands when no one was watching; otherwise she pretended to keep her spirits up.

"She lost more than we did," Serita consoled Jorge one day after he had found Tita at the graveyard crying. "She lived in that house all her life."

"I am sorry to lose the weapons of our ancestors," Jorge said quietly, "and the rifle belonging to my father."

"I know," Serita soothed, "I am sorry to lose things from my father's childhood, too. But we have them in our hearts. We can never lose them there."

"*Tío Capitán* said . . ."

"Run along now, *chico*," she interrupted. "I think I hear him call you."

The boy's eyes brightened, and he raced for the barracks, leaving Serita with a heart pumping at twice its normal pace. She was not the only one who would suffer when Giddeon left; she realized that too clearly. Jorge would surely pine for the loss of his *Tío Capitán*, who had taken the place of a father in the boy's mind.

The last thought left her in a quandary concerning her latest plans. Giddeon had mentioned sending Felix to Texas to pay the taxes with the money they received from selling the mustangs. For a few days now, she had entertained the notion of asking him for half the money to buy lumber to begin rebuilding the house. Timber was scarce here on the coast.

But that would only slow down his departure, and she knew well enough that the longer he stayed, the more difficult it would be for everyone.

The weeks since they had been home from Kinney's Rancho had been among the most difficult in her life. And only partially because of the fire. At night she gave thanks for the straw-filled mattress that kept her awake much of the time. Awake, she could keep from wanting him. Asleep, she dreamed.

A month or so passed—Serita lost track of time with the days filled with so much work—before she broached the topic. Then one day at *merienda*, Giddeon commented that it was time for Felix to head for Texas with the money.

He rarely spoke directly to her anymore, nor she to him, so when he looked at her with the news, she blanched. Quickly, though, she regained her composure and made her request. To her surprise, he agreed.

"Felix can arrange for a shipment of timbers to be sent on the next schooner. We will haul them in from the bay."

"How much will that leave for taxes?" she asked.

He shrugged. "One more herd of horses should catch us up."

"Then we will go after Ebanol in the morning."

His eyes found hers, and she held his gaze, although with great difficulty. It had been so long since she looked directly into those green eyes that she quaked, but she persisted.

"Yes," he said at last, "Kosta and I will go with Jorge and Pablo."

"I will come, too."

"No need." He answered in an offhand fashion, then returned to his meal of tortillas, *frijoles*, and fried quail.

She tore off a piece of tortilla and stuffed it into her mouth. "I will come, too."

He glared at her this time. "No, Serita."

307

"What do you mean, *no?* I am perfectly capable of riding a horse. Every woman in my family rode horses when they were in my condition. I work with *Navidad* every day. And when I start breaking the new *caballado* . . ."

"Serita." His voice held a warning she had rarely heard . . . a warning that the topic was closed.

"Giddeon," she replied in kind, tapping her rolled tortilla against the plank.

Instantly he was reminded of her crop, which she whacked against her thigh when she demanded compliance with her wishes. Daily since the fire they had been reminded of things lost forever.

"We have already discussed this." He glanced surreptitiously at the others at table, then back to her. "No need to rehash old arguments."

"This may be an old argument," she informed him, "but it is not a closed one. I run this rancho. You should know that by now. I will ride with you, if you choose to come, when we drive in the *caballado,* and I *will* . . . I *will* break every one of those damned horses. Myself!"

Before he could reply, she jumped from the table, threw her napkin in her tin plate, and strode away from the camp.

He found her on the hillside overlooking El Rey's valley, sitting on the ground beneath the windswept oak tree, her colorful yellow dress blending with the spring flowers. His breath caught in his throat at the beauty of the scene, and, as he approached, at the poignancy of it. As she watched *El Rey* and his *manada,* tears streamed from her eyes and poured, unchecked, down her face.

"Querida." He had crept up beside her so as not to disturb the horses below. At his whisper, he saw her body tense, and he regretted his early words which had caused her tears, he regretted having hurt her, most of all he regretted her love for him, his baby growing inside her.

He reached to brush the tears from her face, and she flinched.

"Go back to the compound," she whispered. "Please. Leave me alone." With great effort she stemmed her tears and, raising her face to the sky, she felt the cool spring breeze dry her wet cheeks.

"I have the land-grant documents."

She studied him in dismay. "What?"

"They were—Actually, they were never missing. They were in the trunk when I found it."

"Why did you lie?" Her voice was soft, weak, and she sounded as if she didn't care one way or the other.

He diverted his gaze, stared at the *manada,* and wondered the same thing himself. "I'm not sure," he admitted at length. "At first it was an impulse. When Felix asked in the presence of the prisoners, I lied to him. Then when we returned and Trinidad—"

"Trinity had nothing to do with burning *la casa grande.*"

He shifted his eyes to hers. "Perhaps, perhaps not. Anyhow, tell Tita. I didn't mean to worry her . . . or you. And I'm . . . I'm sorry I spoke out in front of the family." Suddenly, his voice became earnest. "But, damnit, Serita, you must respect your condition. The baby . . ."

Swiftly, she turned on him. "Do not mention this baby again. It is *my* baby. I am the person who will bear it, I will raise it, and I alone will be the one to worry about it."

If she had kicked him in the chest, he wouldn't have been left more breathless. He understood her animosity; what she said was true enough, yet . . .

Somewhere inside him jealousy stirred. With difficulty he resisted the temptation to touch her belly, to feel his child. "The baby is mine, too," he responded with bitterness. "Whether you like it or not, you wouldn't be carrying that child at this moment without me."

She answered in icy tones. "Am I supposed to thank you?"

"No." Deep within him a sadness welled and begged to be set loose. "No," he repeated. "But neither are you supposed to kill yourself before he is born."

"Breaking horses by my method is not a strenuous job. For your information, women die *in* childbirth, not before."

"My mother did."

Turning swiftly, she stared at his profile, outlined as it was against the blue, blue sky. He had never spoken of his family before, and now . . . Her animosity toward him dimmed, as though it had suddenly been covered with a blanket of melancholy. Holding back the need to touch him, to comfort him, she spoke instead. "Tell me . . ." The baby inside her kicked, and she winced. "Tell me about your mother."

He shrugged lightly without turning to look at her. Her eyes on him were enough, he decided. If he turned . . . "She died when I was six."

Still she did not take her eyes from his face, and he did not turn around. "How?"

He studied the star on the stallion's forehead. "It was an unlikely sequence of events," he told her. "My father's ship had capsized off Campeche. The schooner that found it towed what remained to shore. My father's body was among the . . . the debris. Word reached my mother, who was carrying her second child. She . . ." He shrugged to belie the emotion recalling these past events evoked within him. Glancing at her, he turned quickly back to the *manada*. "She was running down the street to the docks. She tripped on a loose stone . . . I clung to her skirts. For a long time afterward, I thought I had killed her."

"Giddeon . . ."

Pursing his lips, he absently ran his fingers through his hair, trying to fend off the unwanted emotions.

When she touched his sleeve, his muscles flexed. His jaws tightened. "She and the baby both died, of course," he finished.

With her fingers, she lightly stroked the hair at his temple.

"Don't, Serita." He started to rise, but she pulled on his arm and he settled back down. "I never intended to . . . to hurt you."

"I know," she soothed.

"I came here not understanding. It was

311

stupid . . ." With a heavy sigh, he turned to her, his green eyes grave. "I'm going to leave you — with an empty heart . . . and a baby." Heaving, now, he suddenly turned back to stare at the *manada*. "Forchristssake, Serita. I can't sit by and let you kill yourself in the meantime."

As quickly as her awkward state would allow, she rose to her knees beside him. Grasping his head in her hands, she buried her lips in his hair and clung to him.

At first he tried to resist, but only for a moment. His arms moved to come around her, but, instead, one hand lingered on her belly.

She breathed deeply, feeling faint at the intimacy she had craved for such a long time. Very slowly, she lifted her face from his hair and kissed his forehead as he had so often kissed hers.

"It is *our* baby," she whispered. "I am so very thankful for that."

His eyes found hers and she winced at the torment she saw in them. She lowered her lips, reaching for his.

"No, Serita. No . . . this will only bring you more grief."

Panic raced through her. All she wanted was his touch . . . his lips, his arms, his hands. Her pores burned for him, her flesh ached for him. Her heart was broken, and she knew his touch would mend it . . . if only for a while. Struggling to reclaim what she had lost, she covered his hand with hers, pressing his palm tighter against her. "The deed has already been done," she whispered as lightly as she could.

His green eyes flickered at her words, and she persisted. "What harm can loving me do now?" Then before he knew what had happened, she pulled his face to hers and covered his lips with her own, kissing him urgently.

He resisted but a moment longer. Then he eased her back against the grassy knoll, rested his elbows on either side of her face, and kissed her until the sky above swirled inside her brain.

She reached around his neck and pulled him closer, then closer yet. When still he held himself apart from her, she moved her lips against his. "Hold me, Giddeon. Please, hold me."

Desperately, he planted his lips against her forehead. "I don't want to hurt you."

"You won't." But when he studied her with a skeptical look, she added, "I won't let you."

And at last he lay on his side and cradled her in his arms and kissed her and ran his hands up and down her back, finally fumbling beneath her *huipil*.

And she nuzzled her body against him shamelessly, wantonly, happily. But when he still resisted making love to her, she sat up and stripped the shift over her head, and began undressing herself.

"Hey . . ."

"Hey, yourself," she insisted as she cast aside her chemise and untied her bloomers. "You said you liked . . ." Grinning at him coyly, she pulled his face to her breasts, then gasped as his lips closed over one extended nipple. "Now that there's more of me . . ."

Her words were cut off by the tugging of his lips at her breast, which sent piercing sensations of

313

yearning and desire streaking through every part of her body. Urgently, she pulled at his shirt. Finally, she managed to draw it up and over his head, dislodging his mouth from her breast.

He gazed at her with unmasked passion while she undressed him, then he laid her gently back against the ground and scrutinized her new, fuller figure. "There is more of you," he whispered in a husky voice that set her heart to pounding even faster.

He lifted her breasts in his hands and kissed them tenderly. Almost reverently, he traced his hand down her once-nipped waistline and over her mounded belly. The awe she saw in his face brought tears brimming in her eyes.

"It's hard to believe, isn't it?" he murmured. "That little fellow in there is a part of us."

She smiled and held his hand still. "Maybe he will kick again."

He looked startled. "He really kicks? In . . . in there?"

Laughing, she nodded.

His green eyes caressed her face. "Does it hurt you?"

She shook her head. "It's like a thump . . . a bump," she told him. Then with one hand she brought his hand back to her breast, and with the other she pulled his lips to hers. "Love me now. Please."

But after kissing her with urgent passion once more, he again resisted. "We might hurt you . . . or him."

"Giddeon!" she insisted. "Have you never birthed a colt?"

314

"As a matter of fact, no," he replied. "But that doesn't . . ."

"The young are encased securely in sacks of water. You can't . . ."

"I know. That's why . . ."

Suddenly her eyes gleamed, and she playfully reached to stroke the swollen evidence of his desire. At the startled look in his eyes, she laughed. "Not even *you* are capable of bursting that sack until it is time."

His resistance defeated, he loved her gently but completely, finding in her fuller body fulfillment neither of them had known before. Each thrust of his body within hers spread sweet passion as invigorating balm throughout his being, and as he moved, he watched her face and knew she experienced the same regeneration. Breathlessly they reached the frenzied culmination of their lovemaking. At that moment her black eyes and his green melted and fused with the fire of their desire, and their words, mumbled on ragged breaths, came as from one throat . . .

"A thousand falling stars."

Pulling her with him, he rolled them to their sides, and they held each other while the spring air cooled their dampened bodies. "Are you sure I didn't hurt you?"

She nodded against his chest, snuggling tighter.

He pulled his shoulders back and nuzzled her face up. "Is . . . is he all right?"

She frowned.

"He hasn't moved."

"Giddeon Duval! Are you going to worry every

minute until this child is born?"

He nipped the tip of her nose with his lips and nodded.

"In that case," she told him, kissing him firmly on the lips, "you must promise me something."

He cocked his head. "What?"

"That you will not leave my bed again until . . ." She closed her eyes quickly against the rush of emotion brought on by her racing thoughts. "Stay with me," she continued, "until the baby is born."

His throat tightened as the reality couched in her words hit home. "How could I miss such an important event?" Quickly, he pressed his lips firmly against her forehead and held them there until the emotion-fraught moment passed.

Later, as they dressed, a question rose in her mind. "What was your mother's name?"

He stared at her a moment, then, with a laugh, turned to look at El Rey. "Estelle."

Her mouth fell open. "Star," she whispered, translating the word to English. *Espiritú Estelle*. You named your ship for her."

He took her in his arms and kissed her soundly, with great tenderness. Then holding her head in his hands, he studied her face. "We both have stars in our eyes."

They brought in the *caballado* the following day, and for the next month she worked at gentling horses and he didn't complain. Of course, she didn't do all the work. Jorge had begun to learn the art, and now, under Serita's tutelage, he became proficient.

But Serita held to her plans of overseeing the entire operation. Giddeon held his tongue, more often than not, crediting her with having more knowledge of the situation than he himself.

"However," he told her while they lay in their straw bed one night—he had taken to sleeping with his hand on her belly, waiting for the baby to move inside her womb—"I am only cooperating because you are. If you weren't showing restraint, I would take you across my knee."

She laughed. Then the baby kicked, and she turned solemn. "I won't add to the worries you already carry around."

Trinidad regained strength. He and his men left soon after they began gentling the *caballado,* and he didn't bring his army to Los Olmos again.

Felix returned. "Word is," he told them over dinner one night, "General Arista is preparing for a final siege north of the Rio Grande. We could likely sell a herd of saddle-broke horses at twice the regular price, if we hurry."

Chapter Fourteen

Gentling the *caballado* went quickly, for Jorge learned rapidly and possessed the eagerness of youth. He also had the gift. Everyone saw that, plain as day.

"I'm thankful for it to be passed along," Giddeon told Serita one night after she had tormented and fulfilled his body with her skillful hands. "Now I won't have to spend so much time worrying over losing you to the hoof of a contrary mustang."

The house began to take shape. Not long after Felix returned, the shipment of timbers and supplies arrived in the bay, and they hauled them inland by wagon. Kosta turned his shipbuilding skills to rebuilding *la casa grande*.

To Tita's ill-concealed chagrin, Serita had the style of the house altered drastically. Long and low, with a pitched roof instead of the original flat one, the house sprawled over twice the ground space as before. Deep verandas were overhung by the heavy roof, which was held in place by pillars and *vigas* carved from willow.

318

"The Indians are less a threat now," Serita consoled Tita one night at *merienda*, "so we can afford to let the breeze into the house, along with more light." True to her words, she had twice as many spaces for windows installed in the new structure as in the old, although where and when she could afford to buy glass to fill them remained a mystery. The patio, still enclosed by four sides of the house, was airy and sunny with only the one-story building to shut out light. "The better for the charred stump of our old oak tree to grow back," Serita argued.

"And for your plants," Giddeon added, thinking that all too soon it would not matter how the house was built. They would move to another new home — at Kinney's Rancho. Change. Change was the one constant in a person's life, and he was glad to see Serita adjusting to it. "You can root the camellia cuttings I brought you from New Orleans in pots," he told Tita. "That way you can move the plants about as they need sun or shade."

And take them with you to Kinney's Rancho, he thought. He knew that would be the place for them to move. Tita would be near her brother. Serita would be with family. And his son would have a stable community in which to grow and thrive. She would be happy there, Serita would. Given time, she would learn to love her new home; he was certain she would.

What with General Arista moving from the south and the United States impatiently marking time to the north, he had little time to waste. If Arista made good his hold on the Nueces Strip, McCaulay could well back out of the deal. And if Bustamente lost power—therefore money—the *Espíritu Estelle's* cargo would never be paid for, even if he did manage to salvage it.

The situation came to a head one morning when they arose to find Trinidad sitting before the campfire, alone and terrified.

At first Serita didn't recognize him. He sat on one of the drawn-up logs, his head bowed over a tin cup of coffee he held in both hands.

He looked up at her approach, and she blanched at the animallike panic in his eyes. Quickly he lowered his gaze to the steam arising from his cup.

"Trinity. Whatever is the matter?" She scanned the clearing in back of the barracks, but saw no sign of his army. "Where are your men?"

He mumbled something she could not understand. Taking a cup Abril offered her, she lowered herself cumbersomely to the log beside him. "What happened to your men?"

"They run out," he told her. "It's all over, Serita. Unraveled, like a skein of Tita's yarn. Everything is over. Finished."

Serita pulled the *rebozo* tighter around her shoulders and watched Giddeon saunter to the camp from the training corral. Dread filled her with bitter dregs at the thought of the ensuing fight. She and Giddeon had not argued one time since that day at *El Rey's* valley. Now Trinity had returned. He always provoked an argument between them.

"We heard the Republic of the Rio Grande is crumbling . . ." she began.

"This has nothing to do with the Republic of the Rio Grande, Serita," Trinidad hissed. "Can you not

320

see beyond the nose on your face?"

She frowned at him, but before she could answer, Giddeon cleared his throat.

"Then what does it have to do with, Cortinas? Speak up, and do not insult my wife again."

For a moment Serita thought Trinidad would come to life. He struggled to stand, then slumped back onto the log. "Gringo!" he spat. *That's* the trouble, Serita. Gringos! Greedy gringos!"

She stared, confused. "I thought you were fighting Mexico. What do gringos have to do with the Republic of the Rio Grande?"

"Don't you know anything?" Trinidad gave her a look of contempt. "Gringos are involved in everything . . . everything. Texas gringos are trying to take the Nueces Strip; United States gringos are trying to take Mexico; and . . ." Stopping, he squinted a look of pure hatred at Giddeon, then spat again. "And some gringos, the worst of the lot, are simply trying to take Los Olmos."

Forgetting her awkward condition, Serita jumped to her feet. Giddeon grabbed her shoulders to help her catch her balance. "Careful," he cautioned.

She started to smile at him, but Trinidad interrupted her. "And you, cousin dear, are the most stupid of all."

Fury invigorated her. "You are making no sense. If you came here to insult me or my husband, then you are not welcome. As soon as you have taken *desayuno . . .*"

"You don't care whether I live or die, do you? You don't care anything about your family, your lands. All you care about is this . . . this gringo.

321

He has infected you with more than his seed. He has . . ."

Giddeon grasped the serape draped over Trinidad's shoulders and pulled the man to his feet. "Like she said, Cortinas, you are not welcome here. If you are in need of something. Food, perhaps, or . . ."

"Ha!" Trinidad spat at Giddeon's face, then turned to Serita, his eyes wild, his body trembling as though wracked by a fever. "I may have sold my soul to a gringo, but you gave yours away . . . along with your land. Did you truly believe this man would save you from Oliver Burton?"

Desperately, she wedged herself between the two enraged men. "What do you mean? Why did you come here? What do you want?"

"I came to say goodbye, cousin dear. I made a bargain with the devil, and unless you help me, tonight I must pay . . . with my life."

Giddeon forcibly removed Serita and shook the man by his shoulders. Felix's words came back to him with a jolt. "What kind of deal did you make with Burton?"

Trinidad's enraged face turned ashen and stiff, and Giddeon knew at once his guess had been correct.

Serita blanched. "You, Trinity? You . . . and Oliver Burton? What kind of deal?"

He jerked free of Giddeon's limp hands. "The same kind of deal you made with this gringo. Except I received money for my betrayal, instead of . . ." He sneered at her enlarged belly.

Giddeon struck Trinidad on the jaw, sending the

322

man tottering. He sprawled to the ground, and Serita fell at his side.

"So it was you all along," Giddeon accused above her. "Damnit! I should have known. You knew about the trunk. You burned the house, stole the documents . . ."

Serita covered her mouth with her hands. "Trinity? Tell me you didn't."

Now that the truth was out, Trinidad seemed to regain a measure of sanity. He rubbed his jaw through a week's growth of scraggly beard. "Do you think I am not capable of treason, too? Why shouldn't I steal the documents? You were giving them away. At least I got money . . . up front. Only now . . ."

Serita's head swirled. Her baby kicked and she felt like a wedge had been driven between her ribs, separating her heart and her soul. Unconsciously, she clasped her arms about her belly.

Giddeon knelt beside her. "Are you all right?"

She didn't hear him. Instead, she saw Trinity as a boy, a young *caballero,* dashing and gay. She heard the mournful strains of his guitar when he serenaded in the courtyard beneath the oak tree. The tree of strength. Where had all his strength gone?

And hers? Why was she required to be the strong one always? Giddeon pulled her toward him. He held her with powerful arms; he supported her weight against his sturdy chest. "Why don't you go lie down?" he suggested in a gentle voice.

She stared vacantly into his face. From his strength, hers returned. At length, she turned back to Trinidad, who lay still with one of Giddeon's

323

knees in his stomach.

"Tell me the rest," she demanded quietly.

"I needed the money, goddamnit! You wouldn't help me. You let him turn you against me. I needed the money. I had nothing."

"You had your honor once. The honor of your family. Now you are right, Trinity, you have nothing."

His eyes went from insolent to entreating. He spoke in a placating tone. "Don't worry about Burton. I don't have the documents to give him. I think you already know that. They were stolen from the trunk before Duval here brought it back to you. Those documents are the only things that will save my life."

Serita opened her mouth to speak, but felt pressure from Giddeon's arm restraining her.

"What was the original plan, Cortinas?" he asked.

After a fleeting return of his insolent nature, Trinidad relented. "I am to meet Burton tonight at a cantina over on the road to San Antonio de Bexar — with the documents." He shrugged. "This is the third meeting he has called. I didn't bother to attend the others, since I don't have what he wants. Now he has changed his demands. If I don't show up with the documents . . . Don't worry," he told Serita when she gasped. "It is my blood he is after, not yours."

"Fool!" Giddeon hissed. "What makes you think he will stop with killing you? When he has gone that far, there will be nothing to hold him back. After one murder, the others will not matter." He stared hard at the young man writhing on the ground. "So we must keep him from killing you . . . in order to save ourselves."

Serita's mouth went dry. She could not bear to think of giving up her land. Yet, Trinity . . . any human being . . . was more important than land. Turning now to Giddeon, she asked, "Do you think we should . . . ?"

He replied with a curt "No." Standing, he pulled her to her feet. "We haven't come this far to be defeated by the shenanigans of a lunatic. We'll think of something." He glared down at Trinidad, who had not stirred. "First, we must get the truth out of him."

Calling Kosta, Felix, and the recovering Delos, Giddeon apprised them of the situation, and the four men sat around Trinidad Cortinas the rest of the morning, questioning, listening, planning. By the time their plans were laid, the time had come to execute them.

"We will travel south and approach the cantina from the direction opposite the Burton ranch," Giddeon told the group. "It will take us a good three hours to ride to the cantina in this roundabout way, but perhaps we can go undetected until we get a head count of Burton's men — and test his intentions."

"Humph!" Trinidad snorted. "His intentions should be clear to a blind man. He will either have the documents, or he will kill me." Suddenly, he scooped a handful of dirt from the ground and tossed it into the air toward Serita. "This is your land, cousin! Your land. This is what you are putting ahead of my life."

325

"Trinity." She tried to embrace him, but he pushed her aside.

"Do not touch me with your gringo-infested hands . . . and body."

Cringing, she stifled a cry, and turned away. Giddeon caught her and held her tightly. "He isn't worth it, *querida*."

Her blood flowed like icy creek water through her veins. "He is my family."

Staring at her, Giddeon tried to reason. "He turned against you. You can't blame yourself . . ."

She shook her head in dismay. "I don't understand what happened. Juan is gone; Papá and Mamá ran away; everything is crumbling like the ruins of *la casa grande*." She pulled away from him. "I have nothing left, except . . ."

Except our baby, she thought, watching the men saddle their mounts and check their stores of ammunition.

"I will ride with you, *Tío Capitán*," Jorge offered.

"No, son. You must stay and guard your aunts. I am leaving Pablo and Delos to help you."

"I'm well enough to ride, Gid," Delos objected.

Giddeon shook his head. "I'll need you to help corral those mustangs on the drive to Mexico. Stay here this time and protect . . . our families."

Abril brought food tied in cotton sacks for their trip, and Serita noticed the flush on her face and the smile on her lips at Giddeon's words.

"What did you mean . . . ?" she asked Giddeon, when he ushered her by an elbow into the small barracks room they had shared these last weeks. ". . . *our* families?"

326

He grinned and took her in his arms. "Get Abril to tell you her secret . . . if you promise to keep it yourself."

Serita's eyes widened. "She is with child?"

He laughed. "No . . . at least if she is, I don't know it. Ask her after I leave. But promise you'll keep the secret as long as necessary."

She opened her mouth to respond, and he covered it with his own, kissing her so ardently she soon swayed against him.

"I'm afraid for you," she mumbled at last. "Are you sure this is the only way?"

He nodded, kissed her again, then picked up his spyglass. "We've lost about everything to Oliver Burton we can afford to. If we don't go out to meet him tonight . . ."

"Giddeon . . ."

"If all goes well, we should return by morning. If not, you must be prepared here. Now, listen closely." With that he handed her his empty spyglass case — a long, metal tube, lined with felt. "Put the land-grant documents in here and bury it. Do not let anyone see you . . . not anyone. Do you hear?"

She nodded.

"If we fail, they will come looking for them. They cannot take what they can't find. If Jorge should know . . . or Tita . . . well, we don't want to endanger them. Do you understand?"

"Where?" she asked.

He squeezed her to him. "Don't even tell me." Then he kissed her again and grinned. "For the time being, anyhow. Another thing . . . if they come, I expect you to leave."

327

She shook her head. "No . . ."

"Serita." His voice held a soft command. "You must protect yourself and . . . and our child. If they come, you must leave. Let them have the place. We will figure out what do to afterward."

She followed him outside, where she tried to tell Trinidad goodbye, but he wouldn't look at her. Giddeon mounted, called to his men, and she rushed to his horse's side.

"Please," she urged. "Please don't let them hurt him. He never was very good at . . ." She started to say *anything*, then stopped. "Don't let anything happen to him."

They rode silently, Trinidad between Felix and Kosta, with Giddeon in the lead. As soon as they were away from the camp, Giddeon let Trinidad know in no uncertain terms that he was to cooperate or his life would be in grave danger even before they reached the cantina.

He complied sullenly. And Giddeon recalled Serita's last plea with chagrin. Her last words were not for him, but for this rebel cousin. His distress was heightened by the knowledge that he should not care — that it was, after all, best for her to worry over someone other than himself.

He, who would be gone within the month, two at most, he should wish to be last on her list of people to worry over. It would certainly solve their dilemma when the time came to part.

The afternoon shadows had lengthened before they approached the creek running on the south side of the cantina. Gathering his small band of men beneath a grove of elm trees, Giddeon gave them last-minute instructions.

Trinidad was not happy about being sent into the cantina alone and empty-handed. "What if he shoots me on sight, Duval?"

"Play your part well enough, and he won't," Giddeon assured him. He studied the man with growing aversion. Weak men always riled him, but Trinidad Cortinas created a havoc within him unlike any man he had ever known. Looking at him now, Giddeon thought of his own son, soon to be born. Pray the Lord he did not resemble this part of Serita's family.

More and more these days he thought of his son and wondered what the boy would be like. If he were truly lucky, he and Serita both, the child would resemble her father. The noble, daring Don Miguel Cortinas would be a model for any man's son. But not this simpering idiot of a cousin. Hopefully, Trinidad Cortinas took his temperament from his mother's family.

With difficulty, Giddeon pulled himself back to the present. Usually he relished a good fight, but not this time. This time the margin for error was too great. If he had misjudged Oliver Burton . . .

"Let's ride," he interrupted himself. "Get this shindig over and done with."

Taking the lead, he crossed the creek and kept to the underbrush until they came to the thicket where the other horses were tied: four of them, all bearing Burton's brand.

Trinidad's knees buckled when he stepped down

from his saddle.

"Beats me how you ever led an army," Giddeon hissed. "Straighten up or you're buzzard meat."

Trinidad shot him a hateful glance, then looked pensively toward the doorway of the cantina. From within came the muted sounds of men's voices.

"Remember, Cortinas," Giddeon instructed. "When you step to the doorway, pat your shirtfront as though you have something inside. That should gain you entrance. Then you can bargain with him."

"He won't buy it." Trinidad spat toward a bush at his feet, but nothing left his mouth. "You might as well shoot me right here and get it over with."

"Shut up." Giddeon waited a moment longer until he saw Felix signal from the opposite corner of the cantina, near the window. He looked for Kosta, found him, then gave Trinidad a pat on the shoulder. "Do this for Serita," he said. "You owe her that much."

"Yeah. I save Los Olmos for you. How're *you* going to repay her, gringo?"

The words resounded inside Giddeon's brain with every step Trinidad took across the clearing to the doorway of the jacal that served as a drinking establishment. Trinidad paused at the doorway, patted his shirtfront, as he had been instructed, and stepped inside.

With a suddenness no one expected, the reverberation of a gunshot shook the jacal. The force blew Trinidad backward out the door into the clearing, where he landed with a thud on his back. The sound defeaned Giddeon to all other noises.

Through the smoke-filled doorway he watched four men rush out and kneel beside the body.

"Hold it right there," he called.

The men swiveled on their booted feet and fired in four directions at once. Kosta dropped the man nearest him.

Smoke mingled with dust, gunshots with the repercussion of the first one, with Trinidad's fall.

Felix bounded around the corner, taking out the man nearest him. Giddeon got the rest. Four shots. Four men. With Trinidad Cortinas dead at the bottom of the heap.

And not a one of them Oliver Burton.

"Fan out and find him," Giddeon told his men. He discovered the bartender huddled behind the crude bar. He jerked the heavyset man to his feet and dragged him out the door. "Identify these men."

"Cow Boys."

"I can see that. Who are they? Do they work for Oliver Burton?"

"*Sí, señor.*" The man's voice trembled so, he trilled *señor* into two words.

"Where is Burton?"

"Señor Burton was not in my establishment."

"Then where . . . ?"

The bartender shrugged. "I do not know. One of these men mentioned Los Olmos . . ."

The idea was so unexpected, then so revolting, it took a minute for it to register in Giddeon's brain. "Sonofabitch!" he swore. "What exactly did he say about Los Olmos?"

The bartender shrugged, and Giddeon brought his pistol to bear upon the man's skull. "Think, *señor*. Think hard and fast. Or you will find yourself on top of that heap of dead men."

"It was the man who came here last to join his compadres. He instructed them to . . . to kill the stupid one, then search his body for documents and bring them to *Señor* Burton at Los Olmos."

Giddeon's heart pumped like it would wear itself out any moment. He jumped over the pile of men, then stopped in his race for his horse. "Felix," he called. "Tie Cortinas on his horse and bring him along. Serita will want him brought home."

If she is still there . . . and alive. How could he have been so short-sighted!? His thoughts had been to get the entire battle away from her . . . away from Los Olmos. Her last words had been a plea to watch over her cousin. Well, he'd certainly done that. He sent him into a trap and watched him get his head blown off.

Chapter Fifteen

By the time Giddeon led his troop away from Los Olmos, the daily routine had been interrupted to such an extent that even Tita relaxed her long-standing policies. Without a qualm she granted Jorge's wish to give up siesta in favor of working with the mustangs.

Serita watched the boy race toward the corral, thinking perhaps she should go with him. One glance, however, convinced her Tita needed her more: Her frail shoulders hunched beneath the weight of Trinidad's betrayal; her spirits sagged. They sat beside the window, she and Tita, in Tita's small room in the barracks.

"Are you certain, *sobrina?*" Tita asked. "There can be no doubt? It was our own Trinidad who . . . who destroyed our home . . . the home of our ancestors?"

Serita stroked the thin skin stretched across her aunt's gaunt hands. "It was he," she answered. "He admitted it."

"What reason could he have had? And us, his

own flesh and blood?"

"He said he betrayed us for the money Oliver Burton paid, but I think it was more. I think his anger made him mad — *lunático*."

"Why did he not come to us with his troubles?"

"He did, Tita," Serita said sadly. "Only his troubles were not the kind we could resolve by offering a *novena* in the chapel." At Tita's sage nod, she continued. "Trinity has always been as determined as an outlaw stallion. He would have nothing but Los Olmos, and that on his own terms, to use for his own evil purposes. Perhaps this episode will frighten him enough that we can reason with him."

Tita shrugged. "We had another evil one among us. It was years ago, before you were born. We could do nothing with him, either. Fortunately for Los Olmos, your father and his brothers were strong men who could deal with a corrupt kinsman."

"Giddeon is a strong man also, Tita. He will help us deal with Trinity." *For as long as he himself is around,* she finished silently. "Go to sleep now. I will return after siesta."

Stepping outside, she blinked against the summer sunshine. It warmed her body, at least on the outside, but inside she felt icy cold. She was tired of living in turmoil and uncertainty. Suddenly, she was even tired of fighting for Los Olmos. Nieves predicted the baby would come the last part of September; it was now the middle of June. Two and a half months.

Her heart pounded faster. The *caballado* was ready to drive to market. Giddeon said it would furnish

334

enough money to finish paying the taxes. Then what? She knew he needed additional money to salvage the *Espíritu Estelle*. But how much? Would this herd provide that as well?

Hurrying down the pathway to her own compartment, her mind chattered against itself like the Green Jays in the ebony trees. At least she could count on him being here two and a half more months. He promised to stay until the baby was born. She knew he would keep his word. With rising panic, she recalled his loving touch on her belly, the concern in his eyes every time he thought she might bring harm to herself or the child. He cared for her. She knew that also.

But he would leave, because he loved the sea. He cared for her, but he *loved* the sea. The words swirled in her brain. No wonder she couldn't become overly concerned with Trinidad's treachery. Her husband, her beloved husband . . . the father of her unborn child . . . would soon be gone. The agony that knowledge brought far surpassed any hurt at losing *la casa grande,* at losing the treasures of her family—*relics,* he had called them. Even the thought of losing Los Olmos itself paled beside the anguish of living the rest of her days—she hugged her arms around her shivering body—and nights without her husband.

Why had she been so stubborn about keeping this place anyway? She should have listened to Papá.

As if to countermand her thoughts, the baby in her womb kicked, bringing to mind a new and troublesome thought. "No, little one," she whispered. "I do not wish that. If I had listened to Papá, I would never have met your father . . . and you would not exist."

Sighing, she returned to her own compartment at the east end of the barracks. The moment she closed the door behind her, her eyes rested on the spyglass case. Giddeon's instructions to hide the documents fairly slapped her in the face. Dismally, she chided herself for neglecting such an important task. Not that she envisioned Oliver Burton coming here for the documents. Giddeon's plan was sound. By the time he and his men got through with Burton, she would not have to worry about that gringo again!

Opening the trunk, she took out the ancient documents and rolled them tightly, but with care. They fit perfectly into the slender case, as she had known they would the moment Giddeon made the request. Screwing the cap on tightly, she sighed. They were secure against air and water—now to secure them against corrupt men.

With a thrill, she realized she had the perfect place for that—secure from the elements, away from the living quarters; not an obvious place, but one Gideeon could find later by mere deduction should anything happen to her.

Her hand was on the door handle when a knock came. It was Delos.

"May I come in, ma'am? I have inspected all the locks and windows in the barracks except yours."

"Of course, Delos." Gesturing him into the room, she slid the spyglass case behind the folds of her skirt. Although Giddeon and Delos were as close as brothers, Giddeon had warned her not to let anyone know of her mission. "I am going for a walk," she told him. "Over to the house."

He eyed her seriously. "Giddeon left you a gun. "You'd best carry it along, ma'am."

She watched him close and latch the shutter on the one window. "Are you expecting trouble? Something I don't know about?"

He shook his head. "On the other hand, never hurts to be cautious, 'specially with a varmint like Burton."

She smiled. "I agree wholeheartedly. Although midnight calls are more his style." At his question, she told him of Oliver Burton's nocturnal visits. "An attempt to frighten us away from Los Olmos. But, as you can see, he did not succeed."

"No, ma'am. He surely didn't. You hurry on back, though. Giddeon said not to let anyone stray too far from the barracks. Come dusk, Pablo and I will set up a patrol so's you womenfolk can rest a bit."

Carrying the rifle in her free hand, she headed for the site where the new house was taking shape. Actually, it was four separate houses under one roof. Along one side were the kitchen and dining rooms. Facing Los Olmos Bay, although of course one could not see the water from here, stretched the parlor and entertaining rooms. To the north were a suite of rooms for Tita, a room for Jorge, and additional bedchambers for visitors.

She walked through the building now. The walls were up, ready to be whitewashed with the lime Felix had purchased on his trip to pay the taxes. The four buildings, set in a square, were joined on top by the overhanging roof and on the ground by a tiled foundation, leaving a covered breezeway between each structure.

The empty rooms seemed larger now than they would when furnished; even so, they would be enormous. Kosta had complained that no one needed this much space. But Giddeon understood; at least, he said he did.

Crossing from the dining area into the parlor, she frowned. Of course, she had no furniture. But she had a plan for that, too. She would have Edward Stavinoha, the cabinetmaker she had met at Kinney's Rancho, build her furniture. He and his wife Mary could come live at Los Olmos while he worked. Had they not suggested a visit? They could have the room next to Tita's. Mary was a schoolmarm; she could give Jorge lessons.

Serita's mind swam with the wonderful ideas. She had long felt guilty at the lack of education Jorge received from only herself and Tita. The boy needed more than the two of them could give him. Mary Stavinoha was the perfect answer.

Where she would find the money was a different matter. Straightening her spine, she pressed her fingertips into the small of her back, an act which served to strengthen her determination. Time, she reminded herself. Time was all she needed. In time she could sell enough mustangs and cattle — already more wild cattle were beginning to gather on the plains of Los Olmos. She would have the money, in time.

Precious time. She stooped to walk under a timber Kosta had left propped across a doorway, and

338

the baby shifted position. Time.

Her thoughts turned sour. Time was her enemy. Time for her consisted of two and a half months. Her lifetime, her eternity. Ten weeks. That is, if Nieves were correct. If the baby didn't come sooner.

In ten weeks Giddeon could well be gone. Standing now in the west building of the compound, she grimaced at the pain that knowledge always brought her. This west wing was a suite of rooms—office, sitting room, nursery, and bedchamber. A wonderful baby would sleep in the nursery; in the adjoining bedchamber, she herself would sleep alone. How would she bear to live in this house once he was gone forever?

French doors would eventually open onto the deep verandas from every side of the suite. Stepping through the opening of one now, she stood on the veranda and gazed away toward the bay. She could smell the sea, even from here. But she couldn't see it.

Neither would he be able to, she thought suddenly, recalling the hours Giddeon had spent on the rooftop staring out at his beloved sea. Then, as she stood deep in thought, her body fairly trembling at the image of him, a wonderfully impulsive idea struck her.

She would build him a lookout on top of the house. She would speak with Kosta, and while Giddeon was away selling the mustangs, she would build him an office high above the house from where he could see the sea.

The idea picked up her spirits considerably, and she hurried on with the task of hiding the land-grant documents, a chore that seemed rather foolish now with her spirits lightened. She hoped his confrontation with Burton went quickly and well so he could hurry home to her. Regardless, she would be waiting . . . awake and waiting to hold and be held, to love and be loved.

Crossing through the living space, she passed the metal breastplate, halberd, and dagger which had belonged to her ancestors who came to this new land with Cortés. Jorge had dragged them from the rubble of the old house and polished them with sand and ashes. Stooping, she studied her somber reflection.

Something old, something new. She stepped off the foundation to the east side of the house and skirted the area where they had made the new adobe bricks. They saved many of the bricks from the old structure, but Kosta insisted on using them for only the outside walls, where the burned smell would dissipate.

Trinidad flitted in and out of her mind like a capricious spring shower. She tried to feel sad about him. But there were too many other sorrows in her life for his betrayal to take center stage. Besides, Giddeon would save Trinity's hide this time. Then, after they settled things with Oliver Burton and paid the taxes, she and Tita would straighten him out.

Either that, or she would ship him off to the family in Mexico. She would not allow one so rebellious in nature to influence her child.

At the thought, the baby within her moved again. She paused instinctively, and then she heard the noise, a rumble in the distance.

Horses. Her first thought was of Jorge and the mustangs. Glancing in the direction of the corral, however, she saw nothing.

Her next thought was that Giddeon had finished with Burton and was returning. But one glance at the sky told her sundown was still a good two hours away. Trinidad's meeting with Burton was to take place after sundown. Unless . . .

Unless Trinidad lied again. In which case . . . Her heart froze as she watched a half dozen or so horses race into the clearing between the site for the new house and the barracks. Several more riders followed. So many she couldn't count from this distance.

The barracks were situated a good hundred yards west of the new house. Glancing to her right, she looked furtively toward the cemetery where she planned to hide the documents. It was another hundred yards or so to the east. And here she was, caught between the two.

The horses reared to a stop in the center of the clearing, and Delos came out of the barracks. He must have shouted something, for the men on horseback looked, then turned and rode toward him.

Women came out the doors up and down the barracks. Nieves. Tita. Lupe and Abril. Abril ran toward Delos, but he held her back with a hand.

If he spoke, Serita could not hear. But she saw him look over the group of mounted men, then behind them. She tensed.

Do not let him look this way, she prayed. *Please.* And

341

he didn't.

The instant the men dismounted, she recognized the leader: Oliver Burton! Her fists closed unconsciously around the spyglass case in one hand, the rifle in her other. Why had she tarried?

With one more glance toward the barracks to determine that no one was searching this direction, she moved toward the creek. Holding her breath as tightly as she clasped the spyglass case, she stumbled behind the first elm tree she came to and chanced a look back toward the barracks. Had they been searching, they would surely have located her in her bright yellow dress—at her size!

All appeared quiet. Delos held his ground; at least from this distance, he appeared to. Oliver Burton stood with his usual authoritative stance in front of him. Several men entered various rooms of the barracks. Looking beyond the barracks toward the mustang corral, she searched for Jorge but could see no movement. Then she realized she didn't see Pablo among those in front of the barracks, either.

Where was Pablo? Pray God he was with Jorge. She feared for the boy among all those Cow Boys.

With a flutter in her heart, she hurried on to the creek, where she paused behind another elm. Only briefly this time, however, because suddenly she knew if she were to protect the documents, she must do so now. Her earlier thoughts came back to her with the force of a thunderbolt: the very idea that she would give Los Olmos over to the gringo Burton was spurious. Perhaps for Giddeon . . . Her mind whirred to a stop. Her toe stumbled on a rock, and she landed on her hands and knees. Giddeon. Her heart caught in her throat, and for a moment she couldn't catch her breath. If Oliver Burton had met Trinity, then . . . Giddeon would never have let Burton come to Los Olmos.

Not if he were physically able to stop him. Her heart pounded furiously. She regained her footing and stumbled up the hillside to the family plots. If Burton were coming from the cantina after having discovered the ruse . . .

All the headstones except one were marble crosses. Since the war, there had been no money for marble so Juan's grave was marked by a simple wooden cross. But his cross, like the others, was fashioned with a flower vase attached to its base. After another quick glance toward the barracks, she yanked the flowers from the vase at the base of Juan's grave and stuffed the spyglass case into it. It was a tight fit, but it did fit, as she had known it would. Hurriedly, she stuffed the wilting flowers around the case. It was visible, of course, but only if a person were searching for it. If Giddeon came looking, eventually he would discover her hiding place.

She had worked with numb fingers, her mind only partly on the job at hand. The other part of her brain seemed splintered—a portion with her family at the barracks, another portion with Jorge and Pablo, and a large portion with Giddeon, wherever he was. Now, as she finished this task, she crawled on hands and knees toward the safety of a tall, wide elm tree. She clutched the rifle in damp hands; again her heart lurched to her throat. She swallowed painfully. The baby moved, and she pursed her lips, immediately recalling Giddeon's admonition not to endanger the baby.

Dismally, she realized more lives than that of one baby were at stake at Los Olmos today. Delos was a seasoned warrior, but, outnumbered as he was, he stood little chance against Oliver Burton's Cow Boys. Even if he got off a shot, with the new skin on his hands still tender and the joints beneath stiff, how accurately could he fire?

Pablo possessed a sure and steady hand with rifle or knife. But where was he?

If Oliver Burton had come at last to take possession of Los Olmos, as he surely must have done . . . Inhaling, she whispered a silent prayer and peered from behind the safety of the oak. At first, she had the feeling she had dreamed the entire sequence. All looked quiet. No noises would have alerted her attention. Only the women and one lone man facing another lone man before the barracks, with several mounted men and a number of riderless horses in the background.

Then, watching, she realized the search continued. She forced her brain to quiet itself, her mind to work. Still, she did not see Pablo, nor Jorge. They must have hidden somewhere on the other side of the training corral. Thankfully, Jorge had been away from the barracks when Burton arrived.

A man came out of a room, spoke to Oliver Burton, then headed for the next room in the long row—the east corner room. She held her breath. As quickly as he entered, he returned to the doorway and shouted.

Oliver Burton led the way toward her room, then, turning, he issued orders, which she supposed were obeyed, because, instantly, several horsemen trained their rifles on Delos.

Her mouth was dry now. She licked her lips. Burton headed for her room; the man inside carried her great-grandfather's trunk out the door and dumped the contents onto the ground.

Burton squatted before it, and with the help of his man, belongings began to fly this way and that. In only a matter of seconds, Burton stood and whirled on the group huddled now before the trained rifles of his Cow Boys. A moment passed, two, then the rancher strode toward Delos, backhanded him across the face with a force that sent him stumbling against the hitching rail.

In that second Serita's fear vanished before an onslaught of anger. Who did this gringo think he was? Everyone bowed before him as though he were some sort of god . . . or devil. When, in fact, he was a mere man, and a sorry excuse for one at that. Her thoughts raced furiously, and she was halfway down the hillside before she realized she had left the cemetery. She had to do something. What, she wasn't sure. But whatever help she could give her family certainly would not come from the distance of the family plots.

Cautiously she moved from tree to tree. Where was Pablo? And wherever he was, did he have a gun with him? Or was he . . . ?She swallowed convulsively. Surely they had not already captured . . . or killed . . . Pablo.

The space between the creek and the house was

barren of any trees or shrubbery, and she shuddered to think of crossing it in her bright yellow dress. Even if they were not looking in her direction, anything this bright would be sure to attract attention.

Hadn't Tita said she was too large to wear such bright colors? When she and Rosaria had made this dress, she never imagined herself becoming as large as a sailing ship, as she very nearly was now. Her brain spun mindlessly while she searched for a way to cross the space without being seen, a way to protect her family with only one shot. Finally, she made herself inch straight down the hillside to the riverbank, away from the house. She could hurry downstream a ways, then return from an angle that would afford her the cover of the house. That was a good idea, she thought, just as her soft-soled slippers slid out from under her. She traveled the rest of the way to the creekbank on her behind.

Once she stopped sliding, it took a moment to reorient herself. This made her even angrier. For such a long time she had been conscious of not hurting her baby; now, it appeared her entire family might be wiped out, and she was sitting on her fat rear on the creekbank . . . with only one shot in the rifle she held with a death grip in her fist. One gun. One shot. It would not go far against such a force.

Her mouth was by now so dry her throat rasped when she drew breath. Her brain was fuzzy, but her mind was set. Oliver Burton was not going destroy her family—or at least not any more of it than he already had. If this gringo had killed Gid-

346

deon . . .

Moving stealthily, but with purpose, she gained the veranda of the new house on the bay side, then edged her way around the corner to survey the thicket she knew was to the south. One more small clearing and she would have protection for the rest of the way to the barracks.

That journey seemed to take eons. Before leaving the security of the veranda, she chanced a glance toward the barracks, but all she could see from this angle was the back of Oliver Burton and a few of his men. She dashed across the clearing, caught her breath, and struggled around the thicket.

An out-of-the-way approach that took twice the normal time, she fumed to herself. Suddenly, then, her soft soles betrayed her again. Her toe caught a stump, and the next thing she knew, she lay face-down on the ground, eating a mouthful of grass.

Panic momentarily swept over her, followed quickly by disgust. She had never been so clumsy. Of course, she had always been able to see the ground she stepped on before now, too. She sighed, the scare passed, and she made it to the edge of the barracks undetected.

Now what? she wondered, willing her mind to calm down. She could hear voices from here, and, straining, she could make out the words.

The first of which was her name.

"I am sure the señorita will return before dark," Oliver Burton was saying, "so we will wait. By that time, my men will arrive from the cantina."

Serita exhaled a sigh of relief. So he hadn't been to the cantina, after all. Giddeon was safe.

347

And safe, he would return before—in place of, she corrected—Burton's own men. If they could hold out . . .

At that moment she heard struggles and other voices. Chancing a look around the corner, her mouth gaped at what she saw.

Jorge. Pablo. Two of Burton's Cow Boys dragged them into the clearing. Pursing her lips, Serita watched, forgetful of exposing of herself.

"What's this?" Burton questioned in a belligerent tone. "Two more Spanish hiding in the bushes? Where's your sister?"

Jorge struggled, kicking and flinging his slender body about. "I do not have a sister," he retorted. "Turn me loose. My *Tío Capitán* will kill you for this. He won't . . ."

"Shut the kid up," Burton ordered.

When one of Jorge's captors slapped the boy across the face, Pablo kicked out at him. "Stop that. He is only a boy."

In return, the man who held the rifle on Pablo slammed it into his back, knocking the old man to his knees. Nieves screamed.

"I'm tired of playing games with you Spanish," Burton fumed. "Let's see if a little gunfire will bring that crazy woman out of the bushes. We'll start with the old man here."

"Stop!" Serita called. Coming around the corner of the barracks, she held her arms at her sides, letting her skirt drape over them, concealing both of her arms and the rifle. She walked forward as she spoke. "I am here. What do you wish to say to me, *Señor* Burton."

Burton swirled at the sound of her voice. He stared, his eyes menacing. Then he approached her at a fast clip, his bootheels grinding into the dust at his feet. When they were but ten yards apart, she stopped, and he did the same.

His attention was momentarily distracted by her condition. "I see you have gained something from that fake marriage of yours."

"It is not a fake marriage, señor. If you harm one person at Los Olmos today, let me assure you, my husband will guarantee that fact."

"And where might this so-called husband of yours be?"

She stared at him with a steady stream of pure hatred, wishing her eyes could kill this bastard gringo. "He was expecting you at the cantina."

For a moment, her answer took him off guard. She smiled.

"So, *señor*, you think we *Spanish* betray only our own kind? Were you so foolish as to believe my cousin Trinidad would not in the end return to the arms of his family?"

He glared at her, giving neither tit nor tat. "Your cousin Trinidad is a stupid man. Had I trusted him to bring the documents, I would not be searching these premises now. If I made one small mistake, it was in taking you and that captain for the same kind." His voice showed no remorse, offered no apologies, and when he spoke again, she knew his admission of a mistake in no way kept him from plunging ahead with plans to take Los Olmos.

"A small mistake," he repeated, "which can be easily remedied. Hand over the land-grant docu-

349

ments."

"You burned them with my home," she retorted, hoping to send them away before Giddeon rode into a sure ambush.

"You lie," Burton seethed. Without warning, he shifted his attention to those of his Cow Boys who were still mounted. "Patrol the area. Shoot anyone who approaches." He turned back to Serita with a satisfied smile on his hard Anglo face.

Suddenly, she knew that before Giddeon came into her life, she had judged all Anglos by men like this one standing before her. How wrong she had been. It was as likely, she now realized, that many Anglos judged her people by renegades like Trinidad. This knowledge filled her with a great sadness.

A sadness which in the next instant turned to sickening fear.

"Kill the old man," Burton ordered. "Then we will progress to the traitorous Anglo who calls himself a Texas naval man."

Serita's mouth went dry. Her voice rasped from her throat. "Don't you dare!"

The man holding the gun on Pablo raised his weapon.

Serita was conscious of cries from her family, from Nieves. The sounds tolled like an endless peal of chapel bells, but, of course, lasted only seconds, during which she herself screamed again, "Stop!"

"Kill him, I said," Burton's voice commanded.

And she did. Raising her rifle, she aimed, though later she could hardly recall it, and fired. Oliver Burton pitched forward into the Los Olmos dirt he had tried so hard to wrest from her.

Then she herself crumpled to her feet, falling to the same earth.

She awakened to the sound of hammering, and in the darkened room, the vision of a coffin came into her mind. Juan's coffin.

Shifting her weight to stand up, the straw in her mattress rustled, and her brain froze.

Not Juan's coffin. Oliver Burton's. Cramps suddenly gripped her stomach, and she clutched her arms about herself. Nausea swept over her in waves, leaving her wet and chilled. She had killed a man.

She stumbled from the bed and tore open the door to her small room. Nighttime had settled over Los Olmos. Stars shone from the sky, as though everything was the same as the night before.

But it wasn't. The night before she had not been a murderess. She clung to the doorfacing. The campfire crackled down the way, and she saw figures seated about it. She heard voices, indistinctly. No words. Moving forward on bare feet, she had traveled half the distance separating her from the campfire, before she came to her senses.

The fuzz cleared in her brain, and she recalled not only shooting Oliver Burton, but her reason. He had ordered Pablo killed . . . and Delos. Jorge was held prisoner. As were they all.

Were they still? What had happened since she fired that fatal shot? In the midst of her rising anxiety, the baby inside her moved and set her brain to wobbling. She grasped a pole for support and clung to it.

351

As her mind cleared again, the voices became more distinct. Men's voices. But they were voices she recognized. Not Burton's Cow Boys. She stepped toward them again, and Giddeon caught her before her knees gave way.

While she clung to him as for dear life, tears began to flow from her eyes. "You're safe. Thank God, you are safe."

He held her tightly, thinking the same about her. He had spent the last couple of hours listening to the harrowing tale of Burton's arrival at Los Olmos and of Serita's courageous defense of her people.

Lifting her face away from his chest, she looked at him through the white moonlight. He felt her body tremble beneath his hands, and when she spoke, her voice quivered.

"Giddeon, I killed a man."

He swallowed the bitter guilt he felt over sending Trinidad into the cantina alone and unarmed. "So did I, *querida*."

Chapter Sixteen

They buried Trinidad at first light in the box Pablo had constructed during the night. His grave, however, was at the opposite end of the family cemetery from that of Juan Cortinas.

"Trinity is family," Serita sighed, "but somehow it doesn't seem right to place heroes and rebels side by side. I will not dishonor the family by refusing to lay him to rest with the others, but neither will I dishonor Juan by placing them side by side."

By the end of the week Giddeon had gathered his crew and headed for Mexico with the herd of mustangs. Before he left, however, Serita convinced him to let her move into the new house.

"You have no furniture, no windowpanes," he objected.

"Kosta has built shutters for all the windows," she countered, "and on pretty days we can hang fabric over the openings to keep out creepy-crawly things."

"What about when the baby comes?" The last thing he needed, Giddeon knew, was for Serita to become ensconced in this new house. It would be that much more difficult when the time came to move to Kinney's Rancho.

"The baby," she insisted, "will be much better off in the fresh air of a new house than in these damp and dusty quarters."

He sighed. Agreed. And they moved into the new house. If by moving one meant carrying straw-filled mattresses, a few trunks, and some lanterns. Under Nieves's guidance, Lupe and Abril prepared meals in the new kitchen, happy to have the commodious fireplace in exchange for cooking over the campfire, back-breaking work that filled their eyes and their hair with smoke.

Giddeon left Pablo behind this time. But in his place, he took Delos and Felix and, of course, Jorge. He had reconsidered his plan to take Delos, deciding to take Kosta instead, but Serita prevailed upon him to leave her carpenter.

Obviously, he smiled to himself, she had not spoken with Abril, or if she had, Abril had not revealed her secret marriage.

She walked him to his horse the morning the drive was to begin. "How long do you think it will take?" Inside, she yearned to go. She hadn't ridden a horse in a month now; she had promised Giddeon she would not ride again until after the baby came. A part of her seemed to be missing as a result. She could not recall ever spending so long a time out of the saddle.

And the drive itself would be exciting. She had never been to Mexico, and they were going across the Rio Grande River almost to Monterrey.

"Three weeks," he answered. "Four at the most.

354

We will return before the baby comes."

"Yes," she mused, her thoughts on the weeks to follow the birth of her child. Where would he be then? She didn't ask, nor did she ask for practically the hundredth time whether he really thought this herd would finish the taxes, and what next . . . ?

Except an empty life. What next?

Jorge raced up to tell her goodbye. He had begged to ride Navidad but she put her foot down to that.

"Wish you were coming along, Serita," the boy said.

Reaching, she tousled his hair and was struck with how much taller he had grown. He had filled out, too. Gentling this herd of mustangs had turned the boy into a man.

"You did a fine job, Jorge. I am very proud of you."

Tita rushed up beside them. "If you get a chance," she told Giddeon, "please try to bring word of Miguel. We have heard nothing for such a long time."

Giddeon bent and kissed her wrinkled forehead. "I will, Tita. You take care of our little mother for me."

Tita blushed and turned aside, and Giddeon drew Serita a few steps away and held her close.

"Take care of yourself," he said. "Don't go riding or even walking so far as the cemetery or . . ."

She tightened her arms around his chest and sighed. "Don't carry on so," she told him, relishing all the while his solicitude. She wanted to tell him how much she would miss him, but that would be silly. If she missed him on this trip, what would his permanent departure do to her? She had made a bargain, a bargain she intended to keep, and she would not send him away thinking her a fool. She wanted him to remember her with fondness. "I told you a long time ago, Giddeon Duval, I can take care of myself."

He grunted. "You certainly proved that, *querida*. The only thing in life I regret more than leaving you alone that day is Trinidad's—"

"Shh . . ." Lifting her face, she released her arms and placed a finger on his lips. "Don't. You cannot blame yourself for Trinity's wickedness, nor for Oliver Burton's. Your plan was a good one; you were dealing with unscrupulous men. Sooner or later both of them would have ended up dead by some man's hand." She sighed deeply, trying to dispel the memory of seeing Oliver Burton fall at her feet. "A lot more people would have suffered had they lived longer."

He stared at her silently a while, then lowered his lips and kissed her deeply yet tenderly. She encircled his neck with her arms and pulled his face closer to hers, responding to his kiss with equal fervency. Snuggling closer to him, she felt the bulk of their child separating them and longed for the day when she could once more be alone with him, just the two of them.

But when he rode away, leaving her standing the dust of the *caballado*, she knew the possibility of that day ever dawning was a tale equal in fantasy to those that would be spun around his campfire during the coming month.

Giddeon spurred his horse with vengeance, discontent settling uneasily over the facade he had erected for Serita's benefit. Trinidad's death still bothered him. He had killed men in battle, but this was different.

Rebel that Trinidad had been — Giddeon never doubted Serita's words that the man would have met a foul end sooner or later — still, he was Serita's cousin, and that fact alone left Giddeon more remorseful than he should have been.

The truth of his last thought gave him a jolt. Indeed, he should feel no remorse at all; he should save his contrition for later, when he rode away and left Serita and his baby alone.

He sighed, wishing this entire farce were over. Enos McCaulay had expected to hear from him weeks ago. Not that he envisioned the man backing out of the deal. He didn't. But much remained to be done.

He shrugged and spurred his horse toward a straying mustang, nosing the animal back to the herd. Damnit, he had intended to tell Serita about McCaulay before he left on this drive. That way she could prepare to leave while he was gone.

The last doubt concerning his ability to convince her to move to Kinney's Rancho was dispelled when, after burying Trinidad, she led him to Juan's grave. There she very seriously removed the spyglass case from its hiding place and handed it to him.

"Here are the documents," she told him. "Put

357

them where you think best. After all, you are my husband."

He cringed at her trust. She had come a long way, this beautiful Spanish *señorita*, who had vowed never to relinquish La Hacienda de los Olmos to a gringo.

Of course, he had given the land-grant documents back to her to store inside the old trunk. He knew by this time they were his to keep—or to sell.

Now that she had moved into the new house, however, it would be even more painful for her to move. He should have insisted she move to Kinney's Rancho before the baby was born. Well, he still had time. As soon as he returned, he would tell her about McCaulay and immediately move them away from Los Olmos. A house shouldn't be too hard to find.

The baby could be born at Kinney's Rancho; it would be a safer place to deliver a baby, anyhow—much safer than at Los Olmos, where they were so far from a doctor. They would christen the child in the church at Kinney's Rancho, beginning new family traditions—traditions which would eventually tie Serita and the baby to their new home. Things would work out very well for them there.

Shielding his eyes with his hands, Kosta studied the roof of the new house. "What in tarnation do you mean, ma'am? Build a ship's bridge on top of the roof here?"

"That is exactly what I want," Serita told him. "You are a master shipbuilder; you have done a

358

magnificent job with the house. Now I want a bridge of a ship to sit atop the roof, pointing out toward the bay."

"But I've never . . ."

"Kosta," Serita's voice was firm. "It does not have to float. Seems to me it should be a simple enough task since it will be supported by the roof."

"Simple enough," he groused. "And what might you be intending to do with the bridge of a ship on top of your house?"

She sighed, then turned her eyes toward the sea. "It's for . . ." She swallowed, considered whether to confide in him, then continued. ". . . it will be our office."

He stared at her, shaking his head. "Why not put your office downstairs like we planned?"

"Because I have changed my mind," she interrupted, exasperated. "I know you can do it. Now, get started, please. It must be finished by the time Giddeon returns."

While she talked, his features began to relax, and by the time she finished, his face was a study of earnestness. "Guess it's worth a try, ma'am. Don't count on it working, though." Taking his eyes from her, he studied the rooftop of the new house. This time when he shook his head, she could tell it was with renewed interest, something akin to admiration. "Yes, ma'am. I'll build you the finest goddamn ship's bridge you've ever seen. Just don't be gettin' your hopes up."

He began immediately, and during the next few weeks, the top of the house became the focal point for the entire day's activities. Even Tita, her chagrin at the house evident from the beginning, became so involved with the structure that she carried a hide-bound chair to an oak tree out front and sat hours on end embroidering a christening gown for the new baby and watching the ship's bridge take form.

Sometime during the second week after Giddeon left, laborers — vaqueros and *peóns* — began to appear at Los Olmos. The first to arrive was a married couple and their two small children. Daily after that, workers arrived alone, in pairs, and in group numbering three, four, and one time an even dozen. Soon the vaqueros' cottages and the barracks were full.

When queried, they all replied with the same phrase: *"El Capitán* sent me."

"Sent you to do what?" Serita asked.

The answer, too, was always the same. "To work at Los Olmos."

"I have no money to pay you," she objected the first time.

At that the *peón* grinned. "We work, not for money. For a home. La Hacienda de los Olmos will be our home."

From the moment of their arrival, they began to transform the place from a ranchero on its last leg of existence to a working, living *hacienda* in the old tradition.

The women planted vegetable gardens and set up their looms. They spun the wild flax, then wove the rough skeins into strips of cloth which Serita used to cover her pane-less windows.

The men worked well under Pablo, and he — himself a *corporal* once more — took on new life.

Giddeon had left a number of saddle stock behind, so the men who could ride began riding the range. They herded wild cattle onto the gathering ground, branded them with the ancient *marco* of La Hacienda de los Olmos—a circle with a cross in the middle—then earmarked each animal with a cropped notch on the lower left ear: the *señal* registered by Don Miguel's grandfather in the first official Brand Book for Spanish Texas in 1778.

In their spare time the men hunted peccaries—the gringos called them *javelinas*—whose tanned hides would provide both furniture and clothing for the families on the *hacienda*.

The children hunted birds and fished in the stream below the creek, and laughed and played games and sang songs.

The evenings were full of life as well. While the women cooked and washed dishes, the men propped chairs against the walls of the barracks and strummed guitars, creating both a festive and a nostalgic atmosphere for the entire place.

Tita looked years younger. She had stopped pining over Trinidad. Pablo—as if being rescued from the hands of death wasn't enough, he told Serita one day—now had a ranch to run, and the men to run it with. Life at Los Olmos was beginning all over again. A new house. A new baby on the way. A rebirth of the *hacienda*.

Serita finally remembered to ask Abril about her secret. The girl blushed and ducked her head.

"I promise not to tell a soul until you are ready," Serita told her.

Then with a quivering sigh that concealed none

of her joy nor her fear, Abril blurted out her secret. "But you must not let Doña Ana discover this," she pleaded. "You remember well the time she locked María in the maid's chamber until a priest came. And you know how long it will be until a priest will come to Los Olmos."

Serita laughed merrily. "I am so happy for you, Abril. Yes, of course I recall poor María. Although at the time I had no idea why she was being locked away. I suppose I thought it was to protect her soul." Now she knew otherwise.

The news of Abril and Delos being married brought new hope to Serita. As the days wore on toward the time she would deliver Giddeon's child, she had become more and more despondent, faced as she was with what promised to be the two major events in her life: the birth of her child and the departure of her husband.

The third week after Giddeon left with the mustang herd, the new vaqueros held a *rodeo,* and Serita's feet fairly ached to go along. But she didn't. Nieves still insisted that the baby would be born in five or six more weeks.

"No sense hurrying the little fellow along, *chica,*" she cautioned. "I do not want to do any birthing in the middle of the pasture."

Serita reluctantly agreed; she would never have to miss another *rodeo* due to a coming baby. This baby would be not only her first child but also her last, since she would no longer have a husband.

The fact was sobering, but not half so disquieting as the thought of living her entire life without Giddeon Duval.

Again, she recalled her feelings that terrible day Oliver Burton came to Los Olmos for the last time — her willingness to consider giving up Los Olmos for Giddeon.

It had been a foolishly romantic thought, she now realized. The only way she could live with Giddeon would be for him to take her on board his ship. Such a thing, of course, was never done. Even if it were, a ship was no place to raise a child.

But Giddeon had been reared aboard a ship, she challenged. And without a mother, too, she reasoned. No, Los Olmos was the place to raise her child.

The house was beginning to feel like a home already. Fortunately, one of the men Giddeon sent from Mexico proved to be a skilled cabinetmaker, and she put him to work building furniture.

She still intended to have the Stavinohas come out, but, in the meantime, she needed some of the more necessary pieces of furniture, such as a dining table and real beds.

Her favorite part of the new house was Giddeon's office — the bridge. Kosta finished it a couple of weeks after Giddeon left, and she paced the floor every day thereafter, searching in all directions for his return. On clear days the sea was visible. A sinking feeling in her stomach told her she would be the one to witness the rising of the morning sun through these windows . . . she and her child, alone.

The cabinetmaker fashioned exquisite tables around three walls of the bridge, beneath the large openings for windowpanes. Serita covered the floor

363

with an azure-and-earthen-colored rug one of the new women wove. Even though the climb to the top became more and more difficult as the days passed, this became her favorite place.

One day she climbed to the bridge to commence her daily lookout for Giddeon and was surprised to see a rider approach from the north. A mere dot on the horizon at first, the rider grew larger as she watched, fascinated. Company would be welcome. The thought immediately brought a smile to her face. Since the ordeal with Oliver Burton was over, she had given little thought to other gringo raiders. Now, with all the new vaqueros, no one would dare bother Los Olmos.

She watched the lone rider with growing anticipation. Perhaps it was Padre Alphonse. Although he wasn't accustomed to arriving uninvited, he did know about the baby. Perhaps he thought the time had come and he intended to christen the infant. If so, she thought wryly, he would be disappointed this trip. Nevertheless, Tita would be glad for a priest to say Mass.

The rider approached the creek now and let his horse drink before crossing. No, it wasn't Padre Alphonse.

She shrugged, scrutinizing the vaguely familiar figure.

Her thoughts returned to the padre. She would have to send word to him soon, for she desperately wanted to have the christening during their fiesta on the feast day of San Miguel. Since that was a full month after Nieves predicted the baby's arrival, she should have delivered by then. And she would insist

Giddeon stay—one more month to hold him near.

The embroidery work on the christening gown Tita constructed was exquisite; the gown would be an heirloom to hand down to future generations. And the fiesta . . .

The fiesta would be a christening for the new house, as well as for the new baby. A christening . . . and a . . .

The rider nudged his mount across the creek and up the rise.

. . . and a farewell party for Giddeon.

With the new laborers he sent to work the *hacienda,* she had let herself hope against all hope that he had decided to stay. That, she knew, was folly. He was merely seeing her well situated. And she loved him for it . . .

She loved him for . . .

The rider drew rein in front of the new house. Removing his homburg, he scratched his head and studied the structure with a puzzled look, as if he had stumbled across something he had not expected.

Serita smiled. The ship's bridge would likely draw such expressions for years to come.

The man stepped down from his horse and hitched the reins at the new hitching rail, still scrutinizing the house.

Then she recognized him.

Enos McCaulay.

She made it down the staircase in record time, given her cumbersome state. *Tío* Pepe's warning to stay clear of this gringo land-raider echoed with each step. She flung open the newly carved front door.

For a moment, she merely stared, while he gawked with open mouth at her advanced state. "Miz . . . ah, Duval?"

Her smile was a tentative acknowledgment, nothing welcoming. "Mr. McCaulay, isn't it?"

"Yes, ma'am. I . . . ah . . ." He wiped his brow with a handkerchief.

Regaining her composure, she invited him inside. The ordeal with Oliver Burton had certainly taken its toll on her manners. "Please, Mr. McCaulay, make yourself at home. We see few travelers, but those who do come to our door are always welcome."

McCaulay cleared his throat. "Is the cap—ah . . ." He glanced at her swollen belly and flushed. "Your . . . ah, husband sent word for me to meet him here."

She frowned. "My husband has driven a herd of mustangs to Mexico." His look of chagrin, accompanied as it was by a forlorn expression, caused her to take pity. If Giddeon had sent for him . . . "You are welcome to await his return with us. We are expecting him any day now."

He had been twirling his homburg by the brim in his hands. Finally, he gripped the hat in a tight fist and fairly shook it. "I will," he answered. "Yes, I will definitely stay right here until he returns."

Tita, as expected, was delighted to have a guest in the house. "You have come from Kinney's Rancho, *Señor* McCaulay?"

He nodded, stuffing his mouth with *cabrito*. Serita stifled a smile. He must have ridden the entire route without eating a bite. From the dandified looks of him, he likely didn't know a thing about eating off the land.

"What news do you bring of my brother, Señor Pepe Cortinas?" Tita asked, and was rewarded by a recital of great length concerning practically every person within a hundred-mile radius of the trading post.

Giddeon did not come that day. Nor the next. But Enos McCaulay gave every indication he intended to take up Serita's invitation to remain until the captain returned. With each passing day, however, the man became less and less tolerant of the situation, more and more belligerent toward the family.

After two days of his relentless grumbling, Serita stayed clear of him. He dogged Kosta's footsteps, and she even heard the clear sounds of arguments between them from time to time.

One morning she awakened with a stronger than usual longing to be in the saddle, so she did the next best thing. Before *desayuno* she headed for the corral to pay a visit to Navidad. The filly hadn't been ridden in a month now — not since Jorge left — but Serita visited her every day, feeding her tamales she took from the kitchen, brushing her, mumbling soothing words so Navidad would stay in tune with her voice. Usually her visits to the corral were in the evening around sunset, but this particular morning, she couldn't wait.

Arriving back at the new *la casa grande*, she wondered whether she hadn't been awakened by the devil. When she entered the courtyard, she heard

367

voices coming from the *comedor* beyond. Enos Mc-
Caulay was at it already, she thought, hearing the
argumentative tone in his voice, followed by Kosta's
monosyllabic replies. When she stepped inside the
empty kitchen, the sounds became words.

"I should have known Duval didn't intend to
honor our agreement," McCaulay was saying.

Serita paused to listen.

"Captain Duval always honors his agreements,"
Kosta replied.

"Then tell me why in hell he built this house?
Why is he sending vaqueros here in droves?"

"You do not approve of the house?" Kosta challenged. Serita smiled at the defensiveness in his
voice. He deserved to be defensive; he had build a
sound structure, beautiful to look at, one that would
last . . .

"The structure has nothing to do with it," Mc-
Caulay countered. "It's the money. The money
should have gone to pay those damned taxes."

Serita stifled a gasp. What did Enos McCaulay
know about her taxes? More important, what business was it of his? She started to rush around the
corner and give him a piece of her mind, but his
next words stopped her.

"Duval's man Felix assured me the taxes would be
taken care of before now. I came prepared . . ."

"The sale of this herd will finish off the back
taxes," Kosta replied in a monotone.

She heard a heavy sigh. From McCaulay . . . ?
she wondered.

"I should have known trouble brewed when he
bought that damned Arabian."

368

"The horse was a gift."

"A gift? For a wife in name only? What do you think I thought when I rode up to this door and found her with child? I had heard the rumor while she visited in Kinney's Rancho, but to see the fact . . ." McCaulay fumed. "I'll wager Duval has no intention of returning to sea. He's been leading me a merry chase."

"He'll return to sea," Kosta assured him. "Even the *señora* realizes that, though heaven knows she would like him to stay."

"He'll play hell going back to sea without a ship," McCaulay declared. "I came here, as agreed, with the fifty thousand dollars I promised him in exchange for a clear title to this damned ranch, and what do I find? The taxes haven't been cleared up. Why? Because Duval spent the goddamn money on a wife he professes to be leaving . . . on a horse, a house, and workers for land he agreed to turn over to me."

Chapter Seventeen

Serita stood stock-still for the few seconds it took
Enos McCaulay's words to take meaning in her
brain. Then her head began to swim, and the floor
pitched like a *ladino* mustang at the touch of a
saddle. Quickly, she grasped the adobe wall for
support. The rest of McCaulay's words filtered to
her through a haze.

"That night in Bagdad . . . the crazy old don
. . . my idea in the first place . . ."

Suddenly the four new walls of the kitchen began
to close in on her, and she raced, clutching at the
neckline of her dress, for the outdoors. The last of
July was always the hottest part of the year, and the
muggy air choked in her constricted throat. She
clung to the gnarled, burned trunk of the old oak
tree. But no strength came to her.

"*Señora,*" Abril's voice called from the *comedor.* "Are
you all right?"

Panic-terror stampeded her senses, and she ran.
Away from the courtyard, away from the new
house, away from the damning voice, the condemn-

ing words of Enos McCaulay. But they echoed and grated and clawed at her brain.

At the corral she looked for a saddle, a bridle, finally finding a *jaquima*. All she could think of was getting away . . . far, far away. Away from the awful, horrible lies, away from the possibility those lies were, instead, truth . . . away from reality.

Navidad tossed her head at Serita's skittish touch. "Shh," Serita whispered, but her mouth was dry, and her lips stuck together. "Shh, Navidad, shh."

She couldn't find a saddle, and in her present condition she knew she would have had a hard time heaving it onto Navidad's back had she found one. Leading the filly to the pole fence, she climbed up a notch, balanced precariously in her soft-soled slippers, and after two attempts, finally managed to heave herself onto the horse's back.

Once there, she had forgotten to let down the pole gate, so she bent and tried to reach it. Finally, she succeeded by maneuvering Navidad sideways and close enough to the rail that she could flip the pole out of its socket with her foot. Outside the corral, she gave Navidad the reins and nudged the filly hard in the flanks.

Where she was headed, she didn't think. In fact, her head swirled with everything except her present activities. Her skirts crumpled around her hips, leaving only the thin cotton of her pantaloons to separate Navidad from her own legs. She stuffed some of her petticoats beneath herself, thereby alleviating a measure of the discomfort.

But only a measure. Her heavy body bounced against the horse in a most painful manner. Her physical discomfort was nothing, however, compared to the pain which tormented her mind.

She felt as though someone had whacked her over the head with the butt of a rifle, sending spirals of excruciating pain through her brain—pain which radiated throughout her body in the form of questions too horrible to imagine, much less to consider as fact. But they had been delivered as fact; therefore she had to consider them.

Was it true? Had Giddeon betrayed her to such an appalling extent? How could she not have suspected?

Was it, indeed, true? Had he given her any clues? Was she so stupid as to have witnessed but not seen? Heard but not believed?

Was it true? Had Giddeon all the time intended to sell Los Olmos, leaving her not only heartbroken but destitute?

The country whirred past her. Patting the filly on the neck, she crooned her sad questions in cries that were lost on the wind. She rode without purpose, without direction, giving Navidad rein.

After being cooped in the corral these last few weeks, the filly responded as one set free from prison. "One of us set free," Serita murmured to the horse, "the other, imprisoned by a treacherous man."

A treacherous gringo, she thought fiercely.

As the horse galloped over the swaying switch-grass, the sun bore down on Serita's uncovered head, and she began to feel faint. Her awkward state was most unsuitable for riding. Now she knew why Giddeon hadn't wanted her to ride.

Giddeon! That traitorous gringo! As quickly as

these incensed thoughts entered her brain, they turned to sorrow, and came out as tears.

She had loved him for so long, realizing all the while the futility of her love. But never until today had she recognized the extent of her love for this man.

She had always known giving him up would be painful, but she hadn't counted on the devastation she now experienced.

The wind blew against her, dislodging the last of the steel pins from her hair. The full length of it blew behind her. She lifted her face to the sky and felt the wind dry her tears; her cheeks stung with the salty residue.

From the beginning of this arrangement, she had been prepared for him to leave. Even after Tita's warning on the day of their marriage became a grim reality, she was prepared for him to leave. And although his going would devastate her, she had prepared herself to endure the hurt by clinging to the love she believed he felt for her.

Now, everything had changed. Now, she would not have a lost love to remember, but a treacherous lover; not a beautiful relationship too soon interrupted to recall, but a despicable gringo who used her body and took her land, leaving her alone . . . with his child.

The ride was harder on her than she would have dreamed. Her back ached miserably; she arched it, at the same time massaged the small of it with one hand. When she did so, the baby within her kicked; she gasped for breath. The little foot felt stuck between her ribs, and at the moment it didn't feel so little.

The jolt brought her back to a more conscious state, and she drew up on the reins. If Navidad stepped in a varmint hole while galloping across the country, she would topple onto the ground for sure. And she'd be damned if she would give Giddeon the satisfaction of being right about that! She would not fall off a horse!

With Navidad slowed to a canter, the ride became much easier. She relaxed. Her wits began to return, and with them, her resolve.

Suddenly she smiled in spite of her gloom. She had not been riding aimlessly after all. She was headed straight for El Rey's valley. Leaning forward awkwardly, she patted Navidad's neck. "A look at El Rey won't do either of us any harm," she whispered.

The idea that her brain worked, even when she was unable to control it, encouraged her. Los Olmos was still a very real part of her life. She had the land-grant documents, thanks to Giddeon himself. She had control of her land. And she would remain in control of it. Giddeon could only take from her what she let him. And she had no intention of letting him take her land. She had never intended that, not even in her weaker moments — those times when she thought he was the most important thing in her life. When all was said and done, this land was the most important thing in her life; it was all she had to rely on.

The baby would be wonderful, if things worked out. Often they didn't. Babies were not always healthy and even when they were, they grew to adulthood and left one alone. Babies were not a permanent part of one's life.

No, Los Olmos was the only permanent, indispensable part of her life. And she had no intention of letting anyone take it from her . . .

Not even Giddeon Duval, whom she loved above all others . . . above all reason . . . above . . .

Tears poured from her eyes and flowed unchecked over her dry, stinging face. Not even Giddeon Duval would wrest her beloved Los Olmos from her. Thank God she discovered his deception in time to prevent him carrying it through.

Topping the rise, she stared into the valley through tear-streaked vision. El Rey, her gloriously wild and free stallion, the emblem on his forehead beckoning her as the morning star, tossed his golden mane and stared from the distance. His enormous eyes pierced her with a combination of recognition and mistrust. *He's getting to know me,* she thought. Bending forward again, she whispered to Navidad, "What do you think, *chica?* Is he a suitable mate?"

As she watched mesmerized, El Rey reared on his hind feet. Beauty and grace. His forefeet pawed the air with a furious vitality. Strength and courage. Like a trained army, his *manada* took flight. The earth rumbled and shook at the pounding of hooves; the air quivered with the shrill strains of his cry. The familiar sounds pierced Serita's grief, punctuating it with a resolve to carry forth, to endure, to overcome . . .

Navidad's whinny, by contrast, was a mere whimper in her throat, but in the next minute the filly charged down the rise toward the retreating *manada* — galloping straight into the arms of her lover, Serita thought. Then her own senses were jolted into action.

She pulled back on the reins; to no avail. She signaled with her knees as best her condition would allow. Navidad did not break stride.

Onward she plunged, her delicate limbs rebounding from the hard earth jarring Serita's body with each step. Serita's mind returned fleetingly to Giddeon, but this time it was to his admonition not to ride until after the baby was born.

"I assure you, Señor McCaulay, if they do not find and bring my niece back unharmed, you will rue the day you set foot on Los Olmos." Tía Ana clutched the *rebozo* closer around her frail shoulders.

Somehow they did not appear so frail at the moment, Kosta thought, while the old lady poured her wrath out on them.

Abril had brought the news, and it was soon discovered that Serita had overheard the conversation between himself and McCaulay. Not that they repeated the conversation in detail, but the old lady possessed a sharp mind.

Kosta followed Pablo to the corral at a fast clip, swearing beneath his breath with each step. He hadn't felt right about this gamble, not from the beginning. But as the months wore on, although he was eager to return to sea, the beauty and compassion of Serita Cortinas de Duval worked on his greed, and he began to hope the captain would elect to stay with his wife and child.

He himself of course would return to sea. But

there were many ships, many masters. And this particular captain showed definite signs of capitulating beneath the considerable charms of his lovely wife.

Then McCaulay arrived at the ranch, and Kosta began to consider striking out on his own. He had no stomach for the anguish he knew would accompany Serita Duval discovering her husband's treachery.

But he had not been quick enough about it. At the corral he slung a saddle onto the back of one of the horses Jorge had gentled, hoping the boy had done a good job. He wasn't much for riding horseback.

"If there aren't enough horses to go around," he told Pablo, "I will stay behind. One of the vaqueros can ride; they know the range lands better than I, anyhow."

Pablo seared him with a stare that was obviously intended to send him straight to the devil.

"We will find *la chica*. And you will be there when we do, Señor Kosta."

Those were the last words Pablo spoke until they had been in the saddle over an hour. The vaqueros fanned out on all sides of *la casa grande,* sweeping the country toward the bay and in the opposite direction, as well. Fortunately *Señor Capitán* had seen fit to send laborers to the *hacienda,* Pablo thought. With only himself and these inept gringos, *la chica* would have no chance at all.

Her horsemanship was unequaled by any woman he had ever known. But he had never seen a woman in her advanced state ride a horse, and a young horse only recently gentled, at that. His heart pounded with emotion he had not felt in a long time. Not even when he had looked at Trinidad's bullet-torn body; not when they laid the boy to rest in the coffin he himself had constructed.

Serita had been his favorite, almost like his own *niña,* since he and Nieves had no children of their own. And more than that, much more now, Serita the woman, brave and fearless, had saved him from death not a month past.

His large calloused hands trembled on the horse's rein. Now he had a chance to repay her, but he had no idea where she would be found.

Or did he? Just before he sank spurs to his mount, he turned harsh eyes on Kosta. "You had better pray, *señor,* that we find *la chica* in good shape. If not, *Doña* Ana's wrath will pale beside mine."

And beside Giddeon's, Kosta added silently, cursing the day he joined this star-crossed expedition in the first place. The least he could do was turn back now . . . before . . .

He couldn't leave now. Not before they found her. But afterward, immediately afterward, he was heading for wetter territory. Before Giddeon Duval returned to La Hacienda de los Olmos.

The first thing Serita became aware of when she opened her eyes was an enormous ache in her head. The second thing was that she lay on the ground in the middle of the vast prairie of Los Olmos, alone. Even her mount, her precious Navidad, was gone.

Sitting up, she pressed her fingers into the aching muscles of her back. Finally, the events of the past few hours returned to her, and she bewailed her own stupidity—her rashness at jumping on Navidad and dashing over the prairie like a madwoman.

Well, she conceded, she had indeed been a madwoman for a while. And look where it got her. With a great sigh, she stroked her belly where her unborn child lay.

How could she have endangered this little one's life in such an irresponsible way? And the worst wasn't over. She had a good ten miles to go to reach *la casa grande*. On foot. With dusk approaching.

Exasperated, she rose to her knees, the baby kicked, and she sank back down a moment. Relief washed over her.

"Thank God you are safe, little one." Rising to her knees once more, she pushed her palms against the ground in order to stand up. "Now, it is my job to keep you that way."

She straightened up with less effort than she had anticipated. Every joint was stiff, but by moving each leg separately, then her arms and her neck, she soon satisfied herself nothing had been damaged beyond repair. Then she took the first step, and an enormous cramp gripped her stomach.

Clutching her arms about herself, she doubled forward, waited a moment, and the pain subsided. Anxiety flushed over her, leaving her skin beaded with perspiration. Hurry, Serita, she pleaded. Hurry.

After a few steps, she limbered up a bit, but by

the time she gained the rise from where she had watched El Rey and his *manada,* her legs trembled, and she paused beside the oak tree. Afraid to sit down for fear the cramping would start when she stood up again, she leaned her shoulder against the tree a moment, then started down the hillside.

It served her right, she thought, as her situation began to infuriate her. She had brought this whole wretched ordeal upon herself. Dashing out of the house panic-stricken, like a wild stallion. She walked toward the east, busying her mind with stories Papá had told her about the mustang's tendency for panic-terror. A frightened herd ran without thought to danger, either for the individual or for the herd. Just as she had done. Tales were told of entire herds trampling each other to death, smothering every animal in the herd. She had seen a minor example of it every time she watched El Rey and his *manada.* One whiff of danger, and the herd was off like a fire in a brisk wind.

And she herself had reacted with the same barbaric response to Enos McCaulay's damning words against Giddeon.

Giddeon hadn't even had a chance to explain, repudiate, or refute the claims. She had acted like a panic-stricken animal, when she did not know for certain the allegations were true.

Suddenly her head spun and the cramping overtook her again. She stopped and doubled over. Finally it passed, leaving her heaving for breath and dizzy. And frightened.

She must get home. Soon.

Continuing, she returned to thoughts of her foolhardy race from reality . . . from some fictitious story the gringo McCaulay concocted. Sighing, she wondered what he could have intended, were the story not true. Better leave that for Giddeon to explain. She had much more important things to worry about at the moment. Things she had a measure of control over—like getting home and going to bed and protecting her baby.

How long she walked, she didn't know. Time flitted in and out of her brain like insects darting about on the surface of the creek. Her head throbbed, although she could find no wound by feel. Her body became lathed with a perpetual coating of perspiration which cooled her skin but left her flesh heated beneath.

Her slippers were definitely not made for trudging across the country . . . no more than they had been the night she killed Oliver Burton. She managed to keep from stepping on any of the numerous prickly pear plants, but once her skirts tangled on the thorns of an especially large clump. Finally, in desperation, she ripped the bottom of her skirts off, to keep the thorns from prickling against her legs.

After a while she realized the cramps she experienced were coming in a regular fashion. Every hundred yards or so, she would double over from the ever-increasing pains. At these times the perspiration covering her body would bead her brow and roll into her eyes, stinging. When the pains became almost unbearable, she tore another piece of fabric from her petticoat and rolled it into a wedge, which she placed between her teeth. She wasn't sure it helped, but at least she no longer feared gritting her teeth until they broke.

When the pains subsided, she could walk freely, but each time they occurred, she was left weaker than the last. And the terror in thinking she would die alone on this prairie, thereby killing her own child, was tenfold the terror that had brought her to this situation.

To take her mind off the uncontrollable workings of her body, she recited aloud every poem she had ever learned, sang every rhyme, and repeated the words to all the services in the Missal. All except the service for the Burial of the Dead.

She wasn't dead. Neither was her baby. That was the one thing she still had control over. At least, she still believed she had. And in her mind that made it so.

But when Pablo found her, she was wandering aimlessly, singing the *corrido* that had caused her such pain at the fandango at Kinney's Rancho. If asked, she would not have believed she even knew the words.

"Dashing and daring . . . *guapo ojos de verde* . . ." His handsome green eyes glistened from the leaves of a huisache tree ahead, and she hurried toward them.

"No, *senõr, dice el capitán, jugamos para su hija, Serita* . . .' " Her voice rose and fell with the frenetic timbre of one gone mad. She tripped, caught her balance, and the pains wracked her weakened body.

She fell to the ground, and when Pablo reached her, he knelt and made the sign of the cross.

" '*Jugamos para su hija*,' " she sang, though the words whished from her lips as on a fairy's breath.

382

Unable to understand them, Pablo knew only that she was alive.

"Over here," he waved to Kosta and the two vaqueros who accompanied them. "Can you hear me, *chica?*"

She blinked, he came into focus, and she grinned. " *'Jugamos para su hija,'* " she sang.

"It is I, Pablo," he told her. "We have come to take you home. In a little while, we will have a litter for you to ride on."

Gradually, his words registered. "Pablo."

He brought water and she drank. Then she sat up. The pains had passed once more. "I can ride," she told him. "But . . . I have no horse. Navidad took off after El Rey and his *manada*. She threw me."

Pablo studied her in earnest. Her voice was weak, but she appeared to be gaining strength. If she could ride . . .

"Are you sure, *chica?* It is not over five miles, now."

She struggled to stand, and with his support she succeeded. *"Sí,"* she told him. "All I need is a horse." In fact, she had never felt so weak, but she must get home. She couldn't wait for them to build a litter; she could not wait.

"Is there a horse for me?"

He hesitated only a moment, then his eyes glinted. *"Sí, chica."*

Kosta didn't like it, but he shrugged, knowing what Pablo said, he meant. Anyway, as soon as he got back to *la casa grande*, he was leaving. He wouldn't wait around for Giddeon . . . he wouldn't wait to see whether this woman lived or . . . .

Pray God she didn't die, he thought, assisting her into his saddle. She was a tough one, a mighty strong one. She deserved better . . . much better than the hand that had been played for her, he thought sardonically. And by the time he reached *la casa grande* later that night, he had about halfway decided to stick around and see she got a better deal than was in store for her.

It took longer than Pablo expected to reach *la casa grande.* He sent the two vaqueros after Navidad with instructions not to return until they had the horse in tow. Then he pointed Kosta toward the big house, saying that since he was a sailing man, if he waited a bit, he would have the stars to navigate by.

Afterward, he led Serita home on Kosta's horse. Several times he regretted his decision to let her ride — she grew weaker and weaker, and he could tell by looking that she was in terrible pain. But each time he suggested she wait for him to go to the house and bring the wagon, she resisted, assuring him she could make it.

"*Andale,* Pablo. Hurry, *por favor.*"

Nieves was fit to be tied. "The devil will have your hide, Pablo Ruíz! What do you mean letting that child ride a horse."

Pablo carried Serita to her room as Nieves instructed, followed by Tita, Abril, and Lupe. As soon as she was laid out on the bed, Nieves felt of her stomach and began issuing orders.

"Heat some water, Abril. Lupe, bring clean rags. Doña Ana, you may want to wait in your room. Pablo! Off with you now."

Tita pulled a chair close by the bed, and, taking the rag Nieves had dipped into the basin of water Abril brought, she began to bathe Serita's face and neck. "At least she is still alive," she said, watching Serita's chest move up and down in labored breath.

"Yes, and the child with her," Nieves said. "It will not be long now." Nieves clucked her discontent, however, all the while she removed Serita's disheveled clothing and replaced it with a clean nightgown. "But I must warn you, Doña Ana, she looks bad."

Tita merely nodded. "Yes, I am afraid her bargain with the devil may . . ." Her words drifted off. She was incapable of putting into words her deepest horror, for fear expressing it aloud might indeed make it come true. "Let us pray it will not be so."

As she watched helplessly, Serita's body constricted with pain. Her precious Serita. She remembered calling her impetuous the day of that ill-fated marriage. She remembered, as well, warning her that she might learn to love the green-eyed gringo who at the time so resembled the very devil himself. She had been wrong, but only about the latter. Serita grew to love the handsome sailing man, as she had known at the time she would. Rather than being the devil, however, she had come to think of Giddeon Duval as being sent by the hand of God. Indirectly, perhaps. Actually, she knew in her heart it was Miguel who had chosen this man — Miguel, who knew his daughter so well.

Suddenly Serita screamed in such agony that Tita felt tears behind her own eyes. She watched Serita's body arch and pitch and heard Nieves expel a deep breath.

"Lord help us, it is a tiny baby girl."

Tita stared at Nieves for a full minute, while the old woman washed the pale infant and swaddled it in a blanket. Then she fell to the bed across Serita's cold, still chest. The baby cried. Abril and Lupe gaped. And *Tía* Ana cradled her niece in her arms, desperately praying to the Lord above to suffuse life and warmth into this beloved child.

Chapter Eighteen

For two days Serita remained as in a deep sleep, scarcely drawing breath. At regular intervals, Nieves held her while she nursed the baby, but even at such times, Serita gave no indication of knowing what she was doing.

Tita kept a constant vigil at her bedside, leaving only for the *novena* she began on the second day after the baby was delivered, and then only on the hour for nine straight hours to pray at the new prayer bench the vaquero had constructed for her. She wished for the old chapel, where she could pray as she had done all her life. She hoped the new prayer bench served as well. She prayed she would not have to bury Serita in the family plot, not before she herself was laid to rest there.

She did not worry about the baby. Smaller than any living infant she had seen, the little girl was hardy, with lusty lungs, a vigorous kick, and a greedy appetite. Although from the looks of her, one would not have known it: She was a pale little thing—fair of skin, her hair had a definite reddish hue, and her eyes . . . Yes, Tita mused. The child would one day have the sea-green eyes of her father.

Tía Ana did not worry over anything happening to the baby before Padre Alphonse could come for the christening . . . At this thought, she always forced her mind to other matters. *"Madre de Dios,"* she would whisper. "Pray that Padre Alphonse does not have to bury Serita when he comes to christen the child."

On the third day Serita came back to life. Opening her eyes, she saw Tita beside the window, her embroidery in her lap, Nieves on the other side of the room with her back to her. Moving her head, she took in the strange surroundings; then life began to gradually return to her brain, as well as her body. She recalled the fire, Oliver Burton's death, Trinity's burial, the conversation she had overheard . . .

"Giddeon?" Her voice rasped, harsh and low. But it was enough to bring the two women in the room to attention. Tita dropped her needlework and rushed to the bed.

Nieves turned around. Serita blinked her eyes, staring at the bundle in Nieves's arms. Suddenly, she knew. Her hands found her belly, so long swollen with child. Now it lay flat beneath the bedcovers.

Her mouth dropped open, and Nieves brought the baby for her to see.

"A tiny little girl," Nieves told her.

"Is she . . . ?"

"She is fine, *sobrina,"* Tita assured her. "And thank the Lord, so are you."

388

When Serita attempted to sit up, Tita rushed to prop pillows behind her. Serita held out her arms, unable to speak for the lump in her throat. Nieves placed the bundle in her arms.

Serita felt the feather weight of the baby, even though the infant was swaddled in yards of cotton. She stared at the tiny, wrinkled face. Her mind whirled with the enormity of the moment. She struggled to acknowledge every single emotion which raced through her senses, for this surely was the greatest moment in her life. This one moment would remain etched in her memory forever.

"She is very beautiful," Tita mused.

"Yes," Serita whispered. At first she was afraid to move for fear she would not handle the baby correctly. After a while, though, she gained confidence enough to move one hand, and with it she tugged gently at the blanket, loosening it a bit. With the tip of a finger, she finally managed to touch the little cheek.

The baby's mouth twitched at her touch, and Serita's eyes widened. "Is she . . ."

At that moment, the baby wrinkled her face even more, opened wide her mouth, and let out a mighty howl.

Serita gasped and quickly dropped the edge of the blanket back across her face.

Nieves laughed. "She is telling you it is time to eat." She moved to help Serita pull aside her nightgown. Serita's eyes widened, and her shoulders tensed.

"How do you think we have kept her alive while you tried to die on us?" Nieves chided. Then she

389

studied Serita a moment longer, and finally asked, "Are you strong enough for us to leave you alone with your baby?"

A wave of joy passed over Serita. Alone with her baby! "Yes, *por favor*," she answered.

"I will show you then," Nieves began, and while she talked she washed the nipple of one of Serita's breasts and positioned the baby to nurse. Afterward, Nieves and Tita left the room.

"We will be just outside, *sobrina*," Tita told her. "Call if you need us."

Then, with a suddenness, she called after them. "Is . . . ? Has Giddeon returned?"

Tita shook her head and the two women left, the lightness of their step encouragement to the entire household who had waited with held breath these last days.

The instant they left her alone with her baby, Serita was seized by a feeling of completeness such as she would not have imagined, followed by a sense of alarm of equal intensity. While the baby went after her meal as though she were famished, Serita removed the blanket, then lifted the infant's clothing and examined every inch of the child from head to toe. They were all there, the toes and fingers; her little torso was unblemished, her head was perfectly shaped.

But nothing about her resembled Serita in any way. Her fair skin, her red-tinged hair. "I will call you Estelle," she whispered, "but I fear you more resemble a Stella." Her examination completed, she replaced the blanket and stroked the baby's tiny cheek with her forefinger. "Perhaps you will have

390

my temperament, little Estelle, for otherwise you are surely your father's child."

At that moment, the baby opened her eyes and looked up into her mother's face. Serita stared at the pale-green eyes, knowing they would take depth and substance with the years. Tears flowed from her own.

"My dear, precious child! How will I bear to live with those eyes for the rest of my life?"

Pablo came to see her that afternoon. He neither lectured or admonished her for her perilous flight, rather, in an uncharacteristic show of affection, he patted her shoulder, his eyes glistening with unshed tears. "We brought Navidad home, *chica*. She is in the corral, although I have been tempted to put a bullet through her temple for what she did to you."

"Oh, Pablo. Thank you. Please take care of her. Navidad was not responsible for my accident. That was my fault, mine alone. And you saved my live."

"We are even then," he told her. "You have recovered, so all is well. You have a fine *niña*. What a surprise for Jorge."

For Jorge, Serita thought after Pablo left. What about Giddeon? Little Estelle would be a surprise for him, too. But nobody spoke his name.

Kosta came in, accompanied by Pablo, Nieves, and Tita. He did not mention the conversation that had precipitated her near-fatal dash from reality. Although she wanted desperately to know the truth of the situation, she did not ask him to tell her. She would wait for Giddeon to return and defend himself. Pray God she would be able to decipher the truth from whatever lies he might attempt to pass

391

off.

Enos McCaulay did not come to see her. But she knew he was still around. She heard his voice from time to time during the day, and when she dozed, she dreamed it.

Late that afternoon she tried to get out of bed, but Nieves would not hear to such a thing.

"You were nearer death than many dead folks I have seen," she admonished Serita. "You must stay right here and get your strength back. You don't want that baby to go through life without a mother."

That did it. She settled down and let Abril bring her broth and rice and finally beefsteak. She ate everything they brought, she fed her baby, and she dozed between times. No, she definitely did not want little Estelle to go through life without a mother.

To do so fatherless was enough to ask of any child.

The morning of the fourth day after Estelle was born, Serita awoke to the sound of Giddeon's voice.

Giddeon rode through the night to reach Los Olmos. For the last few days he had been gripped by an unusual restlessness, which he put down to his anxiety over the forthcoming confrontation with Serita.

The more he thought about it, the more he agreed with Don Miguel. Serita must leave Los Olmos; not solely to settle his agreement with Enos McCaulay, either.

She must leave for her own good. Sooner or later

land raiders from north of the Nueces would drive her off. Or, as events of the last week before he left for Mexico proved, worse.

No, he would not be able to leave until she was safely situated at Kinney's Rancho. And he intended to leave as soon as McCaulay delivered the fifty thousand dollars.

His trip to Mexico had convinced him of President Bustamente's deteriorating political situation. If he planned to cash that letter of credit, he had better do it while Bustamente was still *el presidente* and still had funds to pay up.

Jorge interrupted Giddeon's reverie. "How much farther, *Tío Capitán?*"

"Not much, son. Do you think you can ride through the night without sleep?"

"To get home, yes."

Jorge had enjoyed the trip, but Giddeon suspected he had been homesick longer than he himself had noticed. The last day the boy had fallen quiet. He rarely spoke, and when he did, it was not in his usual animated fashion.

"Do you think Serita has had the baby?" Jorge asked.

Giddeon shook his head. "The baby won't come for another month, *hijo.*"

"What do you think we will name it?"

Giddeon smiled. Jorge was as much a part of his life now as a true son would be. It pleased him to know the boy felt the same way about him. "I've considered that, *hijo,*" he responded seriously. "A boy should have an important name. One that represents all he receives from his family, all he is

393

expected to become when he grows up."

"How about 'Giddeon'?" Jorge suggested.

Giddeon shook his head with a deep sigh. No, his son would not carry the name of a man who was father to him in name only. "I will call him Miguel," he said. "Your grandfather is the man I would like my son to emulate above all other men."

"I was happy to see him," Jorge said.

"Yes," Giddeon replied. "So was I. He promised to visit Serita and the new baby in —"

Abruptly he stopped. Jorge had not been privy to his and *Don* Miguel's conversation, thus he did not know of the pending move to Kinney's Rancho. He must tell him soon, however. With the bond which had developed between the boy and himself, he knew he must be the one to tell him. Next to telling Serita, he dreaded this most of all.

Don Miguel had been pleased about the move and about the baby, as well. Once or twice during their short visit, Giddeon had caught the old man scrutinizing him with such intensity that Giddeon squirmed. Don Miguel still gave him the feeling of reading his thoughts, and more — the old man had the visage of one who could see beneath the sur- face — to the very heart of a man, deeper than a man could see himself. And that was unsettling.

Giddeon, Jorge, Delos, and Felix approached from the southwest, and by the time the rising sun fulfilled its late-August promise of a hot and muggy day, they had come in view of *la casa grande*.

"Something is wrong," Jorge said. "It does not look the same as when we left."

Delos agreed, and Giddeon studied the structure

394

while he pressed his tired mount to a faster gait. Indeed, the house did look different.

"Kosta has been hard at work," he mused.

"Yes." Felix nodded. "So it seems. If I didn't know better, I would think we were approaching a ship at sea . . ."

"From the stern . . ." Delos added.

"A ship?" Jorge asked.

The closer they came to *la casa grande,* the clearer the ship took form. They rode past the barracks and the vaqueros' cottages. Jorge and Delos and Felix chatted away. Giddeon observed the early-morning activity with only part of his brain.

"Looks like all the *peóns* made their way north," Delos commented.

Giddeon nodded. He had hoped they would. A working ranch might alleviate whatever jitters Mc-Caulay had fallen prey to during the extra time it took to pay the taxes.

But the better part of his brain was occupied with the structure stretching to the sky. Without stopping at the back of the house, he led the way around the building and drew rein, his eyes transfixed on the ship's bridge sitting atop his . . .

His curiosity turned to anxiety. "What the hell . . . ?"

Hitching his horse at the new rail, he barely heard the exclamations of the others. Their arrival, however, did not go without acknowledgment, for they had no sooner tied their mounts than people poured forth from the massive front doors.

Tita and Nieves and Pablo and Lupe and . . . His mind took them all in; his eyes searched for

Serita.

Abril raced down the path and flung herself shamelessly into Delos's arms. Kosta came out . . .

Where was she? Phrases reached his ears but made no sense, they were so jumbled together in his search for her. It was too early for her to be out rid—

She wasn't supposed to be out riding, whatever the hour.

A final figure came through the doorway and stopped behind the others, but atop the porch, while the family flew down the steps, leaving him alone and visible.

At the sight, fury was born in the pit of Giddeon's stomach. Enos McCaulay! Forchristssake, what was he doing here?

Words took form then—not complete thoughts . . . only words.

". . . birth . . . death . . . baby . . . Scrita . . ."

Before he knew what he was about, he had Enos McCaulay by the collar. "You sonofabitch! If you have harmed my wife, I'll kill you with my bare hands!"

McCaulay struggled to free himself.

Giddeon's voice raised. "Where is Serita?" he demanded. "What has happened to my wife?"

"Giddeon . . ." Serita clung to the doorfacing, taking in the scene with anxiety and confusion.

Her voice came to him as a whisper which exploded like fireworks inside his brain. For a moment he could but stand paralyzed. Enos McCaulay practically dangled from his hand. His eyes swept over her, taking in but not understanding her disheveled

396

appearance, her nightgown . . .

As suddenly as he had grabbed the man, he dropped McCaulay to the steps and swept Serita in his arms. His throat was constricted so, he could not speak.

Finally, the essence of her restored his brain, if not his senses, and he became conscious of her body in his arms. His mind swam with memories of the first time he ever saw her—clad in buckskin breeches and silk blouse . . . her provocative, slender body.

"The baby?" he rasped.

"Come," she said. "I will show you."

Her heart pounded so fiercely, she was left breathless and unable to speak, which was just as well, considering that her thoughts were too jumbled to make sense. He was home; that was all that mattered.

Catching his hand, she led him toward the nursery, hoping she did not swoon. It was the loss of so much blood, Nieves had said, so Serita had eaten more than she wanted in an effort to restore her health before Giddeon returned. She did not want him to see her in such a puny condition. Then they stood above the crib the vaquero had made. It was so new the wood was still pale. Thankfully, Giddeon held her tightly beside him with an arm around her shoulders.

"When . . . ?" he asked. "I thought it wouldn't be for a month yet."

She held him fast about the waist. "This is the fourth day." When he didn't move to touch the baby, she picked up the infant and offered her to him.

"No," he said, almost in panic. "It's too little . . ."

But as he spoke, his hands came out involuntarily and she placed the baby in them.

He stared transfixed, and tears brimmed in Serita's eyes. Her little family was together . . . at last. She would store this memory alongside the first time she held Estelle.

"I thought we would name him Miguel." Giddeon spoke so softly she had to strain to hear him. When his words registered, the brimming tears rolled down her cheeks.

She wiped them away. Then she smiled. "What a lovely thing for you to think. Papá would be honored. But I have chosen a more appropriate name."

He quirked an eyebrow, and her smile broadened. For an instant her thoughts were dazzled by his green eyes. Then she said, quite innocently, "I named her Estelle."

It took a moment more for the idea to settle. Finally he grinned. "No wonder she's so little."

"Yes," Serita whispered, thinking that with a month's more growth, their daughter would have been the size of any son she might have borne.

At the handling, the baby stirred, and Giddeon suddenly held her toward Serita. "Take her."

Serita smiled, but when she took little Estelle from Giddeon's hands, the baby wrinkled her face and wailed.

Giddeon's eyes widened. "What's the matter? Did I hurt her?

Serita laughed. "No, of course not. She's telling us she's hungry."

Nieves rushed in at the sound, followed on the

heels by Jorge.

"You should be in bed," Nieves admonished. "As bad off as you have been. Get on back there, and I'll bring you the baby."

"Serita!" Jorge jumped from foot to foot, unable to contain his excitement. "You had the baby before we got back!"

"Bad off . . . ?" Giddeon asked. His mind returned to the porch, to the words he had heard but not understood. "Was it . . . bad?"

Serita shook her head, but Nieves answered, shooing them away. "Bad? The poor *chica* almost died. For two days she did not even know where she was . . ."

Jorge had worked his way between the grown-ups and now stroked little Estelle's head with a dirty finger. "*Tío Capitán* said you would not have the baby for a month yet." As he spoke he let the baby wrap a tiny hand around one of his fingers.

"She wouldn't have had the baby so soon" — Nieves took the baby from Serita — "if it had not been for that gringo McCaulay."

"What . . . ?" Giddeon began.

"Nieves," Serita warned. "Run along and see that Jorge gets something to eat. I can manage."

Nieves huffed. "If you don't get back in that bed, you will fall down in a faint."

"Giddeon will catch me." Serita's voice was so firm that Nieves looked directly at her a moment, then at Giddeon, and back to Serita. "Are you sure, *chica?*"

"*Sí.*"

Nieves handed Serita the baby. "Call me when

399

you finish." She looked at Giddeon. "Do not let anything else happen to her, *Señor Capitán.*" With that she shooed Jorge ahead of her out of the room and closed the door.

He nodded, chastised for what, he knew not. He stood in the middle of the floor watching Serita pick up a blanket and a couple of white cotton cloths. She walked toward the doorway that led from the nursery to the bedchamber. His mind reeled with the implications of what he had heard. Something dreadful happened to Serita while he was gone; Enos McCaulay caused it; but he himself was ultimately to blame. It didn't take much imagination to figure out what had happened, he thought, as a crushing weight of dread settled over him like a full-grown mustang stallion.

"Come on," Serita called to him from the doorway. "Nieves is right. I should lie down, and this is a good time. When our Estelle wants her dinner, she demands it."

Following her then, he watched as she settled herself against a group of pillows and proceeded to nurse the baby. He stood as though helpless in the middle of the room.

"Serita . . . what happened?"

She looked up at him, his green eyes pleading, his baby tugging at her breast. "Isn't she wonderful, Giddeon? I will tell you something strange. When I feed her, I am overwhelmed by a sense of peace. I cannot explain it, but for a time everything else fades away—all the trials and difficulties we have had lately. For a time, I am filled with such a magnificent peace . . ." Her voice trailed off, and

400

she wished she could tell him the rest—that now with him here beside her, her peace was complete. More complete than ever before in her life.

He studied her, wondering whether he weren't walking through a dream. Emotions smothered him, also, but they were far from peaceful. The sight of Serita with his baby filled him with awe—and with anxieties he could not explain. Her words filled him with a restless anguish.

"Come sit beside us," she said. He obeyed, silently. "No one else has stayed with me while I feed her—not since I woke up. It is so personal . . . so private." She looked into his eyes which were awash with tenderness. "It makes me feel like . . . like we are a real family."

Her words wrenched at his mind and fairly tore his heart from his chest. Bending awkwardly he kissed her lightly on her forehead, leaving the burning imprint of his lips there when he sat back up. "What happened, *querida?*"

"You came home."

She hadn't intended to fall asleep—they had so much to talk about. It must have been the loss of blood, as Nieves kept saying, but by the time little Estelle finished eating, Serita's brain was so woozy she couldn't keep from closing her eyes, and, once closed, she did not open them again for several hours.

The next time she saw Giddeon was when he followed Nieves into her bedchamber with the squalling Estelle. The instant she saw his face, she

401

knew he had heard the story of her flight from reality—almost from life.

Nieves dutifully left the two of them alone with their infant daughter. Giddeon settled onto the bed beside her once more, but he didn't speak until Estelle was suckling hungrily.

"I sent Enos McCaulay packing. The man had no right coming here with his . . ."

The look she gave him stopped his words. "We all do things we have no right to do. I had no right to endanger Estelle's life. You had no right . . ." She paused deliberately. "But this is a special time with Estelle, and we will not ruin it by a recitation of all our shortcomings. Tell me about your trip."

He inhaled a deep breath, studied her a moment, and wanted desperately to hold her in his arms. "I saw *Don* Miguel."

Her eyes brightened, and he reached into his pocket and withdrew a folded piece of paper. "He sent you a letter."

"Read it to me."

He shrugged. "It is addressed to you."

"Read it, Giddeon, while I feed Estelle."

The letter brought good tidings of her mother and other family members in Mexico and wishes for her health and that of his newest grandchild. It ended with a pledge to visit her soon in— Giddeon omitted the final words of the sentence, in respect for her wishes not to discuss unfavorable topics while she fed Estelle. By the time he finished and stuffed the letter back into his pocket, a measure of timidity had vanished, and he reached forward and touched one tiny hand.

"Estelle," he whispered, staring instead at the baby's mother. "Thank you for naming her for my mother."

Serita smiled with a measure of momentary contentment. "As you said one time, we both have stars in our lives. Now we have one more — the most special one of all."

For the first full day after Giddeon returned, Serita kept her resentments at bay. By the second day, however, she had regained enough strength that she dressed and joined the others in the new *comedor* for *desayuno*. Nieves objected, of course, and Tita hovered, but she made it through the morning without any of the fainting spells Nieves predicted.

She didn't see much of Giddeon, because he went with the vaqueros on one of their regular *rodeos*. When he returned in time for *merienda* that evening, he was enthusiastic about the size of the herd.

"It wasn't that many months ago all our cattle were slaughtered," he said. "Now we have several hundred head, including a good number of calves."

She started to ask him what difference it would make, with his plans for Los Olmos, but held her tongue. When she retired to feed Estelle, he followed her, and as in a script, they engaged in an innocuous conversation, during which he told her of his trip and Jorge's experiences and she told him about the vaquero he sent who made furniture. Estelle finished eating and Serita changed her and put her to bed, but Giddeon did not leave as he had the evening before. He stayed.

Her fingers trembled on the blankets she tucked around the infant while she waited for him to leave.

The night before, he had slept in the room originally designed as an office—before she conceived the notion for the ship's bridge. The first day he had treated her with a distant sort of respect—close but not touching, together yet alone. Only his eyes revealed the passion she remembered—and yearned for—so desperately.

Yes, she thought, bending to kiss little Estelle on the forehead, she might yearn for his touch, but that was all. She did not *want* his touch. The closeness she felt for him would probably be with her always, because of Estelle.

But it was a closeness without a future; a hopeless longing that would be sealed with his departure, which, knowing now his true plans, could come any day. No, she did not want to resume a physical relationship with this traitor . . .

"Serita." His voice was low and worked at her senses. She tensed to resist, but he grasped her waist with his hands and turned her in his arms. Without another word, without a struggle, he kissed her.

And she responded. The instant his lips quivered against hers, she was lost. Her hands inched up his arms, around his neck, and at last clasped behind his head, drawing his face closer to hers. Her heart beat faster than it had since she had trudged across the pasture, and with as much purpose. Her mind spun, and she rebuked the thought that she was only letting herself in for more heartache.

He held her tight, pressed her body against his eagerly, and reveled in the touch of her—her full breasts mounded softly against his chest, her flat belly pressed against his, and the idea that he could not make love to her for a while yet distorted his brain.

Sweeping her in his arms, he carried her to her bed and lay beside her, fully clothed. Taking the pins from her hair, he buried his face in its luxuriant mass. When he started to remove her clothing, she stopped him.

"Don't . . ." Her breath blew damp and teasing against his temples.

"I won't hurt you, *querida*. Let me feel you next to me. We will lie together . . . sleep together . . ."

"Please . . . please don't." Struggling, she tried to wriggle out of his embrace.

Their eyes met in the glow of the lamp beside her bed.

"Serita, I have missed you so . . ."

"Don't say that . . ."

"It's true . . ."

"Not true enough."

Their eyes locked; their two separate and distinct wills collided with a hurricane force; yet neither could tear his eyes away from the other. "Yes . . ." he mouthed, his lips barely an inch from hers.

Her fingers twined painfully in his hair. Her heart thudded. How she wanted this man. Before this instant she had never known how much. "No . . ."

"Please," he begged.

"I can't . . ." she whispered. "It will be too hard . . . after . . . after you have gone."

"I'm not leaving."

Their individual breaths tangled as hot and humid lovers between the chasm of their minds.

She curled her lips in and pressed her teeth against them, scarcely able to assimilate her thoughts. "What?"

"I can't leave you."

"What . . . do you . . . mean?"

"You and Estelle are my family. I could never leave you. I will go to sea, but . . ." Pulling her to him, he pressed his lips fervently against her forehead, then continued. "I will never stay gone long at a time. I couldn't."

"When did you decide this?"

"I'm not sure." He grinned wryly. "Could have been the night you wore that flirty black dress and asked me to marry you."

"I didn't *ask* you," she reminded him.

"No, you didn't, did you?"

They slept in each other's arms, stirring only when their daughter called for a feeding, and awoke in the luxury of their bodies and spirits, joined by new commitments—new and sincere vows.

She did not question where he would get a ship in which to go to sea; it was a while yet before she allowed herself to examine that unsettling topic.

Chapter Nineteen

Giddeon spent most of each day with the vaqueros, and Serita took that as a sign of his growing commitment, not only to her, but to the ranch.

When, a couple of weeks after he returned, she put the question to him again about when he had decided to stay with her, he answered; "I suppose it became clearer to me on the trail drive; that was the longest month I've ever spent. I realized it was because I didn't have you beside me."

One afternoon she heard someone on the ship's bridge, so she climbed the stairs. She had not been up there since Estelle's birth, and now as she took the steep stairs she knew why.

When she reached the office, though, he was standing at one of the windows, and her delight at finding him here erased any pain the trip might have cost her.

He studied her with blatant admiration . . . and more. "Where did you get this idea?" He flung his arms about the room.

"Kosta . . ." she began, hesitant to tell him, even

407

now, that he had decided to stay at Los Olmos, how desperate she had been for him to want to.

"Kosta told me," he teased, "that it was all your doing, and that he had a pretty good idea as to why."

She blushed and stepped into his open arms. Quickly, he closed them tightly about her.

"That was before . . ." she began.

"Before I confessed I can't live without you?"

She looked away, toward the sea. The day was cloudy, though, and she couldn't tell whether she looked at water or at sky. Her thoughts were equally muddled. "Before Enos McCaulay came with his dreadful lies," she whispered.

At her words, his arms tightened almost imperceptibly around her, and instantly she knew she did not want to pursue this dastardly topic. She wished she had never heard of Enos McCaulay, yet she had. And since she had, the despicable things he accused Giddeon of must be brought out in the open.

"Tell me about him." She moved from his embrace to perch on one of the hide-bottomed stools the vaquero had made especially for this room.

"Serita, I want you to regain your strength before . . ."

"My ears are as strong as they will ever be. Since we must discuss him sooner or later, tell me now."

He sighed heavily and stared into the misty distance. "What do you want to know?"

"Everything." When he didn't immediately respond, she prompted him. "You can begin with the card game in which you won *me!* Whose idea was

408

that? Yours or . . . or Enos McCaulay's?"

His silence startled her; why, she wasn't sure. "Tell me about it."

"Serita."

"Tell me."

He heaved a deep draft of air and sat on one of the other stools. Still, he did not look at her. "I told you long ago that wagering for . . . for your hand was my idea."

"The game itself. Whose idea was it?"

"It was his . . . but I don't regret it." Turning then, he pierced her with his insolent green eyes. "Do you?"

"No," she whispered, thinking of Estelle. "At least not all of it. The truth would have been better."

"What truth?"

"That you planned to sell Los Olmos to Enos McCaulay for fifty thousand dollars, that's what truth!"

He stared back toward the distant sea. "Would it have made any difference?"

She pursed her lips to keep them from trembling. "Probably not . . . not in the beginning, since Oliver Burton was such a threat. But . . ." I wouldn't have fallen in love with you, she thought desperately. At least, I would have tried not to much, much harder than I did. And I wouldn't have had a baby. A cry escaped her lips at the thought. Estelle was worth everything, but, oh, the pain.

Suddenly his hands were on her, the familiar feel as of heated iron bands that never failed to bring a trembling to her arms. He turned her and the stool to face him. Then, squatting before her on the floor, he studied her intently.

"Listen to me, Serita. This is the only way. Enos McCaulay is our savior. We won't have to worry about the likes of Oliver Burton again."

"Oliver Burton is dead," she retorted, thinking curiously that they were having two separate conversations: she discussing something in the past, a dreadful thing over and done with; he the future. "Oliver Burton is dead. I killed him. I will never have to worry about him again."

"He was only one of many, Serita. You know that." Standing, he stared away to sea once more. "Don't be so stubborn."

His anxiety piqued her own. "Then fortunately you sent Enos McCaulay away. He was no different than Oliver Burton. Why couldn't you see that?"

"No, *querida*, there is one big difference between Burton and McCaulay. Burton was out to steal your land; McCaulay will pay us for it."

Again his choice of words confused her. He was speaking in the present . . . the future. Her present . . . her future. "Money means nothing to me! Los Olmos is my heritage . . . Estelle's heritage . . . Jorge's. No amount of money could or will buy Los Olmos."

"Then you will lose it . . . along with your life, in all probability." He flung his arms in a wide arc around the bridge. "There are hundreds of land-raiders out there still, and very few of them willing to pay. Among those few, fewer yet have any money. McCaulay has both—the intention and the money. He will set us up for life. Can't you see how it will be unless we take this offer?"

410

Her breath came softly, as if from someone else's body. When she spoke, her words, too, sounded as though they had been spoken from afar. "What offer?"

"McCaulay's offer."

It seemed for a moment that every bit of life within her had stopped functioning. Her words were but a vague immitation of sound. "Then it is true?"

"Yes, damnit! Of course, it's true. And if we don't take it—if you don't take it—you will be condemning Estelle to a very uncertain future. They will drive you from this land, Serita. You will have no land, no money, nothing. This way you don't have to worry about Estelle's future."

As he spoke, life returned to her disordered brain, and with it, life-preserving emotions. Anxiety stewed and gave way to anger, red-hot and fierce. "The only thing I have to worry about is believing your lies." Rising, she turned to leave. "And as of this moment, I am through with that."

He reached for her, turned her to face him, but she pulled away. "Serita, I didn't lie. I'm going to stay with you."

She jerked free of his hold. "Stay with me?" Her voice rose in indignation. "Stay with me? How honorable of you. I know exactly what you mean by that. You will take the money from my land, raise your ship . . ."

"Raising the *Estelle* is what will ensure our future . . ."

"*Con permiso!*" she interrupted. "I thought selling Los Olmos would ensure our future."

He gritted his teeth. "With the money from the

Estelle's cargo you will be set for life."

"While you ride the seven seas! When the notion strikes you, *if* the notion strikes you, you will come home to your wife—to wherever you decide to keep her . . ."

"Felix will stop at Kinney's Rancho on his way back from settling the taxes. He and Tío Pepe will find a house." His voice was firm, emotionless, infuriating. "Don Miguel agrees that moving there is best for you, for the baby, and for Jorge and Tita."

"¡Papá! I should have known you were in cahoots with him. He has been trying to make me leave Los Olmos for—"

"He's right. Why can't you understand?"

"Oh, I understand well enough. I understand that you are two of a kind—men who want to roam the world, unheedful of tradition or heritage, unmindful of the women you leave behind. You would stick me in some . . . some house at Kinney's Rancho where you can come for a night or two once a year, sleep with me, leave me carrying another of your children . . ."

He shook her by the shoulders then. "Forchristssake, Serita, listen. Don Miguel wasn't like that, and I'm not, either. It won't be like that."

"You are right, *Señor Capitán*. It will not be like that. I won't stand for such a life . . . not for me . . . nor for my daughter." Her thoughts raced to that night so long ago. The night she wore the black dress and announced her marriage to this . . . this gambling man. The black dress he said bewitched him. "You will have neither my land, Gid-

412

deon Duval, nor my willing body."

It took her a week to change her mind. A week during which she saw little of Giddeon, but thought much of his words. He had said no more than Papá said all along; no more than Pablo said when he cautioned against killing a gringo. *There will always be more of them; there are too many for us to win.*

While she fed and cared for little Estelle, she began to see that Giddeon might be right. If it were only herself, she would never leave. But how could she take the chance of condemning her child to a life of deprivation or even death when it was within her power to do otherwise? And Jorge, she must consider his future, too.

Eventually she came to feel that she carried the weight of the world upon her shoulders, and she stooped beneath the burden. Every time Estelle stared at her with her pale-green eyes, she shuddered. How could she bear to look into those eyes in years to come were she to forsake this child now? To grow up without a father was bad enough. How could she condemn her precious daughter to a lifetime of destitution and turmoil as well?

That she herself was so doomed crossed her mind more than once. For every time she looked into Estelle's eyes, she recalled her first thought on seeing them, and she knew she had been right. Even though he was callous and cold, she would never stop loving him . . . needing him . . . wanting him. Never. Her body ached, even yet, for his loving touch. She knew it always would.

413

Her decision made, several things remained to be done before she could leave Los Olmos forever. She would have to convince Tita and Jorge. That would take some doing, but she would use Giddeon's own argument, that the move was in the best interest of the young ones — Jorge and Estelle. Along with the fact that Tita would be close to Tío Pepe and his family. This, however, she would leave for last.

First, she had one last dream to dispose of. Dressing in a pair of buckskin trousers and a coarse, homespun white shirt, both of which Lupe had made for her since Estelle's birth, she saddled Navidad and rode away from *la casa grande* with Pablo's admonitions ringing in her ears.

"I will return before nightfall," she assured him. "Promise not to tell anyone where I have gone. And let no one follow me."

The old vaquero shrugged, his gaze fastened on the horse she led behind her on a lead rope. "If that is your wish, *chica*. You are sure you are well enough?"

"*Sí.*"

Her ride to the valley was not nearly as comfortable as she had thought it would be, even though a full month had passed since Estelle's birth. In spite of her protesting body, however, she dawdled, committing to memory every rise and fall of the land that was as much a part of her as her own flesh and blood.

Not that she was in any danger of forgetting a place she had viewed from the back of a horse since before she could walk on her own two feet. From the time she was able to sit, Papá had taken her

414

into the pastures, riding with her perched on the saddle in front of him.

No, the old landmarks would remain indelibly fixed in her mind, and she would tell the stories to Estelle every night at bedtime to make sure they were not lost.

First, she stopped by Pablo's Resaca. She had not been born when Pablo took the fall that earned the old mudhole its name. But she had helped pull many a bogged cow out of its sticky mud.

Next, she rode north a few more miles to the gathering grounds. Along the way she studied the cattle and was amazed that the new vaqueros had done such a competent job. Of course, Pablo was an excellent *corporal*.

Sitting her horse in the middle of the gathering ground, the warmth of this early September day suddenly stifled her. Her memories here were *not* of years gone by, but of Giddeon, of the slaughtered cattle, and of Giddeon . . . She sighed. That was the day she first told him she could take care of herself.

Well, she could, she reiterated, heading for the valley. She would have liked to see the corner post once more where the old surveyors set the stone, the place where her great-grandfather accepted this land from the representative of King Ferdinand, but it would require a day's ride to get there, a day's journey to return to *la casa grande*. And she was not up to such a trip.

Neither did she want to take the time. Now that her decision had been made, she was anxious to put the leave-taking behind her. One day of it would be all she could stand, emotionally and physically.

By the time she arrived at the valley, the sun was high overhead. She dismounted at the bottom of the rise, and hitched the horses there. Navidad would likely recall her last spree on the other side of this rise, and Serita didn't want to take a chance on losing both her horses. But she did want a moment to watch El Rey and his *manada*.

Crawling to the top, she lay for a time on her stomach, hands crossed beneath her chin, studying the unsuspecting stallion and his *manada*. He grazed a bit here and there, pranced about, and generally strutted his stuff, king of his world. Free. Spirited. Magnificent.

What a fine mate he would be for Navidad. She wondered whether any of the first generation of offspring would be marked with a star on the forehead. The thought filled her with despair, knowing she would not be able to see the colts—the fulfillment of her dream.

Watching El Rey now, she realized her dream had been much deeper and more personal than mere financial gain. It had not been only to save Los Olmos, her dream.

Her dream had been the dream of the ages—of the past, yearning for the future. El Rey was beautiful and spirited, because his ancestors before him had been. And it was his descendants whose existence she wanted to ensure.

Mustangers were coming into the country as well as raiders, and soon the mustangs would be reduced to the lowest of their form. Since mustangers took the best of the *manadas,* leaving only the less desirable, whether in looks, spirit, or stamina, those remaining would one day be diminished to a poor imitation of the magnificent Arabians and Barbs the Conquistadors brought with them.

The offspring of El Rey and Navidad on the other hand, would be the best of both breeds. Magnificent to look at, a marvel of speed, endurance, grace, and elegance.

Again she wondered about the star and sighed. Star or no star, they would be free. And in being free they would retain their magnificent spirit. Even if she had remained here and had by hook or crook captured El Rey, she ran the risk of breaking his spirit.

Mustangs in captivity, especially superior stallions such as El Rey, often did not survive. The best she could have hoped for was one mating, and if he didn't kill himself or Navidad, perhaps two.

When first her decision to leave Los Olmos became clear in her mind, her thought had been to set Navidad free with El Rey and his manada. Now she knew she had made the right choice.

Like Giddeon Duval, this stallion would never survive in captivity. Like Giddeon, he needed to run free, to breathe free, to live free. Alike in their marvelous bodies and fair, fair looks, they were also alike in spirit. To capture and hold either one would be to destroy him, bringing destruction to captive and captor alike. Tears formed in her eyes and blurred her vision. But she no longer cried for what might have been. Given the choice, at this moment, she knew she would change nothing of the past year of her life.

Staring now at the wild and free mustangs before her, she began to realize that wild and free were two quite separate words. A part of her would always yearn for the freedom of youth. But the wildness was gone, and the yearning was locked somewhere deep inside her heart, guarded by a new sense of responsibility, by a new sense of herself and of her place in the world.

Gone was the impetuous nature Tita worried over; likely it had been killed by the same bullet that took Oliver Burton's life.

Her stubbornness, too, was gone. Giddeon had been right about that. She was stubborn. But for a while, that characteristic had served her well. Had she been less willful, she would have gone to Mexico with Papá—and that would have changed everything.

She would never have known Giddeon's love . . . for she no longer doubted that this freedom-loving man loved her. She would never have known his compassion, his kisses, his body . . . She would never have borne his child.

And those two things changed her as nothing in the world before and after had or ever would: Giddeon's love and Giddeon's child.

She scrambled back down the hillside to her two tied mounts. With trembling fingers, she tugged at the cinch, loosened the saddle, and heaved it from Navidad's back.

After she had transferred her saddle and blanket to the extra mount she brought along, she unhitched Navidad's reins and led her to the top of the hill. As if in a dream, while tears flowed down her cheeks, she paused at the crest and threw her arms around Navidad's neck. She buried her face in the filly's coarse silver mane.

"Dear Navidad, run free and be happy." Quickly then, she unfastened the bridle, drew the bit from the horse's mouth and slapped her flank. "Run, Navidad. Run toward your future . . . and mine."

She rode straight home, determined to have this leave-taking finished tonight. By the time she arrived back at *la casa grande,* although physically weak, she had regained a sense of peace she had not felt since Giddeon made known his terrible plan.

Seeing El Rey again, free and spirited, had given her a new understanding of this sailing man whom she loved with all her heart. For that, she was grateful. Now that she saw him in this light, now that she accepted her own new place in life, she could love him, not hate him.

That, in itself, she thought, striding toward the house, was a major accomplishment. It did not lessen her hurt at giving him up—for her sake, and that of their child. But giving him up was easier knowing she could never have held him, even if Los Olmos were not the center of contention. Los Olmos had nothing to do with his leaving, and she no longer had to pretend it did. Like El Rey, Giddeon was a free spirit who must be allowed to remain free.

It was almost dusk when she entered the house. At her question, Tita nodded toward the staircase.

"He is up there with his man, Felix."

A wave of despair washed over her, followed by

anguish. Felix had returned. Felix, who had paid the taxes so Enos McCaulay could buy Los Olmos; Felix, who was to find her a new home at Kinney's Rancho.

Steeling herself against the lump in her chest, she took the stairs quickly.

Giddeon sat on a stool, facing out toward the sea. Felix sat on another stool but rose when he saw her in the doorway, tipped his hat, and excused himself.

Giddeon did not turn around, so she went to him and encircled his shoulders from behind.

At her touch, he stiffened.

For a moment, she did not say a word; neither did she move her arms. Then, slowly, she began to massage his neck, the back of his shoulders.

"Do not worry," she said softly. "I cannot hold you with my hands, *capitán*. I will not even try."

He inhaled deeply. Still without turning, he reached for her fingers and drew them around him, pressing them against his lips. She could feel his ragged breathing—or was it her own?

"I turned Navidad loose with El Rey."

He tried to rise, then, but she held him back. She wasn't sure she could bear to look upon his face at this moment. "I'm glad I did," she continued. "Seeing El Rey again helped me understand you. The two of you are much alike."

"*Querida* . . ." The word rasped from his throat, and she placed a palm over his open mouth. With the other hand, she withdrew the papers from her shirtfront.

"Don't . . . don't say anything," she cautioned. "I am ready to leave. But first, you. It is time for you

420

to go. Here are the papers—the deed and the land-grant documents, duly signed."

She felt his lips tremble against her palm, and she dropped her hand. He stared at the ancient documents. Then he stood up, in spite of her efforts to keep him from doing so. Quickly, she lowered her eyes.

His arms went around her. "Look at me, *querida.*" She burrowed the top of her head into his chest. "No, Giddeon. There is no sense in this . . ."

His hand found and cupped her chin; he forced her face to his. Lowering his lips, he kissed her, but she remained firm in her resolve and did not respond.

Finally, he lifted his lips and clasped her head to his chest, holding her as in a death-grip. "I'm going to help you move."

"No."

"I want to help. You can't move by yourself . . . with the baby."

"I can do anything." She spoke only loud enough for him to hear. Then she drew a deep breath to steady her racing heart and pulled away from his embrace. "Besides, Delos is staying. He will help us move. Felix found us a place?"

He nodded. "Serita . . . I won't be gone long."

She stared into the mesmerizing vista of sea and land, her heart leaden, her mind numb. "When you leave, Giddeon, it is for good."

His eyes widened. He shook his head. "No."

"Yes. Any money you have left after you raise your ship, you can send to Delos. He will give . . ."

"Serita. I can't leave you."

421

"You made that choice yourself."

"Forchristssake, Serita . . ." He reached for her so quickly she could not escape and drew her to him. "I made it for *you.*"

She inhaled a deep draft of his scent . . . a sweet, delicious scent she would take with her through eternity. How she wanted to give in to him—here and now—just to kiss him if nothing more. To kiss him . . . to kiss him . . . goodbye.

"No, Giddeon. You made the choice for *yourself.* Do not even try to tell me otherwise. I want you to go now, while I . . . I want to love you. Please don't make me . . . please don't make me regret it all."

Chapter Twenty

Of the tasks Serita had set for herself this day, only two remained after she finished giving Giddeon the documents to Los Olmos.

As soon as she left him, she fed Estelle, then called for Abril. All the time she nursed Estelle, tears had flowed down her own cheeks, and the baby fretted. This made matters worse, because nursing her baby had always been a peaceful time . . . always before now.

And it would be again, she reasoned, once she completed the overwhelming task of telling Jorge and Tita, to say nothing of Pablo and Nieves, of their impending move to Kinney's Rancho.

She called for Abril with a purpose. When the young housemaid appeared, Serita found she had been correct. "Delos told you of our move?"

Abril nodded.

"Then will you put Estelle to bed while I tell the rest of the household?"

Abril gladly agreed. The baby held a fascination for her that was obvious to all, even though her marriage was still a secret to everyone except Serita and Giddeon.

Serita had first thought to tell Tita and Jorge together, but at the last minute, she realized she must tell Jorge not only about the move, but also about releasing Navidad. Walking the boy down to the creek, they sat beneath the ancient elm trees, and she first explained the freedom-loving similarities between Giddeon and El Rey. Then she told him about Navidad.

The boy had picked up a smooth pebble and was in the act of tossing it idly into the creek. At her words, he clenched it in his fist. *"Tío Capitán* told to me about our move to Kinney's Rancho." Bitterness clipped his words. "He said we could take Navidad."

"Did he?" Despair mingled inside her with hopelessness and rising anger. She wanted to tell him his *Tío Capitán* was not always right about everything. She wanted to tell him never to use that name again, to stop thinking of Giddeon as his uncle, because he would never see the man again.

Instead he put her arm around Jorge's resisting shoulders. "Navidad would be no happier cooped up in town than Giddeon would be on dry land. I know it is hard now, but when you think about her running free here on the prairie, you will agree."

"I would have ridden her into the country every day," he objected.

"I know." Serita stared at the creek, thinking perhaps it was for the last time. The boy's distress echoed her own. "I know how much you will miss her. I hope someday you can understand . . . and forgive me."

In spite of her best efforts, her voice had quivered, and she felt Jorge turn to look at her. Without warning, then, he placed a protective arm about her shoulders.

"Do not worry, Serita. I will take care of you and Tita and little Estelle. I promised *Tío Capitán* — and I am grown-up enough to do it. Everything will work out. You will see."

She called the family, including Pablo, Nieves, and Lupe, to the parlor after *merienda*, to which Giddeon had not appeared. She wondered whether he had already left.

Her hands were wet with anxiety when she stood before the mantel of the new fireplace, a fireplace they had not yet had cause to use, and now would never have the chance. She had asked Felix to join them.

"As you know," she began formally, "Felix has returned from making the final payment on our back taxes." Looking at each in turn, she saw them nod in agreement.

"What you probably do not know is that he has been tending to some other business for us, too." Her knees went weak, and for a moment she could not go on. How she dreaded imparting such dastardly news to these trusting people.

"Since Oliver Burton's death, we have all felt safe, but we have been deceiving ourselves. There are other raiders from the north who will in time be just as persistent, just as violent, in trying to take Los Olmos from us. So, I have made a decision for all of us." Her voice shook, her words played out. She drew a hasty breath, then hurried on. ". . . I

425

have decided to sell Los Olmos to Enos McCaulay."

Tita gasped. Jorge clasped her hand, patting it in a comforting manner.

"I do not like this, either, but it is the best way — the only way for . . . for our future . . . for Jorge, for Estelle. Señor McCaulay will pay for our land; those who come after him will not be so generous. This way we will have enough money to start over." Her throat tightened over words her father had spoken so long ago. Words she had rebuked at the time. Words she had vowed would never fall from her lips.

"Señor McCaulay will pay us enough that we will not have to worry about our future. Giddeon will handle the details so we can be sure we are not being taken advantage of by . . . by a gringo." She spat the word, and with it the anguish she felt at the entire situation.

She had not intended to let Giddeon off so lightly for his role in this masquerade. Yet, once she started speaking, she recalled how much Tita and Jorge had grown to love him, and she resisted the inclination to blame him for everything that had befallen them.

"Felix has found us a nice house at Kinney's Rancho. It is next door to Tío Pepe. You will love it, Tita. You can walk to Mass every day. As soon as we get moved, we will have Estelle christened in the church there."

Tita's voice cracked with concern, with age. "What will become of our graves, *sobrina?* Who will care for them, the graves of our ancestors?"

Serita crossed the room and took a seat beside

426

her aunt. "Do not worry, Tita. Giddeon assured me he will insist Señor McCaulay agrees to let us visit our cemetery."

Tita shook her head.

"Giddeon will send us the papers Señor McCaulay signs," Serita said. "Giddeon will assure we are not taken advantage of."

At the last, she almost choked on her own words, feeling, as she did, the most betrayed of the lot. She was not protecting Giddeon, she insisted to herself, rather, she was protecting her family.

At the pause of the conversation, Felix stood up and nervously cleared his throat. "Excuse me, ma'am," he began. "I brought news from your family at Kinney's Rancho. They are anxious to have you make the move. They suggested they travel out here and help—"

"That will not be necessary," Serita interrupted. "We will leave within a day or two."

"Don Pepe sent word that they would like to see the homeplace once more before it is sold," Felix continued. "He suggested they send for Padre Alphonse to come from La Bahía to christen the new baby here at Los Olmos on the feast day of Don Miguel."

"No," she insisted. She wanted to leave now. She had said her goodbyes. Now she wanted to be on her way. Everything remaining—the new house, the repaired vaqueros' cottages, the new vaqueros themselves—all reminded her much more of Giddeon than of anything in her past. No, she must leave soon.

"Please, Serita," Jorge cried. Suddenly he was a

427

boy again, rushing to her side, throwing his arms around her neck. "Please. We could have a fiesta, like you planned. Then it would be much easier to leave."

"He is right, *sobrina*," Tita said. "We will stay for Pepe to see the place one last time. That will make it easier for me, too. We will christen little Estelle here at the place of her roots on the feast day of her grandfather. It will be a solid beginning for the child."

They won her over, of course. And although it was painful to think about, Serita was glad to have the christening here at Los Olmos. It would indeed be an appropriate way to say goodbye.

When they finished discussing it, she hurried to the nursery, only to find Abril in the hallway and Giddeon inside the room. She stood at the door on trembling legs, watching him cradle his daughter in his arms. The baby was lost there, with only her blankets draping this way and that. Very tenderly he kissed her on the forehead, then laid her back in the crib.

She had asked him to leave her with a way to love him. What better vision than this? A father kissing his infant daughter. If only she did not know he was kissing her goodbye.

When Serita arose the next morning, Giddeon, Kosta, and Felix were gone. She was possessed by a strong inclination to keep to her room, to be alone. But she resisted.

This was as the first day of her new life — hers

428

and Estelle's — and the sooner she swept away the past, the quicker they could move forward to happier times.

Tita, too, was subdued, but planning the fiesta filled much of her time. Having been informed of the fire, Tía Beatriz sent a trunkful of clothing and linens via Felix — to tide the family over until their move, she wrote. Serita helped Tita go through them.

She recognized Rosaria's needlework on one festive white dress she decided immediately she would wear to the christening and fiesta. Two lovely black silk gowns, one for Tita, and one with delicate lace sleeves and matching *rebozo* for herself; a *charro* suit for Jorge, which, considering the rapid growth the boy had undergone this past year, fit remarkably well.

Nieves put the wives of the vaqueros to work making additional tamales, salsa, and dulces, while she prepared dozens of *buñuelos,* a Christmas treat, but as she said, "This will be a party for the entire year, Christmas included. Especially since we did not have much celebration at Christmas last year."

Pablo caught Serita in the courtyard one morning as the vaqueros were leaving for a *rodeo.* "With the new vaqueros, we can get plenty of cows' heads for the *barbacoa,*" he told her enthusiastically. "How many do you expect we will need?"

"Oh, Pablo, it will be a nice fiesta, won't it?"

"It will indeed, *chica.* And we will have many more when we move to Kinney's Rancho. Just because we are moving from Los Olmos, we do not have to give up our customs."

429

Don Pepe and his family began arriving a week later. "We came a few days early," he told Tita, "so I will have time to look the old place over once again."

"I am sorry to give it up, Pepe," Tita told him. "Times change, though."

He nodded. "And we with them. If we do not give in to some of the demands of the gringos, our children will not survive at all . . . and with our children, will go our culture . . . our heritage."

Jorge had begged Serita endlessly to ride with him to the valley to see Navidad, but she steadfastly refused. That was one trip she did not intend to make again. With the arrival of the Cortinas clan, she thought his mind had been taken from the idea, but one day he and a cousin, Raul, came to her with the same plea.

"If you do not want to go, we will go without you," Jorge informed her.

"Go ahead," she told him. "You and Raul bring me word of Navidad."

Another week elapsed before Padre Alphonse arrived. The first thing he did, after sitting an hour with Tita, was climb to the ship's bridge. "A splendid room," he enthused to Serita when he came down two hours later. This was another trip she did not intend to make again, so she had sent the padre up alone. "I have never felt so close to the Lord as when I looked out upon all His many creations."

Serita inhaled deeply. "Sí, padre. The sea and the land. Sometimes from up there, they look fused — as one."

Rosaria fell immediately and completely in love

430

with little Estelle. "Imagine! She is six weeks old, and still so tiny."

"Seven," Serita corrected. "She will be two months on the day of her christening."

By the day of the fiesta *la casa grande* was overflowing with guests.

"Practically everyone from La Bahía has come and many folks from Kinney's Rancho," Rosario told Serita as they prepared for bed one night. They had turned the downstairs office into a dormitory room, where Rosaria and her sisters shared mattresses and pallets on the floor. With the shutters closed over the pane-less windows, the girls had privacy to dress, but the resulting room was dark and smelled of candle wax.

Many of the boys and men slept on pallets in the parlor, on the gallery overlooking the front of the house, and on the back gallery that ran along the courtyard.

The rooms to either side of Pablo and Nieves's were taken over by the older married couples, like Tío Pepe and Tía Beatriz and Mary and Edward Stavinoha, who were delighted to be included. Serita hoped Edward would be able to get ideas for furniture for the house, which he could sell to Enos McCaulay. No sense everyone losing out.

Mary was delighted to have Jorge join her school. "That will make twenty students," she said proudly.

Serita sighed. Yes, she had made the right choice. All around, for everyone. It was the right decision.

Even insisting that Giddeon not return had been the correct thing to do. Already she was beginning

431

to adjust—at least during the daytime. Of course, she admitted, with a house full of guests it was easier to keep her mind off herself. But at Kinney's Rancho she would be next door to Rosaria and her other cousins. They had always been close.

Rosaria herself had the most wonderful news of all, a secret which she kept until the morning of the fiesta, when Serita wandered into the *comedor* for a simple *desayuno* to find a handsome young man sitting beside her cousin at the dining table.

"Serita, this is Jaime."

Immediately, Serita could tell from the blush on her cousin's cheeks that Jaime was not merely another guest at the fiesta.

"Jaime Estrada. We are to be married in the spring."

"Rosie! How wonderful! And I will be there to help with the wedding."

Guitar music drifted from the courtyard, smells of roasting meat reached *la casa grande* from the pits dug especially for today. When Serita approached Pablo, she smelled the delicious aroma of the *barbacoa*. Pablo had just removed a large sack from the pit. Carefully lifting layer after layer of juice-stained cloths, he invited Serita to peek in at the cow's head.

"It looks wonderful, Pablo," she complimented.

"And you, *chica,* how are you holding up?" As he spoke, he removed the tongue from the barbequed head, recovered and replaced the head among the coals in the pit, then began to peel and slice the tongue on a cutting board.

She sighed. "I am fine, Pablo." If anyone here at

Los Olmos knew the extent of her heartache, Pablo would be the person. He had saved her from self-destruction once, and she knew if need be, he would step in again. "I will be glad to get this over with, though. It is time to go."

He nodded. "*Sí, chica*, it is time to move on. You have a beautiful daughter and a long future. It is time to move ahead."

"I am glad you and Nieves are coming to Kinney's Rancho. It would not be so easy for me to leave without you."

He grinned a toothy grin. "You will always have Nieves and me by your side, *chica*. Do not doubt that."

They had planned the christening for later afternoon, after Estelle's feeding. At that time, she would change into the new dress. Just before she retired to her bedchamber to feed the baby, however, Abril and Delos approached her.

"Do you think Padre Alphonse would consent to marry us after the christening?" Abril asked.

"Of course," she answered.

Delos cleared his throat. "I recall he had questions about whether or not Giddeon was eligible to be married by a priest."

"Not by a priest," Serita told him. "In the church. Since we do not have a church, there should be no problem. Besides, I think Padre Alphonse and Tita were searching for any excuse they could find to keep that marriage from taking place. Come with me. We will talk to him."

Padre Alphonse agreed. He suggested performing the ceremony in the ship's bridge, and Delos and

Abril thought it a most significant place, even though only three or four other people could attend.

"He wanted to christen Estelle up there," Serita confided, "but we wouldn't have room. I am glad he will not leave disappointed."

Then, sending Delos away, she drew Abril into her bedchamber, closed and locked the shutters for privacy, and pulled out the frilly white dress she had planned to wear to Estelle's christening.

"This will be perfect for your wedding gown."

"No, señora," Abril objected. "You will have nothing to wear."

"There are other dresses," Serita assured her. "I want you to have this one."

After she fed Estelle and began to dress for her baby's christening, Rosaria chastised her for her impetuousness.

"This is a christening and a fiesta, Serita. You look like you are in mourning, gowned all in black. Black is for widows."

Serita bit her bottom lip between her teeth. Widows? Well, wasn't she the same as a widow? But she would not let her feelings show. If no one saw her sadness, they would not sympathize, and with no attention, her sadness would die. She knew it would be true.

She prayed it would be true.

"This gown is far from widow's weeds," she declared, swirling the black silk skirt to emphasize her point. "Why, the lace is exquisite. And the neckline dips too low for a widow's gown." She fluffed the delicate lace ruffles that formed the sleeves and smoothed her fingers across the satin of the low, flat

434

neckline. "I haven't had anything this fancy since . . ."

A catch came to her throat at the thought of another black dress. A flirty black dress with multi-colored petticoats. A dancing dress. Well, this could be a dancing dress, too.

Except that she wasn't going to a dance. She was attending her daughter's christening and the marriage of a special couple. But she would not dance at their wedding. Widows did not dance.

Tita brought Estelle in, gowned in the white christening costume that flowed a good two yards beyond the infant's feet. The white, embroidered crosses and seashells gave the gown a richness and depth that even their ancient christening gown had not had.

"You and Jaime must have the next baby to wear this gown," she told her cousin. "Now, where is Jorge? With the two of you as godparents, Estelle will have no worry."

The christening was held in the courtyard with all the guests gathered around, and behind them the new vaqueros and their families. Only once did Estelle stir. That was when Padre Alphonse christened her with three scoops of water, then signed the cross on her forehead with his finger.

When he finished, the guests and the vaqueros' families passed by to offer their best wishes, and afterward Serita returned Estelle to her crib and went in search of Abril.

They had asked her to stand with them, and she agreed without considering the fact that she never intended to set foot in the ship's bridge again. Once

435

there, she knew her first decision had been the correct one, for she was overcome by a nostalgia so great, she thought for a moment she would have to dash back down the stairs.

Fortunately, Padre Alphonse got on with the ceremony. Before he finished, however, he faced the sea, and, in deference to Delos's former occupation, he intoned the ancient prayer for the sailor:

"Oh, hear us when we call to thee, for those in peril on the sea . . ."

Her eyes swam with tears she did not want to shed. Blinking fiercely, she turned her eyes away and stared as far to the north as she could see — to the distant horizon — away from the sea, away from Los Olmos — away from everything dear . . .

"You may kiss the bride."

Still she stared . . . away from her homeland . . . to the new and feared nation . . . to Texas.

"Go, my children, and be happy in the Lord," Padre Alphonse said. "And come to La Bahía to make your communions."

Joy, the required emotion. Turning quickly, Serita hugged Abril. Then Delos. "I am so glad you are remaining here at Los Olmos," she told them. "You will be happy. I'm sure Señor McCaulay will be good to you."

Delos grasped her hand. "Thank you, ma'am. We will not forget you and little Estelle."

He led his bride down the steep stairs, but his words lingered and filled her heart with emptiness.

"Are you all right, dear child?" Padre Alphonse asked.

"Sí," she whispered, afraid if she tried to speak

436

any louder, she would scream. "Please, padre, it has been a long day. I would remain here a while . . . alone."

He patted her head through the mantilla which matched her lacy sleeves. Lacy sleeves, she thought, widow's weeds. What difference did it make?

She dropped to one of the hide-bound stools that in a few days would belong to Enos McCaulay. Bracing her elbows on the table, she stared into the sea so long and with so much will she thought surely she would conjure Giddeon himself, instead of merely his image.

It was there he found her, her head drooped to her arms, fast asleep.

At first he hesitated to awaken her, but he had ridden so hard, all night and all day, and he was here, and . . .

"*Querida.*" His fingers played lightly across the delicate lace of the mantilla that draped her head and shoulders.

She stirred.

With one hand he reached between his legs, found a stool, and pulled it forward to sit on. "*Querida.*"

Later she knew it was the sound of his voice that awakened her, but the first conscious recognition she had of his presence was his sweet, delicious scent.

She turned her head, yet did not lift it from her arms. Her eyes fluttered open once . . .

He kissed her cheek.

Twice . . .

His hand stroked her hair.

"Giddeon!"

She almost toppled them both to the floor in her surprise. "What . . . ?"

He tried to take her in his arms, but she drew away, falling backward. He caught her by the arm. Steadied her. Her body, not her quaking flesh, not her tumbling mind.

"Serita, I've come home . . ."

Her mouth fell open. Her heart hesitated, poised on the brink of expectancy.

". . . to stay. If you'll let me." And even if you won't, he thought, but he would save those words, in case he needed them.

"What do you mean?" Her pores burned with his nearness, with his words, with the very idea that he might mean what she heard, what she wanted him to mean.

Reaching into a pocket, he pulled out the land-grant documents and the deed to Los Olmos and placed them before her on the table. "I didn't go through with it."

She stared, mouth agape. "What about your ship . . . the *Estelle?*"

He rose and, against her wishes, pulled her to her feet, where he held her at arm's length, staring at her with a desperate intensity in his wonderful green eyes. With one hand he pushed her mantilla back, dropping it to her shoulders. His hand stroked the top of her head. "It can wait."

Try as she might, she was wont to keep her emotions in check. She had been disappointed so many times before. She feared this was but another instance when she misunderstood him. "You said time was short. That Bustamente . . ."

438

"Bustamente's money isn't important." His eyes pierced hers like a steady stream of green fire, melting, soothing, as did his words. "With every step my horse took away from you, Bustamente and his money became less important."

Her heartbeat had resumed, when she wasn't sure, and now clamored so loud she could practically hear it. Had she truly understood him? Or misunderstood again? "But the cargo? Aren't you going to salvage it?"

Still he held her at arm's length and stared, his green eyes begging her to understand. The very air around them was heated and fairly throbbed with anticipation — with their fears, with their hopes. Slowly, he shook his head in answer to her question.

"Why?" she whispered.

"Because I love you. You are everything I will ever need or ever care about — you and our baby."

Her arms felt totally useless. She had the disconcerting thought she would never be able to hold Estelle with them again. Then he spoke once more, and she fell into his arms.

"I've even grown to love Los Olmos."

"You mean . . . ?"

"I mean this is the only place we will ever live. Let the gringos come. They will never drive us away."

She clung to him so tightly their bodies molded together, and he held her as if he would never let her go.

Their hearts beat fiercely, in tune each with the other, and in this manner, without speaking, they communicated.

At first, her mind felt as though it had been fused into one unintelligible mass, as the sea and the land, but gradually reality began to take form. She became aware of his body against hers, and she recognized and loved every curve, every hollow. She pressed her face against his chest and felt life return to her spirit with each wild beat of his heart.

"Tell me again," she whispered, still not moving from his embrace.

He tightened his arms, holding her as for his own life. "I'm home, *querida*. We are together, for better or worse, to love and to cherish, until death . . ."

She clutched him tighter, believing, still hesitating . . . believing . . . until at last the metamorphosis was complete. The shell of hopelessness that had formed around her heart cracked, and joy, pure, undiluted joy, joy such as she had never known, burst forth. And she felt free. Free as a butterfly taking wing on a glorious spring day. Free as Navidad herself must feel.

Throwing her head back, she stared into his loving green eyes and received his kiss . . . responded to his kiss . . . reveled in the beauty of his presence.

Finally, he lifted his face a mere inch or so from hers. "I am so very sorry, *querida*, for all the hurt . . ."

She smiled—a smile full of joy now that it was backed by the security of having him with her. "When you wager with the devil, he demands his due, Giddeon. I was as guilty of that as you. After the bargain we forged, we had to earn the right to be happy together."

440

He kissed her again, then led her downstairs to the nursery, where she gently placed his daughter in his arms. "I spoke to Padre Alphonse on the way in," he told her. "I'm sorry I missed the christening."

The image of father and daughter took her breath away. This time is was an image she would *want* to remember. "That's all right. You will be here for little Miguel's."

Tenderly he placed Estelle in her crib, and took the baby's mother in his arms. "And for all the rest . . . how many do you think we can manage?"

This time his kiss stirred yearnings long denied, and she suggested, "I will find Lupe to draw you a bath."

He grinned. "Don't tell me I smell of trail dust. I stopped at the creek and bathed."

Her pores burned, her flesh quivered, and her brain spun. She smiled, beguiling him with her seductive voice. "Then come with me. You must dress for the fiesta."

They did not speak again until they were locked in their bedchamber and in each other's embrace, bare as on the days of their births, clinging flesh to flesh, giddy from their racing hearts.

While his kisses aroused long-neglected yearnings within her, his hands stroked her skin in a way she had believed she would never feel again. She snuggled closer to him, letting his heated skin lift her to an even higher plane of desire.

Trailing his fingers up and down her spine, across her buttocks, around her hips, over her ribs, he reclaimed that which he had forsaken, cursing himself for giving up the one thing in the world which gave meaning to his life, rejoicing that she was not lost to him forever.

"Querida," he mumbled, moving his lips over her face, while his hands unpinned her hair. The feel of its silky strands on his fingers brought a catch in his throat, and he clenched his fists in her hair. "How could I have been such a fool?"

"No more, my love," she whispered. With the heels of her hands, she kneaded his shoulders into pliant masses of heated flesh, and with her fingers she caressed his back, his skin. "Today . . . this moment . . . we begin anew."

Moving above her then, he dropped his lips down her face, across her neck, and stopped at the hollow between her breasts. With his hands he pressed their fullness together and felt them hot against his cheeks. Gently, with agonizing tenderness, he kissed her nipples and laved her breasts with kisses, then dropped his lips to her waist. His hands spanned the newly nipped circumference, and he glanced up at her and winked.

His look, his touch, set her on fire. She would speak, but her mouth was dry, her breath short. She twisted her fingers in his hair, and when he lowered his lips to her navel, she pressed his head to her newly flattened stomach.

Eager yearnings raced through the length of her body, leaving her limbs heavy, laden with desire. When he moved his lips across her belly, she felt consumed by a trail of fire which raged hotter as she lifted her hips and received his lips, his kisses, his desperate attempt to consume and be consumed by a love magnified through denial, now grown to

442

unbearable proportions by their frail, human attempts to reach the unattainable glory.

She demanded, he partook . . .

Her body canted. Her flesh trembled. "Giddeon. Please . . . come to me now."

Reverently, he raised himself above her, and together they joined their bodies and moved as in a fury through the undulating light of the flickering candles. Their eyes held fast, expressing all the while the deepened joy of their reclaimed love. And when at last they lay spent and content, clenched inside each other's embrace, he kissed her forehead, and she held him tight.

Her dream was fulfilled. At last, everything she had ever wished for had come to her. But he had given up his. "You are sure, Giddeon? Will you one day regret giving up your life?"

He kissed her lightly, but his words were deadly serious. "*You* are my life, *querida*—you, Estelle, and Los Olmos. My heart is so full of loving you, I will never have room for regrets."

His words, his touch, his wondrous love healed her wounded heart as with a magical balm, and she sighed, believing him at last. "You are not even a little curious about the cargo?" she teased.

His beloved, lopsided grin sent tremors coursing through her body. He stroked her back with a knowing hand. "Someday when we are old and gray, if we are still curious, perhaps we will salvage that ship together. Right now, we have a ranch to run, a family to raise . . ." His lips descended as he spoke, and just before they covered hers with renewed urgency, he finished, ". . . and a life full of loving each other."

Festive voices and strains of music floated through the locked shutters as from a distance. At last, she became aware of the commotion. "A fiesta is going on in the courtyard, but everything I want is inside this room—you . . . you . . . you."

He studied her lovely face. Then he kissed her lightly on the lips, and from the gleam in his glorious green eyes, she knew he had a plan.

"We will return to our bed, but for now, we must get dressed. Have you forgotten what day this is? The anniversary of our marriage. When I spoke to Padre Alphonse, I told him we want to renew our vows today."

She stared transfixed into his adoring face. "Papá was right. We *can* start over."

Kissing her, his lips lingered on her forehead while his mind strayed to *Don* Miguel Cortinas. Silently, he saluted the shrewd old man who had indeed wagered something of far greater value than an ancient Spanish land grant. "This time we begin with love, *querida*."

Author's Note

In 1839, the "Nueces Strip," that portion of present-day Texas located between the Nueces and the Rio Grande rivers, was claimed by both Texas and Mexico and ignored by both countries, as well.

The resulting no man's land was a hotbed for dissension and turmoil. The short-lived Republic of the Rio Grande was formed by Mexican citizens dissatisfied with both the Centralist and the Federalist governments.

Anglo land-raiders and speculators swarmed into the Nueces Strip from Texas, even though much of its territory was already owned by Spanish and Mexican land-grant holders.

Some of this land, of course, was abandoned, and this book in no way intends to reflect on the honor of the Anglo settlers who searched into Mexico until they found the landowners from whom they could legally purchase the property that had already been abandoned.

The intimidation and thievery did, however, occur. Much of it, too, is documented.

The Nueces Strip is considered the birthplace of the American ranching industry, because it was here on the Spanish *haciendas* that cattle-ranching began, here where the traditions and customs of the American industry, including its methods, its gear, even its language, took form and substance. The first cowboys, referred to in early accounts as Cow Boys, are descendants of the Mexican *vaqueros* (cow workers) and the South American *gauchos*. The original cattle were descendants of Spanish cattle; the mustang, from horses the Spanish explorers first brought to the shores of the New World.

So important was the horse in conquering New Spain that one of the conquerors' first ordinances prohibited Indians from riding horses. Some sources cite the enforcement of this law as late as 1611. When the *peón* (pedestrian) was allowed to ride, he became a *caballero* (horseman), and a greater threat to the conquering Spanish. Since a *vaquero* (cattle tender) must perform his work on horseback, he was considered a step higher on the social ladder than a *peón*.

The end of this story was not told for many years. In 1845, the United States annexed Texas and sent General Zachary Taylor to invade Mexico, where he captured Matamoros and Monterrey. The ensuing treaty established the Rio Grande River as the United States (and Texas) boundary with Mexico. General Taylor's march crossed the Nueces River at Kinney's Rancho (now Corpus Christi) and proceeded to Matamoros along an old trail first used by early Spanish exploration and missionary *entradas* into the Texas wilderness, a route known as

446

one of the several branches of El Camino Real, the King's Highway.

Along this route General Taylor crossed Los Olmos Creek, and were this story history instead of fiction, he would have passed in front of *la casa grande* on La Hacienda de los Olmos.

During the War Between the States, Taylor's Road became known as the Cotton Road, the lifeline of the Confederacy. By that time Stella (Estelle) Duval was a young woman in her early twenties. But we're getting ahead of ourselves. Perhaps we should save Stella's story for another time.

Language and landscapes change through the years. Two examples: According to published accounts, at the time of this story the word *resaca* referred to a mudhole; today it denotes a pond or lagoon. Likewise, before the white man came, this area of Texas was a lush grassland prairie; by the late 1870's, chaparral (brush) was dense, as it is today.

ZEBRA'S GOT THE ROMANCE
TO SET YOUR HEART AFIRE!

RAGING DESIRE   (2242, $3.75)
by Colleen Faulkner
A wealthy gentleman and officer in General Washington's army, Devon Marsh wasn't meant for the likes of Cassie O'Flynn, an immigrant bond servant. But from the moment their lips first met, Cassie knew she could love no other . . . even if it meant marching into the flames of war to make him hers!

TEXAS TWILIGHT   (2241, $3.75)
by Vivian Vaughan
When handsome Trace Garrett stepped onto the porch of the Santa Clara ranch, he wove a rapturous spell around Clara Ehler's heart. Though Clara planned to sell the spread and move back East, Trace was determined to keep her on the wild Western frontier where she belonged — to share with him the glory and the splendor of the passion-filled TEXAS TWILIGHT.

RENEGADE HEART   (2244, $3.75)
by Marjorie Price
Strong-willed Hannah Hatch resented her imprisonment by Captain Jake Farnsworth, even after the daring Yankee had rescued her from bloodthirsty marauders. And though Jake's rock-hard physique made Hannah tremble with desire, the spirited beauty was nevertheless resolved to exploit her femininity to the fullest and gain her independence from the virile bluecoat.

LOVING CHALLENGE   — (2243, $3.75)
by Carol King
When the notorious Captain Dominic Warbrooke burst into Laurette Harker's eighteenth birthday ball, the accomplished beauty challenged the arrogant scoundrel to a duel. But when the captain named her innocence as his stakes, Laurette was terrified she'd not only lose the fight, but her heart as well!

Available wherever paperbacks are sold, or order direct from the Publisher. Send cover price plus 50¢ per copy for mailing and handling to Zebra Books, Dept. 2866, 475 Park Avenue South, New York, N.Y. 10016. Residents of New York, New Jersey and Pennsylvania must include sales tax. DO NOT SEND CASH.